THE TOURIST *ATTRACTION*

SARAH MORGENTHALER

sourcebooks
casablanca

Published by Sourcebooks Casablanca, and imprint of Sourcebooks
P.O. Box 4410, Naperville, Illinois 60567-4410
(630) 961-3900
sourcebooks.com

Library of Congress Cataloging-in-Publication Data

Names: Morgenthaler, Sarah, author.
Title: The tourist attraction / Sarah Morgenthaler.
Description: Naperville, IL : Sourcebooks Casablanca, [2020]
Identifiers: LCCN 2019053648 (trade paperback)
Subjects: GSAFD: Love stories.
Classification: LCC PS3613.O74878 T68 2020 | DDC 813/.6--dc23
LC record available at https://lccn.loc.gov/2019053648

Printed and bound in Canada.
MBP 10 9 8 7 6 5 4 3 2 1

To my husband, Kenney, for making me
laugh every day. You are my joy.

CHAPTER 1

THE BALD EAGLE SOARED OVERHEAD, turning lazy circles against a backdrop of rich forested Alaskan mountainside.

As luck would have it, Graham Barnett had seen this same eagle on the way to work that morning. High above them both, the sun-kissed peaks of the Chugach Mountains glittered with their snowy caps, tree lines receding into grays and browns of weathered boulders.

Graham couldn't have asked for a more peaceful moment to enjoy his hometown of Moose Springs. A moment to sit on the back steps of his diner, take a break, and sip a root beer.

If it just weren't for the moose trying to make love to his pickup truck fifteen feet away.

"Ulysses, we do this every day, buddy." Resting his arms on his thighs, he watched the fifteen-hundred-pound bull moose press his nostrils to the window of Graham's abused Dodge, snuffing along the seal. Long, wet streaks of moose goo smeared on glass still crusty from the previous day's love affair.

"The truck just isn't into you. You've got to let this go, man. Move on to something better."

This was all about Graham's buns. Which was understandable—Graham liked them too—but Ulysses was taking this to a whole other level.

For whatever reason, the moose was obsessed with the smell of the fresh baked bread he picked up from the local bakery every day. Graham didn't have the storage space in his diner's freezer to make this a weekly supply run, and bread was far too expensive to ship into town when he could buy it locally. So Graham's truck always smelled like buns.

And the moose loved it.

Ulysses rubbed his heavy body against the passenger side door, scratching his shoulder and making deep, guttural huffing noises of appreciation. The truck had lost two door handles this way, and Graham had long since given up replacing the passenger side mirror.

"You and I are going to have a talk one of these days. You know this is weird, right?"

Draining his root beer, Graham listened to the volume inside the diner grow louder. Whose great idea had it been to install a jukebox? That was just asking the customers to stay even longer.

When Graham rose to his feet, the bull moose swung his massive head in his direction. Graham went still, partially out of habit but also from respect for the six-foot span of antlers crowning the animal's head. Ulysses considered him for a moment, then went back to wooing the Dodge. If the paint job hadn't already been trashed from this very ritual, Graham would have winced at the sound of antler scraping along the quarter panel.

Movement caught the corner of his eye. A couple were

edging toward Graham's truck, phones out as they shared excited whispers. Graham groaned.

Somehow it had gotten around to the tourists up at the Moose Springs Resort that if anyone wanted to see a moose in the wild, they should park out in his tiny diner's even tinier parking lot. Which was why Graham started leaving his truck behind the building. Still, the more determined tourists always seemed to find the moose when Ulysses came by.

"Hey. Stay back." Graham jerked his head in a curt no as the tourists inched closer, clicking pictures.

At least they didn't have a kid with them. Too many times, Graham had been forced to intervene when someone tried to shove their child on the back of a wild animal. Not a lot of things made him angry, but that always managed to send his blood pressure sky-high.

"He's either going to kill you or date you," Graham warned. "He's got emotional problems."

They were utterly oblivious, which was exactly why Moose Springs had one of the highest rates of human injuries by moose encounter in the entire state of Alaska. Not the animals' fault, either. Still, if one of these days the bull moose with a crush on Graham's truck ended up hurting someone, a Fish and Game warden would have to come and either relocate Ulysses or put him down.

Neither of which the moose deserved.

"Take a picture of us with him." The woman's eyes widened with excitement as her companion continued an endless series of selfies with the oblivious Ulysses in the background.

"Hard pass on that. Okay, Ulysses, take a hike, lover boy. You'll have to come back another day."

Graham clapped his hands in warning. He and this moose had known each other for a while, and they'd come to an understanding. Graham wouldn't use rock salt pellets to drive him away if Ulysses didn't trample his customers. The moose stared at Graham in disappointment, glared at the strangers, then grudgingly moved along.

The couple muttered in equal disappointment, but Graham's sympathy was with the moose. The unending influx of tourists tended to ruin Graham's days too.

Behind him, the music grew louder. Someone must have discovered the volume button on the back of the jukebox.

"I'm going in there." Graham said cheerfully at the couple as he turned to head back into the diner. "Try to make good choices."

Visitors to town rarely did. Walking into the unmanned and packed diner only proved Graham's theory.

When Graham opened the Tourist Trap, he'd meant the whole thing as a joke. He'd never wanted to sling burgers for a living, much less own his own place. All he wanted was to eat free cheeseburgers behind the counter and choose whatever he wanted to watch on the television in the corner. That and a way to pay his bills while not having to answer to anyone.

For some reason, being a yes-man just wasn't in Graham's genetic makeup.

Unfortunately, yes was the word he said most often these days, followed by asking if someone wanted fries with that. When Graham turned the tiny, run-down pizza joint down the road from Moose Springs Resort into an equally run-down, one-man diner, he assumed it would be the type of place where only locals would eat. The last thing he'd expected was for any of the wealthy, entitled tourists to actually *go* there.

With three things on the menu, it barely counted as serving food. Graham had a beer and liquor license, but he refused to make anything that required a blender or a master's degree to remember the ingredients. There wasn't even a sign above the door, just the shadow of wood paneling once covered by plastic letters spelling pizza.

And yet there they were, filling the Tourist Trap to the stuffing point and waiting in line because Graham refused to hire anyone. Which meant working his tail off on any given Tuesday.

For the record, Graham hated Tuesdays. They always ended up more trouble than they were worth.

In his defense, there had only been a couple of people in line when he'd gone outside for his break. Graham hadn't planned on having to shoo away a perfectly innocent moose from his romantic aspirations. Now there were three times as many customers, with the line running all the way to the front door. With a deep sigh of disappointment in his establishment, Graham scrubbed his hands clean and took his place behind the counter. Purgatory was located somewhere between the flat top grill to his right and the fryer behind him.

"You abandoned ship."

From his spot of dubious safety behind his counter, Graham looked up at the familiar voice.

"Even prisoners get time in the yard, L." Graham winked at the woman sauntering toward him. "I almost stayed out there."

Wrapped in a dress that could make one's mouth water, Lana Montgomery didn't just stand out in a crowd. She was the center of every room she walked into. Lana was almost a regular, coming to Moose Springs at least twice a year, sometimes more. Skiing in the winter and as a spectator for the Fourth of July festivities in the summer.

She was also Graham's favorite.

Of all the tourists he didn't want in his diner, he didn't want her there less than the others. And Lana used his dubious affection for her shamelessly.

Slipping to the front of the line despite the others still waiting, Lana leaned her arm on the counter next to a few too many soggy napkins and scattered bun crumbs.

It'd been a busy night.

"Graham, I need a Growly Bear."

"You want *another* Growly Bear?" Graham raised an eyebrow.

"Yes, and make it extra growly." Lana clawed at the air playfully. "Rawr."

Chuckling, Graham took one look at the beautiful woman in her sky-high heels and shook his head in bemusement.

"You've already had a Growly Bear, Lana. Besides, we're sold out." Even as he talked, Graham worked rapidly, dropping baskets of frozen fries in the fryer and slapping fresh burgers and dogs on the grill. He'd done this for so long, he didn't have to think about the actions. Getting customers through the line quickly wasn't a problem. Getting them to leave when they were done eating was the hard part.

"But, Graham—"

"Nope. Growly Bears are a pain in the ass to make one at a time, and I'm not serving any more tonight. And nobody gets them extra growly. I like having my diner still standing. No more fires."

"That was an accident, love." With a dismissive wave of her manicured fingernails, Lana shrugged off one of the more terrifying incidents of Graham's life. "Just a little spark, no harm done."

"Not a chance, L."

Graham softened his refusal with a toss of a broken French fry her way. She caught it with the practice of a woman who had spent two months a year for the last four years doing that exact same thing every time they saw each other.

"It's not for me, I promise." Swallowing her fry, Lana leaned her hip against the counter and hit Graham with the full impact of her smoky eyes. "It's for my friend Zoey. She's never had the pleasure."

Lana pointed toward a small table near the counter, causing him to glance over at the person occupying it, but Graham didn't bother to look closely.

"Then your Zoey needs to order it."

Why did they always order the Growly Bears? The name was dumb, they tasted terrible, and Graham had the distinct feeling they should be illegal. He'd have thought the tourists flocking to his tiny Alaskan town would have learned by now.

Never try to drink a local under the table.

The Growly Bear was Graham's special concoction, crafted the first time someone asked him to make them a drink the locals have. The request left him annoyed and determined to put together the worst tasting thing he could think of drinking.

Leave it to him to start a viral foodie trend when he just wanted to be left alone.

"Zoey's a Tourist Trap virgin." Lana's voice was husky from her first drink, the flush in her cheeks bringing out color in her neck and cleavage. She leaned in further. A little too far.

Graham waved her back. "Your breasts are in my buns, L," he said, loud enough so the customers around them would hear.

"Then charge them extra," she said playfully, glancing at the people behind her.

The man seated at the counter next to them choked on his burger, unable to stop staring. Without asking, Graham reached over and topped off his soda. Being in close proximity to Lana was stressful for all of them.

"Graham, Zoey needs to have a Growly Bear and a Sloppy Dog. This is her first day here, and she has to have the true Moose Springs experience."

Really? The *true* experience? What had his little dive come to?

"The Tourist Trap is everyone's first pit stop," she continued. "Having a Growly Bear is a rite of passage."

Didn't that just run a cold chill up his spine?

Realizing Lana was beaming impishly at him, Graham tossed another fry at her, this time aiming for her forehead. "You're mean, L."

"And you're terribly predictable, love." Dang, she'd caught it, just like the first.

"Fine, you win." Lana was relentless when she wanted something, and Graham was too busy to invest the kind of effort it would take to drive her away. "This Zoey needs to ask for herself."

Lana had a lot of friends, and sometimes one or two never materialized, leaving the extra drinks for her. Since he liked Lana, he let her get away with it, but two Growly Bears was one Growly Bear too many.

Heck, one Growly Bear was one too many, but try telling the masses of resort guests that. A solid third of the night's clientele were drinking Growlies without the decency to feel ashamed of themselves.

"Poor Zoey flew *coach*," Lana continued. "No wonder she's not feeling well. I told her to join me last week, but no. It's all work all the time with her."

"Yes, us selfish plebeians with our jobs."

Graham handed two burgers and a basket of fries to the customer waiting behind her. He didn't bother asking how they wanted them. He'd learned quickly that if he gave a Moose Springs Resort tourist options, they'd still be making him read ingredient labels an hour later.

At first, Graham had exclusively taken cash payment, but there were only so many times he could be stared at with confusion by the ultra-rich before he broke down and bought a tablet for credit card swipes.

Lana leaned further over the counter. Yep. Those were a pair of breasts in his buns. As he added grilled onions to the next order of dogs, he put his palm on Lana's shoulder with the other, gently straightening her. He personally didn't mind, but Graham doubted the next table would like the smell of Chanel in their meal.

Lana snagged a beer from the tray he was preparing. Before he could stop her, she downed it without blinking.

"Hello, Moose Springs," she cried out. "Beers for all my new friends, Graham. Let's get this night started!"

The crowd cheered. Graham groaned.

With a look over her shoulder that could have brought a better man to his knees, Lana sauntered away, beer bottle at her hip as she mouthed "Growly Bear" to him.

With close to forty people in his twenty-five-maximum diner, he'd likely have to bust out the cases of Midnight Sun IPA that had just come in. When Lana said beer, she didn't mean the cheap stuff. It wouldn't be the first time that his repeat patroness walked away with a tab well into four digits. When someone had that kind of money...

"You'd never see me again," Graham murmured as he started making tick marks on a piece of scratch paper to keep track of bottles, adding them as free drinks to the tables of those who claimed their freebies.

Three drinks per customer. That was his rule. One Growly Bear a night. Graham learned the hard way to keep that rule, no matter how ticked off the customers got. They could eat themselves into a coma, but Graham wasn't going to hose any more vomit off his front walk or be responsible for someone wrecking a Ferrari on the winding mountain road back to the resort.

And if anyone got too angry? Well, Graham always enjoyed tossing crappy customers out of his establishment.

When a momentary hush fell over the crowd, accompanied by heavy boots stomping across the wood flooring, Graham's lips curved. And as a body took the seat next to Graham's line of impatient customers, he paused in his work to hand the newcomer a soda and a cheeseburger. No one said a word in protest.

"Thanks." Easton Lockett's deep rumble sounded like a freight train with a smoking habit, even though the owner of the voice would never even consider touching a cigarette.

Some people were tall. Some people were built like tanks, muscular and wide. And some looked like they could sneeze and take down a brick building.

Easton was bigger than all that.

Having to duck when he came through the diner's very normal sized doorway, Easton was beard and man bun above every person in the room. Climbing through the mountains as a wilderness guide his entire adult life had only put muscle on Easton's massive frame, shrinking the rest of the world down a few notches or two. Graham wasn't a little guy, but there was something about being near his friend that made him feel itty-bitty.

Itty-bitty never had been a descriptor Graham enjoyed for himself, but when Easton handed him a ham and cheese hoagie, he decided that he'd let it go for the moment.

"Took your time," Graham told him. "I've been waiting on you."

Glancing at who *wasn't* accompanying him, Graham raised an eyebrow. "Should I bother asking where my dog is?"

"Where do you think?" Easton grunted in response. "Curled up in my sister's lap on the couch."

"You know, most fur aunts and uncles bring their fur nephews back when the day is done."

"She likes him better than the rest of us."

Easton sipped his soda, ignoring Graham's chastisement as successfully as Graham was ignoring his line of customers. People were used to this sort of treatment at the Tourist Trap. From what the reviews online said, apparently Graham's lack of customer service was part of the appeal. Since Graham was all for giving the customers what they wanted, he ripped off a third of the hoagie, stuffing it into his mouth.

"Oh man, that's good. Ash?"

"Yeah. She knows you're sick of burgers." Easton shrugged his shoulders. "And it's not my job to help you with yours."

"Shame on you. What kind of friend do you call yourself?"

"The kind that thinks you should hire an extra cook."

Grabbing his air horn from beneath the counter, Graham smirked at his childhood friend. "Naw. There are plenty of bodies in here to help with the work. Push that trash bin into the middle of the room, will you?"

There was nothing like the piercing violence of an air horn screeching through an enclosed space to make everyone wince. With a sigh, Easton stood up and went to the end of the counter, where a fifty-five-gallon trash can with a construction-grade liner waited. Aiming a look of long suffering at Graham, Easton dragged it to the center of the room. The song on the jukebox ended, and everyone was too busy staring at Graham in surprise to put on another one.

This was just how Graham wanted it.

"All right, you dirty people," Graham called out to his customers. "Time to clean up. No more food until you throw your crap in the trash."

He lobbed a wet dishrag to a woman in diamond drop earrings, then a second to Lana and a third to an annoyed-looking Easton. Graham gave them all a cheerful wave as he added a stack of clean rags and a little red bucket of sanitized water on the counter between customer plates.

"Wipe your tables, folks, because I'm not the maid. If you don't like it, the door's right over there." Graham pointed toward the entrance, just past a life-size cedar moose bust mounted on the wall. Far more impressive work than any he'd ever successfully carved, the moose's rack alone was over five feet across. "Don't knock yourselves out on Frank the Mounted Moose's magnificence as you leave."

For some reason, they laughed, as if this was all part of the fun.

While Easton grunted at the customers to throw their crap away, generally terrifying them with his presence, Graham used the rare moment free of expectations to finish his sandwich.

A soft clearing of a woman's throat was meant to get his attention. Graham ignored her.

"Excuse me."

"No more drinks until the room is clean." Graham kept his focus on the hoagie. "Grab a rag, and we'll get there faster."

"Actually, I was hoping to just have a glass of water."

There was a lot of money in this room—and didn't it disgust him that he could identify an Armani suit on sight—but when Graham glanced up from his sandwich, the woman in front of him looked *normal*. She was wearing a worn Mickey Mouse sweatshirt and torn jeans, traveling clothes most likely, and her brown hair was twisted up in a messy bun. Actually messy, not those artfully staged messes the stylists got paid to create in the resort's spa.

Shoving her glasses further up on her slender nose, the woman dug in her pocket. "Extra ice, please."

In a world of too many Gucci purses, this one used her pockets. Graham liked her already. "Didn't anyone warn you about the water here?"

His customer tilted her head to the side, a long tendril of grown-out bangs falling into her eyes. "What's wrong with the water?"

The tendril wasn't sexy. Lodged in between her glasses and her face, she had to cross her eyes and wrinkle her nose a few times to free it. Amusement curled through him, but Graham didn't let it come through in his voice.

"Ever seen what a three-quarter-ton moose with a full bladder can do to a fresh spring?"

Suspicion and jet lag weren't a good look on anyone, but with one eyebrow raised, her glasses couldn't maintain their perch. If she'd taped them with Scotch tape, it couldn't have been more adorably dorky.

"I don't believe you."

"Don't say I didn't warn you."

Behind the counter, where she wouldn't be able to see, Graham used his soda gun to fill crystal clear water into a glass with ice. Then he added a drop of the yellow food coloring he kept for this exact purpose before giving the water a spin with a spoon. The drink he gave her was tinted faintly yellow, the color of pale urine.

Either she didn't mind a dash of pee in her water or she was too tired to care, because she took the glass. That eyebrow did climb a little higher.

Easton was still pushing the trash bin around the room, so Graham watched her as she lifted the drink to her lips.

"Are you sure you want to do that?" he asked just before she took a sip.

She paused, lips to the rim of her glass. "You wouldn't risk the health and safety of all these people serving tainted water."

Graham chuckled. "Glad to know you have faith in me, Zoey."

Furrowing her brow, she of the glasses and ice water frowned, the tendril of hair falling back in between her glasses and nose. "How do you know my name?"

Graham cut his head toward the stunning woman holding court in the center of the restaurant.

"I remember my customers, and Lana said you were a Tourist Trap"—pausing at the word *virgin*, Graham cleared his throat—"newbie. I'm Graham."

Someone must have said something exciting because a roar of guffaws made Zoey wince. The brief respite from the jukebox ended as they cranked it up again. He blamed Lana. She always loved to blast "9 to 5" every time he made her work. The tourists found it hysterical.

When Zoey glanced around at the cheering crowd and grimaced, Graham rested his forearms on the counter and leaned in toward her. "Yeah, me too. My ears don't work anymore. Not a Dolly fan?"

"Not after a nine-hour flight. I'm not even sure where I am right now."

Customers he had already served started lining up again,

ready for their free beers, but Graham kept his attention on the woman shifting from one foot to the other, her fingers tugging on the hem of her Mickey Mouse sweatshirt. She took a sip of her water without gagging.

"We're in Moose Springs, Alaska. An hour and fifteen minutes outside Anchorage and a thousand miles away from everything awful except your hotel. That place is a dump."

When Zoey choked on her water, Graham admitted, "Okay, it's not too terrible up there. Lana said you wanted a Growly Bear?"

"Umm...I'm worried what that means." She must have noticed what they were doing to the statue near the jukebox. Barley—the life-size carved grizzly bear guarding the far corner—had been groped more times than Graham ever had, lucky son of a gun.

"You should be." Gesturing toward Barley with his chin, Graham added, "Look at that. It's not right."

Zoey swirled her glass of moose pee in her hand, ice cubes clinking. "Do you think the artist meant for that...part...to look like that?"

"True artistic expression should never be qualified or quantified." Graham swallowed the last bite of his hoagie. "Besides, got to let the guy keep his dignity."

"Yes, but why is the grizzly wearing chaps?"

"It's a biker bear."

"Oh. Huh. I guess I can see that." Zoey started to turn, then she hesitated. Curling her finger at Graham to lean in closer, she lowered her voice.

"Watch that guy at the end of the counter. The one in the blue shirt."

Blue shirt, khaki pants, third to enter the diner in a group of six. They'd been working their way through Graham's selection of Alaskan brews, vocalizing their thoughts on each loudly enough to impress the poor schmucks stuck sitting nearby.

"Don't worry. I keep count of how many drinks they're having," Graham promised her in reassurance. "Counting to three is one of my many skills."

"I think you might have lost count on Lana already." Zoey's lip quirked up a little. "And he just took a twenty from your tip jar. Thanks for the drink."

Graham's head snapped around, but all he saw was blue shirt and his buddies lifting their beers and simultaneously chugging, frat boys grown up to be no more refined than they'd started.

When he turned back, Zoey had reseated herself at her small table, book in hand and glasses slipping down her nose.

She was reading a book. In the loudest restaurant ever. Fascinating.

To be exact, she was reading Luffet and Mash's *How to Do Alaska*. There wasn't actually a Luffet, and Mash was a guy named Jerry who had passed out on Graham's floor last year after an ill-conceived notion the entire resort needed burgers after their Christmas celebration. Sobering him up in a snowbank had been fun, but Jerry's idea of how to do Alaska was nowhere close to the real—or right—way.

When blue shirt came up and asked for another round, Graham kept close watch out of the corner of his eye. Sure enough, his elbow was right next to the tip jar.

"Watch out," Graham said in gruff warning as he scooped out

a massive order of fries and grabbed their last beers. "I keep a trap in there."

"What?"

"The tip jar. Be careful. There's a live fox trap in the bottom of the jar beneath the bills. It will shatter your wrist."

Blue shirt looked at him like he was crazy, but he didn't stick his hand inside the tip jar this time when he dropped in a couple dollars. Idiot. Graham wasn't a hunter. Killing defenseless wildlife had never appealed to him, but even he knew enough about hunting to know traps were rarely smaller than seven to eight inches across when set. At most, the tip jar was five.

Maybe he would get a larger jar and actually keep a trap in there. Would serve anyone with sticky fingers right. Speaking of serving...

Zoey and her book were still at the table near him. She should have stuck out like a sore thumb in this crowd, but Zoey blended in to near transparency.

For some reason, he found that refreshing.

Since she had saved his tip jar, Graham stopped what he was doing, ignored the yowls for more food, and leaned over the counter. Easton was still waiting for the last of the tables to finish clearing their trash, much to his friend's obvious annoyance. Graham could have helped him, but talking to her seemed a lot more interesting.

"Hey, Zoey. You want that Growly Bear? Last one of the night."

"Umm...maybe?"

"Yes or no, darlin'. If you're going Growly, you're going all in. If you have doubts, step away from the bear."

When she lifted her chin and pushed her glasses higher on her nose with the tip of her pinkie, Graham couldn't help the wide grin stretching across his face. Damn, she was cute.

"I'm in."

What had she just gotten herself into? She didn't even drink.

Those same words had been replaying in Zoey Caldwell's head ever since she'd gotten off the plane in Anchorage. She wasn't a risk taker, far from it, but she'd dreamed of coming to Alaska her whole life. Zoey had scrimped and saved every spare penny she could scrape together for years. When she had finally saved up enough and Lana mentioned her plans for her next trip to Moose Springs, offering to share a room as she always did, Zoey couldn't pass up the chance at her dream vacation.

A trip to Alaska wasn't just the top item on Zoey's bucket list. Alaska was the whole bucket and the water inside it.

Never had Zoey been so excited, so overwhelmed, and so ready to sleep off the jet lag her nine-hour flight had given her. But Lana insisted on them coming to the rustic little hamburger and hot dog joint, claiming this a rite of passage. The Tourist Trap was charming in the same way the guy at the grill was charming. A little rough around the edges, but amusing. There weren't any menus, only a whiteboard sign with a Magic Marker. It read *Menu: Same crap we always have. Specials: Whatever you jerks didn't eat yesterday.*

Zoey liked it here already.

Swirling her glass idly, Zoey decided the gorgeous cook should have at least added salt to her yellow water and made it room temperature.

If one was going to be a smart-ass, it was important to go all in.

Graham was disturbingly attractive. Too attractive. Grab your moose pee and run back to the hotel on the mountain type of attractive. In Zoey's world, that level of attractiveness was almost off-putting. Medium attractive was more her type. Safer. Calmer. Less...whatever was happening over there behind that grill.

If the Tourist Trap wanted to make money, they needed cooks who were remotely approachable. Not tall, muscled, scruffy-faced men in blue jeans and snug white T-shirts with warm eyes.

He caught her looking at him and winked.

Graham gave exceptionably good wink.

"Oh, you're a bad, bad idea." Zoey groaned, shaking her head. "Nope, not doing that."

"Not doing what, love?" Lana dropped down in the seat next to Zoey, drumming her fingernails on the tabletop. "Who are we not doing?"

"No one." The clack of rattling ice cubes against metal pulled her attention. Yep. Sexy T-shirt man was shaking something in a makeshift cocktail shaker fashioned from a YETI tumbler. Strong fingers held the shaker closed with a single hand, biceps flexing as he absently shook the YETI and scooted fresh-seared burgers to the far side of the flat top grill.

Competent and gorgeous just didn't seem fair.

Lana followed Zoey's eyes. "Oh, trust me. He's not for sale. That boy is locals only. But he can shake a cocktail, can't he?"

Blushing, Zoey took refuge behind her book.

In the land of the midnight sun, June was technically the month with the most hours of sunlight. And since she'd arrived on the summer solstice—the longest day of the year—it was no wonder this day seemed like it had lasted forever. The first flight from Chicago to Seattle had been a series of children kicking her seat back, strangers trying to talk to her despite her earphones, and rushing through the airport terminal because someone—who would remain unnamed—hadn't given herself enough layover time between flights. Added to her natural reluctance of flying, Zoey nearly clawed her way out of the plane from Seattle to Anchorage, the final leg of her trip.

One look at the mountains rising in the skyline surrounding Anchorage, and Zoey knew getting here had been worth every second.

To her pleasure, Lana had hired someone to pick her up from the airport instead of Zoey having to take a shuttle. Lana accompanied the chauffeur, so Zoey had her friend to talk to on the long drive to Moose Springs. The winding scenic road had been stunning, even with her growing headache and jet lag. The deep green and blue mountains with their snowy peaks rising above the hotel and the quaint Alaskan town with its small lake cradled in the foothills below were incredible. Then they'd pulled into the hotel and Zoey's jaw had dropped.

Moose Springs Resort was, to put it simply, absolutely fabulous.

Somehow the rustic luxury of the world-class lodge was even better than what Lana and a hundred internet image searches promised. Lana had invited her to come along every time before, but as with all of Lana's adventures around the world, Zoey had been forced to say no. Just because Lana wanted to fly off to Europe on any given weekday didn't mean Zoey could afford to take off work to go too. Her friend might be a trust fund baby with more than enough cash to spend on them both, but Zoey refused to let Lana foot the bill of their friendship. Besides, she had a waitressing job she couldn't risk losing.

Finally being able to say yes to a trip with her friend was just as fabulous as the resort itself.

"There's just no one interesting here yet." With a dramatic sigh, Lana's eyes swept the room. "It gets better around here closer to the Fourth of July... Oh! I see a familiar face. Come with me, and I'll introduce you."

Nope. Nope nope nope. Theirs was a friendship with long-established rules. Shaking her head, Zoey leaned in. "I don't make you listen to stories about my job, and you don't introduce me to your other friends, remember? Everyone always thinks I'm your assistant."

Lana rolled her eyes. "One day, you will be less of a stick-in-the-mud. I will break you."

Taking a sip of her moose pee, Zoey shot her friend a sassy look. "You're welcome to try."

Theirs was a strange friendship, but somehow it worked. They had next to nothing in common, but they complemented each other well. Zoey didn't want to be the center of attention, and Lana had that covered. Lana needed someone she could trust, someone she could talk to with impunity, no matter what she'd gotten herself into this time. Zoey was good at listening without judging too much...or calling the cops.

Another rattle of ice—this time in a glass—was equally hard to ignore.

"Try not to let your eyes fall out of your head, love," Lana murmured.

"Shut up." Hiking her book higher up, Zoey glanced guiltily over the top. Sexy T-shirt guy's attention was locked right on them even as he worked.

"How's your water, Zoey?"

"Don't tease her, Graham." Lana tsked, a tease-me-instead tsk if there ever was one. "Zoey won't fall for your tricks."

"I have no idea what you're talking about."

Lana rolled her eyes. "Don't trust him, Zoey. Graham might look like a sweet thing, but he's a snob through and through. To him, we're the enemy."

Instead of being offended, Graham just dribbled a splash of red-colored liquor over the brightest, bluest cocktail Zoey had ever seen. "Hey, Zoey. Have you ever read *Where the Red Fern Grows*?"

Zoey blinked at him. "I'm sorry, what was that?"

"So, this kid wants to earn some money, and he decides to do it by catching raccoons for their pelts. He figures out the raccoons will stick their hands in a coffee can to grab a piece of shiny tin and get stuck. Mean, right?"

She tilted her head, confused at the randomness of his comments, then squeaked in alarm as Graham abandoned his counter and headed for their table. "He's coming over here, Lana," she hissed.

"I know." Even her jet-setting friend seemed impressed. "I'm not sure anyone's ever seen his feet before."

Setting down the drink and some unknown kind of bratwurst in front of her, Graham gave them a sexy smile. "My motto has always been not to grab the sparkly stuff. Lana's sparkly, and I'm liable to lose my pelt when she's done with me."

"If Lana lets you get a paw on her, just let go before you get bonked in the head." Zoey returned his smile with a shy one of her own.

"Hey!" Lana protested, but not with nearly enough vigor, her attention already straying across the room. In all their years of friendship, Zoey could count on her fingers how often Lana had managed to sit still for more than a couple of minutes.

Sexy T-shirt guy must have known Lana well. "I'm too lazy to keep up with her anyway. Enjoy your Growly Bear. This one's on me. Just drink it slow."

Mesmerized by how bright and blue it was, Zoey picked up her drink with a murmured thanks. Why were there blue gummy bears swimming in the liquid? Or were they drowning? Currently, Zoey was drowning in the cuteness of her dinner. It looked like a normal bratwurst, but he'd slipped a pair of paper antlers over one end and added two eyes and a toothy grin with ketchup.

"This smells delicious, but it's too freaking cute to eat."

Arching an eyebrow at his generosity, Lana waited until Graham was headed back to the grill before leaning in, her voice lowered conspiratorially. "He only gives kids the antlers. And he never gives anyone anything for free." Lana's eyes sparkled with mischief. "He likes you. I'll ask what he's doing later."

"*No.*" Her face flushing, Zoey gave her a warning look. "Lana, don't you dare."

"I'm doing it."

Just as Lana started to open her mouth in Graham's direction, Zoey squeaked out one of her best threats. "I know your natural hair color."

Lana paused, considering it. "Fine. But you're no fun."

No one should look that good walking across a room or ignoring the customers vying for his attention. Zoey took a bite of the dog as she watched Graham, then immediately spat it out. It tasted awful, the meat filled with a heavy combination of spices that made Zoey gag. In a panic to get the taste out of her mouth, Zoey grabbed for the drink, taking a slug of the bright blue liquid. She was drinking fire. Sugary *fire*.

Lana dissolved into laughter at the expression on her face.

"What's in this?" Choking and sputtering, Zoey took refuge in her pee water.

"It's better not to ask," Graham replied at the same time as Lana patted her hand and said, "Don't worry. Reindeer is an acquired taste. By the time we leave, you'll love them."

"I'm eating a reindeer?" A sweet, cuddly, pulls Santa's sleigh at Christmastime reindeer? Zoey stared at them in horror. She was eating Rudolph. She had just swallowed Rudolph by-product.

Graham said to her from behind his grill, "Welcome to Alaska, Zoey."

Well, there was no going back now. Grabbing the Growly Bear, Zoey took another drink.

CHAPTER 2

LANA'S GENEROSITY HAD LED TO...SHENANIGANS.

Disturbing beer-inspired shenanigans that would have horrified the younger, more impressionable version of Graham. Someone tried to summit Frank the Mounted Moose's impressive antlers and almost succeeded. Another failed in such dramatic fashion, Graham was forced to water down everyone's drinks. Finally, when they were dangerously close to becoming a fun place to hang out, Graham declared it closing time.

It was barely ten.

Sometimes he closed as late as midnight in the summer, knowing his town stayed up and wanted somewhere to eat during the sunlight-filled evening, but that changed depending on his mood. He was less reliable in the winter, and when the Seawolves were playing, he'd been known to not bother opening at all.

Boy, did the tourists online review the snot out of him for *that*.

"Out!" Graham called cheerfully to the remaining stragglers. "Sorry, ladies. You'll have to come back tomorrow."

"But, Graham—"

"Nope. Back to whence you came. Shoo, tourists, you are no longer trapped today."

Locking the door, Graham turned to the mess he'd have to clean up and blinked.

There was a drunk bookworm in his diner.

Somehow during all the craziness of the evening, Graham failed to notice Lana had left, but her friend had not. Zoey had abandoned her table and was now curled up on a seat against the wall, wedged next to a pay phone that hadn't worked since Graham bought the place.

She was still trying to read her book, but she was half-asleep, and her book was upside down.

Huh. He'd only given her the one drink, and that had been hours ago. Joining her by the pay phone, Graham hunkered down so they were eye level, voice softened to sound unthreatening.

"Hey there, Zoey Bear. Where did Lana go? You need a ride home. We're all closed up here."

Zoey peered at him suspiciously, then shook her head. "I need my glasses," she slurred. "I can't see. Danger, danger, Will Robinson."

Graham grinned, because for a tourist, she was kind of growing on him. Trying to adjust her glasses on her nose, Zoey failed to realize that she'd been using them as a bookmark. Taking her very delicate frames, Graham carefully opened them and set them on her nose.

"Imma call a cab." When she started to stand, she ended up staggering. "Whoops."

Graham caught her arm to steady her. "Hey, Zoey? Did anyone else but me give you a drink tonight?"

"Nope. But Lana had some aspirin."

"Are you sure you took aspirin?"

Sticking her nose in his face, Zoey raised an eyebrow. "Are *you* sure I took aspirin?"

Well. This was a first on his watch. "Give me your phone, Zoey. I want to call your friend."

It took her a minute to find her phone in her hand, but with Graham's help, Zoey got there eventually. She proudly presented it to him. Without asking permission, he squished her thumb on the phone to unlock it, then found Lana's name on the recent calls list.

"Yes?" A familiar purr answered on the fourth ring. "I'm rather busy, love."

"Lana, it's Graham. Tell me you didn't give Zoey drugs when she was drinking. Do I need to call an ambulance right now?"

"Oh, no. She's a lightweight. She never drinks."

Graham growled. "And you convinced her to start with a Growly Bear? Come on, L. I trusted you."

"Hmm, I'm sure she'll be fine. You always take such good care of us."

"What did you give her?" Speaking slowly and making sure to enunciate through his gritted teeth, Graham tried to keep his temper. "Lana, this isn't funny. She's looped."

"Zoey only took a couple baby aspirin for her headache. I'll come back for her. In my defense, I thought she'd already gone back to the resort. She never stays out this late."

And he was sure Lana looked her hardest too.

Graham cursed under his breath. "No thanks, I'll handle it. You're a terrible friend, you know that, right?"

Not bothering to listen to her answer, Graham hung up, focusing on the woman in front of him. He didn't take a lot of things seriously, but Graham had a singular distaste for people bailing on each other.

"Your eyebrow is twitching. Up down up down." Zoey tried to waggle her own eyebrows, glasses slipping.

"Yeah, well, Lana makes me twitchy." Wrapping an arm around her waist, Graham helped her to her feet.

"Don't be mad," she slurred. "It's not her fault. Money makes people crazy."

Graham caught a hand in the jaw as she gestured exuberantly in demonstration. "Like, *crazy*. And she's got so much. So. Much. Where's my cab? Imma call another one."

"Sorry, Zoey, I'm going to take you home. I'm not calling you a ride at this time of night, because the good drivers are already taken. Trust me, you don't want the B-team of Moose Springs rideshare drivers."

"What's the mileage on your meter?" One drunken eyeball narrowed suspiciously. "Overcharging is wrong. Is *wrong*." When she poked him in the chest with her finger, Graham's grin widened. "I'm watching you, mister."

This sloshy little bit was quickly in the running for his favorite customer ever. And since Lana had taken a dive off the ladder of Graham's good opinion tonight, the position was currently open.

Juggling Zoey while closing would have been easier with an extra hand, but Graham was dexterous with his feet when needed, and she was determined to help. By the time they killed all the lights and locked the front door, Graham's truck was the only vehicle left by the building. With some effort, Graham pried open the passenger side door, freshly bent from Ulysses's wooing.

"In you go. Seat belts aren't optional."

"Nope. Nope nope nope. Stranger danger."

"I'm not a stranger," Graham promised. "We've already met."

Again with the narrowed eyes. She was a suspicious one. Chuckling, Graham took her phone, snapped a picture of the two of them together, then messaged it to Lana. "See? Now there's proof I was with you tonight. The cops will come looking for me first if you never arrive safely. Lana will tell them."

"What if she doesn't arrive safely either? S'not a good plan." Even as she argued with him, Zoey crawled into the front seat with all the grace and dignity of a newborn baby goat. He clipped her seat belt and closed her door. Graham sighed as he went to the driver's side and climbed in.

There was a burrito at home. He'd planned on eating it by now. But apparently, he was going to the big house instead. This was *definitely* a Tuesday.

"Where's your mirror?"

"Ulysses got it in the divorce."

Zoey tilted her head sideways in confusion and kept on tilting. She tilted all the way over to rest her head on the bench seat back between them, then beamed at him.

"I'm in Alaska."

It had been a long time since he'd seen someone so filled with joy. Even if it was Growly Bear driven, Graham couldn't help but enjoy her happiness.

"You're in Alaska. And you're going to love it here."

If she loved it even a tenth as much as Graham did, she'd never want to leave.

The short night and the angle of the sun below the horizon left the winding mountain road toward Moose Springs Resort blanketed in a soft gray hue. Thick evergreens closed in as they passed a sign for the resort, darkening the blacktop enough Graham finally flipped on his lights.

If he hadn't spent his entire life in Moose Springs, Graham might have waxed poetic about the idyllic setting, a small town nestled in the loving embrace of the towering Chugach Mountain Range. But to Graham, his home was a bowl of cereal. The best of everything was in the bottom of the bowl, with the mountains keeping everything else out. And the resort was a big, crusty piece of cheese that survived the dishwasher and was still stuck to the side of the bowl, currently ruining his breakfast.

The Tourist Trap was near the clustered housing most of the residents lived in, safely in the bowl. Just outside town, higher up in the foothills to give an incredible view of the mountains and access to the best skiing, sat Moose Springs Resort. A huge, sprawling cedar lodge blending high-class luxury and rustic log cabin mountain charm.

If Graham could have scraped the crusty thing off the side of his mountain and flicked it away, he would have in a heartbeat.

When the grass on either side of the road shifted from wild to perfectly mown, Graham slowed down. The entrance sign was impossible to miss, as was the guardhouse everyone had to pass to get inside. Graham knew the bored-looking gate guard, so he didn't bother signing in. Instead, he raised two fingers in greeting as he rolled past, keeping one eye on the artfully patterned concrete driveway and one on the woman next to him as he drove through the resort grounds. At some point during the drive, she'd leaned the other way, her forehead pressed to the window. The moose goo on the outside of the window didn't seem to bother Zoey as she stared at the approaching hotel, lights twinkling in the soft dimness of the mountain's shadow.

"You still good over there?" he asked her.

"S'like Christmas."

"Yeah. You should actually see it at Christmas. It's ridiculous."

"Hmm." A soft sigh escaped her lips.

Graham never—*never*—went up to Moose Springs Resort if he could avoid it. The place was one big playground for the rich, and they all seemed to find him down at the diner, no matter how hard Graham tried to avoid them. But he'd been there enough over the years, Graham could have driven to the resort with his eyes closed. He parked his truck by the hotel's valet station and motioned the valets away when they hurried over.

Graham was more than capable of opening his own doors and collecting the drunk woman staring blearily at his dashboard. When she swayed on her feet, Graham called it a loss and simply scooped her into his arms. She squeaked at the change of elevation, leaving Graham to wave awkwardly at the staff as he strode through the hand-carved entry doors the valets held open for him.

"Nothing to see here," Graham declared cheerfully to the startled desk attendant as he went past. "Continue your lives as normal."

Halfway to the elevator, it occurred to him that he didn't know where he was going. And the bookworm draped romantically in his arms was a solid little thing. That or maybe he needed to start going to the gym more often. Either way, he was going to drop her. So he turned around and headed back to the desk and to the stranger manning check-in, a curly-haired youth named...Grass? Seriously? Who named their kid *Grass*?

Grass must have been seasonal, because Graham knew all the locals. And none of them would have borne that name on a name tag.

When they reached the counter, Graham set Zoey down on her feet, keeping one arm around her waist to steady her. Upon seeing Zoey's confused expression, Graham tilted his head to catch her dazed eyes. "Hey, Zo, you still in there?"

"Violent delights have violent ends." She dissolved into drunken giggles, poking at Graham's white T-shirt. "A sail! A sail!"

Shakespeare. She was quoting Shakespeare while trashed. "Good to know." Glancing at Grass, Graham jutted his chin toward the woman he currently held upright. "This is Zoey. I think she's staying with Lana Montgomery. How do I find her room?"

"Umm, we're not allowed to give out a guest's room location, sir." The clerk typed rapidly at the computer in front of him, but Grass quickly twisted the monitor away when Graham leaned over to sneak a peek.

"Yes, but she's not really all that mobile right now."

"We can take care of Miss..." Grass hesitated, as if unwilling to even share her name. While Graham appreciated the safety in their protocol, it was late, he was tired, and there was a microwavable burrito at home whimpering his name.

"Just call Jackson. Or the Shaws. They know me, and they'll give you the go-ahead. Oh, give me a key to her room too."

Grass looked at Graham in horror. "I can't call the owners or their son this late. It's two in the morning in New York. I'll get fired."

Why was it always him who had to put out the fires? Didn't the world understand Graham was much better left to his own devices? Pulling his phone out of his pocket, he dialed a number. It rang three times before a tired voice answered.

"This better be worth it."

"Women always are," Graham joked. "Hey, man. I'm at the big house. Tell them to call your folks. I need an authorization to drop off someone in her room. One of my customers decided to mix headache medicine and liquor."

"Just let the hotel staff do it."

"I don't know the staff." At the offended look from Grass, Graham shrugged. "What? I don't know you, and you're named Grass. It's weird, man. Jackson says to let me through."

"I didn't say that," Jackson reminded him.

"No, but you're going to say that."

"Let the staff handle it. I'll see you in a couple days." With a grunt, Jackson hung up on him.

"Good talk, Jax." Graham turned to Grass. "Okay, let's start this over. Hi. My name is Graham, and I want a burrito. Give me her room key, or I'll kill you."

Hmm, maybe that should have been his follow-up. The horrified-looking desk clerk reached for the phone and took a step back.

"I have a key." Reaching in her pocket, Zoey pulled out a dollar bill. "Hmm, that's not it."

Tightening his arm around her waist to keep her from tipping over, Graham sighed. "You just called security, didn't you?"

A wide-eyed Grass took another step back before nodding his head. "Sir, please remain calm."

Things probably would have gone downhill after that, but a familiar voice pulled his attention. "Is that Graham Barnett in my hotel? The sky must be falling."

Graham looked over to see the night manager coming down the hall. Every inch of her screamed business professional, from nose to high-heeled toes.

This person he knew. He'd sat behind her in middle school, poking her with a pencil to annoy her in hopes that she'd notice him. Back then, Hannah had been the prettiest girl in Moose Springs. Now, with runway model height, smooth dark skin, and liquid eyes, she was stunning. Hannah was also in the prime spot to take over the world-class resort as manager whenever the current manager retired.

For a long time, Graham had thought he loved her. Too many on-again, off-again, one-more-time's, and this-will-never-work's had disabused him of the notion. She had places to go Graham couldn't follow. Still, he would never mind Hannah's face coming through his door.

"Hey, Hannah, come upstairs with me."

Hannah raised a perfectly sculpted eyebrow. "If that line didn't work after junior prom, it's not working now."

Chuckling, Graham gestured to the woman slumping against

his shoulder, her nose squashed into his armpit, dislodging her glasses. "Just doing my good deed for the day."

"What's wrong with her?"

"Growly Bear and two baby aspirin. Theoretically. I was only complicit in the first, not the second."

Hannah waved away the security guards heading for him. "The day you invented that drink was the day I earned a permanent headache. Do you know how many blue messes the housekeeping staff cleans up? You owe them half your tips, Graham."

"Probably," he agreed. "But first I need to get Zoey here to her room so she can sleep this off."

"Or you could just leave her with us," Hannah pointed out.

"I already said he could do that, ma'am." Grass frowned at him.

Graham frowned back. "And I said I don't know you. Hannah, where did you find this kid?"

Hannah watched the exchange with amusement. "Grass was top of his class's hotel management program."

Hmm. Graham wasn't convinced. Grass swallowed.

"You always did like to be the hero," Hannah said, patting his arm. "Okay, come on. Unlike you, I have work to do."

"I work."

"Do you?"

Maybe he didn't. He certainly *tried* not to, as much as possible.

Graham noticed Zoey had picked up a brochure off the counter and was trying to read it. "You drunk read. That's adorable."

"*You're* arodable," Zoey slurred in retort. "Boom. That just happened."

Could she have been any drunker? Slinging her over his

shoulder would have been easier, but there was—deep in the private parts of his mind where he admitted to eating Frosted Flakes and forgetting to floss—a sliver of Graham who still enjoyed being a good guy.

It had never gotten him anything but trouble, but he still couldn't completely disconnect from his upbringing.

A more practical person would have carried her over his shoulder and lived to bend his elbows the next day. Instead, Graham carefully picked her up, one arm beneath her knees and the other behind her back.

"Okay, upsy-daisy."

He caught Hannah watching him, and Graham gave her a flirty wink. Hannah rolled her eyes and started off toward the elevators. Apparently, she knew which room Zoey was staying in by memory, despite the resort's size.

Speaking of memory, something tickled his. "Hey, Hannah, don't I owe you a drink?"

His ex smirked as she punched the elevator button for Zoey's floor. "A drink because of what you did at Christmas or a drink because of what you did at New Year's?"

Honestly, he couldn't remember much of either of those two days, so he hazarded a guess. "Umm...New Year's?"

"You owe me a drink and about two hundred dollars."

"Ouch."

"Not my fault you can't handle yourself during Go Fish."

"Strip Go Fish."

"We didn't play strip Go Fish."

"Are you sure? Because I feel like I got naked."

"Not because anyone wanted you to, buster."

Well. That wasn't great for the ego. And Zoey wasn't great for his arms. The desire to be chivalrous had been epically destroyed by the time they reached the fourth floor, where Lana and Zoey's suite was situated.

"Could this place be any bigger?" Graham grunted as Hannah unlocked the door. "You need a Segway or something to get around."

"Stop whining." Opening the door, Hannah stuck her head in to ensure the room wasn't occupied. "The exercise won't kill you."

"I'm not whining."

She gave him an amused look. "You're not *not* whining."

The suite was enormous. There was a private bedroom and a full living room, with a kitchenette and a wet bar. The butter-soft leather couch had a pillow and a blanket on it, tidily folded and placed at one end unobtrusively. Instinct told him that of the two of them, Lana wouldn't know unobtrusive if it failed to smack her in the face.

"Okay, darlin'." Graham set her down gently on the couch. "You're going to drink some water and then sleep off the bear attack."

"Don't drink the water." Mumbling, Zoey rolled over into the cushions. "It's…source…moose urine. Don't want to be a zombie…"

Graham's lips curved involuntarily. "What was that?"

"Chronic wasting disease…mostly deer…some moose…don't want to be…zombie moose…end of the world…"

Then she was out cold, leaving Graham to stand there, wondering if zombie moose really existed and if maybe a zombie moose apocalypse might actually be a thing.

Huh.

"You and I are going to have to talk," Graham told the lump on the couch. "You're fascinating."

Under the watchful eye of a woman who knew Graham was more than trustworthy in there all alone, he made sure to tuck a blanket around her and stick a plastic wastebasket next to her head. He slipped Zoey's glasses off her nose and folded them carefully, setting them next to a bottle of water and a worn packet of aspirin from the forgotten depths of Graham's wallet.

Hesitating, Graham glanced at Hannah. "You'll stay with her? Just in case?"

"She's a guest at my hotel." Hannah patted his shoulder and then gently nudged Graham toward the door. "I won't leave this room until I'm sure she's fine. Go *home*, Graham."

Leaving Zoey snoring like a linebacker into her pillow, Graham paused at the doorway, unable to help his tired yawn. "She's cute, right?"

Hannah just shook her head. "Not exactly the word I'd use to describe it. By the way, I talked to the Shaws last week. Their offer still stands."

"Naw, I'm good. I still have some of my pride left." Then, because one of these days, an unlucky guy was finally going to catch a break, he aimed his best smile her way. "So, Hannah. About that drink...?"

"The clock's about to strike midnight, but nice try. Good night, Graham." She gently shut the hotel door in his face.

Yep. Wednesdays. The only thing worse than a Tuesday.

CHAPTER 3

LESS THAN TWENTY-FOUR HOURS INTO her dream vacation, Zoey became a bobblehead.

There was something particularly discombobulating about waking up in a hotel room and not having any idea how she got there. Equally discombobulating was the pounding in between Zoey's ears, like an anvil hammer beating directly on her brain.

She'd been discombobulated. She was a discombobu-head, her skull five times larger than her body, vision bobbing back and forth no matter how hard she tried to remain still.

Groaning, Zoey rolled over and fell straight onto the floor.

The distance between the couch and the carpet was only a foot and a half, but the unexpected drop was enough to land her on her back with a thump and a groan of misery. The worst hangover of her life hadn't been part of the plan. She hadn't scratched this down in her favorite moose-themed notebook, tucked in a bag she hoped was still in her possession.

"I'm going to die," Zoey told the ceiling.

It didn't answer.

"The last thing I remember is a gummy bear."

Again, no help.

Some people could see without their glasses, but Zoey was not one of those people. Everything around her was a smudge of browns and creams and one darkish blob she thought was the coffee table. Fingers scrabbling hopefully at the top of the blob, she found what she was looking for, folded up next to a bottle of water she accidentally knocked over. Stuffing her glasses onto her face, she blinked, hoping to bring her surroundings into focus.

Even with the glasses, the world continued to spin.

Groaning again, Zoey pushed herself up on her elbows. "Lana? Please tell me you're here. I don't have the functional brain cells to track you down this morning."

"Please, as if I'd ever let you wake up alone in your condition."

Wrapped in a silk robe, Lana appeared from her bedroom, bypassing the couch for the suite's modest kitchen. Poking around in the refrigerator, she emerged with two tomato-red drinks filling her hands, bursting with vegetables and bacon, an entire crab leg, and several violently speared cocktail shrimp.

Eyes and legs. The shrimp still had eyes and legs. At eight thirty-five in the morning.

Zoey shuddered.

"Did we have fun last night?" The enjoyment on Lana's face grew. "Whenever I wake up your shade of green, it's usually because I had too much fun."

"I have no idea. Do you have to be so cheerful? Shouldn't you be miserable too? I'm not the only one who made questionable choices last night."

Lana shook her head. "Trust me, the first thing one learns in the Montgomery household is to hold one's liquor in public. I'll rent the Tourist Trap for us one night and show you the difference."

"You mean that, don't you?"

"Of course. Graham would love it. He never passes an opportunity to shirk his workload. Does your head hurt? I'll get you a cold compress."

Clutching her face in agony must have clued Lana in.

Setting the drinks down far too close to Zoey's head, Lana disappeared into the bathroom. Shrimp and tomato smells wafted Zoey's way, making her gag. She nudged them farther away with her fingers, trying not to look directly in the cocktail shrimp's terrified little face.

"Call room service for a pickax," Zoey suggested. "Anything sharp and heavy will be fine."

Lana reappeared with a wet washcloth, carefully arranging it on Zoey's forehead with motherly care. "Sorry, dearest, I'm all out of ways for you to cudgel yourself."

Did she have to look like she'd slept for a month, rested and alert, without a hair out of place? Since Zoey loved her, she didn't begrudge Lana her luck. But as someone who was certain an animal had died in her mouth in the last twelve hours, Lana's lack of so much as a stray eyebrow hair disturbed Zoey. Deep in the dark parts of her primitive brain, she knew it was wrong.

So very wrong.

"Why are you glaring at me?" Lana sounded amused. "I put the Growly Bear in your hand, but I'm not the one who poured it down your throat."

"People who wake up happy aren't to be trusted." Staying on

the floor and squashing the pillow on top of her washcloth was far easier than crawling back up onto the couch. "Or people with hair like yours."

"Hmm? Oh, that's my new sleeping scarf." Hermès, not that Lana would ever be gauche enough to say the brand. "Just wrap and tie, and you wake up smooth as silk. There's aspirin on the coffee table." A teasing tone entered Lana's voice. "A secret admirer left it for you."

"Sure they did. I don't even want to know what room service is charging for painkiller delivery."

Lana sat on the end of the couch that Zoey's nonsilky, far less cheerful body had recently vacated, her expression smug.

"Trust me, no one in this place would dare bring almost expired aspirin made by—" Lana leaned over, peering down at the worn packet. "Dr. Sue's Discount Drugs. Hmm. Maybe you shouldn't take those after all. I have—"

"Nope. Nope nope nope. None of your 'pick-me-ups' or 'right-as-rains,' woman. You need a better labeling system. I don't think your baby aspirin last night were baby aspirin."

"Why is everyone so suspicious of me?" Lana sighed with playful dramatics. "I haven't drugged anyone in months."

"You're joking."

The woman on the couch serenely picked up her Bloody Mary.

"I know you're joking." Zoey looked at the shrimp. "She's joking."

The shrimp stared at her in dismay with beady black eyes and tiny legs that couldn't escape. Zoey stared right back.

"We both deserved a better morning than this."

"Drink, you'll feel better." Taking a sip of one of the drinks and adjusting the second on a coaster, Lana slid it closer to Zoey. "It's my family's special blend. Nothing helps a hangover like a Montgomery Bloody Mary."

"I'd rather take my chances with Dr. Sue."

"If you insist." Seeming disappointed, Lana sighed with a little shrug. "Anyway, you know how my cousin Killian is coming in? He just landed in Anchorage. Brace yourself, because Haleigh and Enzo are with him."

"Why am I bracing myself?"

Lana rolled her eyes. "Because those two haven't been sober since primary school. It gets annoying. But still, one must play nice with friends of the family. They flew in from Italy this morning and are still on Rome time, so I promised I would have a bite with them. You know how Killian is. He can't stand to be alone for a single minute."

Zoey blinked as her brain tried to keep up. "What am I supposed to know?"

"You've met him. The race car Killian, not the polo Killian, although why I have to have two cousins named Killian is ridiculous to me. My aunts are determined to outdo each other, but really, that went too far. Opening Christmas presents was an absolute nightmare of Freudian proportions."

"I don't think you're using Freudian right."

"Besides," Lana continued blithely. "Everyone knows polo Killian is far superior to race car Killian. You met Killian at Killian's polo match. He was so much better, right?"

"Seriously, if you don't stop talking, I'm going to have to murder you. I mean it, Lana. This is an actual threat."

Lana patted her limp, hungover foot. "You remember. We were in Greece."

"Nope. I have been to zero polo matches with you, and I most definitely have never been to polo matches in Greece. That's one of your other post-inebriated friends."

"Are you so miserable?" Offering a true look of sympathy, Lana patted her again.

"I don't even remember my own name right now." Zoey unscrewed the water bottle top, wincing at her breath as she tore into the worn aspirin package with her teeth, then popped the pills. "Did I make an idiot of myself last night?"

"You're asking the wrong person. Something tall, dark, and handsome brought you home." Lana waggled her eyebrows. At Zoey's horrified expression, she laughed. "It wasn't like that. Graham Barnett would rather sit naked on a lake in winter than have a one-night stand with a *tourist*." She emphasized the word as if she'd said Zoey was a pile of moose poop. "Although the hotel is positively dying with the gossip of it."

Which was exactly what Zoey needed. She already felt entirely outclassed by the other clientele, and being the drunk moose poop girl was not on her dream list of Alaskan experiences.

"So, brunch?" Lana nudged the Bloody Mary closer with her manicured fingernails.

"You're serious." Zoey hid her face back in the pillow, where it was dark and nothing spun or stared at her with shrimpy eyes. "She's serious," she muttered to no one specific.

Lana's phone chirped and she reached for it, quickly scanning her incoming messages. "Meatball in my party in an hour? What?"

Zoey's dull brain couldn't help working through that puzzle. "Sounds like his phone doesn't like his voice," she grumbled into the pillow. "That must translate to 'meet me in the lobby in an hour.'"

"I can't believe he's texting through dictation. Yes, I will be there when I'm ready. You have fingers, Killian. Text like a human being." Setting her phone aside, she turned her bright, disgustingly cheerfulness Zoey's way. "You're coming to brunch, right?"

"With your crazy rich cousin and his friends still on Rome time? Oh no. Not a chance."

"But, Zoey—"

"Nope. I am too...what's your word for it? Peaked. I'm too peaked for brunch with the whosits."

"Oh, these are definitely not the whosits. Haleigh and Enzo are firmly in whatsits territory. New money is always about what they are, not who. Don't worry. You'll perk right up. A little smoked trout and toast and you'll be right as rain. The brunch here is absolutely *divine*."

Now, for the record, Zoey wasn't the pickiest of eaters. But in the last twenty-four hours, she'd only consumed a gummy bear drowning in alcohol and a hot dog made of Dasher or Dancer.

There would be no smoked trout and toast. Not over Zoey's dead body.

"Give the whatsits my regards. I'm going to go barf for a while."

"Oh, love. You really are unwell, aren't you?"

"Not really. Just dramatic and embarrassed."

Smiling with sympathy, Lana scooted closer and smoothed her

hand over Zoey's head. "Graham's drinks can drop a tank. If you hadn't gotten tipsy, I'd be shocked. Drink your Bloody Mary."

"Lana? Why *did* Graham bring me home?"

"Because he lit up like a Christmas tree when he set eyes on you. And since you're on vacation and haven't been on a date since—what was his name?"

"We don't say his name."

"Since no-name, I thought it might be fun to see what he'd do about it."

"And that didn't seem like...I don't know...a potentially dangerous situation to you?"

"With Graham Barnett? That boy is as sweet as they come. Besides, I was watching you through the diner windows the entire time." She waggled her eyebrows again. "And then I followed him to the hotel. It was tons of fun, all sneaking about like a Hamburglar, watching him sweep you up in those masculine, rugged arms. Would you like to see the pictures?"

"I don't want to hear any more." Zoey covered her face with the pillow. "There's too much wrong with all of this."

"I've been with you all night. I came in right after he and the manager brought you to the room, so there's no need to be concerned."

"Things happen in cars."

"Yes, but I would have arranged to have him murdered if he tried. See? All's good."

Zoey quit arguing. It was her own darn fault she'd gotten drunk, and things could have been worse. Lana could have flitted off into the night in another stranger's car, leaving her completely alone. Hamburgling it was Lana's way of taking care of her. Just like more alcohol in the morning, her friend's intentions were good, even if her methods were…questionable.

Pulling the pillow down a couple of inches to peer at Lana, she asked with morbid curiosity. "Lana? Do you *know* people?"

A smug expression was not the answer Zoey was hoping for.

"Okeydokey. I might take that drink now."

It was sweet how Lana seemed to find such pleasure in Zoey's attempts to consume her Montgomery Bloody Mary, watching her with hopeful eyes. Zoey almost felt bad about crawling to the bathroom and gagging Lana's handiwork back up again. As she draped herself on the couch this time, Zoey rubbed her forehead.

"I actually feel a little better now." Narrowing her eyes at Lana, Zoey frowned. "You made me drink that on purpose, didn't you?"

"Of course. Well, now I know you're alive, I need to get down to the spa for a quick spiff before finding Killian. There's no time to go afterward. I have an important meeting this afternoon, then finalizing details for my event with the catering director, and after that, I'm meeting someone for drinks. And you know Killian will drag out brunch *forever*."

"Mm-hmm."

A hum of acknowledgment was her standard response when Lana started talking about places and people Zoey didn't know. Trying to convince her friend she didn't run in the same circles Lana did was far too time-consuming on a good day.

But something Lana said finally registered. "Wait." Zoey

narrowed her eyes. "What event? Lana, please don't tell me you planned this vacation around a party."

"It's a bit more important than a simple party, love," Lana told her. "The proper term is a gala, and I didn't bring it up before you flew in because I know how avoidant you get of my friends."

"Are they your friends though?"

"Acquaintances. And I won't force you to go, but I would be very grateful if you did. I even arranged to have a few dresses available for you if you decide to humor me."

In all the years of their friendship, Zoey had never been comfortable with Lana's family or her acquaintances. But Lana looked so hopeful, and Zoey didn't have the heart to tell her no.

"Can I reserve the right to not go? And give you a maybe?"

"Done." Beaming, Lana hugged her. "Okay, off to get ready for the day."

"The spiffing. I'll do it," Zoey valiantly volunteered. "Get your things, because I'm staying on the couch for another hour."

"Are you sure? You really did get a bit more sloshed than I expected last night. There's a perfectly acceptable beautician in the spa who'll do."

"And you'll come back annoyed and frustrated because they never get your eye makeup right. Then I'll end up fixing it anyway. I'll trade you coffee for a spiffing."

She half expected Lana to order the coffee, but her friend went to the room's coffee maker instead. Lana was many things—too many things—but unobservant wasn't one of them. Even though Zoey had maybe consumed half a dozen cups of coffee in front of her friend, Lana fixed it for her perfectly. One and a half creams, half a sugar.

"There you go." Lana smiled at her warmly, giving Zoey the coffee and her makeup case. "Thank you, dearest. Now, make me beautiful."

Even in her post-inebriated state, Zoey couldn't help but chuckle at that. "You're always beautiful."

Growing up within driving distance of the suburbs of Chicago had its perks. Unable to remember a time when she and her family hadn't been strapped for cash, a teenage Zoey had taken an extra job at a local department store in the makeup department. Somehow spritzing expensive cologne in unsuspecting patrons' faces turned into perching on a stool next to the makeup counter.

She'd never had any formal training, but her hands were steady, and she had a good eye for what palettes brought out the color and sparkle in someone's eyes. As jobs went, it hadn't paid as much as she'd hoped for, but as life skills went, her ability to draw a line of liquid eyeliner with surgical precision benefitted her far more often than she would have expected.

Zoey learned what she needed to keep the women in her seats happy, but as a shy teenager with thick glasses and a single outfit nice enough to work in, she had been surprised to find how much she enjoyed it.

Somehow, in her detailed and determined interrogation of all things Zoey, Lana had discovered her past and put it to full use whenever she really needed a "spiff."

Spiffing Lana for a date often took hours, the socialite nothing if not determined to look her best on the rare occurrences someone managed to catch her eye for an entire evening. But since this was just an afternoon rendezvous, whatever that entailed, Zoey made quicker work of her canvas.

"So what's he like?"

"Hmm?"

"The person you're having drinks with."

"I don't know. I didn't catch his name. I was more focused on his hands." Lana sighed lustily. At Zoey's raised eyebrow, Lana added, "During my massage yesterday morning. Don't be such a prude."

"I'm not a prude."

"Really?"

"I'm not a prude," Zoey clarified. "I just don't love being squished and squashed around by strangers."

"Oh, you do *not* know what you're missing."

Maybe she didn't. It had been a long time since Zoey had been squished, let alone squashed, by anyone, stranger or no.

Making Lana beautiful wasn't hard. She'd look great with a soggy paper bag over her head. But since Zoey loved her, she did her best to make Lana as fabulous as the resort in which they were staying. Then, when Lana rushed off to her breakfast, Zoey moved to the window.

Lana had been kind enough to leave the blackout curtains drawn, but Zoey braved the bright light peaking around the edges of the curtains, drawing them aside. She was met with a vibrant blue sky backdropping rows of mountains, jutting up like gorgeous, ragged teeth.

The part of Illinois she came from was flat as a pancake. Back there, she could see for miles, no matter where she looked. Adrift in a sea of cornfields and soybeans, broken up only by subdivisions and strip malls. Here, Zoey felt anchored in place. The mountains and the valley below were all she could see. She'd been in Moose Springs less than a day, and she'd already fallen in love with this tiny Alaskan town.

"Best vacation ever," she whispered to herself. "Worth every penny."

Hannah hadn't let Graham buy her a drink. She had, however, let him pay her back the money he owed her.

It bothered Graham that he hadn't remembered the two hundred dollars, although in his defense, New Year's was his holiday to be the drunk one. To surround himself with his friends and family and take comfort in the oblivion of his own concoctions, knowing they had his back if he got too stupid.

"Too" was a relative term. Graham was well aware of the reputation preceding him.

Even though his night had run later than expected, with a sloshy little tourist to blame, Graham pulled himself out of bed early, determined to make full use of his morning. The Tourist Trap didn't open until eleven, and Graham was an expert at not showing up a minute beforehand.

Even though his body wanted to hide under the covers for a few more hours, he had things to do. Chainsaws to oil. Large chunks of wood to carve.

The thirty-acre stretch of land lining the southern edge of the resort property had been in the Barnett family for generations.

His parents had traded life in the woods for a nice condo near the inlet in Anchorage, closer to his mother's job. Graham could have stayed in the main house, but they visited a lot, and he preferred his space.

Thankfully, the tiny log cabin just off the dirt access road was all Graham's own.

Between the two of them, Graham and Easton built the cabin with their own hands. And okay, maybe the first time around, they kind of botched it up, and the second time, the woodburning stove caught the living room on fire, but the third time around, they crushed it. Maybe if Graham had known that his diner was going to be a financial success, he would have invested more in the size of his house, but interior walls seemed a little too complicated for a first home.

One of these days, if life let him stop making Growly Bears for a living, Graham was going to pack up his belongings and move north of Denali, where no one would ever—*ever*—ask him to take a selfie with them again.

Behind the cabin was a twenty-foot-long steel shipping container, inside of which was the meaning of life and all things that mattered to Graham. The reason why he could spend his days serving food to tourists and nights prying them out of his personal bubble.

His wood.

His glorious, magnificent wood.

The improvised workshop was full of it, from tiny chunks of scrap wood to logs as thick as a man's torso, all in varying sizes and shapes. On one side of the workshop, a long table held Graham's tools, his grandfather's tools, and some bizarre torture-like instruments he assumed were his great-grandfather's tools, but he wasn't willing to put money on them. But the pièce de résistance of his collection was his set of carving tools.

Graham might be stuck in the body of a diner owner, but in his heart and soul, he was an artist, and he chose to express his artistic tendencies using high-powered chainsaws.

Several of his larger pieces wouldn't fit in the shipping container, spilling out with deliberate disorganization in front of the workshop, including Graham's pride and joy: an upright ten-foot-tall cedar log, complete with a five-foot-wide stump base. The piece dominated his carving area as if the tree had always grown there, just waiting for him to shape it into a masterpiece. The gnarls on the log were unique and complicated and could result in either a work of art or a chunked-off piece of junk. The log had stood in front of his workshop for the last six months, staring at him, daring him to have the guts to make something amazing from it.

The thing was—for as competent as Graham was at slinging processed meat—he kind of sucked at being a chainsaw artist.

"What do you think, Jake?" Graham called from just inside his workshop. "What are we carving this bad boy into?"

From his shaded tie-out spot on the cabin's porch, safely out of range of flying wood chips, Graham's furry companion wagged a silky black-and-white tail in acknowledgment.

Normally, Jake had the run of the place, but not when Graham was carving. The border collie had been blind ever since Graham found him as a puppy in a box next to the diner's dumpster. Rage at the animal's abandonment turned into full throttle adoration by the time he drove Jake home from the best vet in Anchorage, complete with puppy-safe chew toys and far too many outfits.

They'd come to an agreement. Jake only had to wear the outfits on special occasions, and when he did, he'd take the indignity without complaint.

Of course, the arrangement never stopped Graham from adding a hat or two to his friend upon occasion. Even now, Jake's floppy speckled ears were topped with a knit cap matching Graham's own. The caps were one of his mother's better attempts at knitting, although she'd taken more care to fit Jake's head than Graham's. Mediocre artistry ran in the Barnett family.

"All right, buddy. I'm going to get the equipment going. Hang tight."

Another lazy tail thump was followed by a yawn, Jake's cloudy eyes covered by the soft wool.

When a head of short, vibrant pink hair popped around the corner of the shipping container's open door, Graham wasn't surprised. Even if he hadn't heard the Jeep's tires crunching gravel as it pulled up his drive, Jake's single warning woof let Graham know not only was someone there to visit but the border collie recognized the vehicle.

"Hey. Is it safe to come in?"

"Safer than out there." Graham finished changing the chain on his favorite chainsaw. "Be warned. I'm excessively rugged and masculine today."

Rolling her eyes, Easton's twin sister set her hip against the steel entrance of his workshop, crossing tattooed arms across her equally tattooed chest. "I'll do my best to control myself. No promises."

In shorts, a tank top, and flip-flops, Ashtyn Lockett looked every inch the born and bred Moose Springs resident she was. Where the tourists were still wearing sweaters and furry boots, Ashtyn looked readier for a day at the beach than a day hauling supplies across the state in her helicopter.

Besides similar eyes and the same rare smile, there was little resemblance between Ashtyn and Easton. Having been at the receiving end of more than one of the prettier Lockett twin's grins, Graham knew how devastating they could be. Too bad the presence of a monster-sized brother always killed any romantic thoughts Graham might have entertained about her. Plus, Ash scared him twice as much as Easton ever could.

Graham hefted his chainsaw up. "I got it fixed. Pretty, huh?"

"Sure. I talked to Easton. He wants a rematch tomorrow at Rick's after you close. Try to run them out early if you can."

Graham started the chainsaw to check he hadn't messed up anything, the meaty growl of the machine drowning out his words. "You could have called instead of stopped by, Ash. You're secretly in love with me, aren't you?"

"What?"

He revved the chainsaw a few times and then let it idle. "I said sure. I don't mind taking East's money."

Ashtyn raised a sculpted eyebrow, her gaze scraping his form, briefly landing on Graham's bare stomach. "Yeah, right. You've always been too pretty for your own good, and you know it. What's the point of the hat if you're not going to wear a shirt?"

"Jake was cold this morning."

The eyebrow arched higher. "And?"

Tucking a welder's mask under his arm, Graham tilted his head. "I don't understand the question."

Snorting, she followed him out into the yard. "Hey, if you want to get impaled by chunks of flying debris, have at it."

Jake whined from the porch at the sound of their footsteps.

"Abs of steel, Ash. Abs of steel."

Ignoring him, Ash walked over to his prized log—the log of which artistic careers were made—and ran her finger along it. "Are you ever going to start this? Or are you just going to stare at it again?"

"Did you hear Jax is coming back into town?" he countered, waiting for her to step out of the way before circling the stump, looking for a proper angle of attack. "He's supposed to be here next week."

Ashtyn made a face. "I'd hoped that rumor was crap."

"Didn't anyone tell you to believe everything you hear?" When she rolled her eyes, he revved the chainsaw loudly. "Okay, I think this is going to be a snake."

"What?" When Ash yelled to be heard over the chainsaw, Graham revved it again.

"A beaver. I'm making a beaver."

She looked at him like he was crazy. "A cleaver?"

"No, just a regular kitchen knife!"

Shaking her head, Ash's lip quirked up. Taking a seat on a nearby lawn chair, intended for that exact purpose of sitting and staring at his soon-to-be masterpiece, Ash picked up a wood chip and lobbed it at his back.

"You can't take anything seriously."

"I seriously wish I'd gotten a couple more hours of sleep."

Letting the chainsaw idle, he turned to her. "Hey, do you know anything about the woman who came with Lana?"

"Why?"

"Why what?"

"You are so annoying." Another wood chip bounced off his shoulder blade. "Why do you want to know?"

Graham didn't have a great answer for that. Instead, he hummed. "I think it should be a fish."

"Keep practicing, kid." Ash rose to her feet and met him. Just under six feet tall, she had no trouble patting Graham on the head. "I'll see you later. Some of us actually have to get to work on time. I'm taking Jake with me. I want some company today."

If Jake tolerated a life of hanging out behind a grill, he'd made it clear he preferred a life spent flying around with Ash. Graham had long since accepted that sharing custody of his puppy with the Lockett twins was for the best, even though he'd have preferred to keep Jake with him at all times. Sometimes—rarely but sometimes—life wasn't just about him.

"Remember Jake's headset. The rotors are too loud. They give him headaches. And I'm not replacing any more of your things if he buries them. You know that's his stress relief, and I refuse to embarrass him for his needs."

Snorting, Ash waved a hand in acknowledgment before stealing his dog, putting Jake and his knit cap in the back of her shiny black Jeep. At least he was riding in style. Gravel crunched as they disappeared up the drive. Left alone in the silence of his manly domain of awesomeness, Graham considered his mighty log.

A snake. It should definitely be a snake.

A shower helped Zoey shed the worst of her muddled thoughts, as did a second cup of coffee. Stuffing her feet into her tennis shoes, she powered through the desire to crawl back onto the couch and sleep off the rest of her hangover. Texting Lana her plans to go hiking, Zoey grabbed her brand-new, airport-acquired Alaska messenger bag and tucked her glittery frog coin purse inside.

There was absolutely no way Zoey was spending her first full day in Alaska inside a hotel room.

When Zoey first realized she had saved enough to make this trip a reality, she hadn't intended to spend her housing money on a couch in the swankiest resort in the state. An off-season visit had been far more in Zoey's budget, but Lana kept pushing for her to come these two weeks, when Lana had already planned on being in Alaska. The Fourth of July was the height of the summer tourism season, and any alternate options within comfortable driving distance to Moose Springs had been booked months prior.

Since Moose Springs was the hub of all amazing adventure excursions a person could hope for when visiting Alaska, Zoey had been unable to resist her friend's offer.

Staying in Anchorage was cheaper, but the lengthy drive and subsequent cost to travel to Moose Springs didn't make the cheaper rooms worth it. Here in Moose Springs, Zoey wasn't near the mountains. She was *standing* on one. Zoey wasn't going to see the wildlife. Wildlife crisscrossed this town like an opening credit for the Discovery Channel, moose wandering across the roads, along the streets, poking their noses out from the tree lines everywhere.

A couch in a luxury suite might be where Zoey was staying, but she would have slept in a bear-proof dumpster to be here.

Zoey already knew her carefully planned budget would only go so far, but as she stepped out of the elevator and saw the closed entrance to one of the resort's internationally touted five-diamond restaurants, curiosity got the best of her. A glass case built into the river rock wall displayed the menu. Pushing her glasses higher up the bridge of her nose, she stared at a piece of paper containing only a handful of dishes she even knew.

"Looks like I could afford the side salad." Shaking her head in bemusement, she glanced lower down the page to the chef's choice seven-course meal. The price listed pulled a loud and unplanned choking noise from her throat.

"Ma'am? May I help you find something?"

A maid with the wildest mass of curly honey-blond hair beamed at her from behind an enormous stack of towels in her arms, both woman and towels dangerously close to tumbling over.

The badge on her chest read "Hi, I'm Quinn, your Hospitality Specialist."

"Oh...umm. I'm just..."

"If you're hungry, there's a great breakfast served in the—ooooh!" With a squeal, Quinn ducked and swerved, rebalancing the towels as they leaned even farther.

"Do you need help with those? I can carry some if you want."

Quinn stared at her, eyes widening. Zoey found herself staring back, unaccustomed to seeing so much of another human being's eyeballs.

"You?" She squeaked. "Help me?"

"Maybe?"

The leaning tower of towels was about to topple, so Zoey grabbed the ones at the top of the stack while Quinn the hospitality specialist still considered her options.

"Thank you." Decision made, Quinn breathed a sigh of relief. "We're dangerously close to being out of towels. I would have gotten in so much trouble for dropping these. They're the special towels."

"You have special towels?"

"Special guests require special towels. Erm, not that all our guests aren't special. But you know..."

"What's a hospitality specialist?" Zoey asked curiously.

"It's their fancy way of saying I'm the maid for the high-profile guests." Quinn made a playful face. "It's still cleaning up people's crap no matter how you spell it." Already widened eyes widened even further, a deer in the headlights look if Zoey had ever seen one. "Oh, I shouldn't have said that. I mean, hahahaha."

Some laughs made everyone else want to join in too. This was not one of those laughs. This was a glance around the immediate vicinity, just a little too loud, awkward kind of laugh. Zoey was tempted to save Quinn from herself by clamping a hand over her mouth.

"I heard nothing," Zoey promised, mimicking zipping her lip. "Where are we taking these?"

"Up to the top. Here, this way."

Following Quinn down a series of hallways to a staff elevator, Zoey balanced her own towels as Quinn used a staff keycard for access. She hit the button for the penthouse suite.

"I didn't bring you up here," Quinn said, dropping her voice conspiratorially. "Hannah would *kill* me."

"Hannah?"

"The hotel night manager. Technically, Mrs. Harris is the general manager, but everyone knows Hannah's actually in charge. We're all just waiting for Mrs. Harris to croak." A naughty snicker escaped around the pillar of towels. "She might have already. Mrs. Harris spends all her time napping in her office with the door closed."

Zoey opened her mouth to say something, but Quinn soldiered on cheerfully.

"The guest list is crazy. We're usually full up during peak season, but there's never been so many high-profile guests in the resort at the same time. And they all need something special." Quinn glanced at her from behind cotton. "Not that we mind. Our jobs are to keep everyone happy."

"There's a silent 'but' in there," Zoey said, squishing her towels to see what made them so special.

"But it's nice when there's only a handful of *you know what*'s in the hotel at once. They're running me ragged." Quinn made another face, her eyes crinkling in mischief. "At least the tips are good."

Considering Zoey's profession as a career waitress, she could appreciate a strong tipper. A few more of them and she might have made it here a couple of years sooner.

The elevator door opened to a private hallway entrance, the staff elevator doors hidden from view at the end of the hall, blending into the décor so no one would notice the elevator—or the people working there. When they stepped into the penthouse suite, Zoey's jaw dropped. Between the massive stone fireplace and a kitchen bigger than her place back home, the suite was the perfect combination of cozy, rustic opulence and space, with window after window revealing an utterly spectacular view of the Chugach Mountains.

"Oh wow."

"Yeah, it never gets old. If you have to clean toilets, there are worse places."

Prying into a stranger's private room was wrong, but as Zoey stood in her spot, towels balanced in her arms with Quinn bustling around her, she couldn't help but stare. The expensive purses just draped over the backs of chairs, bottles of champagne in buckets of ice already chilling despite the early morning hour. Gucci luggage stacked everywhere. She was astonished at the luxury around her.

"What do people pay for rooms like these?"

"More for one night than I make in a month." Taking the towels from her, Quinn offered Zoey a grateful look. "And trust me, it's not worth it. There's nothing in here that we don't have better down in town."

She clamped a hand over her mouth. "I shouldn't have said that either."

Zoey had the feeling Quinn's secrets were secret to very few, if the last few minutes had proven anything. Still, she nodded in reassurance. "Your secret is safe with me."

"I'll have to unpack their things in a moment. They just arrived and went down for breakfast."

"This isn't Killian's room, is it?" Trying not to touch anything, Zoey edged out of the room and into the open doorway, a backward kind of shuffle with her hands firmly in her pockets.

"Mr. Montgomery? Do you know him?"

"We didn't meet in Greece last year."

Quinn blinked, then powered through her confusion with vibrant optimism. "I'll tell him you're here, then. Have you been to the Tourist Trap yet? Everyone *has* to go there when they first get into town. It's tradition."

"Oh, I did. And I will never go back. I made an idiot of myself. The owner had to bring me home."

Quinn's jaw dropped.

"You? You're *her*?" Her. As if Zoey was Moby Dick, an elusive whale of a tourist. "Did Graham Barnett really carry you? Oh, that is so romantic."

Cringing, Zoey edged half an inch into the hallway. "I don't really remember."

"The whole hotel has been talking about it. Poor Grass thought he was going to have to fight Graham."

"What?"

"Then Hannah got control of the situation. She's so good at that."

"Wait, what situation?"

"And all for a burrito. I know Graham is crazy, and not just crazy hot, but seriously. Grass has skills. He trained in jujitsu in Anchorage for a long time. I bet he would have won."

"Won the...burrito?"

Confusion didn't begin to cover this.

"Okay, we're all set! I'll tell Mr. Montgomery you're looking for him. Thanks again! Goodbye!"

With a bright smile, Quinn shut the penthouse door on Zoey's face.

"He doesn't actually know me—" Zoey started to say through the door, then she sighed. "Okeydokey."

It took a while to find her way back to the lobby without a hospitality specialist to follow, but eventually, Zoey managed it. The hotel had several stations posted about the lobby with employees just itching to be helpful. Zoey knew where she was going, and she managed to avoid most of them. As she passed a souvenir shop dripping with handcrafted Alaskan-themed jewelry on display, she spied Lana seated at a table by the window with three other people, one of whom Zoey assumed was the secondary Killian whose suite she'd been in without permission.

Everyone at the table was enjoying themselves and their smoked trout, so Zoey scurried past before Lana could notice her. Zoey turned a corner and ran nose-to-name tag into another body, a tall, rawboned young man in his early twenties.

"Hi, my name is Diego" was trying to beam. This one was definitely trying and failing to beam.

"Did you need any help today, ma'am?"

Diego the bellhop might have sounded friendlier if he hadn't spoken in a monotone, his eyes and voice flat. So close. Freedom and sunshine were within Zoey's reach, but Diego the bellhop was right in her way.

"Oh, I was just wandering around. There's supposed to be some hiking trails connected to the resort."

"Yes." He stared at her. Zoey stared back. Neither blinked.

Maybe it was the starch. His uniform had an awful lot of starch.

When she sidestepped, Diego the bellhop followed suit,

determined to do his job. "On the far side of the grounds, take a left past the miniature golf course. Would you like a complimentary bottle of water and locally sourced organic granola bar to take with you today?"

Why yes. Yes, she would.

Shoving the granola bar at her, Diego continued in his dispassionate voice, "As valued guests of Moose Springs Resort, we encourage our patrons to dispose of all food wrappers in one of our provided bear-proof waste bins. Please refrain from carrying food items on the walking trails."

He forced his lips to lift away from gritted teeth. "A hungry bear is a grumpy bear."

"Umm, yes. I'll eat it on the grounds."

"Also, if you'd like breakfast before you leave, our head chef is world renowned for her fine dining cuisine. Her specialty is a lightly smoked trout on toast, served with house-made wild berry jam."

Zoey shuddered and made her escape.

The instant she stepped through the doors of the hotel, the fresh, crisp mountain air filled her lungs, and the sweet, earthy scent of evergreens washed away the lingering scent of breakfast fish.

The resort was everything rustic lodge glamour, fitting in perfectly with their surroundings. Even in July, the weather was much cooler here than it would be back home in Chicago. Within the grounds alone, there were so many activities, Zoey could have spent the whole summer there and not done them all. As she wandered, smiling shyly at the far more robust guests taking advantage of the on-site amenities, Zoey munched on her granola bar.

Taking pictures on her phone from every angle imaginable, Zoey sighed in pleasure. Perfect. This was absolutely *perfect*.

Despite Diego's lack of personality, his directions were excellent. The resort had paid special attention to providing signs for the trails spider-webbing away from the main grounds. The head of this jogging trail was marked with an information station, complete with a map of the trails and a list of local wildlife that could be found. Even the large government-produced sign was nicer than she'd ever seen, tucked beneath the shade of a log structure and protected from the elements by a thick casing of clear plexiglass.

"Warning. Numerous wildlife encounters have been known to occur on this trail," Zoey read aloud. "Know your bears."

A thrill of excitement flushed through her system.

"Never fear, I have come prepared. Bear bells, check. Bear spray, check. No small children wandering from the trail, check. Make sure to hike with a friend."

Hmmm. If the sign had ever seen Lana in a wilderness type situation, it would have known better than to suggest that.

"Well, I'll just have to be extra person-y."

Ready for her first adventure but just hungover enough to not want to climb a mountain, Zoey picked a wide, sweeping trail with minimal elevation changes. The hike would take her at least an hour, staying within the resort's property. Later, when she was feeling better, Zoey had every intention of exploring every inch of these mountains she could. Taking a picture of the map with her phone, Zoey and her water took off.

The trail couldn't have been tidier unless someone had personally vacuumed the pine needles off the ground. The mountains rose high above the surrounding trees. With every step, her heart swelled wider, her soul flying free. Never had she been happier.

At the unmarked junction, Zoey had the choice to go right or left. On a whim, she went right, when thus far, all her turns had been left.

Zoey knew where she was going. She did. Even when the trail twisted and turned more than the map said it should. Even when it stopped being so well maintained and narrowed on both sides. Even when it became clear that she'd made a wrong turn somewhere and needed to reevaluate her location.

She was a strong, independent woman perfectly capable of taking care of herself in the Alaskan wilderness.

Which was why, when she turned the corner and ended up next to a massive steel shipping container, face-to-welding mask with a man brandishing a chainsaw above them, Zoey knew exactly what to do. She ran away. And when he yelled something, grabbing her arm and pulling her around, Zoey was more than prepared for the situation.

Screaming bloody murder, Zoey kicked him straight between the legs.

CHAPTER 4

NOW, FOR THE RECORD, GRAHAM completely agreed with Zoey's reaction. If he'd walked out of a forest and into a chainsaw, he'd be upset too.

The problem was, when she turned to run away, she'd been running toward the north side of his property, making a beeline for a thirty-foot ravine. The chivalrous part of Graham's nature would never willingly let someone fling themselves to their death on his property, especially when it was all based on a simple misunderstanding.

Unfortunately, it was hard to express agreement while dry retching into a welding mask, injured beyond all hope of recovery. As a person with hopes and dreams and the desire to someday father children, Graham knew better than to remain keeled over with a chainsaw beneath him, even one not running.

All in all, it was a dangerous time to be a man.

He shoved the mask off his face, tossing it aside in an attempt for her to realize he was actually a normal, nonmurderous human being. If the situation had been different, Graham might have tried to console her or at least convince her she didn't need to keep screaming. But alas, curling up in the fetal position was the best he could do.

She screamed all the way to his four-wheeler. She screamed the entire time she tried to start the four-wheeler and failed. She took a breather for a moment as she kicked it a few times and then continued to scream as she ran to the house to—he assumed—barricade herself in and call the police. Let the police come. It was possible Graham needed immediate medical attention.

If he wasn't so busy cursing into the dirt beneath his face, Graham might have screamed some too.

Graham stayed there for a while, letting the white-hot agony roll through him until it dulled to merely a rusty-knife-stabbing-him-in-the-groin type of pain. Then—like any intelligent man would do in the same situation—Graham crawled into his workshop and locked the door.

Until further notice, this was exactly where he planned on staying.

———————

Zoey was a reasonable woman. With the arrival of the Moose Springs police department's finest and the proper displaying of a badge number, Zoey allowed herself to be talked into calming down. The single officer had found Zoey crouched outside the now-closed shipping container, a tire iron she'd procured from the chainsaw murderer's truck held at the ready.

If he'd come at her again, Zoey planned on bludgeoning him to smithereens.

After the police convinced Zoey to put down her weapon and

THE TOURIST ATTRACTION   71

reassured the chainsaw murderer it was in fact safe to come outside again, Zoey had been horrified to find she'd been almost chain-sawed by the nice, handsome bartender who'd so sweetly driven her home the night before, leaving aspirin on the table next to her. Upon further inspection, there was a lot of suitably chopped and chainsawed wood scattered around the property.

It was possible the most terrifying moment of Zoey's life had been an unfortunate misinterpretation of the events at hand.

There was a certain amount of shame in realizing she had attacked a perfectly innocent man. Especially when the innocent man was one Graham Barnett, who had gone to lengths beyond necessary to help her. Yes, it had been scary to turn the corner and come face-to-face with a chainsaw murderer. But now that she knew it was Graham whom she had attacked, Graham who was possibly peeing blood, it only increased the shame.

As the cop took their statements, Zoey kept asking Graham if he was okay, hovering over him like a fretting hen, which he seemed to be enjoying enormously. By the third time he moaned and groaned and asked for her number, Zoey threw up her hands and retreated to the safety of the opposite side of the patrol car, putting the bulk of the vehicle in between them for his safety as much as her sanity.

Ignoring Graham's antics and Zoey's growing agitation, the officer shook his head and asked Graham if he was able to drive into town. After retreating inside his home to get an ice pack, Graham agreed.

Jonah, the officer who'd responded to her call, was a weary-looking middle-aged man, slender and fit, but not for lack of trying for the opposite. Riding in the passenger seat next to him, Zoey kept nudging candy bar wrappers and empty soda bottles with her shoes.

"Sorry, ma'am. Usually, if I'm giving someone a ride, they're in the back." The officer took a long drink of gas station Slurpee, his cup balanced precariously in the squad car's cupholder. It couldn't have been anything less than a half-gallon.

"Do you think I hurt him? I think I hurt him."

A shadow of a smirk crossed Officer Jonah's face. "Well, ma'am. If I had to say, I'd guess he's not going to ask any women out anytime soon."

"He asked for my number three times back there," Zoey groaned. "I almost gave it to him too. Do you think he's okay to drive?" Zoey twisted in her seat to stare at the Dodge truck following behind them. "He might need to go to the hospital."

"Naw, if he needs a doc, he'll let me know. We've had our fair share of tussles and bar fights around here, and Barnett always ends up in the middle of them. I doubt you gave him any worse than he's had before." Jonah rubbed a hand over the back of his neck. "Now that he's not a few feet away from us, are you sure there isn't anything more you want to add to your report? Anything inappropriate Mr. Barnett did?"

"No." Frustrated, Zoey repeated the same thing she'd been telling him for the last hour. "I came out of the woods and saw him with the chainsaw. The rest was sort of instinct."

At the raised eyebrow from the officer, Zoey bristled. "Oh no, I'm not getting any eyebrow judgment thingies from you. You know those women who are too stupid to live? I refuse to be too stupid to live. I don't go in evil basements alone, I don't linger in cornfields on full moons, and I'm definitely not going to let a fully mobile human being with a chainsaw chase me down and stuff my body in a steel shipping container.

"I mean, who even *has* steel shipping containers? In the *woods*?" She huffed.

"They're common in this area, ma'am."

"Anyone in my situation with half a brain would have disabled him. It was the right thing to do."

"Yes, ma'am."

"Seriously. It was the best call I had in the situation."

Jonah took another drink from his bucket of Slurpee.

Sinking down in her seat, Zoey groaned into her hands. "I didn't know I was running toward a cliff. I just saw the bad guy chasing me."

"Of course, ma'am."

When they pulled up to a tiny cement block building on the far side of town, Zoey watched Graham park on the street behind them. He didn't look angry, but he did ease out of the truck with a carefulness that belied his current exuberance. Her agitation at Officer Jonah only increased as Graham grunted in discomfort upon closing the driver's side door. How badly had she hurt him? Was he permanently damaged? Would he never have kids because of her knee-jerk reaction to defend herself in a life-and-death chainsaw situation?

"Are you okay?" she asked under her breath as he held the door for her.

An amused look was all Zoey got in reply.

Zoey didn't think they were being arrested. She wasn't in handcuffs in the back seat, and Graham was driving his own truck. People didn't drive their own vehicles to jail. Then Jonah escorted them inside what must have sufficed as the Moose Springs police station: a building barely the size of a two-car garage, with only a desk, a bathroom, a small refrigerator, and a single cell.

Iron bars, corner toilet, and all.

"We don't have an official station here in Moose Springs, ma'am." Officer Jonah scratched his head, looking around as if uncertain of his options, and then he shrugged. "I suppose the drunk tank will have to do until we get things sorted out."

"Get what sorted out?"

"Well, ma'am—"

"Zoey."

A trace of annoyance crossed his face for half a second before disappearing. "Well, you and Graham—"

"Mr. Barnett," Graham supplied cheerfully, making Zoey groan.

Unfazed, Jonah continued. "You both have conflicting stories about the events occurring this morning on Mr. Barnett's property. I need to talk to my supervisors about what they want done. Barnett, are you pressing charges?"

Zoey felt her eyes widen. "You're joking, right?"

"You did attack me."

"You had a *chainsaw*," she hissed. "People get ax murdered all the time."

"But less often chainsaw murdered." Graham seemed to be entertained by the whole situation. "The survival instinct is strong in this one. I'm lucky she didn't kill me."

Jonah stood there, eyed the situation, and like any other intelligent person, decided he'd rather be somewhere else.

"Why don't you two sit in here for a while and work out your differences? I'll just run out and get us all some lunch."

"The diner is supposed to open at eleven," Graham reminded Jonah.

"I'm sure no one will mind." Taking a fresh ice pack from the station's freezer, Jonah handed it to Graham, closed the drunk tank door, and left them there.

Alone.

Behind bars.

Together.

At least Zoey still had her cell phone in the Alaska bag she'd been allowed to keep after a quick search by the officer. They might have been inside a drunk tank, but at least she could still call for help. Theoretically. Fifteen attempts to try to connect a call through the cement block walls of the makeshift jail only left Zoey ready to screech in frustration.

"How hard is it to get service in this town?" Stuffing her cell back into her pocket, Zoey paced in front of the door.

"Depends on your provider." Graham watched her pace. "Only a couple of them work up here."

"Something that would have been nice to know about *before* being incarcerated."

Seated on the holding cell's lone bench, Graham lounged against the wall, one arm folded across his chest and the other holding a strategically placed ice pack. Obviously, he was more comfortable with the idea of being incarcerated than she was.

Annoyance replaced guilt beneath her rapidly beating heart. A man capable of looking so content in this situation wasn't half as injured as he pretended to be.

"We're technically not locked in." Jutting his chin toward the door, Graham said congenially, "If you want to go all Bonnie and Clyde on this place, I might be willing to be convinced."

"Yes, because breaking out of jail is exactly how I can improve on this experience."

There was only one bench, and it was only four feet long. Given the choice of sitting next to the toilet and sitting next to Graham, Zoey placed herself exactly in the middle, trying not to smell or look directly at the toilet while putting as much distance between herself and the man with an ice pack in his lap as she could.

Stress had brought her headache back full force. Pinching the bridge of her nose, Zoey rubbed the insides of her eyes to relieve the strain.

Calm thoughts. She wasn't in jail in Alaska. Calm, soothing thoughts.

Tilting his head to catch her eye, Graham chuckled. "I bet you're regretting that Growly Bear right now."

"I'm regretting a lot of things."

He saw her looking at the ice pack. "It hurts. A lot."

"Then don't attack people with loud objects," Zoey groaned. "I'm very sorry I hurt you, but you're the one with the chainsaw and a dismembered body box. How hard is it to not be terrifying?"

"You're the one who trespassed onto my property," he reminded her. "How hard is it to not assume everyone is going to dismember you? Did it ever occur to you maybe I'm more discerning about who I dismember than to take any random stranger who trespasses?"

Forgetting to stare straight ahead, she turned away, got a glimpse inside the toilet, and shuddered. Facing Graham was the lesser of two evils. "I was on a *hiking* trail."

"You were on my *private* hiking trail, and you owe me at least two dollars for the use of it. Maintaining that trail for lost tourists doesn't come cheap, you know." His eyes sparkled. "Since we had a misunderstanding, I'm willing to give you half off."

"You want a dollar? I will give you a dollar." Digging through her bag, Zoey growled under her breath, stuffing her glasses higher up the bridge of her nose. "Where's my coin purse?"

"Maybe you threw it at my head." Graham wasn't being helpful.

Another cheerful grin from him, and Zoey was done. Sparkly frog coin purse in hand, she ripped the frog's mouth open, pulling out several dollar bills from her carefully arranged money. "Here. Here's your scaring the ever-loving crap out of me dollar. Here's another. Here's all the dollars, because I'm so sorry for not turning left!"

Throwing each one at his stupid, smug face, Zoey made her displeasure rain.

All the dollars was only five dollars. Graham watched her glare at him for a count of three, then huff a breath of distress as she picked them up from the floor and stuffed them back into her frog purse. "These are my dollars. You can't have them. Put up a sign next time."

Graham's grin only widened. "You are a strange one, aren't you?"

If Officer Dubious didn't return soon, Zoey wasn't responsible for what would happen to him.

Eventually, Jonah did appear, his arms full of plastic-wrapped gas station ham and cheese sandwiches. Too sick to her stomach to do more than hold her sandwich in her lap, Zoey tried to make another call. Lana would know a lawyer. Rich people always had lawyers ready and waiting.

Eyeing the police officer's offering, Graham didn't look impressed. "I mean, Frankie's *is* open, Jonah. I could have gone for a cinnamon roll."

"Aww, Graham, you know I'm on a tight budget. Kelly's pregnant again."

"Really? Congrats, man." Leaning over without looking away from his meal, Graham stuck his knuckles through the bars. "I hadn't heard yet."

Puffing up with pride, Jonah bumped his fist against Graham's. "We've been keeping it quiet. It's gonna be a girl this time. Kel's got a feeling."

"Or maybe she's tired of being outnumbered," Graham predicted.

Watching the exchange, it occurred to Zoey that of the three of them, she was the only one with any significant amount of concern here. Except for wincing a little when he adjusted his ice pack, Graham could have been sitting at Jonah's kitchen table having this conversation instead of in a drunk tank.

"When can we leave?"

Both men looked at her, Graham's lips curving upward in clear amusement. "You got somewhere better to be?"

Pulling a stool over to the door of their holding cell, Jonah settled in with a file in his lap. "Here's what I'm going to do. Ms. Caldwell, I'd like to think this was just an accident, but I've got your police records here. And it's concerning."

"You have a rap sheet?" Graham's eyes widened, like someone had handed him a candy bar unexpectedly. "Oh, I have to hear this."

"No, you don't." Horrified, Zoey made a grab for the paperwork in the cop's hand, but he kept his arm out of reach, leaning back from the bars.

"Indecent exposure—"

"That was not my fault."

"Destruction of property—"

"That wasn't even property! It was just a stupid garden gnome—"

"More indecent exposure."

Sinking down onto the bench, Zoey hid her face in her hands as Jonah continued to list her shame. With every addition to her crimes, Graham's clear enjoyment of the situation grew.

Clearing his throat, Jonah finished the last bite of his sandwich. "Ms. Caldwell, I'd love to let you go on your promise this was all a misunderstanding, but I'm just not sure if it's a good idea to let you run loose up here. We're a small town full of good people, and—" Jonah lowered his voice. "*Public nudity* just isn't something we feel comfortable with."

"Someone please kill me," Zoey whimpered into her hands.

The officer's cell phone rang, pulling his attention. "Excuse me."

Disappearing outside to conduct his call privately, Jonah left Zoey alone in her humiliation, face so hot it hurt her skin. She refused to glance over, hiding from the look she just knew would be on the face of her cellmate.

"So...what kind of indecent exposure are we talking about here?"

If she glanced his way, Zoey knew Graham's eyes would be all sparkly and gorgeous. So Zoey refused to answer, just like she refused to look at him.

"Strip poker?"

It was possible she hated him.

"No, I bet it was a classic teenage streaking gone wrong. Why do people *always* have to lock the doors just when the neighbors notice?"

"Do you have to enjoy this so much?"

"I'm sitting on a bench with a pretty girl. Of course I'm enjoying this."

Risking a glance at him, Zoey was met with—yep. Waving her hand in front of his face in a circular wiping motion, Zoey scrunched her nose and glared at him. "Enough with the sparkle eyes. This is not a meet-cute. This is not a—you know."

"I literally have no idea."

"Oh, *you know*. And it's not." She gestured at his general personage. "Aim all of that somewhere else."

"Incarceration brings out your feisty side."

Shoving to her feet, Zoey resumed pacing the cell, sandwich squishing in her hand as her fingers clenched in an involuntary fist. "You do realize I have a very impulsive friend who thinks I'm out on a hike right now? On the off chance she actually tries to find me instead of hiring someone to do it, the last thing we need is her lost in the woods all by herself."

"I would agree on that." Leaning forward, Graham rested his elbows on his knees, T-shirt hugging his muscled shoulders. "You're much better at being lost than L could pull off."

"Could you just be ugly for a moment?" Zoey asked, aware her voice was a mixture of plaintive and panicked. "You're not helping."

His grin just grew. "You're adorable."

Not attacking him a second time took the willpower of a saint. "Officer Jonah? Can I have my own drunk tank? Please?" When she leaned her forehead against the door, it popped open.

"Better close it," Graham murmured. "Breaking and exiting is looked down on in the state of Alaska."

When she just stood there, staring miserably at the doorway labeled exit, Graham gingerly rose to his feet and met her at the drunk tank door. With a little tug, he pulled the door shut. It clicked as if locking. That amused expression stayed on his face as he pushed the door back open an inch, then closed it again.

"Freedom's tempting, huh?"

She'd had enough of his teasing. "Listen, Mr. Barnett—"

"Graham."

"I'm sorry about your—"

"Ball sack," Graham provided helpfully.

"Your *private parts*, and maybe this is your idea of a great way to spend an afternoon, but I need to make sure Lana doesn't go looking for me. Someone needs to let me out of here or at least let me make a phone call. I have rights."

"Yes, but we kind of do things at our own pace in Moose Springs. I hope you're not claustrophobic, because we're going to be stuck in here a long time."

Feeling her stomach sink, Zoey went back to the bench. She sat down with her now lopsided sandwich in her hand, blinking back tears of sheer frustration. Graham's smile slipped, his eyes and tone softening. "Hey. I was just kidding."

She shook her head, drawing her knees up to her chest. "My stupid cell phone literally only works at your restaurant and if I'm standing on my left foot in the shower in our hotel room."

"Yeah, that happens to a lot of visitors. If you have the wrong carrier, you're not going to get reception for crap up here." Graham passed her his cell phone. "L's number is in there. The security code to unlock it is one, one, one, one."

"You're kidding."

A curve of his lips was his only reply. Murmuring a thanks, Zoey unlocked the phone and found Lana's name, although she half expected him to have her listed as the single letter. The lump of ham and cheese in her now occupied fingers slipped and fell next to her foot as she made the call. Zoey absently picked it up and set it on the bench between her and Graham as Lana's phone went to voicemail.

"Lana, this is Zoey. I'm in—"

"Jail," Graham provided.

"It's not jail. It's a holding pattern. I'm in a holding pattern, and I need you to come pick me up. I don't even know where this place is, but it's a tiny little pretend police station on the far side of town, and my phone won't work in here. Please, call me on Graham's phone. Or just come down here."

Handing the phone back to Graham, Zoey exhaled a sigh of relief. Feeling his eyes on her, she glanced over at him. "What?"

"Are you going to eat that?"

"It was on the floor."

"It was wrapped."

With a sigh, Zoey passed him the sandwich. Destroying it in several large bites, Graham left his ice pack on the bench and went to the entrance of the drunk tank. Raising his voice, Graham smacked his forearm on the bars hard enough to cause a loud bang to echo through the building. "Yo, Jonah. Hey, buddy, speed it up. She needs out of here."

Then Graham sat down next to her, and—much to Zoey's surprise—he offered his hand to her, palm up. "I'm scared," he said in way of explanation.

Rolling her eyes, Zoey huffed a soft laugh. "Yeah, I bet." Still, at his gentle smile, Zoey found herself pressing her sweaty, nervous hand against his ice-chilled one.

Zoey waited, but Lana never showed up. However, Jonah returned, a concerned expression on his face.

"I have bad news. I talked to the chief in Anchorage. Assault is something the DA takes very seriously. She wants me to take you to Anchorage and book you. The DA is pressing charges."

Shooting to her feet, Zoey shook her head, alarmed at the turn of events. "It wasn't assault. He didn't actually attack me."

The police officer cleared his throat uncomfortably. "Actually, ma'am, you're the one being charged with assault. And breaking and entering."

"I was hiding from Reindeer Dog Jason over here!" She pointed at him indignantly.

"Plus trespassing. You might want to call yourself a lawyer. Unless…well…we got the wrong of things."

A look passed between Jonah and Graham.

"What do you mean?"

Graham never once glanced at Zoey as he said in a firm voice. "I kicked myself in the balls."

Zoey stared at him, but Graham continued to hold Jonah's eyes, dipping his chin just a little in a silent signal she didn't understand.

"I kicked myself," Graham repeated. "All this was on me. Zoey was just visiting, and I was showing her some of my art. Then I kicked myself in the balls, and she went inside to call for help for me."

Jonah thought about it, thought about it some more, and then he sighed. "Well, I suppose this was all a misunderstanding. Right, ma'am?"

Graham nudged her in the rib cage with his elbow. "Right, Zoey Bear?"

"If Graham kicked himself...we're free to go?"

"Yes, but I feel obligated to remind you, ma'am. We're a small town of good people. Just because some of us can be convinced to *kick ourselves* doesn't mean we should have to." Without further ado, Jonah opened the door. "Have a nice day."

No one needed to tell her twice. Zoey bolted. Graham followed at a more leisurely pace, stopping to chat with the officer while Zoey headed outside, once more trying to get reception long enough to check her voicemail. Maybe Lana called and she'd missed it?

As Zoey sat on the edge of the sidewalk outside the tiny concrete building, still trying to find a reception sweet spot, their voices filtered out to her.

"They cause more trouble than they're worth." Jonah's pleasant drawl was heavy with annoyance. "Each new batch is worse than the last."

"This was actually an accident, man. Don't hold it against her."

"If she wasn't so pretty, you wouldn't be okay with this. Not like you to get pulled into their kind of drama."

"Maybe, but she's different." A snort brought a flush of color to her cheeks. "She is, Jonah. I don't know, I just think she's a cut above the rest."

Now, in Zoey's life, she had worked her heart out and her fingers to the bone for every single thing she had. She was proud of herself and the accomplishments she had achieved. But she couldn't remember a single time a stranger had said something like that.

A cut above the rest.

Nothing in their interaction thus far should have given this man a good opinion of her. Confused, Zoey watched as Graham Barnett left the station, still walking gingerly as he whistled to himself. He headed to his truck, climbing in with care. Even though she heard the engine start, he stayed parked. After a few moments, he killed the engine and got out again, joining her.

"I could be completely wrong, but my gut tells me L's not coming, darlin'."

"She's coming."

Even Zoey didn't believe herself.

Her spot on the sidewalk couldn't have been easy for him to sink down to. Yet there he was, settling in on cement when it probably hurt terribly, careful not to sit too close. Whatever else he might be, Graham Barnett was kind. Kind enough to hold her hand in the holding cell. Kind enough to lie to keep her from being arrested. Kind enough to care about a stranger not having a ride.

Guilt squeezed like lemon juice on her frayed nerves.

"I tried to call her a couple times. L's not picking up for me either. I'm not saying she won't come get you. I just think it might be a while."

Sighing, Zoey stood. "You're probably right."

Glancing at him, feeling stress and guilt twist her stomach into knots, Zoey added softly, "I'm sorry I hurt you. Thank you for not letting me run off the cliff, and thank you for helping me in there. If you have any medical bills, please send them to me."

Nodding in acknowledgment, Graham climbed back up to his feet.

"It's a long walk back to the resort. Jonah's squad car gets better gas mileage than tennis shoes, but he might be a while. There's a lot of paperwork to go along with our festivities this morning. I don't know how much you remember about last night, but I got you home safe and sound once. If you don't mind, I bet I can do it again."

"I think this tourist has trapped you in enough of her drama for one vacation." Offering him a tight smile, she added, "But if I could use your phone to call a cab, I'd appreciate it. Then you'll never have to set eyes on me again."

"That would be a shame."

An odd expression crossed his face, as if Graham hadn't planned on saying that. Then he held out his phone in one hand and his keys in the other, offering her the choice of either.

"It's up to you. But if I make you nervous, you can drive." Graham jingled the keys enticingly. "I'll even sit in the bed. No chance of mischief."

"What if I steal your truck? Or worse? Women are capable of dismembery-type hijinks too, you know."

"Then at least I went out with a good story. Red pill or blue pill?"

Zoey tapped her fingers on his hand, the one holding the keys. "You drive. My nerves are shot. I could use another Growly Bear about now."

"You and me both."

The truck was a newer model, but something had damaged the side door enough to give Zoey pause.

"Do I want to know what happened to your mirror?"

"Unrequited love. Okay, back to the big house. They're going to start charging me parking if I keep going there."

When he started up the engine, Zoey noticed the time flashing on the Dodge's dashboard. "I thought you had a diner to open. Aren't you going to be late?"

"We're past lunch, and I close between lunch and dinner. A few hours away from the insanity helps me keep my calm. Besides, I need to call Jake and make sure he hasn't abandoned me for my friend and her far more exciting lifestyle. Ash is a helicopter pilot."

"Who's Jake?"

"The cool customer in the sock hat on my screen saver." Like a proud parent, he tilted his phone her way, showing a black-and-white snout on the cutest border collie in existence. "You should meet sometime. He's a great listener."

Her lips curved despite herself. "What do you do when you're not working?"

"Sometimes I sit out back and read. Sometimes I go home and—" Clearing his throat, Graham glanced at her out of the corner of his eye. "Mass murder people."

Zoey groaned. "I said I was sorry."

"I know, but it's fun making you say it again." Chuckling, he turned onto the next street over. "I carve sculptures in my free time, what little of that I have these days. That's what the chainsaw was for."

"What were you carving?"

"You ask a lot of questions."

"I'm working up the courage to ask why you're not furious with me."

As they stopped at a red light, Graham gazed down at her, his tone softening. "Because you were scared, Zoey. I'm not going to hold that against you. Accidents happen."

The light switched to green, but his eyes swept her features. Biting her lower lip, Zoey stared back, wondering just what she was doing.

A car blared its horn right behind them, jerking her back to reality. Graham glanced in the rearview mirror, frowning. "Damn tourists."

The moment broken, he pressed on the gas, deliberately driving slower than necessary to aggravate the person behind him.

"You're enjoying this, aren't you?"

"Absolutely. See that little orange sticker in the top corner of their windshield? It means they're in a rental car. There's tons of similar things planted all over town so we know who to avoid."

"And who to mess with?"

A smug expression was his answer. They turned a corner, driving past the Tourist Trap. "See how I don't have a sign? No one should have known about my place. It was supposed to be locals only. When your town is overrun by tourists, sometimes you just want to get away from them."

"And yet you keep getting stuck in close quarters with me."

Graham shook his head. "Who visits Alaska and doesn't rent a car? We're not exactly known for how little this state is."

"Lana said she had a car we could share." Scrubbing at her forehead with the back of her hand, Zoey refused to look at him. "I'm not stupid, you know. I just thought..."

"She would be a reliable traveling companion?" Graham didn't seem convinced. "L's sweet, and she's got a big heart, but she's the walking epitome of good intentions, questionable follow-through."

"Lana isn't usually this distracted. She's got an event she's planning," Zoey said in her defense.

Graham snorted, unconvinced.

"After today, I'll probably rent my own car. I didn't budget for it, but..." She drifted off, unwilling to add that relying on strangers for kindness wasn't a great transportation plan.

They pulled up to the resort, but Graham set the truck in park a few truck lengths away from the valet station. Turning in his seat, he rested his elbow on the seat back between them.

"That's twice you've let me give you a lift, Zoey. If I didn't know better, I might think you were sweet on me."

His waggling eyebrows were so comical, Zoey couldn't help her small laugh. "Oh, trust me. That's not anywhere close to what's happening right now."

Sighing playfully, Graham rifled through the center console of his truck and pulled out a faded receipt.

"If you decide to get yourself a rental, call this place. They're local, not all the way back in Anchorage, and my cousin Collin owns the place." Graham wrote a name on the back of the receipt, handing it to her. "Ask for his wife, Leah. Tell her I sent you, or Collin will add the tourist reverse discount."

Smiling in gratitude, Zoey stuffed the receipt in her pocket. "Thanks."

"Hey, Zoey."

"Yeah?"

"Next time you want me all to yourself, just ask. No need for the violence."

Stepping out of the truck, Zoey couldn't help but joke. "Yep, lesson learned."

He waited until she almost closed the door, then called out, "Hey, Zoey? Zooo-ey."

"*Yes*?"

"You really should call me. L's got my number."

Zoey shook her head. "I would, but I'm a tourist. Oil and water, local boy. Besides, the melting ice puddle on your pants isn't the greatest turn-on."

"I knew I liked you." He winked at her. "Later, gorgeous."

As Graham drove away, Zoey sighed. He was all kinds of bad ideas wrapped in far too pretty of a package. Thank goodness her phone didn't work up here.

Graham Barnett was the kind of call that should *never* happen.

CHAPTER 5

SLEEP DIDN'T COME EASY.

Graham could have blamed it on physical discomfort, but the truth was Zoey's sweet smile as he dropped her off at the resort wouldn't leave his thoughts. Interspersed with that pleasant memory was her fingertips gripping the edge of the seat in his truck as if trying not to show him how upset she was after their little trip to lockup together.

And when he closed his eyes, Graham kept seeing her startled—then horrified—expression as she stepped out of the woods right next to him.

Knowing he'd frightened her, even accidentally, stuck in his craw far more than it should.

He'd meant it when he'd told Zoey she should call him, but his instincts told him she wouldn't. And why should she? So far, her experiences involving him were less than desirable. Graham shouldn't care. He didn't care. Tourists rotated in and out of town like luggage on an airport carousel. Except...well...he couldn't stop thinking about her.

By the time the morning alarm beeped on the nightstand next

to Graham's bed, he'd been up for hours. Normally, he would have used the time to go outside and work. Today, he sat on his porch, idly scratching floppy ears as he watched the ever-present sun rise higher above the mountaintops, brightening pale gray skies to cheerful blues.

"Well, buddy, what do you think? Should I let it go? Move on with my life?"

A lazy tail thump indicated Jake's agreement.

"Or..."

Placing a paw over his nose, Jake whined. Graham patted the border collie on the head.

"You know me so well. Yeah, you're probably right, but I'm going to do it anyway."

Not generally driven by impulse, Graham still found himself heading up a mountain, parking illegally in the staff parking lot, and walking down a familiar hallway in a familiar hotel, hoping he didn't remember her room number wrong. The clientele in this place rarely appreciated an early morning wake-up call from strangers.

Pausing to reflect on whether this was a terrible idea that might result in further bodily harm, Graham considered his options. Then he rapped on the door with a singsong in his voice. "Good morning! Housekeeping."

Waiting until the count of three, Graham knocked again, louder this time. "Is there a Zoey in the building? Rise and shine, darlin'."

"What's happening?" Groaning loud enough he could hear her through the door, Zoey called to her suitemate. "Lana, I don't understand what's happening."

"Someone's at the door. Make it stop." That particular sleepy grumble was Lana.

Heavy footsteps across the plush carpeting of their suite floor accompanied the door opening to reveal his dream girl. Albeit a rumpled, half-asleep version. Nightshirt twisted askew from sleep, hair a fluffy halo about her head, and eyes blinking sleepily through hastily shoved-on glasses that were in danger of falling off the end of her nose. She was perfect.

"Hey there, Zoey Bear. Not an early riser?"

Stuffing her glasses higher on the bridge of her nose, Zoey looked up in confusion. "Graham? What are you *doing* here? At... how early is it?"

"Six forty-five?" Smiling at her winningly didn't keep her eyes from widening.

"You're insane." She started to close the door.

"Wait, wait. I think you and I started on the wrong foot. Plus, hey, you owe me breakfast. I'm cashing in."

"I'm sorry?"

"I think you've seriously downplayed just how incredibly painful it is to get kicked in the groin. Common courtesy rules say breakfast or at least a light snack is required in said situation. Yesterday, we were both busy, but I've got a solid three, three and a half hours before I have to be an adult today. What do you say?"

Zoey groaned. "I'm sure you'll live. I'm going back to bed."

This wasn't going as well as he'd hoped. Time to up his game.

"I'm peeing blood, Zo. And I *did* keep you from serving hard time. Doesn't that score me any points?"

Long lashes brushed her glasses as her eyes dropped down instinctively. An adorable blush filled her cheeks as she jerked them back up again. "You need to get checked out."

"Naw, I'm good."

"You just said you aren't good."

Chuckling, Graham stuffed his hands in his pockets, slouching his shoulders so he wasn't towering over her. "I'll live. No pressure, but I'd really like to buy you a cup of coffee."

Setting her hip to the door, Zoey peered up at him, arms folded across her chest. "No pressure, huh?" Her eyes sparkled, even though her tone was dry. "You're literally trying to guilt me into doing what you want. Maybe I wanted to sleep in. Maybe you're not welcome here unannounced. Maybe I'm allergic to eggs and bacon. Did you ever think of that?"

Hmm. She had a point.

"What if I promised quiche?"

"Quiche is still eggs and sometimes bacon."

"Yes, but only *sometimes* bacon."

"Doesn't negate the risk of anaphylaxis."

"Are you actually allergic?"

"Not the point."

"It *feels* like the point. Because if this is a breakfast food allergy issue, I'm happy to come back at lunchtime." Setting his shoulder to the same side of the doorframe, Graham gazed down at her. "As a restauranteur, I take food allergies seriously."

Her eyebrow climbed higher.

"Very, very seriously."

"You can't flirt with food allergies, Graham."

"No? See, I thought this was going really well. I can switch topics if that helps. What're your feelings on cinnamon rolls the size of your head?"

"Hmm." Taking a moment to visualize, Zoey sighed. "I bet they don't exist. And you can't flirt with me when I haven't brushed my teeth. I'm not even dressed."

"So? I thought indecent exposure was your thing."

Ahh, too far. With a waggle of one specific finger in his direction, Zoey closed the door in his face. Feeling his lips curving, Graham knew it was time to change tactics. Maybe he needed to be clearer in his intentions here.

"I know you're still there," Graham told her cheerfully. "I can see your shadow through the eyehole."

"You're an eyehole."

"Probably, but I'd like for us to be friends. Come on, ballbuster. Let's get some breakfast."

"Or I could just call security."

"Naw, I'm buddies with the owner's son. They're used to me." He did his best to appear charming through the eyehole. "It's my treat."

"I don't eat breakfast."

"Everyone eats breakfast. Some just start later in the day than others. Let me make yesterday up to you. I don't make a habit of scaring women, and I'd like a do-over."

The door opened just wide enough for her to peer out. "I thought you said I owed you?"

Graham shook his head. "Naw, I think it's mutual owing. I know a place that makes an excellent egg-free omelet with no bacon."

"The five-star restaurant in the world class resort where we're standing right this very minute?"

"Someplace where the napkins aren't folded into swans or fans or dorkfish. Cinnamon rolls the size of your head. Warm, yummy cinnamon rolls." He lowered his voice to sell the deliciousness of the offering. "But they run out quick. Are you in or out?"

Never one to fear a little pain, Graham risked the tip of his nose as he stuffed it into the one-inch opening of the door, earning himself a view of her pretty eyes and the curtain-darkened room behind her. Then a close-up of the security chain as she smirked and chained him out of her room.

"I take it that's a no?"

Even though it was stupid, he found himself dreadfully disappointed. Graham didn't know why, but he was dangerously close to liking this one, tourist and all.

"I'm in," Zoey admitted, still leaving the chain up. "But if you're lying about the cinnamon roll, I'm going to get revenge. I don't know how, but the retribution will be swift and the justice ample."

"How ample?" Graham murmured.

"Oh. *Ample*. Teenage daydream ample."

"My favorite kind of revenge, gorgeous." Dying to reach out and brush an errant strand of hair away from her brow, Graham had to content himself with stuffing his nose farther inside the door, earning a soft snicker for his efforts.

"You're like a puppy desperate to come in and play. Okay, out, so I don't squish you." He did as she asked, and Zoey closed the door enough to unchain it before opening it all the way. Rumpled and sleepy looked far too good on her.

"Hey there, Zoey Bear," Graham murmured, softening his voice.

"Wait out here until I get ready. Lana's still in bed."

"I wouldn't dream of intruding."

"You're incorrigible, aren't you?"

This time when the door closed between them, it stayed that way. Graham settled in to wait for a woman, leaning back on the wall across the hallway. He'd been called worse, and he'd rarely had the chance to wait for better. Zoey appeared only a couple of minutes later, her black-and-white Alaska bag over her shoulder.

"A part of me was hoping this was all a bizarre dream."

"Really? Because I feel like you and I are becoming fast friends." Graham tossed her the keys. "You drive. This is way too early for me."

Maybe he deserved the rolled eyes, but he'd earned the tiny curving of her lips fair and square.

Hannah was just coming off her shift as Zoey headed for the exit, Graham at her heels. When Hannah tilted her head, silently mouthing "What are you doing?" Graham shrugged, giving his ex a helpless look.

"She's kidnapping me," he stage-whispered back. "Call Jonah."

Hearing him, Zoey turned, confused. "What was that?"

Hands in his pockets, Graham lengthened his stride to fall in next to her. "Nothing. Oh, I'm parked with the rest of the staff. Hang a right."

Someone was waiting for them in the bed of the truck, floppy ears perked to listen for Graham's voice, furry tail wagging.

"Who is this?" Her voice shifted to one of delight. "He's wearing *pajamas*."

"That's Jake. He's the love of my life." Confessing his everlasting devotion to the wriggling ball of fur and joy didn't bother Graham one bit. "Jake prefers the snug comfort of long johns, but he's been known to rock a sleep set if the cartoons are right. We're all about the choo choos and Ninja Turtles, aren't we, buddy?"

Aware his dog was adorable on the level few living beings achieved, Graham was used to strangers reaching for Jake without asking. Already shifting to intercept if her hands went for him, Graham's instincts weren't necessary. Zoey's fingers stayed clasped behind her.

"Can I pet him?"

"Of course. He's blind, so hold on. Jake. Introduction time."

The border collie sat up at attention.

"Jake, buddy. This is Zoey. She's trouble, but so far, she's made this week more interesting than normal. Don't bite her, okay?"

With a yip, he dropped to his belly, tail wagging furiously.

"He promises he won't bite," Graham assured Zoey. By the look of utter delight on her face, he knew Jake had won her over already. Still, something about this girl made him want to show off, just a little.

"Give the woman some space, Jake. You just met."

The border collie literally hopped backward, then he rolled over, sticking out one paw and curling the other across his chest.

"Yeah, I know. She's a heart stopper, isn't she? But try to play it cool, man. Just say hello."

Trotting up to the edge of the truck bed at Graham's verbal cue of "hello," Jake held out his paw in introduction.

Taking his paw in her hand, Zoey melted into a standing pile of goo.

The border collie wiggled and wagged until his body couldn't handle it anymore. Flopping over, he shoved his furry belly into Zoey's slender fingers. Graham watched her coo over Jake like he was the best dog in the world—which he was. Nose-to-nose, Zoey dissolved into giggles as Jake licked her from chin to cheekbone.

"Way to make me look bad, buddy," Graham murmured. "He's such a ladies' man."

"On the contrary. He more than makes up for you waking me up so early this morning. Your daddy owes you, doesn't he?"

Jake wriggled in agreement.

"Actually, we're more like human/canine bros. His mom was a real piece of work, and dad left when his eyes were still closed."

"Hush. I like you more when you're just standing there, all sexy guy with a cute puppy."

Graham hushed. As compliments went, he'd take it.

"Is it safe for him to be in the bed?"

"Nope, but I wasn't going to leave him in the cab while I was inside the big house." Picking Jake up under one arm, Graham carried him to the back seat of his truck, belting him in securely.

In the end, Zoey did drive, although she had to scoot his seat up as far as it could go to reach the pedals. Settling back in the passenger seat, Graham kicked a foot up and enjoyed not driving for a change. A few eyebrows raised in curiosity as Graham's truck drove past with a Zoey-shaped driver, but Graham waved cheerfully, letting them look.

"You'd think they'd never seen us on a date before, Jake."

"This isn't a date. Well, not with you. Jake still has a shot."

"You get all the ladies, don't you, buddy?" Graham sighed

mournfully. "It's just not fair. You were born with all the looks, and I got stuck with the charm. Turn left up there."

"I can't tell if you're the most confident or most self-deprecatingly insecure human being I've met."

Chuckling, Graham closed his eyes. "Tell me when we get there."

A couple of hard steps on the brakes later, Graham finished giving Zoey directions to the modest, two-story strip mall downtown. The bottom three units were easily identified, with signs hanging for all the world to see: the local daycare, a family law office, and the town's life-weary therapist. Upstairs were three more units, two with newspapers covering their windows and one with a simple unmarked door.

There wasn't a single person in town unaware of the culinary bliss housed in the far-right unit. But like all the other tourists, Zoey's eyes went to the signed units first.

"Is it weird those businesses are together?"

"It's strategic. Kirk thought it was clever to set up right where the stressed-out, new parents dropped off their kids. But then he got divorced three years ago and quit trying to save everyone else's marriages out of spite. So Catey opened up her law firm right in between. Of course, the bulk of us just go upstairs to Frankie's and eat our feelings."

"You know a lot of people, don't you?"

"I know the whole town." Graham got out of the truck, setting Jake and a collapsible bowl in the bed. He always kept a jug of water in the back seat just for this purpose, and he made sure the water was where his pup could find it.

"Stay, Jake. The lady and I will be back soon. Sorry, but no dogs in this establishment. We'll hang out at the Trap later."

Zoey blinked in surprise. "Are you allowed to bring him to your diner?"

"Nope, not at all."

A soft laugh matched the sparkle in her eyes. "But you still do."

Running a hand over Jake's floppy ears, Graham looked down at his friend. "Wouldn't you? Sometimes he stays with his aunt Ash and uncle Easton so he doesn't get too bored. They have a cute little pit bull he's sweet on. Right, buddy? How any of the ladies could say no to you is beyond me."

When he looked up, he saw Zoey watching him. The scent of baking bread hit them in a wave, causing Zoey to inhale deeply, her eyes fluttering closed. "Cinnamon rolls?"

"Unless you'd rather try couple's counseling." Smiling at her sigh of pleasure, Graham led her to the stairs around the side of the building. "Right this way."

The bake shop didn't sell egg-free omelets, but Graham hadn't lied about cinnamon rolls the size of a person's head. The pans of sugary deliciousness were lined up for them to see, although half of those trays had been emptied by earlier customers.

"We should have hurried, Zoey."

"Why does this place smell so familiar?"

"They source the bread for my place. Speaking of, hey there, Frankie."

The Native Alaskan woman behind the counter waved a hand at him in greeting, hustling around to take and fill the orders.

"Frankie, this is Zoey. She's a friend. Zoey, ignore what Frankie says. She loves me dearly."

"Depends on the day," Frankie joked.

Frankie gave Zoey a friendly but wary smile. Which Graham completely understood. He felt the same way with the strangers always wandering his town. But unlike Frankie, Graham was rarely nice to them. Zoey was an exception.

She looked around, taking it all in. "Your store looks amazing."

"Remind this one," Frankie teased. "He's always on me for more bread, more bread."

"Not my fault." Leaning comfortably against the counter, he watched Zoey explore the bakery. Frankie watched her too, curiosity growing. "Frankie's family has been here—"

"Forever." The bakery owner nodded at Graham. "Before the Barnetts arrived here. They've been thorns in our sides for four generations."

Frankie flicked her eyes toward Zoey, then raised a curious eyebrow. "A tourist, Graham? So the rumors I've been hearing are true?"

"Lies, all of it. But yeah, Zoey's good people," Graham promised, vouching for the woman busy doing math problems in her head. She pulled out her travel book to confirm something before turning back to him, excited.

"So you've been here since the late 1800s? That was when Moose Springs was founded. Did your families build this town?"

"You're not going to find everything worth knowing in a travel book, Zo." Graham put his hand to the small of her back, smiling down at her. "You want anything else?"

"Besides the monster pastry? I'm good." Without warning, Zoey started to crack up. Turning to follow her line of sight, Graham spied a pair of antlers very slowly rising in the window behind them. A massive lip wiggled into view, rubbing a wet smear across the clean glass.

Chuckling, Graham walked over to the window, catching Zoey's hand in his and drawing her with him. "This is Ulysses."

Ulysses was impressive, tall enough he could almost see through the second-story window if he stretched his neck as far as it would reach. "Appropriate name," she murmured, wide-eyed and breathless.

"I thought so."

"Joyce?"

"Homer. I like to keep it old-school." Graham tapped a finger against the window fondly. "Poor guy loves the smell of these things, and he never has been able to get one."

Kneeling down, Zoey placed her mouth next to the moose's snout. "'Take courage, my heart,'" she said sweetly, quoting Homer's *Odyssey*, the animal's namesake. "'You have been through worse than this.'"

Graham dropped down next to her, watching Zoey lean forward and breathe against the glass, her fingertips tracing a heart in the condensation.

"'For a friend with an understanding heart is worth no less than a brother,'" Graham murmured in a husky voice.

Turning his way, Zoey pushed her glasses up her nose with her pinkie. "Or a sister."

"Even better for Ulysses."

Graham was seriously considering if it would be inappropriate to kiss her when a moose's lips were right there too, the most awkward of threesomes. Unfortunately, an annoyed huff broke the moment.

"Your moose is as much a pain as you are." Frankie softened the comment with a fond smile. "Please run him off before he causes trouble." After Graham rose to his feet, holding out a hand to Zoey to help her up, Frankie pressed a take-out bag and two coffees into Graham's arms.

"That's her way of saying she loves us." Graham said dryly. Zoey fought to keep a straight face as Graham handed her their food. "Stay here, if you don't mind. He's usually pretty chill, but bull moose are unpredictable."

Ulysses was not interested in leaving, so by the time he convinced the moose to take a hike and go find something else to snuff, the coffee had cooled to perfect drinking temperature. Zoey had waited for him, watching the fun out the same window she'd drawn her heart on.

There were a few cozy, two-person bistro tables tucked in the corner of the bakery, but they must have seemed too cozy for his companion. When Graham started to head toward the closest one, Zoey and her massive cinnamon roll rolled right on out the door, across the parking lot, and over to one of several heavy cedar picnic tables set up in the grass.

It had rained the night before, even though none of the weather channels had predicted rain the whole week. Swiping her hand over the bench seat to knock away the worst of the standing water, Zoey flopped down, eyeing her breakfast with enthusiasm.

"You know, the tables inside have cushions." Graham settled

in far more carefully on his side of the picnic table, grimacing when he shifted on the seat.

"Sore?" She almost sounded sympathetic.

"The projectile vomiting has passed," Graham replied. "I'll survive."

"Should we get Jake?"

"Naw, he's a weenie about wet grass. He's happy where he's at. So. Let's start with apologies. You can go first."

Mouth full of frosting, Zoey's eyes widened. "Oh no," she mumbled around her food. "I'm blameless. Blame. Less. With a capital B."

Stealing a bite of her cinnamon roll, even though he had one of his own, Graham watched as she stabbed her fork at his hand.

"That doesn't actually hurt."

"It's not supposed to. I'm establishing a defensive perimeter." Content she was successfully defending her territory, Zoey reached over and stole a bite of his breakfast. Graham could have defended his own territory too—his reflexes weren't that bad—but her little smirk of victory was worth it.

"You're dangerous, Zo."

Misunderstanding his meaning, Zoey sighed. "Yes, but a girl needs her Krav Maga. If it means anything, I just wasn't expecting a chainsaw. And you had that super scary mask."

"Which was protecting my face from wood chips."

"So you claim."

When he leaned in, resting his weight on his forearms and wiggling his fork at her, Zoey flicked his arm in warning. Graham relaxed backward in his seat, nudging his plate toward her so she didn't have to reach as far to steal from him.

"So did you make up for lost time yesterday?"

Zoey cringed in remembrance. "Lana felt bad about missing my calls, so she 'made it up to me' too."

"Something tells me her version of an apology isn't quite as carbo-loaded as mine."

"No, she felt like taking me to have our body hair violently ripped out by the roots by a woman with anger issues."

"Ahh. You met Grace."

"*You've* met Grace?"

"Of course. Grace is my go-to when I need some manscaping."

Zoey's jaw dropped in shock. He leaned over and brushed his thumb over her chin to close it. "Haircuts and beard trims only," he promised. "But I like the way you think."

Blushing furiously, Zoey scrunched her nose at him. "You don't get your hair cut at the resort."

"No, but I've been known to sneak in a mani-pedi or two. A guy can care about his cuticles too, you know."

"I have no idea how much of what's coming out of your mouth is true or just your own personal brand of passive-aggressive societal mockery disguised as a sense of humor."

Pleasure spread across his face. "Maybe I just call it like I see it."

They ate in a silence far more comfortable than should have been expected from a pair with their deeply sordid history of mutual histrionics.

"Graham? You wanted me to go out with you to breakfast,

but I saw the looks they were giving you. I wasn't supposed to know about this place, was I?"

"Busted." Rubbing an awkward hand over the back of his neck, Graham glanced away. "Yeah, part of not getting overrun by the tourists is not letting them know where our favorite places are. I broke the rules. Frankie wasn't mad, but she was eyeing you to figure out why."

"So...why did you?"

"Honestly? I really don't know. I just wanted to see you again, and I thought you might like it here."

As admissions went, it wasn't a great one. Yet she didn't seem to mind. In fact, a defensiveness in her shoulders started to slide away. This time, the silence was awkward, but as he caught her eye, finding himself smiling somewhat stupidly, that same blush was back on her cheeks.

"This is a really great cinnamon roll. You're forgiven."

He knew she'd see it his way.

Killian Montgomery was exactly what Zoey expected him to be. Handsome, charming, and rich enough to have the grace not to rub it in her face or the face of anyone else around them.

The whatsits, Haleigh and Enzo, were far less secure in their importance in the world. There was money and then there was *money*. And while Enzo seemed to love throwing around names and places as much as Haleigh loved throwing around her designer clothing, Killian just relaxed back, taking it all in.

Even though Zoey couldn't eat another bite without going

into a diabetic coma, she agreed to join them for a late breakfast, sipping water while Haleigh gave the waitress a hard time over the toastiness of her toast, the saltiness of her caviar, and the freshness of the orange juice watering down her champagne.

Not for the first time, Zoey saw the bored, disillusioned look in a member of the Montgomery family's eyes, although with far less eye rolling than Lana was currently doing. The Montgomerys might have been jaw-droppingly wealthy, but they were always exceedingly kind to the people around them. Zoey bet Killian and Lana had never given anyone a hard time over toast in their lives, and clearly neither were impressed by Haleigh's attitude.

With a promise she would spend the evening with them, Zoey called a rideshare to take her from the hotel to the car rental place just outside of town. The driver was young and drove a bit fast, but he was far cheaper than arranging a shuttle with the hotel and easier than catching a ride with the preoccupied Lana.

To his credit, Graham's suggestion for where to get a rental car was a good one. She'd asked for Leah and got her husband, Collin, instead. After an awkward exchange in which Zoey learned she absolutely sucked at name dropping, a woman with a "Leah" name tag showed up, two young boys at her heels.

The undeniable smell of reindeer dog and fries wafted from the unmarked paper take-out bag in her hands.

"You would not believe the line today," she told her husband. "It actually went around the corner of the store. If he didn't let me cut in front of everyone, we'd never get anything over there." Leah shook her head in disbelief. "Here, eat while it's still warm. I'll finish up."

Sure enough, when they set the contents of the take-out bag on the waiting area coffee table, the hot dogs had cute little paper reindeer antlers.

Zoey's stomach rumbled despite the fact Vixen and Comet were being slathered with ketchup in the corner, and she wasn't even hungry.

What was the man doing to her? He and his food had crawled into her brain.

Leah picked up the rental paperwork Zoey had started, read the name on the top, and then she glanced up.

"So you're Zoey. Graham said you might be coming by. Can I see your driver's license? Thomas, James, share with each other. Those fries are for both of you."

Convinced it was easier to get ax murdered up here than previously assumed, Zoey had kept her driver's license in her pocket since the chainsaw, crotch kick debacle. If someone found her beneath a cedar stump, she wanted at least to be identified. Handing the license over, Zoey glanced at the kids. Their fries smelled so good, Zoey's stomach rumbled a second time, loud enough for the other woman to hear.

Leah palmed the license and set it on the scanner. "Yeah, me too. I snuck a few fistfuls of fries on the way home. I'd say go get some after you leave here, but it's brutal over there right now."

"Is the Tourist Trap always busy?"

"From the moment he opens the doors. He started closing between lunch and dinner just to have a chance to breathe. They wait outside like a pack of wolves."

As she made a copy of Zoey's driver's license, Leah asked, "How do you know Graham?"

"I kicked him in the groin" seemed bad, especially since this was a friend of his. Or at least someone the diner owner knew well enough that his name meant Zoey not paying the exorbitant prices listed on the sign behind Leah. "He recently kept me out of prison" seemed equally awful.

Curious eyes locked onto her, and Zoey realized she'd hesitated too long. "We met at his restaurant." Yes, that was safe.

"You mean the bane of his existence," Leah chuckled. "Graham is my husband's cousin. He's our sons' godfather. Thomas and James adore him." Nodding her head toward the two boys playing in the corner, she added, "I'm praying nothing ever happens to us, because they'll have to take care of Graham, not the other way around." Even as she said it, a fond look crossed her face. "Okay, here."

"Don't you need my credit card?"

"This one's on the house." Leah wasn't hiding her curiosity very well. "Graham asked for me to be nice to you, and he's never personally referred anyone to us before. So I'm guessing you did more than just meet at his restaurant. He actively dislikes most of the people who come through his door."

"I think he's tired of having to drive me around," Zoey said awkwardly, pushing her glasses up on her nose. One day, she would have a pair that didn't slip, but first she needed a rental car. Still, it felt wrong to have these nice people think the wrong thing.

Leaving the keys on the desk between them, Zoey hesitated. "This is really nice of you, but you might not want to do me any favors. Full disclosure, I sort of attacked him, got us both arrested, and he might not be able to have children now because of me."

Unconcerned, Leah's grin just grew. She picked up the keys and placed them in Zoey's hand.

"Bring it back with the tank full. Don't worry about the scratch on the door; we know it's there."

The car they'd given her was a cute little SUV, and while it had a few marks on the outside and one deep gouge in the paint near the passenger side mirror, it was clean and smelled like fresh air, not air fresheners, when she climbed in.

The freedom of having her own vehicle left Zoey feeling like that fresh air was filling her with new life. Okay, so maybe the first day...two days...of her vacation had gone awry. But this was her dream trip.

She was going to make the most of it.

The day started so well. Then the customers showed up, and it all went to hell.

Being sore hadn't helped, especially when it meant Graham couldn't move as quickly as he wanted. And while he normally would have ripped through the lunch crowd by two and felt little to no remorse closing the doors until the dinner shift, for once, Graham stayed open, trying to get the line somewhere close to gone. Finally, he gave up and acknowledged that he was working a double shift. Or a full shift. Whatever.

He'd trained the town and the resort to not bother him between the hours of two and six, so it died down to a reasonable trickle by the time trouble in Jimmy Choos came walking through the door.

"What's a dame like her doing in a place like this, Jake?"

The border collie at his feet whined.

Lana always looked like a million bucks. But when she walked into his diner this time, she was dressed a little closer to the actual number. The slump in her shoulders didn't match the perfectly tailored, cream-colored jumpsuit and black designer heels. The man with her seemed more interested in talking on his phone in the corner of the diner than ordering, so she approached the counter alone.

"Sorry, L," Graham said in greeting. "I can't serve you anything today. I've seen what you do with the ketchup bottle, and I can't afford the dry cleaning bills."

Flapping a hand at him, Lana focused on the customer seated closest to where Graham worked.

"May I sit here when you're done?" She asked politely, unaware of the effect of her thousand-watt smile on the poor fool. Lana waited patiently for him to decide if the comfort of a highly coveted seat at the counter was worth accommodating her request.

Apparently, it was. "Erm, yeah. Sure. I'm done anyway."

Taking a napkin from the dispenser, Lana settled into the seat, delicately wiping residual crumbs from the previous occupant into a little pile.

"Is it time for the air horn?" she asked hopefully. "This place is starting to look hammered."

"I'm not closing today. I'll wipe things down in a minute."

"You? Clean? Love, the day you lift a finger to do work you

don't have to is the day I renounce the family business and go bunk up with Zoey."

"What's wrong with bunking up with Zoey?"

"Absolutely nothing, which is why I would stay with her. Although she has a turtle. I'm not sure I can live in a house with a turtle."

"It would be a travesty of epic proportions," he murmured.

"You *do* know they carry salmonella." Lana shuddered. "I'm not interested in a repeat of that particular experience. Once was more than enough."

"The turtle's named after a Renaissance artist, isn't it?" When she raised a confused eyebrow at him, Graham shook his head. "Never mind. Hey, Lana? You and I need to talk. Something's off with you. Since when do you bail on friends and not pick up your phone?"

Lana hummed playfully. "I'm in trouble. Be careful. I might like it."

"I'm serious. What are you doing?"

"That's what I've been trying to figure out." Sighing with feigned distress, Lana leaned against the bar. "What would you say if I bought the resort?"

"I'd say I'm packing my belongings and running north as fast as humanly possible. You don't have the staying power for a business like that one, and by the time you were bored enough to sell it, my town would be ruined. Don't. Buy. The resort."

Graham held her eyes, trying to use his frown and all his nonexistent telewhatever powers to psychically influence the most dangerous person he knew.

With an actual sigh, Lana set her elbows on the bar and stared sightlessly at the wall behind him. She only pulled out of her head when Graham set a shot glass in front of her with a single fry in it. Then, because he genuinely liked her, no matter how much of a pain in the butt she was, he added a second one.

It just seemed wrong to have an L without some resemblance of happiness on her face. "You look like you need a double. Talk to me, goose."

"If I do, you're going to be mad at me."

"You're not actually buying the resort, are you?" Concern creased his brow deep enough he could feel the lines digging into his skull. "I'd love having you around more, but it's a bad idea."

"Why?"

"Because the only positive thing about the place is the Shaws. Jax grew up with us. They raised their son here. They're not local but they aren't—"

Pursing his lips, Graham stopped himself from saying something hurtful, no matter how much he believed it.

"They aren't the enemy," Lana provided, her beautiful features hardening, even though her voice was soft.

"No. The Shaws are just the people who made it easier for the enemy to cross behind friendly lines."

Awkward silence fell between them until Lana frowned, reaching for a fry. "I'm not buying the resort. Your deepest, darkest fears are yet to be realized. Speaking of..." Lana waggled her eyebrows comically. "I've been busy, but I'm not blind. *Someone's* been consorting with the enemy."

Leaning on the counter, Graham stole her second fry and shot that sucker without a chaser. "L, do I have a story for you."

CHAPTER 6

THE ADVENTURE EXCURSIONS WEREN'T CHEAP. When she had booked them nearly six months prior, Zoey hadn't cared.

There simply wasn't any way she was traveling all the way to Alaska and not doing every single thing possible to make the most of her vacation. Digging deep into her daily living money, Zoey paid ahead of time for a "Deluxe Excursion Package" through Moose Springs Adventurers, the top excursion package the budget off-site travel company offered. And if she lived off ramen and peanut butter for months to compensate, it was worth every penny.

Moose Springs Resort provided their own arrangements for experiencing Alaska, but those catered to a clientele financially superior to herself, starting with a deluxe excursion package about four times pricier than the one Zoey reserved, with fewer activities on the list. Their "Luxury Package" and the "Too Stupidly Expensive for Any Mere Mortal Package" were heavily advertised in her and Lana's room, but she doubted that was the limit to what the resort was willing to offer. With their own helicopter landing site on the grounds and a fleet of staff ready to jump when a guest

THE TOURIST ATTRACTION   117

so much as sneezed, they could have arranged any type of adventure Zoey could dream of, as long as the price was right. Which… well…it wasn't.

Zoey was going deluxe with Moose Springs Adventurers, and that was that.

Now that she wasn't drunk on a Growly Bear, incarcerated, or letting herself be stranded somewhere, Zoey was ready. She was pumped. She was driving down small, winding mountain roads, singing at the top of her lungs to the radio, and letting the wind whip through her hair and fill her nostrils with the scent of the Alaskan wild.

When a small sign poked out of the tree line, Zoey almost missed it. "So much for advertising," she murmured, performing a careful three-point turn in the middle of the road. "Come on, tires. Stay out of the ditch."

Ditch wasn't the right word. Cliffside drop-off was more accurate.

Her first excursion was a guided horseback ride through the mountains, the brochure provided by Moose Springs Adventurers promising wildlife sightings of everything from deer to grizzly bears. Two and a half hours of tranquil hoofbeats, softly swishing manes and tails, and stunning terrain.

Zoey turned onto a rough, uneven lane with heavy, large-stone gravel difficult to drive over. The tires on her SUV slid, fighting for traction, so she slowed down to a crawl. At the end of a mile-long drive, Zoey turned a bend and inhaled a breath, eyes wide. The heavily forested road opened to a clearing, blanketed with rolling pastures, a small pond, and several barns dotting the landscape.

There were even those big round bales of hay stacked along the side of the largest building where everyone was parking.

Only a few horses remained in the pastures, wandering around and nibbling on the short green grasses available to them. The rest were tied up beneath a long, open-sided barn, already saddled, their noses clipped to the gate and a row of round, beautiful horse butts swishing their tails to shoo away flies.

Zoey had made sure to leave early in case she had gotten lost, but she'd underestimated how long the line would be, how many liability release forms she would have to fill out, and how chaotic the group of riders would be as they raided a stack of protective riding helmets.

A harried employee took Zoey's paperwork and marked down that she was indeed carrying a helmet beneath her arm, never once looking up to her face. "Caldwell, you're stall sixteen. Go down to the end, far side."

"Over there?" she asked, nervous and excited as she peered at the line of horses, the open barn now swarming with their soon-to-be riders.

"Huh?"

The helper was too busy, so Zoey edged aside to let the impatient group behind her—two adult women and a heavyset man—move up. "Never mind. I'll find it."

Stall sixteen wasn't easy to find because the animal tied in that spot was trying his best to go unnoticed. Ears pinned and a sour, pinched expression on his velvety nose, he eyed her balefully as she approached. Zoey didn't know a lot about riding, but as she stood next to the short, brightly patterned mount she'd been assigned, she could feel waves of resentment rolling off the animal.

If the universe had put polka dots on a barrel and made it look bitter about life, that was her horse.

"Hi," she tried, hoping to start this temporary relationship on better footing.

The horse turned his head, staring at the pipe gate he was tied to instead, deliberately ignoring her.

A single guide moved from horse to horse, giving the same directions on how to go forward, stop, and turn to every rider. When the guide reached her, Zoey realized she was a teenager, not the tall handsome Alaskan cowboy she hoped would be part of this adventure.

"My name is Riley, and I'll be your trail guide for the day. If you have any questions, just ask me." The statement was delivered in a monotone, as if she'd repeated it so much, she didn't hear her own words. "This is Mugs, your horse for the ride today. Appaloosas are known for their speckled coat patterns."

With bored eyes, Riley droned a rehearsed spiel specific to every horse, adjusting the stirrup length for Zoey with the automatic actions of someone who had done this on twenty horses three times a day, all summer long. "Mugs here gets picked on a lot by the other horses because he's so brightly patterned. It makes him cranky."

"Oh no. I'd be cranky too." Zoey's heart went out to her mount. She reached out to pet his velvety nose, then squeaked when his ears flattened and his lips wrinkled.

Well, that wasn't reassuring.

"Why do you call him Mugs?"

"His name's Mugshot, because he always looks like he's about to get sent to prison. Okay, picture time." Riley stuffed the reins into Zoey's hands. Stepping back, she pulled out her phone and in an equally bored voice said, "Say cheese."

Waving the phone with the image beneath her nose, Zoey caught a glimpse of her startled eyes and Mugs's flattened ears, his expression one of serious disgust.

"Stick your foot in the stirrup and use his mane, not the saddle horn, to pull yourself up. Horses don't have nerve endings in their manes, but they do get sore backs."

Was that true? The idea of pulling a poor animal's hair while awkwardly climbing up its side sounded mean. With the grace of a sack of potatoes, Zoey did as directed. Mugs grunted dramatically, then swung his head toward her leg, massive square teeth bared. Yelping in alarm, Zoey jerked her heel up to her hip, looking to the guide for help.

"What did I do wrong?"

"Nothing, he's just in a mood today. Shove your foot out when he does that. He won't want to bite your shoe. I'm sticking you in the back. Normally, my other guide would take the last place, but she called in sick. Mugs knows these trails better than I do. Just kick him if he falls behind."

"Won't that hurt him?"

The tiny smirk broke through the boredom in her eyes. Smacking her hand down on Zoey's tennis shoe, Riley said, "Not with these little nubs."

Now, that wasn't fair.

As Riley turned her back, Mugs swung his head again, aiming for Zoey's shoe to prove her wrong. Riley moved on to the next horse and rider, a beautiful sorrel gelding, half dozing as he waited patiently.

"My name is Riley, and I'll be your trail guide for the day. If you have any questions just ask. This is Patch. He's—" As Riley started a new spiel about this horse, Patch nuzzled the other rider's hand, tickling her with his long whiskers and wiggling lips. Zoey eyed him wistfully.

"You see them?" Zoey muttered to Mugs. "He doesn't hate his rider."

Mugs snorted in equine contempt.

When everyone was on their horse and ready to go, Riley swung up on her own gray mount—a tall, energetic animal who hadn't given up hope of a different life yet—and called for them to line up. A rich hodgepodge of variously skilled riders managed to form themselves into a semblance of a line, although the three who ended up behind Zoey at check-in now were in front of her. Listening to their conversation wasn't intentional. The two women—sisters from what Zoey could glean—had the kind of voices that carried, even if the people around them would rather those voices didn't.

Mugs dug in his heels when the group took off at a walk, but with a sigh of disgust and some nudging and cajoling on Zoey's part, he finally shuffled forward.

"I bet Patch isn't giving his rider side-eye," Zoey told him. Mugs ignored her.

They hadn't lied about the stunning scenery. As the trail wove in and out of the forest, through open glades, the mountains rising tall and glorious above them, Zoey's heart swelled. If she could have jumped off her horse and rolled around on the ground, she would have, so happy as she was to be there. To see this. Then they descended into a shady glen, the afternoon sunlight filtering through the evergreens, and Zoey fell in love.

Complete, unadulterated love. There was literally no other place on the earth she would rather be than exactly that spot.

As for wildlife...well...the current volume of conversation in front of her had Zoey wanting to shrink away. No wonder there were no deer to be seen.

The two sisters had traveled everywhere, and they wanted everyone to know, sharing their stories as loudly as they could in an effort to regale the others around them. As they talked and argued over details, the husband kept slipping something out of his pocket and taking sips of it, ignoring them both.

Mugs wasn't enjoying himself, especially when the one sister's horse—a very pretty palomino—started misbehaving. Now, Zoey had been trying to see any kind of wildlife at all and was twisted around in her saddle when it all went wrong, so she didn't know exactly what happened to start everything. The palomino started bucking, sister one screamed bloody murder, convinced she was going to die, sister two screamed at sister one to stop screaming, and husband one and a half pulled the flask out of his pocket and started to drink hard.

Stuck at the front, Riley tried to yell back what to do, but the trail was too tight to let her get there to help them. An aggressively bucking horse butt was not as picturesque as one standing in line or grazing in a meadow. Mugs snorted with surprise as he caught a tail beneath the chin, startled to the right, and ended wedged between two trees, Zoey clinging to the saddle horn.

Backing himself out from in between the trees, Mugs ignored Zoey's attempts to help by tugging on the reins. Zoey realized a moment later than her horse that they were pointed with his nose back to the barn.

Mugs was done with this foolishness. With a derisive snort to the rest of the group, he started back up the trail.

"We're going the wrong way."

Mugs ignored her.

She tried to turn his nose, but he tensed his neck and ignored that too.

"Riley, I need some help here," she called out, waving frantically, but the teenager was too busy trying to contain the screaming situation, the bucking situation, and the drinking husband situation. The poor girl looked like she wanted to scream or drink too, up until all of them disappeared because Mugs topped the hill and was resolutely headed down the other side.

Pulling on the reins, stuffing her nubs into his sides, verbally appealing to his better nature...none of it worked. There was nothing Zoey could do. The horse was determined on going back to the barn, and her options were to bail from a moving equine vehicle or just let this play out.

"Okay, what do I do? What do I do?" Frantic, Zoey looked around at a much more peaceful but far more frightening expanse of wilderness.

"I'm not calling Lana for help. One, my phone doesn't work, and two, I have my pride. So we're going to turn around. I'm sorry if this hurts your mouth, but I have no choice. I'm not getting lost a second time in two days." Stuffing her feet into the stirrups,

Zoey stood up with both hands hauling on the reins as hard as she could. "Mugs, *whoa*."

Mugs thought about it. He paused. There totally was a pause. Then a derisive snort and a shake of his head later, he continued on, a trail horse untrailed, a beast of burden now free.

"I'm going to die in Alaska. We're going to get lost, and my horse is going to eat me to survive."

Abruptly, they came to a split in the path, and Mugs stopped without warning, pitching Zoey forward onto his neck, saddle horn digging into her stomach.

An equine ear flicked back as if in question. "Oh, now you want my opinion? Now?"

She was not concerned. She was cool, calm, collected. This was all okay. Death by being lost and eaten by the only carnivorous horse in Alaska was okay. Deep, soothing breaths. Deep, soothing—

When her phone rang, Zoey nearly lost her reins in her desperation to answer it. "Hello? Lana, thank goodness."

"I just heard the *best* story about you." Lana's voice cut in and out among the sounds of voices and music in the background.

"Lana, listen to me. My horse went rogue."

"What did you say? It's hard to hear you. I think she's on her adventure still."

"My horse went rogue! I think he's plotting against me. Lana, I need you to teach me how to ride."

"That's what the guides are for, love. Besides, those trail horses don't care you're up there. They just follow the line."

"Well, mine's having an existential crisis and just quit his job. I can't figure out how to get him turned around."

"It'll stop eventually, then hop off and ask for your money back. We're all at the Tourist Trap. Meet us here when you're done." Even with the terrible reception, Zoey could hear Lana cracking up. "Graham says you attacked him."

"I didn't! It's complicated." Even here, in the middle of the wilderness with nothing but Mugs around, Zoey could feel her face and neck heat up with embarrassment. "There was a misunderstanding."

"Is that what we're calling it now?" His warm, sexy chuckle in the background only made things worse. "Let me talk to her."

"Graham wants to talk to you."

"Lana, no. Don't you dare pass over the—"

"Hey there, Zoey Bear. How's my favorite ballbuster?"

Distracted by his flirty tone, Zoey failed to get her leg out of the way when Mugs drifted too close to a tree trunk. With a squeak, Zoey hung up the phone, scrambling for the reins.

Lana promptly called her back, but there was no way Zoey was going to answer. If Mugs wanted to scrape her off, Zoey had bigger concerns than a hot diner owner.

Carnivorous or not, she'd rather be lost with the horse than without him.

"This was not on the plan, Mugs. Him, you, any of this."

Mugs ignored her and continued with the kind of resolve only a twenty-year-old barn-soured trail horse with polka dots could maintain. The trail was more peaceful without her companions, but Zoey's stomach stayed twisted with nerves until the barn finally came into view in the distance. Mugs saw it too, his flattened ears finally perking up. With renewed enthusiasm, the Appaloosa surged into what might have been a trot at an earlier point in his life but now mostly consisted of several strides of lumbering faster, then a jerky slowing to accommodate his freaked-out passenger.

Then, instead of helpfully returning to stall sixteen, Mugs did what Mugs did best. He walked up to one of the massive rolled bales of hay, stuck his face in muzzle-deep, and he stayed there.

They didn't give Zoey her money back. They did, however, give her a stern lecture about respect for the rules and the group and how leaving endangered not only herself but everyone on the trail.

Standing up for herself worked about as well as it ever did. There was just something about her that made people not take her seriously, which was super annoying when Zoey was not at fault here.

Her excuse—the horse made me do it—only would have worked if the riding outfit wasn't convinced Mugs was the best horse on the planet and would never do what she was suggesting. Unsaddled and turned out to pasture by the time Zoey was done not getting reparations, the horse eyeballed her from around his mouthful of grass as she drove past.

"Well played, sir," she muttered. "Well played."

Once back at the resort, she met up with Lana and her cousin, who were just returning from the Tourist Trap. Both seemed to find the entire thing far funnier than she had. The closest either Montgomery got to sympathy was Killian saying he'd treat everyone to a night out on the town. Other than showering the smell of horse off her, Zoey had nothing better to do, so she agreed.

If anyone had asked, Zoey could have told them they wouldn't be welcome at the small pool hall just off the main street running through town, the one with only the tiniest "open" sign in the window. She didn't even know why they were there until she realized Lana had noticed the receipt Graham had written the car rental information on. But Killian and his crew were determined to do something "fun," and in cruising the tiny town in his sleek black Lamborghini, nothing else so far had sufficed. Rick's it would be.

Zoey didn't know if he actually found a place to rent the thing or if Killian's Lamborghini was shipped in for him to use, but either way, she felt more than awkward parking her rental car near his. She nearly lost a hip when Haleigh whipped into the spot next to them, squealing her Porsche SUV to a stop.

"I didn't realize they even made Porsche SUVs," Zoey murmured, earning an amused look from Lana as they headed toward the unmarked building, noticeable only for the number of cars out front and the sound of music playing inside.

Inside, the building was exactly what a dive pool hall should be, complete with dark wood paneling and a short bar at the far end of the room. Nearly every table was full, and the air smelled of pizza and thinly veiled hostility. Walking into Rick's was like walking into the high school lunchroom at a new school. Everyone looked, but not one looked happy.

"Someone spilled the beans."

The smooth, masculine rumble was familiar. The sharp edge to that smooth voice was not.

"Don't be a grump, Graham," Lana said breezily. "It's a free country."

Despite Zoey's heels, she was still shorter than her companions and had to crane her neck to see the owner of the grumbling voice.

In a room full of strangers, Graham Barnett was a sight for sore eyes. Or just regular eyes. All eyes. All eyes enjoyed Graham Barnett, especially in dark jeans and a snug black T-shirt.

He'd pulled a ball cap down over his hair, cell phone and leather wallet tucked in his back pocket, and Zoey couldn't keep herself from staring at the broad expanse of his muscled shoulders as Graham bent over his group's pool table, taking—and making—a shot.

"It's free, but sometimes it feels a little crowded, L."

"We can leave." Zoey touched Lana's arm to get her attention. "There's plenty of other things to do."

Graham blinked, then the annoyed expression was gone, instantly replaced by the sweetest, sexiest smile.

"Of course, some crowds are better than others." Abandoning the table, even though it was still his turn, Graham approached, smiling down at her. "Hey there, Zoey Bear. I thought I might have to go back to the big house to see you again."

"How are you feeling?" Lowering her voice so as not to announce anything embarrassing to the people around them, Zoey glanced down—then very quickly back up again. "You know...*there*."

"In my balls? Where you kicked me?"

His voice was so loud. Graham's cheerfulness was infectious, but the attention they were receiving with his antics made Zoey want to disappear beneath the plank flooring.

"You kicked yourself in the balls," she shot back. "I have the police report to prove it."

"So do I."

Graham leaned in and took her completely by surprise with an unexpected hug in greeting. The hug was brief, just his palm touching her upper back for a moment, hers braced awkwardly on his muscled arm and the pool cue wedged in between them for safety.

Still, he was warm and smelled like buns.

Crap. She was as bad as Ulysses.

"It's good to see you, darlin'."

"Thanks for not having a chainsaw in your hands," Zoey quipped in reply.

"Don't knock my preferred art form." Lingering just a moment in their still awkward hug, Graham added, "One day, I'll be famous."

"You already are, love. For all the wrong reasons." Lana set a hand to her hip, raising an eyebrow at Zoey. "Are you playing with us or playing with the handsome boy tonight? I know it's been a while for you."

One of Graham's companions tried to cough to cover a snort. Could her cheeks be any hotter? Zoey's entire front side was on fire from embarrassment.

"That's why we're friends," Zoey grumbled. "There's not enough abject humiliation in my life without her."

Graham's grin just grew. "Save me a game, Zoey?" he asked her, sounding far sexier than the man had a right to.

Aiming a look her friend's way, Zoey immediately scooted back out of the range of hugs and misunderstandings. "Sure...ummm... yeah. Maybe. Good luck to you...and all your...evening endeavors."

Killian had already secured a pool table on the other side of the room. With an awkward wave of her fingers, Zoey scurried over to the dubious safety of Lana's cousin and his acquaintances. Lana followed, a knowing look on her face. Slipping an arm through Zoey's, Lana glanced over her shoulder at Graham.

"Good luck to you in your evening endeavors?" Her eyebrow rose.

"Shut up." Zoey all but dragged Lana toward their newly acquired table. "I didn't know what to say."

"How about 'the pool table looks nice and sturdy, but let's check to make sure before my vagina gives up all hope, withers, and dies'?"

"You don't get to voice my vagina's opinions," she hissed.

"Free that speech, love."

"You're actually the worst human being I've ever met. You know that, right?"

Lana's laugh pulled the few eyes that weren't already following them. At least Zoey knew their attention was firmly on her friend and not herself. No one ever managed to stand next to Lana Montgomery and be noticed.

"Who's that guy?"

Curious, Killian lifted his chin slightly to indicate the table of Graham and his friends.

"He's a long story." Zoey picked up a cue stick. "Okay, boys, you might as well get comfortable. It's my break."

———

"I don't like that guy."

Graham didn't know who the man was who'd accompanied L and the Zo-ster into the pool hall, but he had that look.

The look. The pinched nose, squinty eye, chin to the ceiling, stick rammed super far up the ass *look* Moose Springs residents got drunk and made fun of every time they were together. Was it too much to ask to have one night, just one single night, without being overrun by the rich and infamous? Wasn't that why he kicked all his customers out early?

"What's she doing with them anyway?"

Ash raised a dubious eyebrow. "She looks like she knows them. Why do you care?"

"I don't."

She snorted, shaking her head.

"I mean. Just look at him," Graham continued. "Five bucks he goes in for the 'Here, baby, let me show you how to shoot' routine."

"I don't care," Ash reminded him as she missed her shot. "Easton, do you care?"

A grunt of reply was muffled by the beer stein against Easton's mouth. "Nope." Draining half the beer in one long swig, Easton set it down, wiped his mouth free of foam with the back of his hand, and grunted again. "But he does."

The language of Easton was deep, multifaceted, and consisted of varying intonations on the same guttural noise. Being fluent in Easton had saved Graham a lot of trouble having to actually communicate in words. Still...

"There he goes. Lean in, let me help... That's right, send that jerk packing, Zoey. You don't need him. Use that stick if you have to. You're not above a solid groin shot."

"It's your turn," Ash reminded him.

"Yeah, I know." Grabbing a cue chalk, Graham ran it over the end of his cue more times than necessary, grinding the chalk down with a squeaking noise. "Do you think she actually likes him? Because she looks annoyed to me."

"Really? You seem like the type to totally miss female annoyance." A boot kicked him in the back of the calf. "It's your turn."

"Oww. What's with all the violence lately?" Limping over to the far side of the table, Graham haphazardly bent over and missed his shot. "I should go over there."

"And say what?"

"I don't know. Hey, Ash, did you know moose can become zombies?"

Ash sighed the sigh of someone on their last nerve. "There are literally no words for what's wrong with you."

"Did you see that? He just offered her a drink. What a schmuck. She clearly doesn't like him, which is to be expected. The Zo has discerning taste."

"You know this from—?"

"Breakfast. And one accidental encounter where she thought I was going to murder her. What's this jerk's problem? I really should go over there."

As he started to move, Easton reached out a hand and clamped it down on Graham's shoulder. "Stop picking fights with the tourists," Easton rumbled. "Jonah said the next time he gets called, he's going to charge you with assault. No more warnings."

"It's fine. I'll let him have the first swing."

"Why are the pretty ones so stupid?" With another, more

expressive sigh, Ash rounded the table. "What exactly will you accomplish by doing this?"

Graham didn't know. But as the rich son of a bitch put his hand on her shoulder, he decided Zoey Caldwell might be worth it.

———————

Zoey wasn't sure what had caught Killian's attention, but from the moment she returned to their pool table, he was laser focused on her. At least he wasn't trying to "teach" her how to play a game she was better at than he was. That would have been beyond annoying. Instead, Killian kept leaning in as if to impart wisdom and murmuring jokes to make her miss her shots. So far, Zoey had indulged his antics, if more for Lana's sake than anything. After all, this was the second-rated Killian of the family, and by his self-deprecating humor, he knew it. Still, Zoey took her pool seriously. And seriously, if the others around her would drink a little less and focus on their game a little more, she wouldn't be cleaning the table with them.

In between calls for more shots, Enzo and Haleigh showing far too much of their mutual enjoyment of each other's company, and Lana's constant tapping at her phone while standing in other players' ways, they were making quite the spectacle of themselves.

"So, Zoey." Killian glanced at her. "Tell me something about you."

"Oh. Umm. I'm not very interesting."

Actually, Zoey thought she was at least adequately interesting, but she didn't want Killian to get the wrong idea. He was nice enough and attractive when he wasn't staring into space with bored eyes, a thousand miles away, but not her type. Zoey wasn't sure what her type was—her past was filled with an eclectic hodge-podge of the yawn-inducing, a few solid disappointments, and at least two unsavories. But instinct told her Killian was as much her type as she was his. Like the only blueberry muffin at an empty breakfast buffet, it was either her or a plate of cold, soggy bacon.

"Tell me one thing interesting."

"I can't ride a horse for shit."

Barking out a laugh, Killian nudged her pool cue with his elbow right as she lined up her shot. "That makes two of us. My cousin is a genius with the brutes."

"No! Why don't I have any battery left?" Letting out a frustrated thump of her heel on the floor, Lana was oblivious to the irritated look from the player behind her, the one who couldn't line up for their shot. "Ugh, this is ridiculous."

"Because you've been glued to that thing since I arrived?" Killian rolled his eyes, bending over to take his shot. "She's addicted."

"She's work-*ing*," Lana singsonged, obediently sidestepping when Zoey pulled her over, mouthing a silent apology to the table behind Lana's back.

"On her secret project none of us get to know about, but we're all expected to show up for and donate to." Haleigh rolled her eyes.

Lana didn't even glance at her. "Trust me, no one is expecting much from either of you."

Enzo snickered, taking his own shot and earning a dirty look from his girlfriend. "What?"

"She insulted you too," Haleigh reminded him, smacking him

with a cue stick. Which turned into a cue stick battle, which was not how these things were meant to be used.

Chuckling, Killian placed his hand on Zoey's shoulder. "Okay, pool shark, it's your turn."

"I'm not a pool shark. Pool sharks pretend they aren't good. I don't mind you knowing."

The curve on her lips turned to a grimace when Enzo's cue came dangerously close to whacking them in the knees. "Seriously?"

"I'm pretty sure that's Zoey's take-a-hike face."

Zoey didn't even notice Graham approaching until he appeared behind her elbow.

"Of course, the lady and I are still getting to know each other, so I could be wrong." Shooting her a wink, Graham handed her a cube of chalk. "You ready for that game you promised me?"

Maybe it would have worked, but Haleigh dissolved into laughter, and her boyfriend turned to Killian in challenge.

"Are you going to let this guy snake your date?"

"This isn't a date." Frowning at Enzo, she chalked the end of her stick so hard the chalk squeaked in protest. "Not a date."

"I don't know," Killian teased her, squeezing her shoulder just to annoy Graham before dropping his hand. "I was hoping it might turn into one."

Enzo glanced at Zoey. "He did pay for your drink and for the table. Just saying."

"My ice water was free," Zoey growled back, but no one was really listening to her, their focus on the two large men with friendly expressions, clearly squaring off.

"So you're saying if I want to snake your date," Graham said, eyeing Killian, "then I have to reimburse you?"

"Or just play for her," Enzo added.

"Uh-oh," Lana murmured, her eyes flickering up as the table finally became of more interest than her phone. "She's going to eat you."

The pool hall went red around the edges. Zoey could feel the hair on the back of her neck bristle with rage. "I'm sorry, but *what* did you just say?"

"He said—" Haleigh started helpfully, but Zoey held up a hand, shutting her up.

"All of you better *not* have just insinuated that I can be bought, traded, or won. Because if any of you did, I'm going to kill *all* of you."

"Watch the feet, gorgeous," Graham murmured playfully. "At least last time, you weren't wearing heels."

"Of all the ridiculous, sexist, misogynistic, Neanderthal *bullshit* anyone has ever said to me. You. And you. Oh, and *you*—" Sputtering in fury, Zoey turned to each man as they all involuntarily stepped back out of self-preservation. Zoey cracked her cue down on the floor. "And if anyone is playing for anyone, I should be playing for Graham. I'm better at pool than any of you."

"Done." Pulling a roll of bills out of her purse, Lana slapped the money down on the table. "A thousand for the burger boy."

"Burger boy?" Graham looked pained. "I have hobbies, you know."

"Who's playing for me?" Killian looked back and forth between them hopefully.

"*No one*," Lana and Zoey replied simultaneously.

Since Killian was race car Killian and not polo Killian, he must have been used to this sort of treatment. With a chuckle and a murmured "ouch," he settled down on a stool.

"We're playing for Graham. Right, Zoey?" Waggling her eyebrows at Zoey, she stuffed her phone in her purse.

"Lana, what are you doing?" Zoey hissed, following her around the end of the table, where the pool triangle was hanging.

"Just having some fun, love." Eyes twinkling, Lana made quick work of racking the balls. "I think the lovely diner owner's company is worth at least that much. Your break or mine?"

"Mine. And I don't have a thousand dollars." Bending over the table, she shot Lana a look.

"Then you better win. Because trust me, if I win, he's going to be my new pool boy. Speedo and all."

Zoey missed her shot.

For some reason, her hand slipped right off the cue and the cue right off the ball, resulting in the worst break Zoey had ever made since she had turned eleven and was tall enough to hold her own stick. "That wasn't nice."

Lana took a delicate sip of her drink. "No, but it was funny."

"I feel like I should be protesting this." Graham leaned a hip against the table. "But I'll just sit here and try to look pretty."

"You're in my shot." Scooting him away with a nudge of her foot, Zoey sighted along the cue. Right as she was about to hit, she noticed Graham's face at eye level with her from the other side of the table.

"Don't miss, gorgeous. I'm scared of what Lana will do to me."

Zoey shook her head, murmuring, "You and me both."

Killian's phone rang, and he excused himself to take the call, leaving Enzo to eye Graham in a way that made Zoey want to smack him. Clearly, Enzo didn't think much of Graham, his loyalty to Killian written all over his face.

"How about a real bet?" Enzo tossed a much larger roll of bills onto the table. "Twenty thousand to the winner. Loser gets the loser over there. Don't worry, man. You're the conciliation prize."

Choking at the sight of so much cash, Zoey went still. Twenty thousand dollars was as much as Zoey would make in a year. Sometimes it was *more* than she made in a year. To Enzo and Haleigh, it was nothing. To Zoey, that amount of cash could make serious changes for the better in her life. But one look at the expression on Graham's face, his jaw tensed because he knew as well as she did why Enzo had done it, was all it took for Zoey to know she'd never touch it in a million years.

Not when Enzo just wanted to put Graham in his place.

"I don't want your money, Enzo," she said softly.

"Everyone wants my money, sweetheart," Enzo promised. "Some just play hard to get first."

"I may end up punching it out in the parking lot after all," Graham joked. Despite his laid-back posture and easy smile as he watched Enzo, there was a heat in his eyes none of them could miss.

Feeling her face burn with humiliation, Zoey picked up the cue ball. Deliberately rolling it into the closest pocket to her, she glared at Enzo, so furious she was shaking.

"Scratch."

"Why is it new money always insists on carrying that much

cash?" Lana rolled her eyes, plucking the white ball out of the corner pocket and placing it down where it suited her the best. "Let's have a little class, shall we? Oops, missed this one. Zoey, it's your turn."

Once again, Zoey picked up the cue ball and shoved it in a pocket. "Scratch."

If looks could have killed, Zoey was sure the glare she aimed Enzo's way would have been a particularly painful version. Much worse than a carnivorous horse. Three scratches from Zoey later, Lana sank the eight ball with a solid thump of victory.

"Well, that wasn't nearly as hard as it should have been. Sorry, love. Some people just have to ruin the fun." Peeling off a thousand of Enzo's money, presumably to cover what Zoey didn't have, Lana picked up the rest between two manicured fingertips and dropped it in his lap. "Really, I don't know why he likes you two."

Lana's bored tone of dismissal left Enzo flushing a particularly dark shade of red and Haleigh's eyes widening.

Killian ambled up, stuffing his phone into his pocket. "What did I miss?"

"Your choice in friends sucks," Zoey said, so angry she couldn't look at any of them. Hard, quick movements of her hands had the balls racked and ready.

"Would you like to play again?" Lana asked her, because Lana knew how much Zoey loved pool, but she was done. With a tight shake of her head, Zoey left the table and headed for the bar.

She needed a moment free of these people, to swallow her anger and try not to think about the money she'd left on the table.

Money that could have made a real difference.

"Water please," she said to the attractive but shy-seeming man working behind the bar.

The bartender gave her a wary look, which she didn't blame him for. The people she'd arrived with had done nothing but make spectacles of themselves. Even now, she could hear them carrying on as if it meant nothing.

Fingers trembling in anger, Zoey scooped a couple of pretzels from the little bowl he silently set in front of her.

"Well. That was interesting."

Zoey wasn't ready for tall, scruffy, and handsome to lean against the bar next to her, so she buried her face in her hands.

"That was exactly why I don't like to be around Lana's friends. Or friends of friends. It always starts fine and ends up with—"

"You taking double shots of ice water? Hey, Rick, keep them coming for Zoey here."

The bartender, Rick, snorted but played along for Graham, adding a shot glass of water next to her larger glass. When she lifted her head to murmur a thanks, Graham caught her eye. "If it helps, I can go beat up those two, no problem. But I might need some help beating up myself if I'm getting lumped in with the Neanderthals."

Rolling her eyes at him, Zoey groaned. "I'm refraining from judgment, but only until I've finished my water."

"Which means I have ten sips to redeem myself."

"I'm sorry about them. I don't even think they realize how they act."

"I'm used to the type." Shrugging off the situation, he caught her gaze again, smiling sweetly. "You won me, fair and square. Or lost and got me, technically. Now that you're stuck with me, what are you going to do with me?"

"I can't believe I let Lana goad me into that. I'm a female Neanderthal. A Neanderthaless."

"You're also a better pool player than Lana." Graham's eyes crinkled. "You could be buying us all a round right now."

"He was trying to embarrass you and bully me. Screw him and his money."

Zoey didn't realize her hands were still shaking until Graham gently took her fingers in his larger, rougher ones. Squeezing lightly, he sat backward on the barstool next to her, body facing the room but his eyes gazing down warmly at her.

Holding her hand in front of far too many curious eyes.

"Trust me. I'd put up with his type to get to spend time with you any day of the week." Voice softening, Graham asked again. "So, since you have me, what are you planning on doing with me?"

Zoey would never know what she would have answered, dangerously distracted by Graham's proximity and far too focused on the feel of his thumb tracing the smallest of patterns on her wrist.

"Well, tonight's a bust. Are we bailing? Or are we throwing them out?" A slender woman approached, her features creased in annoyance. The stone-faced mountain of a man behind her was impossible to read, but he certainly wasn't smiling.

"Ash, Easton, this is Zoey. Zoey, welcome to the Lockett twins. They're trouble. Keep an eye on them. Guys, Zoey's even more trouble. You're going to love each other."

"Twins?"

"I know. Spitting image, huh?"

Never in her life had Zoey ever seen two people who looked less alike. They were both tall and they had the same warm brown eyes, but everything else was completely different. Easton was the tallest man she'd ever been next to, with shoulders that wouldn't fit through most doors. Ash was slender, maybe six foot if she went on her tiptoes. Ash's short, spiky hair was bubblegum pink with turquoise tips, and she had more piercings in her ears than Zoey could safely count without staring too long. She was easily one of the most beautiful women Zoey had ever met.

Zoey supposed somewhere beneath all that beard, Easton had a face.

"Stay if you want. I'm out." Ash shot a disgusted look at Zoey's companions, then headed for the door. Easton stayed, dropping down to a stool several seats away, focused on the UFC fight on the television behind the bar.

Graham turned to Zoey, lips curved with amusement. "Ash doesn't like tourists."

"I'm beginning to see why." When Zoey frowned at Enzo, he caught her glaring at him and gave a cheeky smirk. Turning her back on him, Zoey focused on Graham instead.

"I didn't win you. But I'd like to buy you a drink in apology."

"We spend a lot of time apologizing to each other. I don't think you have anything to apologize for." His kindness cut through her displeasure, bringing her focus right back to him. "How about we make a deal? No apologies unless someone really deserves it."

They shook in agreement, and when he hooked her pinkie

finger and made her pinkie swear on top of it, the rest of Zoey's upset disappeared.

"You're doing it wrong," she insisted. "That's not how you pinkie swear."

"That's not how *you* pinkie swear. Alaska is more adept at these things."

Somehow it turned into a heated discussion while simultaneously becoming a pinkie war, which Zoey lost badly because Graham might play fair, but he sure wasn't going to take it easy on her. Pinkie muscle for pinkie muscle, he had her solidly outmatched.

Zoey didn't see Lana approach until she was right there, watching them in their finger death battle.

"We're taking off," Lana told Zoey before turning to Graham. "And I'm stealing Zoey this time. Sorry to ruin the fun, but she's mine tonight. We've got some hot tub time to catch up on."

"That's just rubbing salt in the wound," Graham decided. "All right, ladies, a guy knows when he's second-best. See how they treat me?"

Rick and Easton just ignored him. Easton focused on the fight, and Rick was trying to cover how uncomfortable being around Lana made him. The poor guy had cleaned the same glass four times since Lana had stepped up to the bar. As Lana headed toward the door, Graham didn't watch her go. Hmm. Zoey liked that. She waved her fingers in goodbye and started to leave, but Graham caught her hand halfway to the door, again asking her to wait.

"Hey, Zoey? Have you noticed L's been off today? More distracted than normal?"

"Yeah, a little. I know this is a work trip for her, but I haven't seen her as much as I thought I would. She seems stressed."

Brow furrowed, Graham glanced at the door, to the woman waiting outside. "That's what I thought too."

Warmed by his concern, Zoey squeezed his hand. "It's nice of you to worry."

"I don't like tourists, Zoey." Leaning over, Graham spoke quietly in her ear. "But I love my friends. Keep me in the loop, okay? If something's wrong, we'll take care of it."

And as he headed to the bar, back to Easton and Rick, back to a life and routine foreign to her, Zoey couldn't help but smile.

She didn't know this man, but somehow, she believed him completely.

CHAPTER 7

"YOUR MOTHER MADE POT ROAST last night. The really good recipe from Easton's grandmother. You know the one."

As he pulled out of his drive, Graham put his cell phone on speaker and set it on the seat next to his hip. "Yeah, Dad, I know the one." Half-asleep, he eyed the bucket of coffee balanced between his legs.

Graham's family was a close one, and he made a point to call his parents as often as he could. He knew they missed him since moving to Anchorage for his mother's work. But he hadn't factored in enough time this morning to cover a detailed explanation of the week's activities. They kept busy, the Barnetts. As the designated lazy one of the family, Graham highly suspected he was adopted.

"She's also knitting you a scarf. Make sure you love the scarf."

"I always love the scarves." He did. They were good scarves.

"Did you tell him about the scarf?" His mother's voice called in the background. "I made him a new scarf."

"He knows you made a new scarf," Graham's father replied.

Both had become harder of hearing in the last few years, so the volume of the phone conversation had grown increasingly loud. "Does he want some leftover pot roast? Ask him about the pot roast."

"I don't need the pot roast, Dad." Trying to interject failed. Neither one was listening to him, so Graham waited patiently until his mother replaced his father on the phone.

"Hi, sweetie. We missed you last night. I made that pot roast. You know Ruby Lou Lockett's recipe?"

With an indulgent nod, Graham agreed. "Yep, Ma. I know the recipe."

"I'm having your dad drive the leftovers down to you. It's your favorite."

Knowing he was outmatched, Graham capitulated. "Okay, but I have to work all day. How about we have the pot roast the next time I see you? Maybe in the next couple days?" Before she could ask when that would be, Graham's phone beeped with another call. "Hey, Ma, I've got to take this other call. Love you."

"This better be important," he drawled, switching to the other line. "I'm going to have to start that whole conversation over again." The truck's front right tire caught a pothole, splashing coffee in his lap, bringing a curse to his lips.

"Food safety is in town," a teenager's bored voice told him. "They just caught Mom."

"Harold alert, huh? I'll pass it on. Tell Luce I'm sorry, and thanks for taking one for the team."

Hanging up, Graham pulled to the side of the road. "On a Friday too. You sneaky son of a bitch. You think we won't duck you on the busiest day of the week, don't you?"

The Alaskan Food Safety and Sanitation inspector was getting inventive. Unfortunately, Lucy's One-Stop was closest to the main highway running through the mountains, just before the turn-off to Moose Springs. Everyone in Moose Springs knew everyone else, and Graham kept the numbers of every single restaurant owner, bar, and food-serving establishment in his phone. One mass message was all it took to warn the town to gird their respective loins.

As he received a plethora of thank you messages, general grumpiness, and a few choice phrases about timing, Graham absently scratched the ears of his passenger.

"Well, buddy. Looks like today was the wrong day for me to sneak you into work with me."

Tongue lolling out, Jake wagged his tail furiously.

"Who am I forgetting? I feel like I'm forgetting someone."

The border collie barked twice, his blind eyes turning toward the window, nose snuffling at whatever scent he caught in the crisp morning air.

"Yeah, I suppose. Think she'll be excited to hear from me?"

Jake whined.

"Good point," Graham agreed as he dialed her number. "I don't think she's ever forgiven me for—hey, Hannah. It's me."

"It's a little early for you to be bothering me, don't you think?" She yawned, clearly tired from coming off a midnight shift at the resort.

"Early or late?" Graham joked. "Hey, FSS is on their way."

There was a pregnant pause, followed by the kind of sigh only the truly exhausted could utter. Then a string of expletives that made Graham snicker into his coffee.

"And you warned everyone already?"

"The least I can do," he replied modestly.

"Looks like I'm going back to work. The day manager has a doctor's appointment and isn't coming in until eleven. You suck, you know that, right?"

"Love you too, Hannah."

A growl and the ending of their call was her reply. Chuckling, Graham took another sip of his coffee, just as a familiar patrol car pulled up next to him.

"Everything all right, Graham?"

"Yeah, it's a Harold alert. Lucy's boy called."

A pained expression crossed the police officer's features. "Dang. I was looking forward to breakfast too. Do you think Frankie's will still be open for the next fifteen?"

"I doubt it. Better luck tomorrow, Jonah."

Making a second person sigh that day, Jonah drove off, heading toward the One-Stop out near the highway. If Lucy had already been hit, at least she would stay open today. And with two small children, a pregnant wife with her own job, and as much overtime as he could handle, Graham doubted Jonah had more than some Slim Jims and a few energy shots in his squad car.

This would be a long, hungry day for Jonah unless someone had mercy on the poor schmuck and snuck him something from the resort.

Graham pulled onto the road, resisting the urge to drive faster than normal. When FSS came to town, it was every man, woman, and moose for themselves. Jonah was on his own.

The last FSS inspector had been a kind, no-nonsense Native Alaskan woman whom Graham adored. She'd spent too much of

THE TOURIST ATTRACTION   149

her very precious time helping him get his diner up to code before opening. He'd been there for her first baby's christening, and he still exchanged Christmas cards with the family every year. But three years ago, she had been promoted, and the town's beloved FSS officer was replaced by Harold.

And oh. Did they *hate* Harold.

Moose Springs wasn't big on change, especially not the kind of change that took away the people they cared about. Still, no one would have been actively unfriendly if it weren't for poor Rick down at the pool hall. On his first surprise visit into town—because Harold preferred his surprise visits to a friendly message saying he was coming by—Harold had taken Rick entirely by surprise. Rick only served frozen pizza and alcohol as snacks for his customers, but Harold had gone through the place with a fine-toothed comb and a point to prove.

By the time he was done, he'd had Rick's now ex-wife in tears and the quiet, kind pool hall owner ready to take a swing at him. Harold moved on to Frankie at the bakery, then Graham himself that day before heading up to wreak his personal havoc on the resort.

Graham wasn't fond of the power hungry, especially when they actively hurt his friends and community. So they'd started a "Harold watch" program. Undoubtedly, he'd get one of them. There was no helping it. Harold was as determined as he was mean.

But Moose Springs jumped for no man. Especially not one who liked making people sweat.

When he reached the Tourist Trap, Graham parked in the back out of habit. Whistling a little tune to himself, he wrote a paper sign saying they'd be closed for the day, taping it to the inside of the window. He'd learned his lesson about just leaving the doors closed on an unexpected day off. At least his lunch shift in lockup with Zoey had only been met with a few angry reviews and one strongly worded phone call.

Sometimes the tourists got a little unruly when denied their food. Graham had a cracked window and some dented dumpsters to prove it.

Even as he hung the sign, Jake's ears perked up. A sleek black Lamborghini pulled in front of the diner. Two familiar people in the previous night's clothes tumbled out of the sports car, leaning on each other as they staggered toward the front door.

"Great," Graham murmured to his dog. "These two."

"Are you open?" Enzo knocked loudly on the glass door, even though Graham was standing right there, face inches away. "Hellooooo."

"It's nine in the morning. What do you think?"

"Come on, man. My woman's got the munchies."

"And yet I still won't be opening."

Enzo flipped him off, which Graham chuckled at, shaking his head good-naturedly. But when he saw Enzo pull a small bottle out of his pocket and take a hard swig before climbing back in the sports car, Graham saw red.

Graham was out the door, hearing it hit against the side of the diner with a loud crack. "Hey!"

"Maybe they're opening?" Haleigh paused halfway to the passenger door, glazed eyes sparking with hope. "I want a burger so *bad*."

Striding to the driver's side door, Graham smacked his arm on the top of the Lamborghini. "There are people here, jackass. This is a town with kids who play in their yards, and you're driving drunk."

"Bite me."

Okay. Well, if that was how today was going to play…

Graham wasn't the biggest of guys, but he'd earned his fair share of strength hauling downed logs out of the woods for his carving. He was more than capable of snagging this idiot by the collar and hauling him right back out of his car. Enzo took a sloppy swing at him and missed, stumbling. Graham didn't bother returning the favor. In another time and place, Enzo might have put up a better fight, but his eyes were glazed with more than alcohol.

"Do you know who I am?" Enzo demanded.

Graham frowned at him. "I couldn't care less. Get in the back seat."

"What?"

"Either I call the cops on you and risk getting stuck here to be Harold-ed, or I drive you two idiots home."

"There isn't a back seat."

"Noooooo seat…" Haleigh echoed before dissolving into mindless giggles all over again.

"That's your problem to figure out."

Every moment Enzo and Haleigh blinked stupidly at him, Harold got closer. So Graham just aimed them both at the passenger seat and gave a little nudge, letting the pieces fall as they may.

Which was how Graham ended up in a stupidly expensive sports car, his dog's wagging butt on a Prada purse. A drunken Haleigh cooed and petted Jake, her own butt in the way every time

Graham had to shift. Beneath dog, purse, and woman was a very squashed Enzo, half-passed out.

"Someone kill me," Graham muttered to himself.

Haleigh poked her half-conscious boyfriend with a long fingernail. "Killian's going to kill you if he finds out someone else drove."

Enzo's response was a garbled mumble.

"This is your idea of a vacation, huh?" Graham ignored the confused gateman at the resort entrance and just kept going. When he pulled up in front of the hotel, the result was too many bodies tumbling out into the waiting valet's arms.

Jake wasn't as familiar with their location as other places in town. Tucking his tail, he whined as all the new smells assaulted him.

"Jake, *stay*." A firm barking order glued his pup's paws to the pavement as Graham tossed the keys to a second valet and rounded the back of the car. He scooped Jake up under one arm, catching Haleigh around the waist to keep the weaving woman on her heels and not face-planted on pavement.

Since Enzo had been an ass last night to Zoey, Graham didn't mind watching him trip and tumble to the concrete sidewalk.

"These belong to you," he told the staff, shaking his head at the two drunks. "Don't let them drive until you're sure they're sober."

"Sir, we can't—"

A snarl of frustration pulled from Graham's throat as he handed Haleigh off to a valet. "They're. Drunk. Handle it, or I'm going directly to the Shaws."

"Sir. Remain calm. Please, stay calm."

Closing his eyes, Graham counted to ten, then counted backward from ten, then thought about football for a while. Then he opened his eyes and looked at the kid standing in front of him. Good old Grass had come to the valets' rescue, eyes reddened from the night shift and expression determined. Armed with a cell phone and some sort of martial arts stance, Grass edged between the valets and Graham, keeping one eye on the inebriated pair being helped into the hotel and one on Graham. The phone was probably already set to 911.

"I have a puppy." Hoisting Jake higher up his side, Graham tried to look unthreatening. "Can't ninja-kick a guy with a puppy."

"Sir, that's a full-grown dog, sir."

"Kid, you have got to lighten up."

"Sir, remain calm!"

"I *am* calm!"

Hmm. Yelling hadn't helped because Grass had his hands up, ready to rumble. Groaning, Graham stepped back from the situation.

"Okay. I really need to stop coming to this place."

Moving away from the hotel's entrance, Graham pulled out his phone, deciding of all his friends, Easton would give him the least amount of crap for having to come pick him up. Before he could make the call, Jake began to whine, his "I recognize someone" whine. Or maybe it was an "I have to pee" whine. He stepped on the wide, manicured lawn and set Jake on the ground.

"Fine, buddy. Do what you gotta do, then we're out of here."

Jake was off across the grounds like a shot. Cursing at his own stupidity, Graham jogged after him.

Coming around the corner into another one of the resort's lawn areas, Graham found himself nose-to-yoga pants with the second set of bottoms of the day. But since one was Zoey's, he found this situation far less annoying than the first one.

"Suddenly, my day has gotten so much better," Graham murmured, watching his dog fall in love with her all over again.

"Jake!" Zoey burst into giggles.

The border collie wriggled and waggled and licked Zoey's face until her glasses fell off. With his exuberant attentions, she was unable to maintain her sun salutation or Chaturanga whatever thingy the overly pacified instructor droned at them.

At Zoey's side, Lana was doing the moves flawlessly, her cell phone under her nose and her nails typing away.

Ambling over, Graham joined the two women in their line. "What are you two lovely ladies doing this fine morning?"

"Mountainside Morning Yoga." Lana didn't look up from her phone.

"Sounds like a breakfast," Graham decided, squeezing in between Lana's and Zoey's yoga mats. "L, no cell phones in class."

Stretching out comfortably on the grass, he flicked her phone with a finger before turning back to Zoey. "So, yoga, huh? I pictured you more of the running through the woods screaming type."

She opened her mouth to retort, then started giggling again as Jake scooted on his belly through the grass, resting his muzzle on the mat between her arms.

"Yes, I love you too," she promised. "But I paid for this, Jake. I did; I paid way too much for it."

"To see him? This guy?"

The instructor opened one eye, aiming it Graham's way.

Graham jutted his chin upward in greeting. "Heya, Russ."

"Good morning, Graham. If you're joining our class, please lower your voice to pleasing levels and take a downward dog position. Feel the stretch."

"Feel the stretch, Zoey," Graham stage-whispered to her. Her glasses had slipped down her nose in this position, and he wanted to nudge them back up for her.

"Deeper," Russ instructed. "Let the stretch take your mind off your worries."

"This guy used to be so uptight in school. I used to cheat off his papers in kindergarten, and he'd throw a fit."

"Sun salutation," Russ hummed. "And greet the morning."

"How do you cheat in kindergarten?" Zoey asked, giggling.

"I'd just copy what he drew."

Clearing his throat, Russ raised his voice. "*Greet* the morning in *quiet* reflection."

Zoey lowered her voice to an actual whisper. "Aren't you supposed to be at work?"

"We're closed today. There was the possibility of being criticized, and I don't take criticism well, constructive or otherwise."

"Graham. Greet the morning or please leave my class."

Well, when Russ put it that way... Greeting the morning popped his back in the kind of way he'd feel for the rest of the day.

"Hey, Zo." Getting her attention, he waggled his eyebrows at her. "What are you doing today? Besides this?"

Her already bright eyes brightened even more. "I have a shuttle to catch in forty-five minutes. Lana and I get to go whale watching out of Seward. Oh my gosh, I've been dreaming about this for years, and suddenly, it's today. It's in less than an hour! I couldn't sleep last night."

Could she have been any cuter? Graham wasn't sure he'd ever been as excited about something as she was about this. Russ called for them to go back into downward dog, and for a moment, Graham watched his actual dog touch noses with Zoey, Jake shivering with pleasure and Zoey looking just as happy.

Okay. So *that* might have been the cutest thing he'd ever seen in his life.

"Sorry, love." With a sigh, Lana shook her head. "It seems my work trip has become more work than trip. I'm going to have to sneak away from this one too."

When Zoey's happiness slipped, it took Graham's heart right along with it. "What do you have to do?"

"Nothing for you to worry about, just a little investment meeting or two. Maybe Graham wants to go."

Whale watching? With a whole bunch of tourists? Nope, Graham most certainly did not want to go. He glanced at Zoey and realized his reluctance must have shown on his face.

"Or Killian," Lana continued, aiming a knowing look Graham's way. "I bet he's free, and you two get along well."

Ooh. L always could hit a man where he lived. It was probably why these two were friends.

"How's that fair? You offer a guy a fun-filled day of whale watching with his favorite Zoey and then take it away?"

"You snooze, you lose."

"I'd enjoy the company," Zoey said shyly, sounding embarrassed. "You don't have to though."

THE TOURIST ATTRACTION   157

"Sadly, I'm going to have to pass." Softening his tone, Graham scooted his hand over an extra inch and hooked his pinkie finger over hers. "I'd love to spend the day with you, but I have a feeling there's a no Jakes rule on this trip. Even if I booked it out of here, I couldn't get him home and get back here again in forty-five minutes."

Despite her clear disappointment, Zoey gave him a reassuring smile. "It's okay. I'm fine going alone."

"Just go with Killian," Lana pressed. "He likes you. He won't mind at all."

Now, why did that stick in his craw so much? Graham grunted, glaring at the grass.

"Don't force him, Lana. I'm perfectly fine on my own. I don't need a babysitter."

"No, but I promised you I would go with you, and this is the second thing I have to miss." Lana sounded embarrassed and more than a little frustrated.

Eyes closed, Russ raised his voice to be heard over them, smooth and peaceful but so loud.

"Everyone rise to your feet. Now, take a deep breath. Reach for the sky, opening your chest and your shoulders and your mind. Let the mountain air wash over you. You are the mountain. As you go into mountain pose, be the mountain. Let its slopes be your slopes."

"Be the mountain, Zoey," Graham told her as they stood. "Be it."

She shushed him, but her shoulders were shaking from containing her mirth.

"From mountain, we go into tree. As you were the mountain, you now become the tree. You are the tree."

"I think inner me is getting confused," Graham murmured out of the side of his mouth to Zoey. "Excuse me, Russ?"

"Yes, Graham."

"What kind of tree am I? Cedar? Evergreen?"

Russ ignored him.

"I think you're a leaning log," Zoey murmured back. It was true. Graham was doing a significant amount of leaning toward the woman next to him.

"Is there a downed tree pose? I can stick my sticks in the air."

This time, Russ opened his eye and trained it on both of them.

"Remember, Morning Mountain Yoga is for opening yourself to the beauty of the world around you. As we mentally prepare ourselves to go into happy baby pose, first stretch your toes to the heavens, legs open, vagina to the sky. Lift with your hips, open and welcoming to the new experiences of today."

Now, Graham had done many things in his life, but he had never once pointed his vagina to the sky.

But hey. It was always good to try new things.

"Hey, Zoey. Psst, *Zoey*."

"Mm-hmm?"

The sexy little bit beside him was trying desperately not to fall out of position, her face purple from holding in her laughter.

"Am I doing this right?"

Jake had the decency to turn away.

By the time they came out of happy baby pose and relaxed on their backs for a while, Graham had to admit he felt more pelvically open to the universe than he'd ever felt before. That and bizarrely sleepy, but it might have had more to do with listening to Russ hum for a solid ten minutes than anything else.

Having Zoey by his side, Jake snuggled between them, felt oddly pleasant. And yes, they'd only known each other for a few days, but when he looked over and saw her stretching out comfortably on the grass, gazing up at the mountains rising above them, Graham couldn't help but want to spend a little more time with her.

Hooking his pinkie around hers, Graham tugged lightly to get her attention.

"Hey, Zoey. Why don't we drive down to Seward together? If we leave now, I can drop Jake off at home and get us down to the boats in time. I promise you won't miss your ride."

She hesitated, then shook her head.

"Learning about everything from the tour guide is the fun part." Zoey reached over and patted Graham's arm. "Thank you for being sweet, but it really is okay."

Throughout their exchange, Lana stayed quiet, but Graham felt her eyes flickering over to them more than once.

"I could puppysit for the day," Lana offered. "You know Jake and I are super tight. If not, Killian would *love* an excuse to get out of today's meeting."

While Graham was fairly certain this was manipulation, it felt a lot like her being an actual friend at the moment. Because when faced with the idea of his Zoey on a boat with tall, dark, and fancy pants, Graham was pretty sure he would much rather spend the day with her.

"Are you sure, L? Jake gets scared when he's alone with

strangers, and he gets sick from the stress. He needs to be with you or at my place."

"I solemnly swear I will take the best care of Jake that anyone has ever taken of anything ever. Now, are you going, or am I calling Killian?"

Well. It wasn't like Graham had anything better to do. He'd already opened his pelvis to new experiences for the day.

Zoey really was beautiful. And with the look of hopeful excitement back in her eyes, Graham realized he would do far too much to keep it there. Finally allowing himself the luxury of carefully adjusting her glasses high on her nose, Graham gazed over at her, voice softening.

"Whale watching it is."

When Graham agreed to go on the whale watching trip with her, Zoey's first inclination was relief. But when he turned his head her way, playfully squeezing her pinkie finger, it occurred to her Graham might be a problem.

A sexy problem, but a problem nonetheless.

After a quick change of clothes and a phone call to Moose Springs Adventurers to switch Lana's name to Graham's on the reservation, Zoey grabbed her Alaska bag and hurried down to the lobby. She found Graham just inside the hotel with Lana, ignoring the lurking Diego and his brochures, Jake at his feet and a worried expression on his face. Somehow, they'd procured a leash—one of the rules of the resort—but no one was actually holding the thing except for the dog. Ears perked and leash folded neatly in his mouth, Jake turned his cute little nose back and forth between the two humans, following their conversation.

"It's going to be fine. Stop being a worry wart."

"L. He's my baby."

"You're so dramatic."

Graham frowned at that. "I'm a responsible pet owner."

"Are you? Because I'm pretty sure you showed up here in a sports car, and he wasn't wearing a seat belt." The dog turned toward Lana.

"How did you know that? And the situation wasn't conducive to seat belts. Jake understands the limits of reasonable expectation. Right, Jake?"

Ears perked, he turned back to Graham.

"I have eyes everywhere," Lana reminded them. "And I would have found him a seat belt. Jake, your daddy doesn't take care of you at all."

"L, you literally ditched your so-called best friend sloppy drunk the first night she was here."

"And see how nicely that turned out? You two are delightful, by the way. Much better than the last one she was dating."

Zoey's face heated up at the insinuation of Lana's comment, and she was glad neither one seemed aware of her presence. To her horror, Lana kept going.

"I've never met someone so boring in my life. How she managed to climb in bed with him—"

Graham must have been horrified too because he shook his head as if to shake free the images.

"Okay, so I'm going to stop that line of thought. Lana. *Lana*."

"Yes?"

"Please don't forget my dog. Don't forget his water. Don't forget he exists. And please, for the love of everything, don't forget he can't see."

"I will send you pictures on the hour to prove that we are having nothing but the most fabulous time." Lana picked up Jake, even though it took both of her arms to Graham's one. "Say bye, Graham. Bye-bye. We're going to be so much chicer by the time daddy gets home."

Graham whimpered.

Jake had the gall to look pleased.

"She's good with breakable things," Zoey promised him.

"Come on, handsome," Lana cooed. "You and I are going to get a makeover."

"Don't listen to any advice she gives you, buddy. You aren't an autumn. Poodles make terrible girlfriends. Make good choices!"

Zoey patted him on a muscled arm, watching Lana sashay off with Graham's fur baby. "Don't worry. I think she's joking."

"Think or know?"

"I hope? Come on. Our shuttle should be here any minute."

Graham allowed Zoey to herd him outside where the Moose Springs Adventurers tour shuttle was supposed to pick her and Lana up. As Graham held the door for her, he returned Zoey's murmured thanks with a nod, then his eyes flickered over her shoulder to a woman hustling down the sidewalk. She was beautiful, from nose to high-heeled toes, in a perfectly tailored suit with the managerial bearing to match.

Shifting out of her path was instinctual, but Graham

continued to hold the door for her and the breathless desk clerk at her back.

"Morning, Hannah. Grass. As always, a pleasure."

Grass narrowed his eyes, edging through the door sideways so as not to offer his blind side to Graham. Huh.

"How's Harold this morning?"

"He's already made the sous-chef weep." Hannah the—oh. She was the night manager of the hotel, or at least that was what her name tag said. Hannah turned to Zoey. "I hope you're enjoying your stay, Ms. Caldwell."

"I hope you're enjoying your stay," Graham mimicked in a squeaky voice, earning himself a swat of Hannah's hand.

"Don't start, mister. Graham, today has been a nightmare." As she went through the door, the hotel manager put her hand on his arm and squeezed. "But it would have been a worse nightmare without the warning. Thank you."

"I know it's stressful up here, and they have you way overloaded." He gave Hannah a softer version of his normal greeting. "Anytime you want out, let me know. I'm down for a rescue mission."

"If I ever need rescuing, I'm more than capable of doing it myself." Hannah bumped her shoulder to his playfully. "And I like running this place, even on the bad days. Now get out of my hotel. You always cause trouble when you're here."

Graham let the door close, following Zoey to the sidewalk.

"You're friends with the manager?" she asked cautiously, aware she was prying.

"Hannah's my ex. I'm the one that got away."

"Does she think that?"

"I assume she does." Graham glanced down at her. "Why, are you jealous, Zo?"

"Nope." Definitely, probably nope. "I just think it's nice you're friends with your ex."

"Hannah's good people. Besides, I think I'm just acquaintances with my ex," Graham told her, eyes sparkling in amusement. "I may have lost actual friend status the third time we broke up."

"Was that recently?"

"About a year ago, give or take a few months."

Zoey nodded, unsure of what to say.

"You know how some things seem like a good idea when you're tired or lonely or you had a bad day? I'm Hannah's too much whiskey, didn't get the raise, current boyfriend and she broke up call. By the next morning, everyone involved remembers it's a bad idea."

"Do you pick up?"

Amused eyes gazed down at her. "Depends on how good an idea it seems at the time."

His statement hung between them for a moment, leaving Zoey feeling awkward and oddly unhappy. Then Graham shrugged. "Hannah's great, but we've never been in sync. Even when we were together, I wasn't what she really wanted. Opposites attract, but some people have forward momentum, and some prefer their lives to be in a holding pattern."

"Are those your words or hers?"

"My mom's." Graham flashed a sexy grin. "It's her nice way of saying I'm lazy."

"You're not lazy," Zoey teased just as the shuttle bus turned up the Moose Springs Resort's drive. "You seem like a conservation of energy type of guy, not the truly unmotivated."

"I knew from the moment we met, you get me, Zoey."

A middle-aged man in a collared shirt half a size too small trudged out of the shuttle bus, mustering up a polite greeting. "Welcome to Moose Springs Adventurers, where all your adventures are moose-tastic. Caldwell and Montgomery?"

Zoey stuck her elbow in Graham's side to quiet his snickers. "Caldwell and Barnett, actually. We called the office a minute ago and changed everything."

"They didn't call me."

"I'm sorry. But yeah, my friend had to work and he—"

"Played hooky," Graham provided cheerfully from behind her.

"Had to close his business for the day for—"

"Nefarious purposes."

"Yes. Nefarious purposes. So we called and changed Lana Montgomery's ticket to Graham Barnett."

The driver frowned. "I can't let him on the shuttle if he doesn't have a ticket."

At which point things went downhill. Not drastically, but a soft, gentle slope downhill, involving twitchy passengers aiming some serious side-eye in Zoey and Graham's direction through the window. Both Zoey and the driver ended up on the phone with the reservation office at the same time, while Graham leaned a shoulder against the side of the shuttle, every so often rapping his knuckles against the fiberglass.

"Nice shuttle. What year would you say this is?"

"'Ninety-three." Their driver grumpily turned back to the phone. "No, she said Barnett. B-A-R. N-E-T."

"Double T. Two T's." Zoey waved her hands in front of the driver's face, raising her voice to get his attention. "You have to tell her *two* T's. That's why you can't find him."

"What is this? Fiberglass? I bet this gets cold in the winter. Do you do a lot of tours in the winter?"

The driver gave him a pained look.

"Graham. Barnett." The call kept cutting in and out, not helping the situation. "No, *Barnett*. Oh, for the love of…just give me your phone too. No, seriously. Give me your phone. Okay, I'm on speaker phone with both of you. You're both in the same office. It's Barnett with two T's! Come on people, focus."

"You probably need a good strong heater, huh?" Graham murmured. "But that's a lot of people in there. Body heat's good in the winter. Still, fiberglass…I wouldn't have chosen—"

"*Graham*. Shut. *Up*."

"Yes, ma'am."

Zoey didn't buy his easy, aww shucks agreement for one second. But then the office finally figured out their tickets, and the even surlier bus driver stepped aside to let them on.

The bus was packed, with no spots together available, and thirty sets of eyes all glaring at her and Graham in varying forms of disgruntlement and impatience.

"Ooh, tough crowd," he murmured from behind her. "Hey, has anyone here ever heard of the Tourist Trap? I know the owner. He'll hook you up with a free meal if someone lets us sit together."

"That was shameless," she whispered back.

"Never be afraid to use your gifts, Zoey."

In the end, even the promise of reindeer dogs wasn't enough to break the ties holding seatmates together. Graham ended up squashed next to a family of Australian tourists halfway toward the back of the bus and Zoey next to a couple on their honeymoon in the front.

"Hey, Zoey Bear. How's it going up there?" Graham called before they even made it to the main highway leading to Seward.

A thumbs-up wasn't enough to entertain him. Graham waited a moment before calling up again. "Hey, you might want to take some motion sickness medicine. Don't want to barf all over the whales, right?"

"I am all set." Zoey raised her Alaska bag and waggled it at him. "Do you need to take any? I have nondrowsy, nondrowsy extra strength, and one prescription-strength, nothing's going to make you sick, but you'll probably pass out medication."

"Born and bred Alaska. If I couldn't keep my sea legs, I'd get kicked out of the state."

His eyes lingered on her, causing Zoey's face to heat up at his attention. It was impossible not to, even with all the passengers in between them. Smiling at him, Zoey turned around in her seat, keeping her legs tucked in and her elbows to herself. Yes, they had started this trip out annoying everyone, but she was determined to be a good passenger.

"Oy. Zoey. Zooooooooooey. Psssst, Zoey."

"What?"

"Hey, you know the humpbacks are—"

"On the left, you'll see the Chugach Mountain Range," the

driver droned into his intercom, the loud shrill speakers above their heads squawking in protest and cutting Graham off.

"I can't hear you," Zoey mouthed, teasing him. "Sorry."

Graham rolled his eyes and settled into his seat with a clear sigh.

"She's so mean to me," he said to the man next to him. "You should see how she is with the kids. All sweet as sugar to them, but I'm chopped liver."

Zoey listened intently to the guide's spiel, ignoring Graham's increasingly detailed and forlorn description of his and Zoey's married life. His imagination was impressive, and as she made mental note of the inconsistencies between the guide's talk and the extensive research she had done on the area, Zoey found herself growing increasingly distracted by Graham's tale.

"Oh, and the fights we have over the bills. Don't get me started. I mean, I work hard every day to make sure the Hamburger Helper is on the table when she gets home, but does she appreciate it? Nooooo. She's always saying, I make more money than you. I don't forget to mail in the mortgage check. *My* boss doesn't think *I'm* a drunk."

Graham sighed so loud he drew nearly all the bus passengers' eyes. "It's just rough. I think she needs to go to rehab."

Twisting in her seat, Zoey gave Graham her best death stare. "Seriously?" she stage-whispered.

"What was that, dearest? I couldn't hear you over the factually inaccurate account of our homeland."

A modest wooden sign appeared in the distance, next to a building that Zoey had been waiting to see.

"Oh. Oh! Can we stop?" Half standing in her seat, Zoey nearly jumped with excitement. "Please, just for a moment."

"No stopping."

"Hey, man, my emotionally unsupportive spouse wants to see something. We're good on time. Ten minutes won't kill you."

Bless the man. He might be annoying, but he was quick to jump on her side. The tour guide frowned in the mirror.

"No stopping. Please remain seated until we arrive at our destination."

Disappointed, Zoey slid back into her seat.

"I would remain seated," Graham drawled loudly, "but I'm pretty sure someone in here's about to have a bathroom emergency." He waited, then said, "And you're gonna get stuck cleaning it, buddy. Sure you don't want to stop?"

The guide's eyes narrowed, just a little, then he slowed down just in time to make the turn-off into a tiny gravel parking lot. As soon as they came to a stop, Zoey rushed outside, the crisp mountain air hitting her nostrils, wiping away the scent of stuffy, grumpy bus.

Graham joined her, hands stuffed in his pockets. "You know about this place, huh?"

"Of course." Zoey pulled her well-worn travel book out of her bag, thumbing open to an earmarked page and reading aloud the words. "'Bob's Banana Blasters. An oddly non-banana-shaped and non-banana-flavored treat that will change your existence as you know it. Do not miss this one if at all possible.' And I do not intend on missing it."

"This thing again?" Graham scoffed playfully, tapping her

copy of Luffet and Mash's *How to Do Alaska*. "I've got to find you a better tour guide."

The shuttle driver gave them a dirty look. Biting her lip to keep from giggling, Zoey slipped her arm through Graham's and tugged him toward the building. The actual shop was the length of the single-wide trailer it once started as, but in the years since inception, the shop owner had added more than a few lean-tos off the exterior. It was also a knife shop, and inside, dusty glass displays stuffed with all kinds of weaponry filled the trailer, with a few stools pulled up in front of carved animal horns. And at the far end was an overweight man on a stool, beard halfway down his paunch, standing guard over an old freezer and a bucket of cash.

"You ran screaming from me, but this place you want to go into?" Graham murmured in her ear.

"Your steel box of horrors wasn't non-banana-shaped."

"Do you think he calls himself the blast master when he's alone?"

Snickering, Zoey hurried to be first in line as the busload of tourists obediently shuffled toward the blast master. Graham followed at her heels.

"Buy a guy a blaster?" he asked hopefully.

Zoey was more than happy to peel out enough bills to cover two of the oddest treats she'd ever seen in her life. And Luffet and Mash weren't wrong. It didn't taste like a banana, even though it was vaguely flesh colored, yet whatever it was she put on her tongue melted with utter deliciousness.

"Thanks." One single word, but the way he said it had her

toes curling. While Zoey was busy hiding behind her treat and uncurling them, Graham peered around the establishment with a critical eye.

"I bet Harold would eat this place alive."

"Who's Harold?"

"Long story."

"Graham, look." Grabbing his hand in excitement, Zoey pulled him to a glass counter, her focus on the wall behind it instead of the artifacts inside. "See that picture? I read that all the movie stars coming through here used to stop and take their pictures with the original Bob."

"I think the original Bob retired somewhere warmer a long time ago."

"I think the original Bob is hiding beneath that beard. Do you think he'd take a picture with us?"

"I think going whale watching is as close to tourism as I can conscientiously endure. No selfies."

Grinning around her provided wooden spork—because whatever they were eating had enough lumpy parts to require some stabbing—Zoey shook her head.

"You're a selfie snob."

"You're…" He paused, considering it. Finally, Graham said, "You're trouble. Do you like your goop?"

"I love my goop."

"Yeah, me too. Damn that book."

It wasn't fair how good-looking this guy was. Zoey licked her spork nervously. Was he thinking about kissing her? Because she was thinking about—

Pain. Lots and lots of pain.

"Whoa. What's wrong?"

Zoey gestured frantically at her face. "Splinter in my tongue! Spinter in mah tongue!"

"Let me see."

"No, you can't—ahh! Let go!"

"That's right, say ahh." Graham winced, a mixture of concern and amusement in his eyes. "Ooh, that looks painful."

It was. It really was. Graham pulled out a knife from his pocket, flipping it open. "Hold still. Come on. Don't be a baby. I'm not gonna—oops."

For a horrifying moment, Zoey's brain refused to acknowledge what that oops might mean. Then Graham, beaming with pride, held up a half-centimeter-long wooden splinter.

"All good."

"Did you use the knife?"

"Only a little." At her look, Graham chuckled. "I have godsons. That's not the first tongue splinter I've plucked."

"Thank you," she mumbled, feeling her face heating. He must have known she was embarrassed because Graham scooted closer, arm brushing hers.

"Had to earn my keep, gorgeous."

His eyes dropped to her mouth.

The blare of a megaphone made them both jump. "Back to the bus," the tour guide said. "Please return to the bus."

"An air horn is better," Graham whispered to Zoey as she worked her jaw, squishing her tongue back and forth to make sure it was there. "Come on. Let's beat the masses."

This time, Graham darted in and took the front seat, pulling Zoey in next to him.

"That's my seat." A disgruntled passenger said, glaring at them, but when Zoey went to move, Graham snuck his pinkie around hers, tugging lightly in silent request to stay.

"Yes, and I totally stole it. What the wife wants, the wife gets."

After patting the free seat next to them, Graham handed the guy a Tourist Trap business card, printed in the style of a Monopoly "go directly to jail" playing card.

"Life's rough, isn't it? Here's a coupon."

CHAPTER 8

THEIR BOAT WAS NOT THE stuff dreams were made from.

Graham didn't consider himself a particularly picky man, but even he gave the vessel some serious side-eye as they boarded. Zoey was either oblivious or even less picky than Graham because she ignored the ship completely in favor of reading aloud from the brochure.

"Even though peak gray whale viewing season is during their migration in April, a variety of sea life can be seen in the summer months in Resurrection Bay. Sea otters, sea lions, killer whales... oh! Listen to this. Dolphins often swim next to the ships."

Lost in her reading, she was oblivious to everything around them. Graham placed his hand on her shoulder, gently steering her forward as they did the tourist shuffle toward the SS *Problematic*.

"Watch your step, Zoey."

Graham didn't make it down to Seward much, and he never came during summer. Unlike the Cook Inlet outside Anchorage, Resurrection Bay was more than deep enough to accommodate the massive cruise ships visiting during peak tourist season. The little coastal town was a nice place to get lunch and maybe hike up Marathon Mountain for some fun. But the sheer number of tourists waiting around for whale watching tours in Seward was overwhelming.

Their boat was decently sized, but it seemed like far too many people for comfort. Graham didn't love how everyone was stuffed elbow-to-elbow with each other or how they ended up wedged into an assigned seat with another couple with only inches of tabletop and a solid twenty-five years of life between them.

"Hey there," Graham tried to greet the other pair cheerfully, earning himself a kick in the knee from the little boy and the girl bursting into tears.

The family seated in the next table over turned around and gave Graham nasty looks.

"What did I do?" he asked plaintively.

"Maybe kids don't like you," Zoey teased, setting her Alaska bag on her lap so there was room for the Styrofoam cups being placed in front of them by the boat crew.

"My godsons love me. I'm cool."

The captain's voice over a scratchy loudspeaker cut off whatever she would have said next, although by the sparkle in her eye, Graham doubted it was flattering to his godfather awesomeness.

"We're having reports of a rough sea today, folks. If anyone would like to disembark prior to leaving port, now would be a good time to do so. If not, enjoy your lunches."

Pushing one of the cups his way, Zoey said, "You get what Lana ordered. If you don't want the vegetarian chili, you can have my fish chowder."

"Hmm. I hate to say it, but there's fish chowder, and there's fish chowder. That is neither one."

"You know the millionaire heiress who was my travel partner would have eaten either one of these without complaint."

"Yes, and she won my last reindeer dog eating competition. Proper chowder is an art form."

"Mmmmm. It's soooooo good." Zoey moaned in pleasure.

"Don't go all Sally on me now."

She popped an oyster cracker in her mouth, then squeaked as the boat dipped, splashing water over the bow and chowder over her lap. With a sad little noise, she uprighted the Styrofoam cup and scraped the last third of her meal off her jeans.

"Karma." Graham nodded sagely. "For saying I'm not cool."

"I didn't say it," Zoey replied, a cute little smirk on her lips. "I thought it, but I never said it."

Graham winced as he got kicked in the shin this time. "I really do love kids," he promised her, eyes watering.

"There's a viewing deck," she offered. "It's probably less violent."

"Yeah, let's do that. Children, have a lovely day and enjoy your whale watching."

The little girl stuck her tongue out at him, and Graham almost—almost—caved to doing the same right back at her.

As the boat left the harbor, they found a little coffee station near the center of the main deck. Unfortunately, everyone else had discovered the same thing, meaning they had a wait on their hands. At least no one was kicking him anymore.

"You said poodles make terrible girlfriends," Zoey said

randomly, causing Graham to blink and try to catch up. "Back at the resort. Is this experience talking?"

"If you think I'm dumb enough to go down that train of thought, you're crazy," he said decidedly. "But I will say that I like women who wear mud boots just as much as women in Manolo Blahniks. Maybe more."

"Lana thinks you're a complete snob." She arched an eyebrow. "I might be starting to agree with her."

"It's possible." Chuckling, Graham poured himself a cup of coffee, then stepped aside and waited while Zoey fiddled with her own. The line was impatient, but Graham took position beside her, smiling congenially at the other passengers while guarding her right to get her coffee to creamer ratio absolutely perfect. "Hey, Zoey?"

"Hmm?"

"I'd like you even if you had fuzzy duck slippers."

A cute blush reached her cheeks. But was that guilt in her eyes? Unable to stop himself, Graham shifted closer, smiling down at her. "You have some, don't you?"

"I have no idea what you're talking about."

Coffees in hand, they stationed themselves at a window near the front of the viewing deck. The intercom screeched, making them both wince as the captain came back on. "Brace yourselves, ladies and gentlemen. The next few minutes will be particularly rough."

No kidding. As they picked up speed, heading out of the harbor, the boat rose and fell on the waves so aggressively, Graham felt like a bobber in the ocean.

"To distract yourselves, I'd recommend looking out to the left.

Sometimes we can see dolphins swimming alongside the boats in this passage."

Zoey went up to her toes as she looked out the window, trying to see anything remotely close to a splash caused by an animal.

"Graham, I don't see anything."

"Don't worry. These guys get paid to find—oh crap."

The boat hit rougher water, sending them staggering and Graham's coffee nearly spilling onto Zoey. "Sheesh, level it out, man."

"The captain wants everyone in their seats for the next couple minutes," a crew member said, coming past them.

Neither of them wanted to return to the still-crying little girl and her leg-attacking brother, so they found a small bench against the wall, barely big enough for the two to sit squished together. Graham's stomach lurched at the roiling of the vessel, and he focused on the view outside to distract himself.

"See that?" He nodded at the shoreline in the distance.

"What am I looking at?"

"I don't know. I figured you would."

She gripped the wall for purchase. "Landmasses aren't my expertise."

"I'll make it up for you. Okay, right there, that's Moose Turd Isle." When Zoey slapped his arm lightly in admonition, Graham wondered if she knew her attempt not to giggle was all the encouragement he needed to bust out his inner thirteen-year-old.

Amid his describing Big Bazonga Mountain far off in the distance, a look of disgust passed Zoey's face. "Eww. Another one?"

"Another what?"

"Have you noticed how many people are throwing up?"

Honestly, Graham had been doing his best not to think about it. Even as they reached relatively calmer water, the waves were still enough to have the boat pitching about.

Now that she pointed it out, though, there really were a lot of people growing sick.

"We got another one. The kid with the pointy shoe."

"Eek, his mother too," Zoey added.

Everyone was throwing up. With each new gagging noise, another broke ranks and began hurling too. Even Graham was getting grossed out, the smell leaving him more than a little nauseous himself.

Zoey kept twisting around, looking at the other passengers in concern. "Do you think they'll cancel the trip if too many people get sick?"

Graham didn't know, but his heart went out to her.

"Come on," he said. "They opened the doors. Let's get outside and get some fresh air. Maybe we'll see something."

They weren't the only ones with the idea. The bow was stuffed with green faces and bodies pushing for room on the rail to see… nope. Not to see anything. Just to use the rail as a launching pad for their lunches.

"This is so disgusting." Zoey started laughing, her eyes filled with tears.

"You have the worst luck, don't you?" The bow dipped, spraying them with droplets of frothy ocean water. Graham braced his legs wide apart, gripping the handrail closest to him for balance.

She did the same, hand brushing his, but Zoey kept turning around, clicking away with her phone, even though all they could see was the cliffside and two sea lions sunning themselves on a partially submerged rock.

"Ladies and gentlemen, we've heard from another vessel there's a pod of killer whales nearby. Let's see if we can catch them before they go deep."

With a squeak of excitement, Zoey went up on her toes.

"Graham, I don't see them."

Did she have binoculars? Of course she did. But even with the bulky things squashed to her eyeglasses, she still looked disappointed.

Graham's stomach lurched when the boat crested a series of strong waves, and Zoey nearly ate it, juggling her binoculars and phone instead of holding onto the rail. Normally, Graham made sure a woman wanted his arm around them before doing so, but as she scrambled to keep hold of her things, he doubted Zoey even realized his arm was around her waist.

"Sorry, folks. Looks like they slipped away from us. Keep on a lookout for blowholes. We might see something yet."

Dropping down to her heels, Zoey's shoulders slumped. "At least we didn't get sick, right?"

Graham squeezed her waist, drawing her just a little closer. "That's something. And the view is—"

"*Stunning*," she breathed, finishing his thought.

The captain cleared his throat. "Ladies and gentlemen, there seems to be some activity on our starboard side. It appears—oh."

"Don't say it," Graham murmured. "Don't say it."

"It appears the dolphins are chumming the waters."

Large, horrified eyes turned to Graham. "They're eating the vomit?"

"They're eating the vomit."

It happened so fast, Graham was utterly unprepared for it. One moment, he was staring at the dolphins eating a tour boat's collective breakfast in equally horrified fascination. The next moment, the largest killer whale he'd ever seen in his life rose up from the water right next to their boat and crashed back down, the force of the whale's mass rocking their boat sideways.

Graham lost his balance, but two arms wrapped around his waist, holding him up as the boat dropped down into the trench of the wave caused by the jumping whale.

Zoey's eyes were huge, her hair soaked, her glasses beading with water and askew. "Did that just happen?"

"That just happened, Zo."

The utter joy on her face wrapped around Graham's heart and hauled it down somewhere in his stomach, right where it was easier for her to hold on tight. With a squeal of sheer excitement, Zoey let go of his waist and flung herself into his arms.

"I just saw a killer whale! Graham!"

"We just got beaten up by a killer whale," he teased, unable to loosen his hold on her. Instead, Graham pulled her closer. "See, gorgeous?" he murmured in her ear. "Not a waste of time at all."

It would have been the absolute perfect moment to kiss her. Which was why it made complete sense that Graham turned and lost his lunch over the side of the railing.

———

When the violent rocking of the tour boat caused what few passengers who hadn't gotten sick to turn green, the captain called it a loss and headed back to shore. Killer whale shower or not, some things simply weren't salvageable.

As for Zoey, her feet were floating ten feet off the ground, even as they were told everyone had to come back inside and stay in their seats.

The ride back to shore was even choppier than the ride out. Every time the boat rose and dipped with the waves, the group would collectively groan. Waves crashed into the bow with heavy slaps of water, the resultant boom vibrating the air around them, turning the tour boat into a metal drum.

To his credit, Graham kept the rest of his insides in, but he had to fight for it. They found a pair of seats away from everyone else near the bow, since so many passengers were gathered back by the coffee station, where the rise and fall of the turbulent waters weren't as pronounced. The ride was rougher, but at least they had some space. Large hands gripped the edge of his seat until Graham's knuckles were as pale as his face. She gave him some motion sickness medicine when he asked, but it was too late to help him. Like the rest of the boat, Graham was screwed.

When they finally docked, it was a stampede to get back to solid ground.

"I like you, Zoey," Graham decided as they grabbed their things and tried to escape the vessel before the masses. "But the next time L says to hop on a boat with you, my answer's going to be a hard pass."

"Don't worry. My glacier tour tomorrow is just me," Zoey told him, trying to force away her disappointment. It didn't matter that the tour had been cut short or that so many other tourists had been irresponsible with their motion sickness preparation. She'd not only gotten to see a whale, she'd been drenched by the amazing creature from head to toe.

"No shuttle bus," Graham groaned. "Leave me. Save yourself."

"Come on, big guy," Zoey said, pulling his arm around her neck and wrapping hers around his waist, giving him something solid to lean on. "It's not so bad."

"Zo, I will give you anything you want to convince you to take a rideshare back to the big house. I know people. Good, smooth-driving people who will come pick us up."

"All of whom will have to drive here first and then take us back. The sooner you toughen up your squishy little spine and get on the shuttle bus, the sooner you can be home."

"Women aren't the gentler sex."

"No, we aren't. Okay, handsome, in you go."

She pretty much had to stuff him through the door, and Zoey wasn't surprised at all when he took a three-seat bench all for the two of them, flopping down dramatically and telling anyone who tried to sit with them they'd rue their decision for the next hour. Unsurprisingly, the sheer volume of space Graham took up encouraged the others to accommodate him.

"I know you feel terrible, but there's no excuse for this kind of manspreading," Zoey chided him. "At least get your legs in our area."

"Manspreading?"

"You know, when guys take way too much space because they think they inherently deserve it."

Tucking his legs in a few inches more, Graham sighed. "Better? Because my manness can only inverse spread so much."

The shuttle bus rolled a few feet, then lurched to a stop, turn signal on. Graham groaned and turned his face into her shoulder. Zoey patted him on the back of the neck.

"You're manspreading again. Tuck 'em up there, handsome."

"Sorry. It's been an educational day for my pelvis."

To his credit, Graham tried to keep his long limbs contained from there out. But the motion sickness medicine finally kicked in, along with the drowsiness. The face hiding mournfully in her shoulder became an actual head sleeping on her shoulder.

And a sleeping Graham sprawled.

"I don't actually know him," Zoey told the others in the bus as he began snoring. Aggressively. Taking his chin in her hand, she gave him a little shake. "Graham. You're driving everyone nuts."

He blinked at her, gave her a sleepy smile, and then winked. *He winked.* Then he was out again.

The bus driver picked up his piece of paper, the bus wobbling as he jostled paper, steering wheel, and his intercom.

"On the left, you'll see the Chugach Mountain Range—"

He was reading the *same thing*. The exact same spiel that had interested her on the trip there, except they weren't in Moose Springs, and the mountains were on the right, not the left.

Sleeping Graham said what they all were thinking, a loud snort of disgust, followed by a few choking noises.

About halfway into the trip, Zoey gave up trying to wake Graham and looked out the window. As they drove higher into the mountains, Zoey sighed wistfully. She would have given anything to stop and look around, to hike into these mountains and feel the earth beneath her feet. Smell the fresh air and hear the birds singing in the trees above her head. The need was visceral, like a hand wrapping itself around her heart and pulling her.

Smooshing her forehead against the safety glass and staring longingly was the best she could do.

Only in the last few minutes leading up to their arrival in Moose Springs did Graham start to stir, a feat requiring some significant effort on Zoey's part. The speed bump just after the Moose Springs Resort gatehouse finally pulled him awake.

Thank goodness, because there was only so much drool her shirt could soak up, and he'd reached maximum capacity.

"Hey there, Zoey Bear." Sleep made his voice rougher and sexier, lashes framing those warm eyes as he gazed at her.

"Are you feeling better?"

Graham yawned, a mighty yawn, and stretched his muscled arms above his head, vertebrae cracking in a way that must have been pleasant. "Yeah, it was a good nap. How about you?"

"I'm thirty seconds from clawing either my eardrums or your eyeballs out. So please. Pretty please. *Move.*"

Blinking, Graham stood up, backing into the aisle to give her a clear escape route. "Was I snoring?"

"There are no words for what you were doing. You need a sleep apnea test. You're at risk for a stroke."

"Hmm. Would you believe you're not the first woman to tell me that?" Graham followed at her heels, giving a parting wave to the rest of the bus.

Zoey dutifully tipped the tour guide, then headed inside, sidestepping Diego and his pamphlets as she pulled out her phone. "We may need to use yours to call Lana."

"What. The. Hell."

At Graham's horrified tone, Zoey looked up. Instead of having to track her down—a feat proven difficult this trip—Lana was waiting for them in the lobby, ever-present phone in one hand and a glass of champagne in the other. Head to toe glam luxury, Lana was dressed in the kind of silky red and gold romper that only women of her level of attractiveness could pull off. Not for the first time, Zoey felt woefully outclassed by her friend, but it was impossible to hold it against her when Lana beamed at her.

"Oh, I was hoping you would be here soon. How was the tour?"

"There was a whale." Zoey tried desperately not to let her disappointment show through.

"Just one?"

Just one. And a lot of vomit.

"What the hell did you do to my dog, L? Did you bedazzle him?"

"Stop being such a baby. It's just some bling."

Graham whistled for Jake, but the animal stretched out at Lana's feet never moved.

"I told you," Lana said smugly. "You don't take nearly as good care of him as you should. Right, dearest?"

Jake barked in complete agreement.

———————

Since Graham was sick, Zoey drove him home this time.

Having left his truck at the Tourist Trap earlier, he promised he could catch a ride into town tomorrow with Easton. Zoey didn't doubt his ability to find someone to help when Graham clearly knew everyone in Moose Springs.

Even though his land was right up against the resort property, the actual access road took a while to reach, meaning he had time to fiddle with the settings on her rental car, finding the better stations—so he claimed—and not making it as hot as a desert in there. Then he went about trying to scrape the crystals cemented to Jake's freshly clipped and painted toenails with his pocketknife.

"This was invasive," Graham grumbled. "Who blings someone else's fur child?"

"Keep those crystals," Zoey advised. "They're probably diamond chips."

"That's absurd. Even L wouldn't do that."

"Wanna bet?"

Shaking his head, Graham kept working, but he did make a careful little pile of crystals on the center console of her rental. They pulled up to his house right as the light started to shift from the bright blue of day to a softer, yellowing color, the only indication evening was approaching.

"Violent illness aside, did you have fun at all?" Zoey asked, setting the car in park.

"I always have fun with you." He seemed loathe to leave, and to be honest, Zoey wasn't ready to part either. "Walk a fellow to his door?"

Charmed despite knowing better, Zoey climbed out and offered him her arm. Like the gentleman he was, Graham took it and made a deal of leaning on her for help.

"It was so awful, Zoey." He turned his head, groaning into the top of hers, leaning in playfully. "Everyone thought it was fish chowder, but no one realized it was poison. My pain is still palpable."

"You had the chili." Unable to help pointing that out, she patted his head. "I promise you'll live."

"You're not as cruel as I thought." Stepping away when they reached the door, Graham started to open it for her, then hesitated.

"I'd invite you in, but I have a firm no tourists rule."

A quick glance of apology wasn't quite enough to take the sting from his rejection.

"It's fine."

As she turned to leave, Graham caught her fingers, drawing her back. Stepping close, Graham rested a warm, strong hand on her hip, gazing down at her. "It's not you, Zoey; it's me. I set a no rotating door policy on my life a long time ago. I'm not wired to live that way, so I keep some boundaries. But that doesn't mean I want you to leave."

Softening the words with a sweet smile, Graham held up a finger to say he'd be right back. Disappearing into the house, Graham left Zoey and Jake on the porch, a scratchy puppy tongue licking at her fingers and a strong tail thumping against the back of her knee. He returned moments later, leaving the door open but the screen door shut behind them. Sitting down on the porch steps, Graham lifted a pair of old-fashioned bottled root beers in his hand.

"Thirsty?"

"Definitely."

Tilting a bottle her way, Graham handed the drink to her.

Zoey took a sip of her root beer as Jake stretched out on the step below them, resting his chin on his furry paws. "This is good."

Jake's ear flicked between Zoey's direction and then Graham's, following the conversation as they spoke.

"Ash's aunt home brews the stuff and sells it in town if you want to take some home. She sets some aside for the rest of us, because the visitors usually clean her out."

Us. Them. Clearly, Graham had a line drawn in the sand between the two, and the distaste in his town for "them" was impossible to ignore. Zoey took another sip, tipping her head. "All jokes aside, you don't like the tourism in town, do you?"

Graham opened his own drink and took a long swig, draining half the bottle. "I wouldn't say that."

"You hate it?"

"Closer." Shrugging, Graham nudged Jake's furry tail with the toe of his boot. "Let's just say, I like my town a lot better when we're left to our own devices. This is a great place. We don't need idiots wrapping their Ferraris around trees in our front yards."

She waited, letting him choose his words.

"I was just a kid when the Shaws built that place. Their son, Jackson, and I grew up together. Jax is a good guy, and we had a blast running around up there, causing trouble. But the older I got...I don't know. Too much crap goes down that shouldn't. We're a good town with good people. We try to be welcoming, but at some point, enough is enough."

Pursing his lips, Graham finally grunted. "I keep telling myself that one of these days, I'll pull stakes and move north where I won't have to deal with any of this anymore."

"But then you'll have to leave everyone that matters to you," Zoey said, not unkindly. "That's a hard choice."

"Yeah. Which is why I come home every night and secretly hope the hotel goes belly up and we all get our lives back." Chuckling, Graham leaned back on his elbows, feet stretched out in front of them. He shot her a boyish look. "It would make one great bonfire up there, wouldn't it?"

"I plead the fifth." Playfully, Zoey added, "Jonah didn't get all of my rap sheet."

With a sigh of pleasure, Graham settled into his slouch. "I knew I liked you."

Graham leaned over and lightly bumped his arm into hers. When he did it again, even softer, this time it was Zoey who leaned her head on *his* shoulder. Inhaling the scent of the evergreen forest around them, of cedar wood piled haphazardly about his yard, and of expensive shampoo on Jake's coat. Enjoying the hard muscles beneath her cheek and the sweet soda on her lips.

Tilting her bottle his way, Zoey murmured, "To one day being left alone?"

"To one day being left alone."

Clinking bottles, Graham gazed down at her, expression unreadable. Then he smiled gently and leaned into her just a little before taking a sip. "But not quite yet."

CHAPTER 9

THE NEXT MORNING, GRAHAM WOKE up with Zoey Caldwell overtaking his brain. Seasickness aside, he'd had far more fun with her than a guy had a right to, and he kept hoping Zoey would call him up, maybe demand a repeat of their breakfast date or save him from another day at work by dragging him back out to sea.

She didn't.

Even though he hadn't technically given her his number, Graham occasionally checked his phone to see if she called. She hadn't. And yes, Graham had just seen her the night before, but still. He'd bothered her first thing in the morning to get breakfast. Was it too much to hope for Zoey to do the same?

Deeply disappointed by her perfectly acceptable behavior, Graham started his morning as normal. Working out in his shed, then ordering new summer clothes for Jake online. Staring at his log and making sure if any other lost tourists randomly appeared out of the woods, he wasn't as terrifying as he stood rooted to the ground in artistic indecision. Checking his phone again to see if maybe he'd missed a call from her, Graham gave up and drove Jake to Ash's place, where his pup could spend the day outside with her.

Then, when there was nothing else Graham could do to avoid it, he dragged himself in to work.

Easton was a creature of habit, so he showed up at the diner around lunch, giving Graham someone to talk to other than the strangers massing through the doors. The relationship worked well for them. Graham gave East food. East dragged the trash can out and made people pick up their crap. In between still checking his phone and grudgingly serving customers, Graham told Easton about his impromptu afternoon with Zoey.

"You. Went whale watching. Voluntarily."

Easton's voice rarely changed in tone, but his lifted eyebrow spoke volumes.

As he worked, Graham shrugged. "Zoey was all alone. I kept her company. It's not a big deal."

"Whale watching. On one of those overstuffed tour boats."

Graham shoved a burger at the next customer, only half listening to the order being told to him. "It was miserable too. I can't believe they convince people to give them their money. But she loved it, man. Like a kid at Christmas."

Easton's eyebrow climbed higher.

"Okay, judgy. Like you've never gotten roped into some stupid crap because of a woman."

"Name anything I've done that comes close."

Hmm, point to Easton, because Graham couldn't. East kept his mortifying experiences close to the chest and not for general consumption. "Well, it's not my fault you have the emotional range of a tennis shoe."

And then she was there, the next customer in line, hair falling over her eyes and that one strand stuck between her lashes and her glasses.

"Hi," Zoey said shyly.

Feeling his face split with the widest, stupidest grin, Graham nearly dropped a burger patty on the floor.

"Hey there, Zoey Bear. We were just talking about you."

"Should I be worried?"

"Always." He flipped a burger higher than normal, maybe to impress her. "So what's on the menu today?"

"Umm, just a…" She glanced at the prices on the menu board, hand fidgeting in her pocket. "Just a dog please."

"That's all you want?"

Pulling her hand out of her pocket, she added softly, "And a water."

"Wow, you're really paying into my retirement today," Graham joked. When he glanced up from his grill, he saw her face had gone a particularly unhappy shade of red.

Graham told her the price, watching as she counted out her change. The next customers in line shifted impatiently as she dug deeper into her pocket. Her flushed face went even redder as it became clear to everyone in the room that the two dollar and change meal was more than she could afford.

"I'm sorry," she whispered. "I'm not as hungry as I thought."

"Hey, I've got this one," Graham started to say, but Zoey already had turned on her heel, hustling out of his restaurant as fast as she could go. Head held high, even though everyone was looking at her.

"Take the wheel, will you?" Graham clapped Easton on the shoulder.

"What?" Easton gave him a horrified look as Graham stripped off his apron and lobbed it at Easton's face.

"Flip twice, don't let anything burn. This isn't rocket science, buddy."

"What about you?"

Graham was going after a girl.

Somehow, Graham's teasing hit Zoey hard. Too hard. Like a punch in the guts when she already wanted to puke.

Abandoning the Tourist Trap, Zoey hurried across the parking lot, avoiding the eyes of the other customers joining the line. So focused on just getting out of there, Zoey almost missed the voice calling after her.

"Hey, Zoey. Darlin', slow down."

Hard pass on that. She just wanted to be away from all the people inside, even Graham. Still, he followed her as she paused just long enough to pull the keys out of her pocket with a shaky hand. So *of course* the keys hooked on the inside fabric of her pocket, turning it inside out and sending her money—what was left of it—flying.

"No, no, *no*."

Dropping to her knees despite being in the middle of the parking lot, Zoey scrambled to catch her change, frantic not to lose a single dime more. Collecting them carefully, Zoey crushed the handful of coins to her chest, bursting into tears.

"This isn't the safest place to take a pit stop. You should see how people drive around here."

A heavy hand rested cautiously against her shoulder, but when she didn't pull away from the man now kneeling on the ground next to her, Graham curled his arm around her shoulders and drew her into his muscled torso.

"Hey, what's wrong?"

His voice was soft, nearly crooning to her as she sobbed like an idiot into his chest. It was a good chest—a great chest, really— and designed to be cried into. But Zoey barely knew Graham, and her mortification only rose.

"I'm f-fine."

A low chuckle met her warbled insistence. "Sorry, Zoey." Graham kept her tucked to his chest. "For some reason, I'm not inclined to believe you. Was it me? I'm sorry. I never meant to come off rude. It's been a long day, and it's still the lunch shift."

"It's not you." Valiantly, Zoey forced herself to pull it together. "They canceled my glacier tour today. Everything was refunded, and they said I could reschedule for later in the week if I put down another deposit, but when I went to get my purse, it was gone."

"The little frog one?"

"Yes. And I've searched everywhere. I don't even like reindeer dogs, but everything at the resort is so expensive, and—"

Wiping her eyes with the back of her hand, Zoey sniffled. "It's so stupid. My coin purse had everything. I know I had it yesterday on the tour, because I kept checking. I didn't want anyone to pickpocket my bag when I was distracted with the whales."

When Graham didn't say anything, Zoey bit her lip to force it to stop quivering. "I'm not like them. I know you think I am, but I'm not. I saved every penny I could for years to take this trip. Do you know how much ramen I ate? And not the good kind in the cup. The cheap blocks from the dollar store kind of ramen. My blood pressure is like ten points higher now from all the sodium."

"That's some serious dedication." Using both thumbs, he wiped away her tears.

"I know, right? But I knew it would be worth it if I could just get here. Only it's not. Everything isn't what it was supposed to be."

"What was it supposed to be?"

"Beautiful. Perfect. Fun. Not so expensive that I can't even afford to eat reindeer dogs."

"Ah, and here I thought it was my company you couldn't resist."

Rolling her eyes, she still couldn't help relaxing a little as her stress eased in response to his joking. "Shut up."

Dipping his head, Graham murmured into her ear. "I know you're not like them. They drive me crazy, but you I like. Come on. Off the ground. You're far too gorgeous to be down here."

Slipping his hand through her arm, Graham stood, drawing her with him. "There. No one puts Zoey in a corner."

"I'm literally in a parking lot with no corners."

"Don't make me dance with you." His biceps flexed as he kept her close. "I might like it. Have you checked in your rental?"

"About ten times. It's not there."

"Do you mind if we check again?"

"No offense, Graham, but I'm an intelligent woman more than capable of looking under a seat."

"True. But I have something you don't have." At her quizzical look, Graham waggled his fingers. "Longer arms. Where's your rental?"

"Next to your truck. I couldn't find anywhere else to park. But Ulysses was across the road. I don't know if he's still there."

Taking her hand in his, Graham led her around the building, ignoring the gathering line inside the diner and the glaring faces watching them through the windows.

Sure enough, Ulysses was in full courting mode of the truck next to Zoey's SUV, snorting and slobbering away.

"Buddy, my woman needs to check the car."

Ulysses huffed, eyeing them.

"Come on, man. Catch me a break. I don't want to get stomped on today."

Abruptly, the moose spun, darting across the back parking lot and into the road. Gasping at the speed of his escape as much as the power of the massive animal, Zoey watched vehicles slow down for him. Ulysses ran alongside the road for several strides before cutting across, bolting for the protection of the forested mountainside.

"How fast was he going?"

"Maybe twenty-five, thirty miles per hour at the most. They've clocked 'em at thirty-five, but he's like me. Too lazy to invest that much effort."

Even as he said it, Graham opened her car door and started proactively searching through the driver's side, checking the door pockets and under the seat.

"I already looked," she said, defeated. "It's not there. I drove you home, and—"

"And my dog was in your back seat." Graham crawled in the back, wedging himself awkwardly so he could reach beneath the back of the seats. "Jake loves anything and everything he can get his cute little paws on. It's as if he instinctively knows things are shiny, even though he can't see them. Like…yep." With a flourish, Graham lifted her sparkly green frog coin purse. "My dog hid it for a rainy day. Don't feel bad. He buries my crap in the truck all the time."

Zoey opened the purse, checking to make sure it was all there, not out of suspicion but from the need to reassure herself. Graham watched her counting with sympathetic eyes as she leaned against the side of the SUV.

"I can't believe I spent all morning eating my heart out over this when I was sitting on it the entire time."

"I'm sorry Jake caused you to be so worried. But everything's better now, right?" he asked, cupping her face in his hands.

"Yeah." Blinking rapidly at his kindness, Zoey stared at his chest, feeling so lost. So alone.

"Not really better, huh?" Strong fingers wiped away her tears.

"I just need to readjust my expectations."

"Maybe. Or maybe you need to have this place cut you a break. Come on. It's almost the end of lunch." Graham led her back into the diner and flipped the closed sign. "All right, everybody out. I'm closed until dinner."

"Finally." Easton expelled a heavy breath from his place behind the grill, looking beyond ridiculous in an apron several sizes too small. Pointing a large finger at Graham, he growled, "You. Hire someone."

"Yeah, but then they'd have to work for me. And I'd feel guilty about shoving everyone out the door."

As Easton stalked out of the restaurant, muttering to himself, Graham turned to the other patrons. "Hey, this is not a drill, people. The Tourist Trap is closed. Please head to the closest exit in whatever disorderly fashion you prefer. If I hurt your feelings, remind me tomorrow, and I'll give you a free…I don't know… something."

"Fries?" a hopeful patron asked.

"Sure, free fries. Just get out of my diner."

Watching the grumbling masses shuffle out, Zoey shook her head. "I don't understand how you stay open."

"Neither do I." Graham sighed mournfully as he prepped something behind the counter. "The harder I try, the worse it gets."

"Most people would kill for a thriving restaurant."

"Yes, but most people aren't us." Setting an iced tea and plate in front of her, Graham leaned on the counter between them. "And I know you don't like them, but here. Eat something."

"I don't not like them. I just don't like them. They're growing on me."

The reindeer dog had antlers like always, but this time, he'd drawn a little sad face on the reindeer. Despite her wet cheeks and puffy eyes, Zoey couldn't help but exhale a soft laugh. She pulled her glasses off and set them on the table, scrubbing roughly at her eyes and wiping away the remains of her embarrassing meltdown.

"I'm sorry about out there. I kind of got all—"

"Real? Validly upset?" Graham came around the counter to sit next to her, dropping a basket of fries in between them. "Zoey, do you know how many times just this summer I've watched someone have a complete meltdown over something completely stupid? Like chipped paint on a sports car's undercarriage after someone drove on gravel roads. Stupid. Complete freak-out."

"If you're trying to make me feel better, you're doing a really good job at it."

Zoey smiled at Graham. Or she smiled in the direction of Graham. Her glasses were still on the table. Unable to resist the allure of fresh fries, she let her nose guide her hand.

"Can I wear these?"

She guessed he had picked up her glasses. "You're seriously the weirdest person I've ever met."

"I'm not the one with a coin purse that looks like a bedazzled frog princess. How do I look?"

"I'd have to put them on to tell you."

"You're blind as a bat, aren't you? I bet they couldn't make contacts thin enough to fit this prescription in your eyeballs."

"Now you're just being mean. And I like my glasses."

"Yeah, me too." Chuckling that low, warm rumble of his, Graham carefully set them back on her nose. "I like a lot about you, gorgeous."

From past experience, Zoey knew her face was always a splotchy, reddened mess after she cried. But Graham's eyes were sweeping her features, gaze lingering on her mouth.

"Your tour got canceled?"

She nodded. "Technical malfunctions with the boat."

"That sucks," he murmured. "You can't come all the way to Alaska and not get to see the glaciers."

"I guess I'm the special one."

His lips curved. "Yeah, I was just thinking the same thing."

Graham picked up his phone. "Hey, Ash? It's Graham. I need a favor."

———————

When Zoey had planned her dream trip to Alaska, she'd known from the beginning there would be certain things she'd never be able to do. As the helicopter tilted to the right, circling the glacier below, she couldn't help but inhale deeply to slow her racing heart.

This right here. This was what she'd known would never happen.

"Pretty, isn't she?"

A heavy headset protected Zoey's hearing from the loud chopping of the helicopter propellers. Through the headset, she could hear Graham's voice in her ear, a slight buzz distorting his words.

"How long has it been since we've been out here, Ash?"

With a casual shrug, Ash made a second, lower sweep over the river of solid ice, blues and iridescent rainbows reflecting across the surface of the glacier below.

"Since we've been here? Not since Jenna. Since I've been here? Last week."

"Have you been sight-seeing without me? I'm crushed." Graham's teasing tone came through clearly, but when Zoey glanced over her shoulder at the man in the back seat of the helicopter, he gave her an amused look. "Jenna's my cousin, in case you were burning alive with jealousy." A warm voice came through the headset. "I know you have it bad for me."

"Zoey, let me know if you want to leave him out here. I wouldn't mind."

"Do you think a polar bear will eat him?" Zoey quipped.

"This far south? Naw. But he might die of despair without someone to pay attention to him."

"Ouch."

"And he's sensitive."

"I'm actually sitting right here, ladies."

"And I heard he's got a short—" Graham whistled loud enough to cover whatever she was going to say. Voice filled with humor, Ash continued, "Temper. A very short temper."

"Please, I'm the *epitome* of laid-back." Stretching out his feet as far as the cramped quarters would let him, Graham tipped his head to the window. "You're missing the view, Zo."

They made another pass, so close to the glacier Zoey could almost taste it. "Aren't we getting too low?"

"We're setting down." Graham nudged her seat with a knee. "You wanted to see a glacier, right? Well, here it is."

A squeak of excitement escaped her throat as Ash landed the helicopter on the glacier and killed the engine. "Take your time. Just don't do something stupid like carving your initials in the ice. No one wants to read *Graham loves Zoey* for the next thousand years."

"The next million years," he grunted as he swung out of the helicopter, for once flushing at the teasing. "Read a book."

"Global warming, five hundred years at most." Ash smirked. "Kiss my ass, baby doll."

"Not with a lady present."

As they started out across the ice, Zoey glanced at him out of the corner of her eye. "Are you sure you two weren't ever...?"

"A couple?" Graham shook his head. "I'm more the annoying older brother type. Besides, Easton terrifies me."

"I thought he was your best friend."

"Ulysses is my best friend."

"He just likes you for your buns."

Graham nodded sagely. "Can you blame him?"

As Zoey scooted forward on the ice, careful to keep her balance, Graham followed, hands stuffed in his pockets and shoulders relaxed. He never seemed this calm at work or on the boat, she noticed. Maybe it was the isolation. Out here, it felt like they and Ash were the only people in the world.

"So all you had to do was pick up a phone, and suddenly a private helicopter glacier tour appeared."

"Small towns are like that. Oy, Zoey. Stay to the left. You'll want to see that."

Bearing to the left as suggested, she gasped in pleasure at the shallow pool of brilliant blue water in front of them. As they knelt by the glacier pool, cupping handfuls of ice-cold water, Zoey nearly thrummed with excitement.

She pulled out her phone. "Graham, will you take a picture with me?"

Hesitating, she glanced at him, curious at his pause.

"Of course I will, gorgeous," he murmured. So he held up the phone and let her move it around and add all the filters she wanted before clicking away. He didn't even grumble when she added the puppy dog filter, giving them both wriggly noses and puppy ears as they leaned their heads in close to fit in the photo.

Zoey bounced forward, still snapping pictures for all she was worth, then suddenly, she hit the brakes. Her eyes widened, her jaw opening in shock.

"*Graham*. It's an *ice cave*."

There was a reason he'd asked Ash to take them here specifically, and it was worth every favor he'd have to trade for the inconvenience just to see the look on Zoey's face and hear her breath catch in her throat.

Now, for the record, Graham knew far too well ice caves were dangerous. But this ice cave had been there since he was a child, and the shifting climate patterns had yet to cause any noticeable structural integrity losses this far up the glacier.

"There's a climbing rope."

"Hold on, Zo."

It was adorable how excited she was, but the idea of a med evac for a broken neck was far less exciting for Graham. But there was joy in her eyes, and no matter what else he did or didn't do, Graham was not going to be the one to take that from her. If Easton thought he was crazy for the whale watching, who knew what he'd say about this. Selfies, ice caves, letting Ash have a first-row seat to his insanity...Graham would never hear the end of it.

"I weigh more than you," he told her, tugging on the rope to check it. "Let me try it first."

"That's nice, but you have a better chance of pulling me out if I fall than I have of pulling you out if you fall. Plus, I'm a better climber."

"How do you know that?"

"The same way I knew I was the better pool player."

"Tell me how you really feel." Chuckling, Graham knelt next to the stake securing the climbing rope, gripping it securely. "Okay but try not to fall. We lose tourists every year, but you're more enjoyable than most."

More enjoyable. Funnier. Sweeter. Basically, she was the last person who Graham wanted to lose life or limb because of an error in judgment on his part. She couldn't have been any happier. Zoey was practically bouncing with pleasure. Graham wasn't immune to the beauty of the glaciers in his home, but he couldn't take his eyes off her.

"Be careful, Zoey," he added gruffly, looping the rope around his hand a second time and feeling the tension of her weight dig the heavy nylon braiding into his skin. She climbed quickly, then held the rope steady as he climbed down to join her.

"Graham. Look. It's amazing."

Over the course of his lifetime, Graham had watched a lot of strangers ooh and aah over his corner of the universe. He'd spent a significant portion of those years mentally or physically rolling his eyes. But as he stood there, watching Zoey turn in a circle, her face alive with sheer joy, it occurred to him that familiarity too often bred contempt.

Surrounded by walls of ice, something inside Graham thawed, leaving him unable to keep from closing the distance between them.

She caught him watching her, looking far too pretty to be with a guy like him. It wasn't the first time Graham had been off his game in this place.

"I lost my virginity here."

Which wasn't the best conversation starter he'd ever had.

"What? No."

Graham couldn't keep the sheepish expression from his face. "It was awful. I'm assuming it was awful, but on my end, it was amazing. All thirty-three seconds of it."

"At least you didn't have time to freeze your dangly bits."

"My dangly bits are made of steel. It comes with the territory of living up here." He scratched the back of his head, adding, "And maybe there was one dangly bit that didn't escape unscathed."

"Your dangly bits have had a tough life."

"So they remind me regularly."

When he winked at her with what he hoped was sexy roguishness and probably more like prepubescent awkwardness, Zoey blushed again. Then she slipped her hand into his, and Graham was a goner.

As they stood in the corner of an ice cave, Graham allowed himself the luxury of enjoying how much Zoey Caldwell was enjoying herself.

"Show me where."

"There."

"Right there?"

"Right in that spot. Although it technically started over there."

"That's a lot of ground to cover."

"Especially when you're trying not to let anything important hit the ice." Graham squeezed her fingertips in his. "Zoey? How long are you here?"

He'd never asked anyone before. He'd never wanted...or needed...to know.

"Eight more days. This was a two-week vacation."

"You leave next Sunday?"

"Sunday afternoon," she corrected him. "I'm planning on making those couple hours count."

Eight days wasn't enough time for anything. If Graham was the kind of guy for whom just over a week was enough, he wouldn't be standing there with the kind of woman who had no clue he couldn't stop staring at her.

"Zoey? If I asked you to go somewhere with me tonight after work, what would you say?"

Glancing at him shyly, Zoey bit her lower lip, worrying at it. Graham wanted to kiss her and steal that lip away, make it his for a while and treat it better than she was currently doing. But eight days just wasn't enough time.

"I'd say yes. But on one condition."

"What's that?"

Her eyes reflected the blue glacier ice like stars in the night sky. He was waxing poetic. It was a bad, bad sign.

This time, Zoey was the one who winked, flashing him a naughty grin.

"You have to tell me which dangly bit."

CHAPTER 10

CLIMBS BACK UP ALWAYS SUCKED more than climbs down. At least Zoey had a great view.

Graham went first, climbing with the competence of a man who was used to this sort of activity. When he reached the top, he whistled loudly to signal to Ash they were ready to start back. Then Graham turned and knelt by the rope ladder as Zoey followed suit. She climbed up more slowly than Graham had climbed, taking one last look around to memorize the moment.

"That was amazing." Unable to keep from beaming at him, Zoey accepted Graham's offered hand, getting a foot safely on the ice. "Did you see—"

It wasn't the rope's fault that things went to hell in a handbag. It was all the ice's fault. Or maybe it was the stake having wriggled just loose enough in the warming surface of the glacier. Or maybe, just maybe, the glacier was as fed up as the locals were at having their home territory crisscrossed by the curious feet of exuberant tourists, because when the rope went, it took the stake and Zoey right along with it. That would teach them to not pay attention to climate change.

With a squeak of surprise, Zoey slipped. She kept slipping, right off the edge of the shelf into the cave. Graham lunged for her, snagging her wrist as she went over. Dangling twenty feet above the floor of the cave, only Graham's strength keeping her from falling.

"Hold on!" Graham bellowed, tightening his grip on her wrist. "Ashtyn, get a rope! Zoey, give me your other hand."

She tried to stretch, but the movement only made them both slip more. "Graham—"

"No way." A feral snarl escaped his throat. "I'm not letting you go."

"Actually, I was going to say please don't let me go. I will eat every reindeer dog in Alaska until Santa's sleigh is permanently stuck on the ground if you don't—"

A cry of fear escaped her lips as Graham's purchase gave a few inches.

"*Ash, move!* She's slipping."

Not just Zoey. They both were slipping. As terrified as she was, it occurred to Zoey maybe it would be a good thing to make Graham let her go. If someone was going to get eaten by an ice cave, it was better for her than him. He had a much better chance of getting help.

At first, Zoey thought they were falling. It took her a moment to realize that they were both dangling, only now he had a two-armed grip around her waist from grabbing her. Graham's face squashed painfully into her left breast as he cursed like a sailor.

"Did we die?"

"Not yet, gorgeous," he grunted. "I'm going to hoist you up. Grab onto Ash and don't let go. If you have any muscles, you use them."

"I have muscles."

"Prove it, Zo, because I'm not at my best position to be tossing tourists right now. One, two, three."

Maybe he wasn't in his best position, but when he hit three, Graham muscled her up past him. If he had been cursing like a sailor, up on the ice, Ash was as foulmouthed as the sailor's disreputable uncle, ice ax clenched between her teeth as she rewrapped the rope that now held Graham's leg secured around a new stake in the ground. Between the two of them, Zoey and Ash grabbed Graham's legs and hauled him high enough he could get the top half of his torso out of the ice cave.

Graham dropped back on the ice, inhaling deeply to regain his wind. "Thanks for saving our bacon, Ash. That was exciting, wasn't it?"

It took a moment for Zoey to realize that the pounding in her ears was actually her heart beating violently in her chest.

"I think our versions of exciting may be a little different," Ash groaned, sitting on the ice near them, winded.

Zoey looked over and realized Graham's face was two shades paler than it usually was, and his hand was tight around her own.

"That was brave," she whispered, rolling over and wrapping her arm around his waist. "Thank you. Both of you."

He hugged her tight, a much-needed comfort for both of them. Smoothing his hand over her hair, Graham looked into her eyes.

"You know how life-and-death situations bring things into sharper clarity? I just realized something very important."

"What is it?"

Nose-to-nose, Graham panted, "I am so glad I'm not a wuss."

"Did you ever see *Dirty Dancing*? You're carrying a watermelon, Zoey." With that, Graham dropped something bulky in her arms. It wasn't a watermelon, but the sticks of firewood he gave her sure weren't light.

Grunting under the weight, Zoey followed Graham down the sandy beach where a party full of strangers waited for them. "I feel like you use too many pop culture references."

Graham hefted his own firewood bundle up higher, balancing it in one arm and taking a handful of her top pieces to add to his own.

"I have it."

"Yes, but I don't want you to fall the wrong way. Stick a foot in a mud flat, and I won't be able to get you back out again before the tide comes in and you drown or freeze to death."

"Ha ha."

"No joke. Stick to the dry stuff, and you'll be fine."

Eyeing the frothy, crashing waves next to them, Zoey stepped closer to Graham's side. "It's a dangerous day to be us, huh?"

"Don't worry," he said, eyes sparkling in the soft July sunlight. "When a guy finds a woman he likes, he tends to not let her die of exposure in a mud flat."

Not letting her die seemed to be Graham's mission of the day.

His friends were having a late-night bonfire along the coastline, and Graham had invited Zoey to come along. They dropped off their armfuls of firewood, and Zoey helped pull pieces of driftwood over to the slowly growing fire for seating, careful to keep a safe distance from the mudflats Graham warned her about.

Zoey was grateful he was such a large, talkative personality. Even though she had come with him, there were certainly some curious looks and a few less than enthusiastic ones. But everyone loved Graham, and the more he pulled her around introducing her, the more Zoey started to enjoy herself.

She knew more people than expected, and it was clear Graham knew them all. Easton and Ash, Rick from the pool hall, and Frankie from the bakery were familiar faces in the group. Diego, the resort pamphlet pusher, sat silent at the edge of the fire, carving a piece of cedar and ignoring the rest of them. Leah gave her a nice hug in greeting, although Zoey would have preferred not to have Officer Jonah there, even if he was distracted with his kids and a newly pregnant wife. Despite the late hour, several families had brought their children to make s'mores. Flirting teenagers played a game of touch football just past the firewood, and one infant was sound asleep in his mother's arms.

Watching Graham play with his godsons was so much fun, and it was clear as the three played a game of soccer that Thomas and James were far more skilled. After Graham's pride had been crushed and no one could eat another bite of graham cracker, melting chocolate, or fire-toasted marshmallow, they all settled in around the bonfire. It was a teeny tiny little thing, not nearly large enough to fit this many people around comfortably. Zoey perched on her allotted section of driftwood, hoping there weren't too many creepy-crawlies making their way toward her, Graham on the ground at her side.

Ash pulled out a guitar, skilled fingers strumming the chords quietly, drawing the attention of the entire group.

"I didn't know she played," Zoey leaned over and murmured to Graham.

"The Locketts are a talented family," he agreed. "But don't tell them. Their heads are big enough as it is."

Ash snorted without missing a chord. "Shut up, Graham."

Ignoring Ash, Graham stretched his legs out in front of him, relaxed and at peace.

The wind was crisp, blowing strands of her hair across her forehead and into her eyes. Zoey pushed them away, then glanced over and saw Graham watching her. Was he shivering?

"Are you cold?"

"Are you offering to keep me warm?" Graham asked hopefully.

Rolling her eyes, Zoey couldn't help but laugh when he rubbed his arms with dramatic excess.

"Brrrr." Leaning his shoulder against hers, Graham adopted an expression of shivery misery.

He was a lot taller than her, but seated on the ground as he was, it wasn't hard to drape her arm across his shoulders.

"You just want to cop a feel." Graham sighed. "Women are all the same."

Which wasn't true at all, because Ash was *amazing*. As her fingers strummed the strings, Zoey found herself entranced, drawn into the music that somehow fit perfectly with the low crash of the waves against the shoreline. The flickering firelight left the forest behind their circle in darkness. She might have been nervous if she had been alone, but these strangers were as relaxed and comfortable as Graham. The wilderness was their home.

A deep longing hit her hard, a desire to be here, not as a person who'd carried a watermelon but as an actual person who belonged.

Even though the fire grew in warmth, the wind still left her chilled enough that Zoey leaned into Graham's shoulder, unconsciously seeking the heat of his body next to her. His hand rested loosely on the driftwood between them, and when she shivered just a little, Graham slipped his arm around her. He tugged her those few critical inches from the driftwood seat onto his leg.

"Is this okay?" he murmured.

When Zoey nodded, he curled his muscled arm around her waist and snugged her against his chest.

"That was *almost* smooth," she said, smiling.

Graham returned her grin with a quick one of his own. "I do my best."

His best wasn't too bad. To his credit, Graham was very good at holding a woman. His strong torso was the perfect place to cuddle into, her head resting on his collarbone as he traced lazy patterns with his thumb on her knee.

Warm breath on her neck, just beneath her earlobe, made her shiver. "Do you want to take a walk?" His low masculine rumble left her knees weak.

Murmuring a yes, Zoey rose to her feet. Eyes followed their

movements, causing her cheeks to heat at the raised eyebrows and speculative looks.

As soon as they slipped out of range of the firelight—and curious ears—Zoey gave Graham a rueful look. "They think we're hooking up."

"Hey, whoa there, killer. What kind of guy do you think I am?"

As he teased her, Graham wrapped his arm around her shoulders, keeping Zoey tucked to his side as they skirted the beach. He was much better at it than she was, and the warmth of his body cut the chill significantly.

Even in the land of midnight sun, a cloudy sky could cover the landscape in a softer version of the darkness Zoey was used to at night. The waves crashing against the shore were so soothing, Zoey paused, drinking in the moment. But even the waves weren't as good as having Graham's arms slip down around her waist, turning her to face him. He touched his thumb to her jaw, a silent request for permission.

In answer, Zoey nodded into his palm, turning her face and pressing her lips to the base of his thumb.

"You just kissed my thumb."

"Was that weird?" Zoey asked. "That was super weird, wasn't it?"

In answer, Graham took her hand, his eyes locked on hers as he kissed each of her knuckles, slow, soft kisses that made her legs shaky.

"It was the weirdest." His eyes sparkled in the soft light, reflecting off the waves like dancing, broken glass. They started walking again, rounding a bend just as a cloud rolled away from the sun, leaving them once more in that strange, soft midnight sunlight.

A quiet squeaking noise pulled her attention, followed by a series of clicking. More joined the first, then several loud huffs.

"What is that?" she whispered, trying to see out into the water. All she could make out were shapes in the distance.

"A narwhal pod. You're lucky. They usually don't come this close."

Mesmerized, Zoey leaned into his side, trying her best to find the long horns the whales were renowned for. Instead, there was only the soft slap of their bodies slipping beneath the surface.

"Graham, can you see them?" When Graham shook his head, Zoey sighed. "That would have been perfect."

"We can wait awhile, see if they come back," he offered kindly.

But the sounds of the narwhal pod were gone. Taking his hand, Zoey started walking again. "I wish I could have seen them."

He glanced down at her in consideration. "We could always go swimming."

"Could we? I feel like maybe we shouldn't. Isn't the water freezing?"

"Naw. It's fine. Come on, Zo. Where's your sense of adventure?"

"I'm pretty sure being in the middle of the wilderness with a stranger thousands of miles away from everything I know pretty much entails that I am all about the adventure."

"Are we? Still strangers?"

"Aren't we?" she murmured, countering with his own question. Zoey really hoped not.

"You're in love with Easton, aren't you?"

Zoey sputtered. "I'm sorry, what was that?"

"I see the way you look at him." Graham sighed in mock misery. "I get it. The ladies always liked him the most. I don't know. The rippling muscles thing never really did it for me. I was always a sucker for the artsy types."

"You don't like me for my rippling muscles?" Holding up her arm, Zoey flexed. "You see that? It's impressive."

"There are no words." Even as he agreed with her, Graham's large arms curled around her, tugging her closer.

"You're about to show off, aren't you?"

"I'm considering it. Do I need to?"

"You definitely need to."

"Since you asked so nicely…"

Even though she expected it, Zoey still squeaked when he scooped her up. But unlike a far sexier picking up situation, where her legs would be wrapped around his waist and Graham would be gazing down at her with lust in his eyes, she somehow ended up sitting on his shoulders facing the water, with his head between her thighs and her hands gripping his hair for balance.

"Don't worry. I won't drop you," Graham promised as he ambled down the beach. "Not unless I have a really good reason to."

His hair was soft, and since his head was right there, she ran her fingers through it. "Graham? What exactly are we doing out here? Other than defying gravity and giving you a neck ache?"

"I wanted to show you something."

"What did you want to show me?" Zoey asked the top of his head. They skirted another boulder and then stopped.

"This."

Beyond them, the rough, dark gray waters of the Turnagain

Arm rose and crashed, widening from the narrow passageway to a broad, violent sea, ringed in jutting mountains. The low hanging sun cast yellow and orange hues across the far-off mountain-tops, the highest snowy peaks reflecting that midnight sun. And somehow in that moment, on the shoulders of a man she was only starting to know, this wild, strange place was the most beautiful thing Zoey had ever witnessed.

"There's this moment," Graham said quietly. "A moment everyone who decides to live in Alaska has, where they know without a shadow of a doubt that this is where they belong. I'd been here a hundred times, but the first time I truly saw this place was after I came back from college. I knew nothing out there could be better than what I had here. No matter what else you do or don't get to experience, Zoey, I wanted you to come here, to my moment."

And maybe it was his moment, but as the clouds parted again, the narwhal pod surfaced, so close Zoey could see the reflection of their horns. She'd never seen anything so incredible, so other-worldly in her life.

Utterly mesmerized, she couldn't breathe.

"Do I get points for summoning a herd of sea unicorns for you?" he murmured.

"*Graham.*" She couldn't put to words what she was feeling, but never had anything been so *right*.

She didn't know why—when there was something this amazing in front of him—Graham chose to lean his head back and gaze at her. "Looks like it's your moment too, darlin'."

"Thank you." Zoey was almost moved to tears. "Graham, tonight was…everything."

She'd never known anything could be this perfect, then Graham blew the rest of it out of the water when he whispered, "That's how I felt the night I met you."

Zoey would never regret missing the narwhals disappearing into the water. Trusting Graham wouldn't let her fall, Zoey bent over and kissed him instead.

CHAPTER 11

EVERY SUNDAY NIGHT IN MOOSE Springs was karaoke night at the Tourist Trap.

No one had bothered to ask Graham if that was okay with him. If they had, Graham would've said emphatically no, it was not okay with him. He couldn't imagine a worse situation than one in which the customers of his diner found an excuse to stay around even longer, driving him to stand behind his grill until nearly midnight, listening to the off-key musical stylings of those who should know better.

Some days, Graham truly hated his life.

By the time Lana's "crew" came through the door, Zoey a quiet presence at their heels, the party was in full swing. From across the ridiculously packed diner, she raised an eyebrow at him as the group approached. He recognized Killian—*grr*—and Enzo and Haleigh, but the others were just more nameless, faceless strangers. Zoey seemed lost among them, dressed in her worn jeans and faded Wonder Woman T-shirt. She hung back, letting the rest of them order their mass of Growly Bears and food. Only when they moved off to find an empty table did she approach.

"This was not my idea," he assured her in greeting, indicating the cleared area that made up the makeshift stage.

Graham winced at a particularly bad blond woman attempting a Righteous Brothers' cover. The two backup singers with her weren't going to be enough to save her, not when her voice entered the vicinity of a warbling screech.

"Definitely not my idea."

"Why did you give them a karaoke machine?" Zoey asked, accepting the glass of water he gave her with a nod of appreciation. "It's a truth universally acknowledged that a drunken mass who see a karaoke machine must use that karaoke machine."

"I *didn't*. They just kept bringing one. I threw two out in the dumpster, but karaoke machines are eviler than Ouija boards. They just keep coming *back*."

At his feet, Jake whined.

"I know, buddy. It's breaking my ears too."

"Is it okay for him to be in here?" Zoey asked, noticing the tail wagging furiously next to Graham's leg.

"Yeah, Harold already caught me this morning. He's not coming back anytime soon." Graham gave her a mock worried look. "Are you going to tell on me?"

"Depends," she said flirtatiously. "What's it worth to you?"

Oh man. She was killing him.

"We're in trouble, Jake," Graham murmured.

When Jake whined in reply, Zoey headed behind the counter, kneeling down and taking Jake's furry nose in her hands. "Don't worry, you handsome devil, you. I'd never tell on your daddy. But I will give him a lot of crap for the horrible sounds coming out of that speaker."

"He gets lonely. It's the classic, age-old fight. I'm always gone at work; he's always stuck in the house. He thinks I'm out playing with other dogs, and it's always a fight when I get home. If I didn't take Jake out and show him a good time every now and then, he'd up and leave me."

Zoey dropped a kiss to Jake's snout. "Sounds like you deserve it. Right, baby? Your daddy deserves it. If you were with me, I'd treat you better. No one keeps Jake in the corner. Not with your new bling. Aren't you gorgeous?"

"Now who's quoting too much pop culture?"

"Alaska is rubbing off on me."

"Alaska wishes."

Sometimes things just slipped out. Wincing at his own choice of phrasing, he glanced at Zoey out of the corner of his eye. Her cheeks had turned an adorable shade of pink, and she was clearly taking refuge behind her glasses, hand partially obscuring her face as she fiddled with them.

"Alaska also thinks you could use a real drink. It's on the house."

"I thought you didn't give away anything for free." Zoey shot him a cute little grin. "Especially not to those who rotate in and out of your sphere of existence without remorse."

"Haven't you noticed, Zoey?" Graham moved closer, because she wasn't the only one who could flirt. "I keep making exceptions for you."

Zoey declined the drink but did take a soda, a small order of fries, and Jake, insisting on paying for everything except his border collie. Graham didn't think of himself as a hoverer or invasively nosey, but he glanced at her wallet when she counted out the bills. Even someone not paying attention could tell her cash stash was shrinking. So he snuck an antlered reindeer dog onto her plate while she focused on Haleigh's rousing and entirely believable rendition of Katy Perry's "Last Friday Night." And because it was Zoey, he drew little music notes falling out of the reindeer's open, singing mouth in ketchup.

While Graham was busy finishing Zoey's perfect, musically inclined dinner, Easton abandoned his own table, joining Graham at the counter. "So."

"So what? Hey, can you give this to Zoey? And tell the rest of them to come get their crap? It's ready."

Easton gave him a look that spoke volumes. "You need to hire help."

"Yeah, yeah, but if someone was relying on me for their paycheck, then I'd actually have to care about this place."

"You mean it, don't you?"

Choosing not to answer, Graham split his focus between laying out a fresh set of patties and the sexy little bit in the corner. Easton came back, looking just as annoyed as when he left.

"The one with the weird makeup made a pass at me."

"Who, L?"

"No, the brunette."

Six feet if she was an inch, the woman in question wasn't the first supermodel to come into his diner. Graham didn't recognize her, and he also didn't like how she was seated next to Zoey but wasn't acknowledging her presence. "Eh, don't bother, buddy. Not worth the headache."

"Looks who's talking," Easton said, making Graham frown.

Over with Zoey, Jake was having a blast. Zoey had found his dog a seat and a pair of noise-canceling headphones. Her hands in his coat and the leash draped over her knee seemed to be all the security blanket Jake needed.

"You jealous?"

Looking away from her table to the hulking beast of a man standing at the counter, Graham snorted.

"Of her? Naw, Jake still loves me."

"I meant of him."

Graham opened a bottle of beer and passed it over to his friend. "I plead the fifth. But if I don't stop staring at her, people are going to talk."

"People are already talking."

Graham shook his head. "Great."

"It's your own fault. You've been following her around since she came to town like she's got a leash on both of you."

"Lovely imagery, buddy. My male pride thanks you."

Easton shrugged. "Just calling it like I see it."

"Zoey, Zoey, Zoey."

The table of awfulness began chanting her name. Poor thing's face was bright red, and she kept shaking her head with the kind of vehemence of someone who really, really didn't want to sing in front of a group of strangers.

"You're staring again," Easton rumbled. Smug jerk had the audacity to look amused.

"She's a customer. I have to pay attention to my customers."

Even Graham wasn't buying it. Easton took a long draw on his beer, then he said, "You're screwed. Ash wanted me to tell you that."

"Thanks, man. Duly noted."

Leah and Collin had joined Ash and Easton's table, along with half a dozen others who found karaoke night to be better than a movie for entertainment value. The thing was, too many of these people were so utterly convinced of their own masterfulness that they took it way, way too seriously. Every once in a while, one of his people would go up there too, a passive-aggressive mockery of those attempting to sing their hearts out.

"Lana, I don't want to sing!"

"You'll be fine."

"Come on, Zoey. I bet you have a great voice." Killian squeezed her hand in encouragement.

Graham's own hand squeezed the ketchup bottle so hard the top popped off.

Easton grunted. "Is he a problem?"

Graham didn't know. What he did know was marching over there and throwing Killian Montgomery the fifty-eighth through the window was not in his best interest. All the effort would gain him would be an embarrassed Zoey, perhaps another trip to the drunk tank with Jonah, and a potential lawsuit Graham would not win.

But it sure was tempting.

"Don't let them bully you, Zoey Bear." Graham popped a fry into his mouth, ignoring the curious eyes his comment drew. "They only want you up there so they don't have to sing."

Lana twisted in her seat, still sipping her Growly Bear. Usually, she chugged the things, but she was milking it tonight. "Killian wants her up there because he can't sing. I want her up there because she can."

"Lana, *no*," Zoey insisted.

"Come on. Your signature song. Just one song, and I will leave you alone the rest of the night."

"The rest of the night, Lana. You promise."

"I *swear*."

Grudgingly, Zoey rose and went to the cleared area, Jake's leash in her hand. She fiddled with the microphone with her free hand, not looking anyone directly in the eye.

Up until this point, it had subconsciously occurred to Graham that Zoey was as close to perfect as he could have imagined. And there was a very big difference between perfect and perfectly real.

As she stood there with Jake at her feet and a shy blush on her cheeks, she was perfect. Then Zoey opened her mouth and showed Graham how real she could be.

It wasn't that she had a bad voice. Zoey had a good voice. Not an award-winning voice but a second row in Sunday's choir type of voice. Pleasant. Sweet. Comforting. None of which matched her...unfortunate...choice in songs.

Easton stopped drinking his beer, for once startled. "Is she singing—?"

"Yeah."

"By—?"

Graham tilted his head, brain trying to understand what he was hearing and seeing. "Oh, yeah. East, is this really happening?"

"It's happening," Easton grunted, a note of confusion in his voice. "But I don't think it should."

"Is that interpretive dance?"

"It's...something." Her performance was the most glorious of train wrecks, and he couldn't force his eyes anywhere else.

To his credit, Jake did his absolute best to support Zoey in her current decision, adding in the kind of arr-arr-ooo's the original artists never thought to incorporate in their music. And when the pair of misfits were done, there was a full standing ovation, with screams and cheers and pounding of hands on tables.

"East, buddy? I think I might love her."

Easton just took another pull from his beer.

There was nothing else he could do. Raising his fingers to his mouth, Graham let out the most piercing whistle he could. "Zo-*ey*. You show 'em, darlin'."

The adorable, disturbed woman beamed at him, Jake a wriggling mass of happiness in her arms as they left the stage. Easton stared at Graham, incredulous.

"What? I'd like to get laid again at *some* point in my life," Graham muttered out of the corner of his mouth.

The only good thing about karaoke night was the food requests slowed as the singing ramped up, and the bulk of his work was just keeping track of and serving drinks. It took a lot less time to pop open a beer bottle than it did to grill a burger, leaving Graham time to breathe every so often.

And to think of something to say to the woman headed his direction.

Happiness lit her features as she leaned against the counter at Easton's elbow. "What did you think?"

"You're a woman of many talents, Zoey." That was safe enough, right? But Zoey was no fool, and she narrowed her eyes until Graham cleared his throat awkwardly.

Easton snorted but saved him. His man was predictable, and having consumed two beers and a burger, Easton rose to his feet, grabbed a chair, and dragged it to the makeshift stage.

Zoey slipped into Easton's vacated stool, eyes widened. "Is he going to sing?"

"Looks like it."

Forearms resting on the counter, Graham mentally acknowledged his arm was too close to hers. Zoey twisted in her seat, and their shoulders bumped together. A surreptitious glance in his direction, as if she were checking to see if he minded.

Oh, he definitely didn't mind. What Graham minded was the inch still between them.

Since everyone was paying attention to Easton instead of them, Graham slipped his hand between her rib cage and elbow, brushing his thumb across the inside of her elbow in silent question. She leaned into his shoulder, turning her arm into his touch. Permission granted, Graham ran his thumb gently down her arm to her wrist, then entwined their fingers.

"That was smooth," she murmured.

"I have my good days every once in a while."

Easton's voice had brought utter silence to the room, his deep, rumbling croon of "Blue on Black" almost as good as the original. Maybe better, in his own way.

Zoey leaned into Graham's shoulder throughout the song, her hair brushing his bicep. "Oh, he's really talented."

"I knew it. You're in love with Easton," he grumbled as Easton finished the final chorus. "He gets all the women."

A snicker escaped her mouth, not loud but loud enough to draw the attention of half the room. Stiffening at their curious eyes, Zoey started to pull away. Tightening his hand on hers to keep her right where she was, Graham frowned at the people staring. He didn't give a crap what the sea of strangers thought, but he did care what his people thought. And if they were going to stare, he'd stare right back.

Lana always was good at breaking the tension. She lifted her Growly Bear up into the sky, saying cheerfully, "Graham, you dog, you."

"Thanks, L," he drawled.

"I think the cat's out of the bag." Biting her lower lip, Zoey glanced at him. "Is this going to be a problem for you?"

"No, but it's going to be a problem for anyone still staring at us in the next five seconds."

The growl rolling from his throat wasn't supposed to be that harsh, but he didn't like the way she was shifting uncomfortably from all the attention.

"Easy, killer." Ash rose and met them at the bar. "It's just weird seeing you with someone."

"Oh, we're not..." Drifting off, Zoey glanced down at their joined hands. "I'm on vacation."

"Then you better work fast." Ash smirked at him. "Glacially slow is not going to win this race, and that one is hot on your heels."

Tilting her head in confusion, Zoey followed the direction of Ash's chin nod. "Who, Killian? Oh, no. He's...no."

Graham chuckled, squeezing her fingers before letting them go. "Good, because he drives me nuts."

"I mean, he is really hot. And if you get past the chiseled muscles and dangerously good looks—"

Keeping the growl out of his throat wasn't even in the realm of possibility, even though Graham knew she was just teasing him. Since the little minx was grinning openly at him, Graham didn't feel bad at all leaning over the counter and stealing her hand again, tugging her close enough he could wrap an arm around her waist and haul her up on the counter. Zoey squeaked in surprise, then snickered as he rested his forehead against hers.

"What are you doing later?" he murmured.

"Making sweet love to your nemesis."

"I knew it." With a dramatic sigh, Graham pressed a kiss to the tip of her nose. "Fine. Just as long as you're both thinking of me the entire time."

"I mean, was there any other option?" She ran her fingers through Graham's hair. "I'm stealing your dog."

"That's not all you're stealing."

Hmm. Maybe he still had a chance after all, because even a room full of strangers cheering for her singing hadn't brought this much sparkle to her eye.

Lana sidled up, finishing her Growly Bear as she did. "We're moving the party to Killian's suite," she informed Zoey, leaving the unspoken question hanging between them. Lana didn't seem quite her normal self, strained around the eyes and not nearly as carefree as usual. Zoey must have noticed too because she glanced at Graham.

"I should go."

Graham gently tugged the end of a tendril of hair with his finger. "Sounds like a lot of fun."

He wanted to ask her to stay with him, but the last thing he was going to do was keep her from enjoying herself. The rest of the night went about as expected. Drunken eating. Drunken singing. Drunken selfies. A fight broke out, giving Graham an excuse to kick everyone out, then he spent a solid half hour stuffing the bulk of his glassware in the oversized commercial dishwasher in back.

Since Ash and Easton offered to take Jake home, Graham was all alone when he closed the diner and locked the door behind him, root beer in hand. He wasn't terribly surprised to turn around and see someone sitting on the tailgate of his truck, legs swinging. Between local kids sneaking a place to mess around and drunken...well...anyone...his poor abused truck had been molested by more than Ulysses for being alone in a dark parking lot. But instead of strangers or local teens, Graham realized his truck's companion was none other than the woman who had carved her way into his thoughts.

"Hey, gorgeous." Bending down, Graham kissed her cheek without thinking about what he was doing. Then, because thinking about what he was doing didn't seem to affect his less than stellar decisions, he added softly, "You're a sight for sore eyes."

"You saw me two hours ago."

"It was a long two hours." This time, he kissed her other cheek.

"What are you doing right now?" Zoey asked hopefully.

"Hmm. I was aiming for a hot date with some woman I barely know. How about you?"

"There's this guy who pulled a sexy helicopter excursion out of his back pocket on me yesterday, and I was thinking of seeing if he was up for a little mischief."

"Mischief. Zo, you're talking my language." Taking a sip of his root beer, Graham asked, "What's the game?"

"I stole Killian's car."

"What?" He choked on his drink.

Dangling a pair of keys in front of his face, she bit her lip to keep from laughing.

"Technically, Lana and I stole Killian's car. He's busy ripping Enzo a new one for being an ass to the hotel staff, so we figured that he could deal with some cooling-off time. We were wondering if you'd like to go for a joy ride in a Lamborghini."

"And be an accessory to felony theft? I may have to pass on this one."

"That's what Lana said you would say. She's actually on the joyride right now. These are your keys. I just stole them too."

Amused, Graham offered Zoey his hand as she slid off the tailgate. She wrapped her arms around his waist, squeezing him tightly.

"Hi." Zoey beamed up at him.

"Hey, gorgeous."

"How was work? Before all the singing tourists showed up and made you miserable. Did you have a good day?"

Her question was so normal, so expected from two people

who knew each other. And yet Graham was taken back. He couldn't remember the last time someone asked him how work was or how was his day.

"My day was good; my night was better. And right now is fabulous."

Graham wasn't ready to fall for anyone, but her slender fingers had a grip around his heart, squeezing for all she was worth. And she didn't even know it.

"Where are we going?" he asked.

If she said his place, Graham was tempted. Deeply, sorely tempted, no matter how much of a bad idea it would be. Graham knew himself, and he knew that temporary wasn't what he needed. But when she said to hop in, Graham did exactly as she asked.

"I heard that on clear nights, you might still get to see the northern lights, even in summer. There's a scenic lookout not far from here that's our best shot."

She sounded so excited Graham hated to tell her she was wrong. They were too far south and the summer sun too bright to see what Zoey was hoping to see.

"Luffet and Mash again?"

"Diego and Grass. They argued about it for a while. Diego said no, but Grass was sure he'd heard others had luck there."

"Trust Diego. Kid's not seasonal; he knows what he's talking about."

Still, Graham settled into the passenger seat, his arm on the back of the bench and hand lightly gripping her headrest. Zoey shifted so that her shoulder pressed into his wrist, a small movement inviting the connection growing between them. Good, because it was getting a lot harder to not scoot over, to not put his arms around her. Wanting her was grinding on his self-control almost as much as every time she glanced over at him, biting the side of her lower lip.

"I promise I'm not taking you out there to ax murder you."

"I might let you, gorgeous," Graham murmured, voice husky.

Flushing visibly in the dim light of the wooded roadway, Zoey took a breath and a chance, her hand slipping over to rest on his leg. The combination of shyness and strength turned him on so much Graham took a deep breath of his own.

Yeah. She was killing him.

The lookout was a ten-minute drive up the mountain, leaving them higher than even the resort. Thick tree cover blotted out the bulk of the resort grounds, but soft twinkling lights of the town filled the basin below them.

Zoey parked with the truck bed facing away from the view, blocking the lights as much as possible. Then they climbed in the bed. Zoey held up her stuffed Alaska bag. "Hand towel from the kitchenette as our tablecloth, check. Alaskan wilderness soundtrack on my iPod, double check. But I had to get creative with our four-course meal."

"You don't actually need the soundtrack," Graham reminded her, tugging the corner of her towel into place between them. "There are lots of noises around us."

"True. But can you hear...bubbling brook?" She switched the track, smiling at him. "Or eagle in sky? How about...oh, this is a good one. Moose mating call."

Graham lunged for the player, scrambling to turn it off. "Oh no, bad idea. The last thing we want is a lonely bull ticked off we tricked him."

"Oops."

"You keep me on my toes, darlin'." He changed the player back to bubbling brook, turning the volume low enough she wouldn't miss out on the natural sounds of the forest around them.

Upending her Alaska bag, a variety of food products tumbled onto the towel. "Every day, the resort gives us these granola bars as a way to make sure we have all the snacks we need. I've been hoarding mine, and Lana prefers her carbs at your place or in alcohol form. These are all ours, baby."

Organizing her stash of food products, Zoey continued cheerfully. "We also have cookies from last night's cookie tray, complimentary oranges and yogurt, some packets of saltine crackers, and the pièce de résistance, not one, not two, but *three* frozen Hot Pockets."

"We don't have a microwave," Graham reminded her, chuckling at her enthusiasm.

"Oh, we don't need one. They were frozen two hours ago. Now they're lukewarm."

"This is disgusting."

"I know. But it's so good. What do you want? Ham and cheese or the remaining pepperoni pizza? There were two, but a girl gets hungry when she's survived a near-fatal ice cave adventure."

Opening his mouth to say pizza, what actually came out was, "Ham and cheese. I can't take what you love."

A rosy blush filled her cheeks. "Oh, I do love them. There's no doubt about that."

Leaning back comfortably against the side bed of his truck,

Graham stretched his feet out in front of him, munching on a too-cold Hot Pocket, deciding it was pretty much as gross as he'd expected. But the woman across from him was munching her pizza pocket like it was high-dollar cuisine.

"If I'd met you in college, we'd have fifteen babies by now."

Huh. That was one of the things he probably shouldn't have said. But Zoey just snickered, tucking her legs beneath her.

"Because of my choice in snack foods? You have a short list of requirements in a partner."

"It was a simpler time," Graham acknowledged with a sage nod, snagging one of the bottles of water. "If I'd known we were having an impromptu picnic, I would have added to the stash. I make a mean salmon tartare."

"I'd rather have more reindeer dogs."

"Admit it. They're growing on you."

"Or maybe the guy dishing them out is growing on me." Zoey glanced at him shyly. "Yesterday, you could have dropped me. Some people would have, knowing they were slipping too, but you just held on. You saved my life. It was the bravest thing I've ever seen someone do. Thank you, Graham."

Unable to formulate a proper reply, he chose instead to pull her feet into his lap.

"Did you know the human foot is as long as a person's arm from elbow to wrist?" Slipping her shoe from her left foot, he placed her polar bear sock against his forearm. It was barely half the length of his arm, and her wriggling toes were tiny. "You've got some growing to do, Zoey Bear," Graham murmured, covering her toes with his cupped hand.

"Graham? Why are you single?" She gazed up at him beneath her long lashes. "You're too nice to be this available."

Heart warmed at her compliment, Graham squeezed her toes.

"Probably for a very similar reason as you. Were there no guys in Chicago that could catch your eye?"

"Well…" Zoey hedged, and when she shifted in her seat, he could see the guilt in her eyes. "Lana's from Chicago. It's easier to let them think I am too."

"The plot thickens."

"I'm from Mudgeton, Illinois. It's theoretically close to Chicago. Close enough the truck stop outside of town catches a lot of commuters. That's how I met Lana. I was working a night shift, and she was driving to some estate a friend of hers owns outside the city. She got bored, stopped for a cup of coffee, and we got to talking. I don't know, we just clicked."

Zoey's lips curved in remembrance. "Mudgeton didn't know what hit it when she decided to stay awhile. I didn't even know I had a millionaire sleeping on my grandmother's couch, eating her casseroles all month."

"Knowing L, the casseroles are what made her stay so long." Graham pulled out his phone. "All right. I need to see this town."

With her feet safely tucked in his lap, there was no way for her to get the phone out of his hand.

"Argh! Why is it that everyone has phone service up here but me?"

"Wrong carrier. Okay, so I see. Wow. And I thought Moose Springs was small."

"We're not small," Zoey insisted. "We're spread out. It's a farming community, so most of the place is crops, not people."

"No one in Mudgeton caught your eye? No sexy farmer boys?" He waggled his eyebrows at her.

Leaning against the side of the truck bed, Zoey sighed lustily in remembrance. "There *was* Derek Lowman. He was so cute, but he was too busy making an idiot of himself for the girl down the street, Cheryl Ann Parker. It was all very dramatic teenage angst. No one was left unscathed."

Graham was busy clicking away at his phone. "Cheryl Ann Parker... Oh. Yeah, she's a hottie."

Since his phone was out of reach, Zoey tossed a package of crackers at his head.

"Jerk."

"Did she end up barefoot in Derek's kitchen?"

"No, she ended up with a college scholarship to the Ohio State vet program."

"What about you?"

Zoey hesitated, then added in a quieter voice, "I ended up waiting tables on the night shift at the Mudgeton truck stop. Twenty thousand cups of coffee later, I had enough tip money to come here."

"You think I'm going to judge you because you didn't go to college?"

Zoey gave him an awkward shrug. "Some people do. Most everyone made it out of Mudgeton. I made it to the highway and stopped."

"Do you know what I studied in college?"

"It's definitely not business management," Zoey teased. "You're terrible at it."

"The worst." No arguments there from him. "I studied how to get kicked out of art school."

"Too much partying?"

"I wish. I worked my heart out, but I wasn't good enough. It was either change majors or limp home with my tail between my legs, so I took the money I would have spent on the rest of an art degree and opened the Tourist Trap. I didn't want my parents and grandparents feeling like I wasted the money they worked so hard to save up to send me to school."

"They must be proud of you." Zoey nudged his stomach with her toe. "You've done so well."

"Have I?" he wondered quietly. "I'm not so sure sometimes."

Leaning over, he brushed the hair from her eyes, those same tendrils that always got stuck in between her nose and her glasses. Finally letting his gaze drift over her features, Graham didn't try to hide how mesmerized he was by her.

"I should have kissed you in the ice cave," he murmured.

"Mmm. You should have kissed me on the boat."

"Yeah, but that would have been a cliché." His lips curved with affection for this woman, an affection he never expected to have. "Pretty much the same as a first kiss in the bed of a guy's pickup truck."

"First kiss? I remember a kiss on the beach, mister."

"You kissed me. I didn't kiss you. And upside down first kisses don't count. We could work on that if you were interested." Graham waited patiently, giving her the chance to decide what she wanted. When she scooted in, his breath caught in his chest, his stomach tightening.

"Oh really?"

Lips mere centimeters from hers, he nodded. "Really."

"Did you ever see *Lady and the Tramp*?"

"I'm not rolling a Hot Pocket toward you with my nose," Graham said, voice husky with desire. "My nose isn't clean."

"You're not making the best case for yourself," Zoey observed, but her eyes had started to close as she leaned into his touch.

"I'll work on making a better one."

"Oh, look! Graham, I think I can see—"

Then he kissed her, beneath what wasn't even a hint of the northern lights, threading his fingers into her hair and drawing her close.

Slender hands traced up his chest, and he wondered if she could feel his racing heart. This one had stolen his heart: hook, line, and sinker.

"You taste like Hot Pockets."

Smiling against her lips, Graham kissed her again. He'd take whatever advantage he could get.

———

They'd eaten her picnic and listened to a bubbling brook until Graham's bladder protested the torture. But he wouldn't have moved for anything, not with Zoey leaning against his chest, curled up in his arms as they stared up at the sky. One kiss had turned to two, then to more, but he almost liked this most. Having her resting against him, a quiet companion drinking in the beauty of the place he loved.

"You know, Zoey," he murmured into her ear. "There's a scene in *The Last of the Mohicans* where—"

"Book or movie?"

"Does it matter?"

Zoey nodded emphatically. "It definitely matters."

"Movie. I couldn't make it through the book. Too boring."

"You don't stop reading a classic because it's boring," she argued.

"Maybe *you* don't stop reading a classic because it's boring. I do it all the time."

"Was there a point?"

"I'm getting to it." Inhaling the scent of her hair, Graham rested his chin against her shoulder, then placed a single kiss to the side of her neck. "There's this scene in *The Last of the Mohicans*."

"Is it a good scene?"

"It's the best scene. They're sitting like this, and he's holding her, like this." Graham wrapped his arm across her chest, his hand covering her stomach. "And then she's dramatically craning her head off to the side while he stares into the distance."

"Like this?" Giggling, Zoey tried to stretch her neck out, head tipped.

"Almost, but I think there was more postcoital, heaving bosom action."

She heaved as best she could.

Graham squeezed her into a hug, resting his chin on her head. "Good try, but you look like you're having an asthma attack."

"No, I'm sexy. I promise."

She was more than sexy. She was perfect. And like a bad

karaoke song with interpretive dance, she was one hundred percent real.

"Hey, Zoey? How many more days?"

"Seven," she whispered, threading her fingers through his own. Graham held her tighter, and when her smile slipped, he found it again with soft kisses and gentle teasing. But inside, Graham knew the truth, and he knew why this was a terrible idea.

A week would never be enough.

CHAPTER 12

THE LINE FOR THE TOURIST Trap started early. Zoey knew Graham didn't open for lunch until eleven, but when she drove through town at half after ten, she couldn't resist going past.

To her shock, the line was a solid twenty people deep already. Zoey parked behind the building next to Graham's truck because there wasn't much room in the parking lot, then she pulled out her phone. Fiddling with it to try to get at least one bar of reception, Zoey stood in the back of a growing line. On the third attempt, her call finally went through.

"Hey, darlin'," Graham greeted her in his lazy drawl. He sounded sleepy, which was to be expected. They hadn't come back from their picnic until almost dawn. "Tell me you're coming to save me from the masses."

"Technically, I'm part of the masses. This is nuts, Graham."

"You're outside?"

"And way back in line. I was just coming by to say hi, but..." Zoey looked at the line, already shifting and grumbling to themselves. "They seem to be an aggressive group today. Might not be the best idea to get in the way of these people."

"Just cut the line. I'm at the door."

Easier said than done. With every "excuse me," "sorry," and promise she wasn't actually cutting line, the looks grew meaner. When she reached the front of the line, Zoey found a man with legs braced outward glaring her down with the determination of one who wanted lunch and would be getting it. The door swung open, and in that moment, Zoey worried as much for Graham's safety as she worried for her own. She was already regretting this idea.

"Just her," Graham told the crowd in a deep, authoritative voice. "We open at eleven. Back off, man."

Graham stepped forward, his sheer size and hard frown forcing the belligerent crowd to give way. Zoey squeezed in the space between his rib cage and the door, grateful for his bulk between her and the angry muttering accompanying her entrance.

"Wow. I knew your place was popular, but this is ridiculous."

"That's what I keep saying." Turning the dead bolt on the front door, Graham pulled a shade down so they were out of view of prying eyes. Then he turned, leaning a shoulder against the door, arms folded over his chest.

"Hey." One single word and those warm eyes sliding over her was all it took to roll a shiver of anticipation down Zoey's spine. "What's the plan today?"

That was a normal question. There was no reason to feel like this, except for the fact Graham was standing close, voice lowered and attention completely on her.

"I didn't plan anything. Today was supposed to be an unscheduled spontaneous adventure day."

"Tell me you have unscheduled spontaneity written in your planner."

"Maybe...probably."

Graham was extremely handsome, but somehow just standing there, gazing down at her, reaching over and tucking an errant strand of hair behind her ear, he was the most attractive man she'd ever seen. Momentarily overwhelmed, Zoey took a step back, retreating to the safety of somewhere not within arm's reach.

Just because they'd kissed the night before didn't mean Graham wanted her to launch herself at him in the middle of the morning with a mass of hangry customers outside.

It wasn't so much like being hunted as there was an invisible rope between them. Zoey moving back meant he was going to follow. And she was fairly certain if he had gone a different direction, she would be following him. When Zoey's hips bumped the table, it occurred to her that she may have deliberately lured him somewhere she could shove him down and have her way with him.

This morning was becoming increasingly confusing.

"What do I owe the pleasure of your company, darlin'?"

"I wanted to make out with you."

Had that actually slipped out? Zoey tried to cover her slip-up with a laugh. What came out was a strained little squeak.

"You didn't mean to say that." Graham shifted in closer, thumb tracing the curve of her jaw with the lightest touch.

"Nope. I think. I have no idea. I accidentally probably meant to say it."

A smile curved his lips, a softer, far sexier smile than she had ever seen him give. Graham's eyes searched hers, his voice low and husky. "If you did mean it, you should know I've been thinking the same thing since last night."

Did she mean it? "Umm, I actually had a legitimate reason for bothering you at work...I think."

Warm breath brushed the rim of her ear. "Trust me. You are *all* the excuse I need to be bothered at work."

Oh, screw it.

Graham was a lot taller than she was, but when she pulled him down to her, the height difference wasn't nearly as bad as she'd expected. Especially when Graham wrapped his arm around her waist, lifting her up to her toes.

Last night had been soft, sweet, the slow burn kind of kiss that had made her heart flutter and her defenses weaken. This kiss burned her alive.

Twisting in place, Graham sat back on the edge of the booth's bench, hauling her into his lap.

"We still good?" he asked, placing warm, open-mouthed kisses down her neck.

"As long as you stop talking," Zoey promised.

His voice softened, emotions she couldn't read flickering across his features. "Whatever you want, gorgeous." He gazed down at her, eyes flickering from her own, then down to her lips. Shivering in anticipation, she leaned in, but still Graham held back, his mouth centimeters from hers.

As if counting. Deciding. One. Two.

With a groan, he kissed her before she reached three.

Keeping her hands off him was impossible. Every inch of his neck, his chest, his arms was wrapped in rock hard muscle, softened only by the worn white T-shirt between them. He smelled like bread, because he always smelled like bread, but also of shampoo and deodorant. Every time her palms slid over his chest, down his stomach, across his sides, the muscles beneath her hands would flex as if subconsciously trying to impress her. But when her fingernails dug into his shoulders, that strong body shivered beneath her hands, pressing into her touch.

Even as desire tried to wipe out every coherent thought from her, it occurred to Zoey maybe Graham was as starved for human contact as she was.

"This is a lot better way to start my day than coffee," Graham murmured. Unlike her wandering hands, his had stayed firmly glued to her hips, but his eyes were drinking her in.

Zoey knew it the instant Graham's control cracked, because it was the instant after her own did. Moaning in appreciation of his hard body against hers, Zoey wrapped her arms around his neck, plastering herself all over him. With a jerk of his hands, he hauled her tight to him, mouth slanting over hers. That slow burn between them flaring hotter with every breath they couldn't catch.

A bang on the door jolted her back to the present, causing her to jerk in his arms.

"Shh," he murmured when she started to turn around. "Ignore them."

"It's past eleven. They're breaking down the door."

"You're breaking me." He carefully pushed her glasses back in place on her nose. "Two more minutes."

"One more minute."

"Okay, Zo. Just one."

The things this man could do with a single minute...especially when that minute turned to four and a half.

"We know you're in there!"

"Then you should know I'm busy!" Graham growled back.

Biting her lip failed to hide her mirth. With a groan of defeat, he rested his forehead to her chest. The same hands that had traced fiery patterns over her skin now wrapped around her like she was a teddy bear.

"Why me?" he groaned. "Why can't they just leave me in peace?"

"Because then you'd be unemployed like me," Zoey joked, sliding off his lap. "All right, handsome. Time to earn a living. You already played hooky enough this week."

"You're unemployed? And yet able to jaunt off to a vacation of a lifetime?"

"Jaunting off to the vacation of a lifetime is the reason I'm currently unemployed." Zoey offered him a wry look. "They promised the vacation time and then went back on it. They said if I left, I wouldn't have a job to come back to."

"And you left."

"They pay me," Zoey told Graham, going up on her toes to press a kiss to his strong, stubbly jaw. "They don't own me."

"You've got balls of steel, darlin'." He walked her to the door, then caught her hand. "Hey, Zoey. A friend of mine is in town. Want to have a late lunch with us after I close?"

Did he just ask her on a date? Lunch with someone else didn't count as a date, right? Because Zoey was ready for an actual date with him. To see where this could—

Nowhere. This could go nowhere.

"Uh-oh. What did I say wrong?" Focused on her, Graham didn't miss her hesitation.

"Nothing," Zoey promised. "I'd love to. When and where?"

"I'll meet you at the resort at two thirty." With a quick kiss to her temple, Graham opened the door, letting the line trample past them first so she could slip out unharmed. "Poor schmuck has to stay there too."

The first time Graham met Jackson Shaw, he'd punched him in the face.

Maybe they'd only been in kindergarten, but to this day, Graham maintained Jackson had it coming.

As an only child, he'd never learned to share well. Take a Barnett's Transformers sticker at your own risk.

In the years since kindergarten, Graham's relationship with the son of the resort owners had been far more positive, even if the face punching had sort of become their thing. So when he heard Jackson was back in town, the first thing Graham always did was hop in his truck and drive up to the big house to see him.

The fact that gave him an excuse to see Zoey was only an added bonus.

She was waiting for him near the gift shop, staring longingly at the jewelry displayed in the window while resolutely ignoring the brochure dude edging toward her.

"Diego." Graham nodded in greeting to the other Moose

Springs local before stepping up behind Zoey and wrapping his arm around her waist.

"What are we drooling over?" he asked her, pressing a kiss to the rim of her ear, knowing his breath would tickle her neck. Graham liked knowing that. He wanted to know more, every little bit of information he could about her. Including what had her gazing so intently through the glass. "Is it the earrings?"

"No, although those are pretty. Stupid expensive though. Do you see that piece of old newspaper they're using as decoration in the display? That's from the 1920s, Graham. It's almost a hundred years old. It should be in a museum."

"No one goes to the Moose Springs Museum. It smells like formaldehyde."

"Why?"

"Because it's in the same building as the taxidermist."

"You're lying," she accused, but Zoey was giggling as she turned around and stepped out of his arms.

Graham opened his mouth to proclaim his innocence, but then he saw stars. Everything blurred for a moment, but as he staggered back, he could hear Zoey yelling.

"Hey! Get off him!"

Vision clearing, Graham saw who had sucker punched him. Jax always could get the jump on him. But Zoey had planted herself between them, hands up and stance ready, like she was prepared to kick Jax's head off.

Someone had taught this girl some serious self-defense, because Graham was still working his jaw, trying to keep his feet, when Jax moved in for the hug that always followed their ritual greeting. Zoey, his tiny slip of a perfect person, grabbed Jax by the wrist and did some sort of Jedi thumb trick thing that had him yelping in pain and jumping backward.

"Trust me, buddy, I have had a long morning, and I'm not in the mood to watch a friend get attacked. So back off or I will go full spider monkey on your ass. *Security*!"

Her only weapon was a worn water bottle, but she brandished that sucker like a broadsword, braced and ready.

Grinning, Graham stepped behind her, draping his arm around her collarbone and pulling her shoulders back into his chest.

"Jax, this is Zoey. She's cute, right?"

"She's *mean*. I think she broke my thumb."

When Zoey twisted her face around to look at him, Graham caught a glimpse of actual concern in her eyes. Graham rested his chin on the top of her head, hugging her tighter to him. "You're not mean. He's a baby."

"He hit you."

"It was his turn."

"That makes no sense at all."

Groaning, Zoey leaned back into him, just a little. The smallest of actions, just an involuntary need to take shelter from a stressful situation, but Graham liked her leaning into him for comfort.

"Mr. Shaw?" A blond, curly-haired hotel worker with massive eyes stared at them in concern. "Are you all right? Do you want us to escort Ms. Caldwell off the grounds?"

Zoey's own eyes went wide with horror, even if not nearly as big as the blond's eyes. "No, Quinn. I was just...argh."

"Naw, it's fine," Jackson promised. "Graham's taste in women has always been off."

"Did he just call me *off*?"

"It was a double insult, darlin'," Graham said in her ear. "If he riles me up enough to hit him, then Jax gets first punch next time."

"This makes no sense. Which, considering it's you, makes complete sense."

Slipping away from his hold, Zoey stepped sideways, looking at both of them as if they'd lost their minds. With a grin, Graham moved in and gripped Jax in a massive bear hug.

"Let's start over. Jackson Shaw. This is Zoey. She's taken me down, and I promise you, she can do the same to you. Tread lightly, my friend. She has pointy toes and knows how to use them."

She offered him a pained look. "Really?"

"Zoey, this stuck-up rich boy is Jax. Believe it or not, he's not half-bad."

"Don't wax poetic on me," Jax teased, then said to Graham, "Where are we going? I don't want to eat in this shitbox."

"You're reading my mind, brother."

Their usual haunt was Rick's pool hall, and Zoey agreed to share a pizza with them. They piled into her rental car at Zoey's insistence. Hands tight on the wheel, Graham wondered if she was still upset at Jax or if there was something else bothering her.

Rick didn't say much, but he gave Jax a rough hug in greeting before sticking a pizza in the oven for them. The pool hall was empty at that time of day, leaving the bar-height tables free for them. Even after consuming a mass quantity of bread, cheese, and meat, Zoey seemed frazzled. More so than a simple accidental thumb-breaking situation would have caused. Wrapping his arm around the back of her chair, Graham tilted his head to catch her eye. Only then did he notice the hairline crack in the center of her glasses or the tiny piece of scotch tape holding the delicate frames together over the bridge of her nose.

"Hey, what happened? Did your glasses break on you?"

"That's one way of putting it."

Graham slid his arm down to her shoulders, hugging her tight. "Should I ask? Did the planned spontaneity not go as planned?"

Zoey groaned. "I'm at the point I don't even want to talk about it anymore."

Jax raised an eyebrow.

"Her vacation is trying to kill her," Graham supplied helpfully.

"It started with a zip line. A spontaneous, exceptionally long zip line, which sort of...stopped."

"How far in?"

"About halfway." Zoey put her forehead on the table, her mangled glasses digging into the bridge of her nose. "And they argued awhile about who would have to come get me. Then I was hooked up like the bad end of a tow truck and hauled to the next line. Which, again, was really long."

Oh, this poor woman. Even now, her face flushed with the embarrassment she must have endured.

"How many times did you get stuck?"

"Every. Single. Time. At least until they started sending me out with someone else to make sure our weight kept us moving."

"Did it?"

"Nope. They decided halfway through the course that my

equipment was faulty and needed replacing. They held up not just our group but every single group following us until they could get my entire butt sling thing changed out. Guess who was everyone's favorite zip line companion today?"

Graham squished her sideways into him, as much as he could safely squish her and not break her or her taped glasses.

"I think you get the record for having the worst luck on excursions."

Jax frowned. "This wasn't one of ours, was it?"

She shook her head. "No. I booked all my excursions in a package deal with Moose Springs Adventurers. They gave me a discount for adding this last minute."

"There's your problem," Jax decided, lightly slapping his hand down on the table. "They suck. Like, they seriously suck. Don't go anywhere with them. I mean, I get that people want to save money, but if the price is bargain basement, you're probably going to get screwed somewhere. Just stick with us, Zoey. I'll tell the concierge to make sure you get in one of our zip tours today."

Despite his friend's intentions, Graham felt Zoey tense.

"Drop it, man," Graham warned in a light voice, catching Jax's eye and giving a hard shake of his head.

"What?"

"Thank you, Jax." Her appreciative words didn't reach her eyes. "I'll talk to the concierge later."

"Naw, let me call them now. Freaking Grass is over there. Who names their kid Grass?"

"That's what I said. Hannah called me a jerk."

"She's called you a lot worse," Jax said with a smirk.

Even though Zoey knew about Hannah, having the other woman mentioned casually in front of her left Graham uncomfortable.

"I'm going to find the restroom," she decided. "Excuse me."

Jax might have been cut from the same roughneck cloth Graham was, but he'd spent too much time in the kind of circles Graham never would. When Zoey pushed her chair out, Jax rose to his feet, the manners drilled in automatically. The moment she was gone, Jax dropped down to his seat with a grunt and a curse.

"What's with the death glare?" Jax asked.

"She can't afford it. And before you do, *don't*. You'll only make her feel worse."

Jax gave him a considering look. "That's disturbingly astute of you."

"Keep calling me names, and this shit's going south fast."

Barking out a laugh, Jax settled back in his chair, manspreading for all he was worth. "Okay, seriously. What the hell are you doing? Last I checked, you wouldn't touch a girl like her with a ten-foot pole."

Bristling, Graham sat up straighter in his chair. "What's that supposed to mean?"

"I mean, she's hot enough, but come on."

"You're more of a jerk than I remembered."

Jax snorted, shaking his head. "Maybe I'm just tired of being around people I can't speak my mind to."

"Well, how about you don't start by running your mouth about Zoey? Cause all pleasantries aside, you and I are about to speak our minds outside."

A massive grin spread across Jax's face. "No shit. When Ash told me, I didn't believe it. You're screwed, man."

Gritting his teeth, Graham looked away. "You didn't come all the way here to mess with me about my love life or lack thereof. What's the deal?"

"I don't know. My folks are acting real weird, and they told me I had to come. There's some benefit or something I'm supposed to represent the family at."

"Lucky you."

"You think I like going to that crap?"

No, Graham knew Jax didn't. There was a reason they were sitting in Rick's instead of eating up at the resort.

"By the way, they said to ask you if I saw you—"

"No way. Hannah brought it up the other night too. I'm not opening a second location, and definitely not at the big house."

Jax hit him with a calculating look. "It could help the foot traffic at your place."

"Low blow, man, using intimate knowledge of my misery to advance your mother's agenda." Graham shook his head. "I'm not hiring employees. The last thing I need is someone depending on me. It makes being undependable too hard. No, but thanks."

"Hey, I told them you'd say no, but you know how Ma is when she wants something."

"Yeah, I remember." They had constantly been in trouble with Jax's mom when they were little. "The woman has eyes on the back of her head. So you go to this thing, watch some rich morons spend their money to save whatever the cause of the month is, catch some fireworks, and then what? Are you staying for a while?"

Jax frowned. "I don't know. My gut says to get out and back to New York while I can. Have you seen the guest list this week?"

This time, Graham was the one who snorted. "Since when did I ever pay attention to who's up there?"

"It's a lot of money. Too much money. And the timing? I know the fourth is big around here, but my gut tells me this isn't all about some fireworks. But everyone I talk to seems closed lipped about it."

A door swung open at the far side of the pool hall, catching Graham's eye. As Zoey appeared from the bathroom, she smiled at him, a real smile that reached her eyes even from across the room. Yeah, he probably was screwed when it came to her.

Funny how it didn't bother him half as much as it should.

"You have the dumbest-ass look on your face," Jax teased. "That woman's got you by the balls."

Graham didn't bother to deny it. "Remind me to tell you how hard she kicked me in them. I still pee too far to the left."

When she sat back down, Jax turned his focus on her, eyes bright with curiosity. "So, Zoey. Since my buddy is totally smitten with you, I'd love to know more about you. The good stuff, not the bullshit stuff."

He was a direct guy, Jax. Unfortunately, Jax had always had a thing for the shy, sweet type.

"He's going to try to steal you from me," Graham warned her. "He started with my favorite trading cards when we were kids, then spots on the school's sports teams. Jax actively tried to seduce every girlfriend I've ever had."

"And you're still friends?" She raised a skeptical eyebrow.

Leaning forward on his elbows, Jax aimed a lazy smirk at her. "He didn't tell you what he did to *me*."

When Zoey leaned forward too, taking a long sip of her water, Graham groaned. He recognized that sparkle in her eyes.

"By all means," she said. "Enlighten me."

They'd lingered in Rick's too long.

By the time Zoey realized what time it was, she had to rush Graham back to his truck so he could get back to work. Even though Zoey was worried about him arriving late to open for the dinner shift, Graham didn't seem in any hurry, spending too long telling her goodbye in the parking lot. As goodbyes went, it was beyond satisfactory if far more discreet than their morning in the booth.

Zoey would take it.

Lana was deep in conversation with Hannah and Quinn when Zoey walked through the lobby, but she caught Zoey's eye, holding up a finger to ask her to wait.

Finishing whatever they were speaking about, Lana hustled over. "Were you just out with Jackson Shaw?"

"Yeah, he's a friend of Graham's. Why?"

Lana pursed her lips, glanced at the man leaning on the front desk, talking to Grass, then flapped her hand. "It doesn't matter. I'll catch up with him later."

"You've been very mysterious this entire trip. Are you ready to spill the beans?"

"Let's get to the room, then we'll talk."

Patiently, Zoey waited to grill her friend until they had ridden the elevator to their floor and safely closed the hotel room door behind them. Bending over sideways, Lana pulled the four-inch stiletto pumps off her feet.

"Oh, I've wanted to burn these since I put them on this morning."

"Then why did you wear them?"

"Power shoes, dearest. Men have power ties; women have power shoes. I had a lot of people to talk to today, and I needed all the power of persuasion available to me." Tossing her purse on the counter, she rolled her shoulders, then twisted her neck to ease the strain. "In answer to your question, my mysteriousness is not drama so much as discretion. And if I tell you, mum's the word."

"I'm mum." Zoey perched on the kitchenette counter next to Lana's purse. "Swearsies realsies."

"You Mudvillians say the weirdest things."

"Mudgetonians."

"Yes, that's what I said. I'm working on a project for Moose Springs. An important project that will really help the town, but it needs to stay under wraps until it's...well...not. There's going to be enough red tape to jump through, and I'm still working on financing the project."

Zoey leaned over, stretching so she didn't have to abandon her seat while pouring herself a glass of water from the sink. "Lana Montgomery, are you actually worried about money?"

"Darling, I think you have far overestimated what I do and do not have access to. The Montgomery Group's assets are not my personal piggy bank to break open anytime I want a new toy. Especially not when those toys are spectacular." With a sigh, Lana dropped onto the couch. "I've finalized all the plans for tomorrow night's gala, but I'm still nervous about it." Turning hopeful eyes Zoey's way, she perked up. "Have you decided if you're coming with me?"

Zoey cringed. "I was kind of hoping you'd forgotten about that. Are you sure you want me there? I'm not going to fit in with your people. I never do. We have three disastrous New Year's Eve parties under our belts to prove it."

"They're just people, and you've already met some of them. Besides, you can bring a date. Graham cleans up handsome, and he'll love an excuse to get out of work early."

"Lana, I can't ask him to go to something like this. He'll hate it."

"But you'll come?"

When Lana gazed up at Zoey, for once looking vulnerable and uncertain, Zoey felt her last resistance cave.

"It's just for a couple hours?"

"Black tie, a couple hours, and it will be fabulous. Bring Graham; everyone else will have a date. Trust me, you'll have an amazing time."

The only thing Zoey trusted was how much Graham was going to hate this idea.

"He'll say no."

Finally, the stress in Lana's eyes shifted to mirth. "Zoey, a boy like him risk messing things up with a woman like you? He wouldn't *dare*. Now come on. We need to pick out a dress. I brought three for you, but if you don't like them, we'll take a quick jaunt to Anchorage."

THE TOURIST ATTRACTION   261

"You have all the answers, don't you?" Zoey slid off the counter and followed Lana into the bedroom.

"Mm-hmm."

Zoey flopped dramatically down on the bed, defeated. "And you're sure I can't prove my friendship to you in any other way? Maybe by donating a kidney to you?"

Lana just disappeared into her closet, humming cheerfully to herself. She came out holding three hangers, face triumphant. The dresses were floor length, haute couture, and probably cost more than Zoey's car back home. "Rose, wine, or mint?"

Zoey cringed, knowing she wouldn't feel safe taking a drink of water in any of them. "Whatever I'm least likely to ruin."

"Mint it is. Oh, dearest. Graham's going to just *adore* you in green."

CHAPTER 13

"I CAN'T BELIEVE WE AGREED to this."

Graham adjusted his tie in the hotel's oversized hallway mirror. "I didn't agree to anything. You were the one who wanted to recreate *Titanic*, darlin'. Nice dress, by the way."

Grinning up at him, Zoey exhaled a laugh. "You know they all drown in the end, right?"

"Not me. I'm with you on the door." He leaned in, whispering in her ear. "Never let go, Zo."

"I wouldn't dare," she promised.

Determined to use her car as much as humanly possible, Zoey had offered to pick him up after work when Graham shoved his dinner guests out at a paltry 8:00 p.m. He'd been tempted, but knowing he was about to spend an evening with the resort's finest left Graham twitchy and in need of an escape route. After closing, he drove to the resort in his truck instead.

The Tourist Trap's dinner crowd was more passive than usual, and whatever event Lana had planned up at the resort had thinned their ranks. Even though consistency was the key to any business's success, Graham knew he could get away with it. For every tourist he ticked off today, a fresh one would take their place next week. Frankly, it didn't matter.

Being Zoey's date to some gala did matter, so Graham pulled his best—and only—suit out of the closet, dusted it off, and had it hanging in the back ready for after his shift. Reassured by Zoey's promise to help him clean up tomorrow morning before opening, a quick change of his clothes in the bathroom was all Graham needed before zipping up to Moose Springs Resort.

The dress she'd slipped into was more than enough to have him willing to follow her into any crowd, including this one. As they stood down the hall from the resort's banquet room, Zoey hesitated, fiddling with her hair and checking her makeup in the reflection of the mirror next to them.

"You look great," he promised. "Come on. This is going to be fun."

"You think so?"

"No, but we're supporting L. And she's fun. It's close enough."

"What time do you need to get back home for Jake?"

"He's staying with Aunt Ash and Uncle Easton tonight. He likes them better, and I couldn't get the adjustments made to his tux in time. Who knew dog tailoring would be such a nightmare?"

She was so nervous, her voice shook. "Are you sure you don't want to go spend the night with him instead? We could have a gala for three."

Graham didn't want to be there, not for a single second, but one look at Zoey in her soft green dress, pale and trembly from nerves, and he knew he was right where he belonged. Resting a hand at the small of her back, Graham shifted closer to her side, letting her feel his presence beside her. Reminding her she wasn't alone.

"This is important to L," he reminded her gently.

Inhaling a deep, steadying breath, Zoey nodded. "You're right. Lana needs us here. We're being good friends. And there's probably food."

"Theoretically."

The ballroom had been decorated with a similar kind of understated opulence as everything else in the hotel. Round tables glittered with polished silverware and crystal wineglasses. A massive hearth dominating the far wall burned with an attended fire, where a disgruntled Diego stood, balancing a silver platter of miniature s'mores in his hands, complete with tiny, perfectly charred marshmallows. A private balcony stretched the length of the ballroom, with two-story sheets of glass separating those guests still inside and those mingling around stone fire rings outside. Everywhere he could see, glasses of champagne were held carelessly in hands glittering with diamond tennis bracelets or expensive-looking watches.

Graham was a confident person, and validated or not, very little intimidated him. But even he took pause for a moment as they stepped deeper into the ballroom, overwhelmed by the elegance surrounding them. Somewhere in all this mess of music, hors d'oeuvres, and candlelight was Jax, and out of sheer self-preservation, Graham scanned the crowd looking for him. He finally found his friend next to Lana, both of them looking far too comfortable in their formal wear. Fingers moving to his tie unbidden, Graham hated his knee-jerk reaction to make sure he looked okay.

At least no one would be paying any attention to him. Not with Zoey stunning everyone's socks off.

"We should probably go say hi." Clearly steeling her nerves, Zoey pushed the glasses higher up on her nose and headed for the woman holding court in the center of the room. Graham stayed at her side, catching her nervous, clammy fingers in his warmer ones and squeezing in reassurance.

"Maybe I'll carve you into my log when this is over," he murmured to her, lips brushing her ear.

Good. That brought some color to her cheeks.

"Don't threaten me with a good time," she whispered back.

"So do we get to know what all the excitement is about yet?" Jax was asking Lana as they approached, draining his champagne. "You throw a good party, Ms. Montgomery, but my curiosity is getting the best of me."

Utterly unfazed by his charm, Lana delicately sipped from her own glass. "After dinner, we're announcing the surprise. Until then, enjoy yourselves."

"Save a dance for me?" Jax asked her.

This time, Lana paused, letting her eyes drift down Jax's strong form, then back up again. She tilted her head as if considering it, then smiled serenely.

"I'm working, but perhaps another time. Zoey? Come sit with me. Our table's at the front." Arms linked, Zoey and Lana left Jax to pick up his wounded pride and Graham to enjoy the view.

"She's amazing, isn't she?" Graham sighed in contentment, taking a deeper drink.

"She's something."

At Jax's somewhat offended tone, Graham clapped him on the shoulder. "Wrong she. Sorry, man. Did L hurt your feelings?"

"Well, she didn't *not* hurt them." Jax snagged another glass of champagne off the tray passing by. "Come on. Let's see if I can get my feelings hurt again. So far, tonight's better than I expected."

They ended up at the same table as Killian, Enzo, and Haleigh, much to Graham's chagrin. At least Jax ambled along after them, stealing a seat next to Lana that had been marked for someone else.

Knowing they didn't fit in one bit, Graham focused his attention entirely on Zoey, playfully entangling their fingers and distracting her by whispering things in her ear. Distracting her had become his new favorite pastime. Unfortunately, despite his best efforts to the contrary, the others at the table pulled her attention. A deep discussion between Haleigh and another woman had turned into a sort of verbal sparring match over who could insult the town more. Graham was good at ignoring complaining tourists, but Zoey was new to the experience. Even as he tried to distract her, he could see her eyes flickering back to the two women.

"I mean, really. Let's try to be as utterly ridiculous as possible." Haleigh rolled her eyes. "I don't know why Killian keeps insisting on going to places like this. I was perfectly happy in Italy. But no, we had to come to *Moose Springs*."

The way she said the name of his town rubbed Graham the wrong way. It must have rubbed Zoey the wrong way too because she frowned across the table.

"At least there are people here worth talking to," the other woman said. "I was down in town today, and I think I ran into an actual Neanderthal. He was so tall it was insane. You should have seen the beard on this one." With a naughty giggle, she pulled out her phone from her purse. "You *have* to see him. I took a picture when he wasn't looking."

The snickering pair didn't bother to hide the phone screen from curious eyes. And yeah, it annoyed him to see they had taken a picture of Easton, but it wasn't the first time. Graham didn't want to know how many social media posts he'd been an unwilling participant in. But he wasn't nearly as upset as the woman sitting next to him.

"He might have been cute with the man bun," Haleigh decided. "But that beard? Eww. And the flannel? I can't even."

"That's Easton." Zoey was clearly angry. "He's really nice."

"Maybe if we let him cut some wood for a while, I could get on board," Haleigh's friend said, the pair snickering again. "He has some muscles; I'll give him that."

"I'm putting him on my feed." Haleigh's thumb moved over her phone. "I'm tagging him as 'Sasquatch Man.'"

Shifting on her seat, Zoey pushed her glasses up on her nose, glaring. "No, don't do that. You shouldn't take pictures of people without their consent."

"It doesn't matter." Haleigh dismissed her. "There's no way that guy even knows what a smartphone is."

"I bet he has a *great* personality," Haleigh's companion joked, completely ignoring Zoey.

"He also likes long walks on the beach and sharing hot cocoa," Graham drawled. "East's only half-Neanderthal. There's nothing wrong with that."

Graham glanced at Enzo, where the other guy looked bored to death. "Right, Enzo?"

"What?"

"Enzo agrees."

Covering her mouth didn't smother his date's snort. Even though Lana beamed their way—pausing from her conversation with Jax to see what had made Zoey laugh—the snort drew Haleigh's attention. Haleigh arched an eyebrow at Zoey. Champagne made some people mean. A bottle of champagne made Haleigh...something else.

"So, Zoey," she asked, raising her voice so everyone around them would pay attention. "Since you don't approve of us, why don't we talk about *you*?"

Such an innocent question, but there was an undercurrent of malice beneath. He didn't understand the source, other than Zoey's closeness with Lana. And maybe that was all she needed for Haleigh to set his date in her sights.

Zoey looked up, momentarily startled at being pulled into the conversation. Leaning forward on her elbows, a tipsy Haleigh smirked. Graham stiffened, because he knew that kind of look. He'd seen it far too many times, and it always made his blood boil.

"I'm not that interesting," Zoey told the table, but Graham knew her deflection wasn't enough.

"She saves herself in high-intensity situations," Graham spoke up. "She gets out of jail free, dangles above certain death, gets kissed by whales, and generally is the coolest person on the planet."

The smirk on Haleigh's face grew. "Is that before or after

she finishes serving the midnight special at a truck stop? Tell me, Zoey. Is it hard to cut the pies just right?"

"I'm good at my job," Zoey said tightly. "I *like* my job."

Haleigh raised her voice. "If anyone ever hears me say I enjoy serving sloppy seconds to truck drivers, *please* kill me."

Gritting her teeth, Zoey's face reddened as she glared down at her food. Eyes flashing, Lana opened her mouth, but Graham doubted anything she had to say would make this any better.

"So basically, you just called my date trash." Graham sighed in resignation, cutting Lana off. "Okay, we're going to have to fight now."

"Excuse me?" Haleigh looked at him in astonishment.

"No excuses. You called my date trash, and now I'm going to have to fight you."

And with that, Graham took a spoonful of whatever the creamy, glittery gunk on his plate was and flicked it in her face.

The silence at the table was deafening as goop slowly slid down Haleigh's long, perfectly aristocratic nose.

Then everything got a bit noisy for Graham's tastes. Someone demanded to know his full name because lawyers would be involved, and who did he think he was, and blah blah gluten allergy blah. Graham ignored it, because he couldn't have cared less what they were going on about. Instead, he braced his arm on the back of Zoey's chair, smiling down at her as she tried and failed to keep from dissolving into helpless laughter.

Hannah hurried over, took one look at Graham and his spoon and the shrieking woman, and she gave him her look.

"I need to leave," he murmured in Zoey's ear. He liked

murmuring in her ear, because she always leaned in, the smell of her shampoo filling his nostrils. "Hannah *will* actually fight me."

"If you're leaving, I'm going with you."

"Dramatic escape?"

"Definitely."

Well. Since she asked.

Graham hopped to his feet. "Lana, our apologies for causing a scene. Your gala is as fabulous as you are. Unfortunately, a man's dignity was at stake, and there are some things we just can't let slide. Easton would never forgive me. Ladies. I hope I see none of you in my near future." Then he scooped Zoey off her feet and into his arms, bolting for the exit.

As runaway attempts went, it was fabulous until they hit the elevator. And waited for the elevator. And were forced to make small talk with the confused-looking couple in the elevator, who were too close to Zoey's feet.

Then the doors opened in the lobby, and Graham darted for the front doors.

They hit his truck running, and Zoey was almost crying from laughter as he stuffed her and her dress into the driver's seat and kept squishing her over until he could fit in there too. They peeled out of the valet station in dramatic fashion, tires squealing loudly.

"Graham, did you see her face? And then it was all gloop, gloop, plop?"

That had been the best part, next to having an excuse to get out of there. "Never say I won't defend Easton's honor. Or yours."

"My hero." She batted her eyes, gathered her skirts, and leaned over to press a kiss to his cheek.

And maybe she was just joking, but Graham...well...he wasn't. Because deep down, he was ready to throw a whole pot of goop at anyone who put her down.

When she scooted over, Graham slipped his arm around her waist and pulled her closer. He hit the hazard lights and pulled off the side of the road, not caring if the truck's tires left ruts in the perfectly manicured lawns.

"I like waitresses." He touched her face, silently asking her to look at him. "I like your dress, but I like your Mickey Mouse sweatshirt even more. I like your hair in a messy bun, with these always sliding down your nose." He nodded at her glasses. "And I like you not wanting to eat whatever they were serving in there, because I didn't want to eat it either."

"You have weird taste in everything," she decided, but her voice had softened. "I'm not Cinderella, Graham. I have a good life, and I don't need to be rescued."

Graham chuckled, low in his throat. "No rescuing from me, gorgeous. I'm definitely not the prince. But I know a great place to get away from here and get a real meal."

"Is it weird? No more weird meat. Please no more weird meat."

"It's only a little weird."

And as she leaned in and kissed him, Graham knew that a little weird was good enough for both of them.

For the second time that night, Zoey walked into a room feeling entirely out of place, her clothing far too dressed up for Shorty's, the dive Graham drove her to. But this time, Graham was in his element, his arm heavy over her shoulders and folded back across her collarbone in a protective gesture she wasn't sure he was even aware he was doing.

Normally, she would have sat across from him, but when Graham scooted into the booth their server led them to, Zoey followed suit.

He kept his arm around her, and yes, it might have made looking at the menu just a little harder than it should have been. But she liked staying close to him. A familiar pink head was seated across the room. Ash said something to her companion, one of the women from the bonfire, and then she came over, sliding into the other side of the booth.

"How did the party go?"

"About as expected. We had to make a quick exit before the cops were called."

"Sounds about right," Ash said. "Zoey, never take him anywhere you need to make a good impression. He's going to humiliate you as thoroughly as possible."

"I'd rather be with him than anyone else in that room."

The words left her mouth without Zoey meaning them to. She glanced over at Graham and found him watching her, his eyes holding hers.

"Be careful, gorgeous. I might start to think you actually like me."

His normal teasing was gentler, his eyes and tone softening. The thing was, Zoey did like Graham. Far more than she had ever expected or wanted to.

Without thinking, Zoey leaned in and kissed him, right in

front of Ash and all the rest of the people who knew him. She started to pull away, but Graham's fingers caught hers, tugging her back to him.

"I'll just leave you two alone." Ash scooted out of the booth. Graham waved goodbye but didn't try to stop her.

The server arriving to take their drink order interrupted them, breaking the moment. Graham glanced at the menu, shaking his head. "Do you have any idea how sick I am of hamburgers and reindeer dogs?"

"And yet, here we are at a place that lists those at the top of the menu."

Graham nodded. "Yes, but right below are the next thing for your bucket list. Welcome to Shorty's. If you can eat ten hellfire wings, I don't have to pay for our drinks."

"So you're taking me out, but I have to burn my taste buds because you're too cheap to actually pay for our meal?"

"Think of it as you earning our meal."

"What's the likelihood that I'm going to barf from this?"

"I'd give it about a fifty-fifty."

Zoey adjusted her glasses on her nose and nodded gamely. "Bring it on, hot stuff."

Unlike Graham, Shorty had plenty of help. Within minutes, their food was in front of them. Wing for wing, Zoey took him down. And okay, maybe there was going to be some severe gastric distress when this was all over, and she had tears and snot openly running down her face, but someone needed to put Graham Barnett in his place, and Zoey was going to be the one to do it.

"Boom. That just happened." Zoey mimicked dropping a mic. "But it was cute how hard you tried."

"I think I'm in love." Graham leaned back in his seat and held out a saucy fist. "Marry me, Caldwell."

"Only if I get Jake in the prenup."

"Done." They bumped fists.

"Prenups are bullshit." Graham drained his beer, then settled into the basket of cheesy bread they had ordered. "If you don't trust someone, don't marry them."

"There wasn't a single couple in that ballroom tonight with anything less than an ironclad prenup."

"Sucks to be them." Graham stuffed a hunk of bread in his mouth, mumbling as he chewed. "If she can't rip your heart, guts, and bank account away from you, then she wasn't the right one in the first place."

"You really mean that, don't you?"

"Yep." He handed her the cheesiest piece of the bread dripping with garlic butter. "Anything else is a waste of time."

"You're a closet romantic, aren't you?"

"If I was, I'd never tell you."

Even as he said it, Graham draped his arm over the back of their booth, giving Zoey the perfect place to cuddle into his warmth.

On a whim, she tore off the end of her bread and offered it to him. That dangerously sexy smile reached his eyes, and it was only sexier when he nipped it from her fingertips. Zoey's breath caught, and even as the server brought the check, her heart continued racing.

They drove back to the resort, Zoey figuring they owed Lana an apology for disrupting her important night. Graham parked in the employee lot, getting out and walking to Zoey's passenger door. Sticking as always, he wrestled with it while she watched him with amusement. Finally, it popped open, but only when she unlocked the door.

"Ooh, good one," he murmured.

"Remember, never be afraid to use your gifts." Zoey slipped out of the truck, accepting Graham's helping arm as she wobbled on her heels.

"I'd walk you to your door, but Hannah would kill me."

"Are you scared of her?"

"Absolutely."

They snuck in a small side entrance rarely used by other guests, back into the building they had darted away from only hours before. This time, they were alone in the elevator, and as it started to climb toward her floor, Graham drew her closer, pressing the softest kiss to her earlobe.

"I had a great time tonight, gorgeous."

"Graham Barnett, are you serious?"

The doors had opened, revealing the woman in question. He squeaked. "Umm, hey, Hannah. About earlier..."

"It was me," Zoey spoke up. "I hit his hand. And aimed the spoon. I hit his hand after aiming the spoon, which happened to be in Haleigh's direction. It was a magnificent display of accidental food aggression in which he's utterly innocent. I'm pretty sure it was a ghost."

"A ghost," Hannah repeated flatly.

"Yes. Two ghosts. I really think so. Do you have haunter's insurance? Because that would be terrible for business."

"Terrible," Graham agreed, edging around the manager. "Super awful. Let's look that up. Call me; we'll talk about it."

Then they bolted for Zoey's door, leaving a disgusted Hannah muttering to herself in the hallway about there being two of them.

Zoey opened the door and pulled Graham to safety inside her room. She opened her mouth to tell him something but immediately lost all thought as his lips found hers.

The kiss was soft, undemanding, giving her a chance to pull away. When she didn't, choosing instead to lean into his hard, strong body, a noise of masculine pleasure rumbled from his throat.

"Did I tell you I like your dress?"

"You told me you like my Mickey Mouse sweatshirt."

"Good."

Then he kissed her again, and Zoey's hands were in his hair, pulling him to her as she went up on her toes. Graham was tall, tall enough that he had to lean down to kiss her, an action that lasted only for a second. Strong hands slid down her rib cage, wrapping beneath her hips, then dug in. He picked her up, bringing her to his height.

Her dress hiked up as her legs wrapped around his waist, heart racing as Graham took a step. Where he was headed, Zoey didn't know, because the door swung open again, whacking them both.

"Oops." With an impish look, Lana swished past them. "Ignore me. Carry on."

"Is it just me, or did she deliberately show up right now?" Graham murmured into Zoey's ear as he set her back down to her feet.

"Trust me, it's all you. I can't turn around without accidentally running into the two of you getting all tryst-y with each other. Speaking of which..." Lana winked at Zoey. "Congratulations, love. I knew he would be the perfect thing to clean out the rafters."

Groaning, Zoey looked at Graham. "Please tell me she didn't just say that."

"Which part is your rafters?" Graham asked curiously, earning himself a swat of Zoey's hand.

"Are you mad we wrecked your gala?" Zoey cringed. "I'm really sorry. Haleigh just really gets under my skin."

"Oh, that? That was nothing. A party isn't a party unless someone calls a lawyer." Lana didn't seem bothered at all. With a dismissive flap of her hand, she moved to the wet bar in the corner of the suite and poured herself a drink. "Graham, I'm glad you're here. You two left tonight before I could start the program."

Graham's sharp eyes missed nothing. "I've never seen you drink brandy," he noted.

"It's an easy swallow when I have some difficult news to share." Taking a sip, she hummed in appreciation, then turned her eyes to Graham and Zoey. "Graham, you might want to sit down for this."

Folding his arms across his chest, his brow furrowed. "You're not giving me warm fuzzies here, L."

The ring of his cell phone interrupted whatever Lana was about to say. Graham glanced at it, then frowned deeper, holding up a finger. "Sorry, ladies, I need to take this. What's up, Jonah?"

Standing at his side, Zoey could hear the officer's voice on the other end. "I've got some bad news, Graham. I'm real sorry to be the one making this call."

Zoey watched the blood drain from Graham's face, his fist balling at his side.

"Who is it?" he asked quietly.

"That moose that's always hanging around your place charged some tourists tonight. Someone got hurt."

The tension in him didn't ease, but he did inhale a tight breath. "Start with that next time, man. I thought it was Mom or Dad. Did he kill anyone?"

"No, but they're airlifting the husband to Anchorage. He hurt the guy pretty bad. Easton's tracking the moose, and you know that only takes so long. We need to relocate him, but we thought… well…you might want to say goodbye."

Graham hung up, turning to them, clearly shaken. "Zoey, I'm sorry. I need to go. L, can you catch me up on your big news later?"

"Of course, Graham." Lana dipped her head in understanding. "It can wait."

Halfway to the door, Graham stopped. Turning, he gazed down at Zoey then reached for her hand, wrapping his fingers tightly around hers. "I'm sorry this is how our night is ending."

"Me too." Zoey said quietly, "Do you want me to come with you?"

Exhaling a hard breath, he nodded.

"Yeah. That would be nice."

———

The Tourist Trap still had people gathered in the parking lot—a fire engine and various trucks from volunteer emergency responders and Jonah's police cruiser. Another squad car with two state troopers was parked near the building, and their flashing lights reflected off the diner's windows.

Graham pulled up as close as he could get, setting the truck in park.

"You might want to stay here," he said in a tight voice. "Sometimes the aftermath of these kinds of things are rough to see."

Jumping out of the truck, Graham strode right into the middle of the fray as if unfazed. But since his hands had clenched the steering wheel white-knuckled the entire drive down from the resort, Zoey didn't heed his warning, following at a distance. Jonah met him, a hard look on the trooper's face. Glancing at Zoey, Jonah turned back to Graham.

"There wasn't any damage to your place, but we're going to be here awhile. Easton called, and he's tracked the bull just north of Rick's home. We've got a transport ready, but they need to tranq him before he gets somewhere more heavily wooded."

Graham nodded tightly. "Thanks for the heads-up."

Disappearing for a moment into his diner, Graham came back out with a paper take-out bag in his hand. When they got back in the vehicle, Graham was furious.

"This shit right here is why I'm so over this place," he snarled. Nearly crushing the paper bag in his hand, he thrust it her way to hold. "There was no need for any of this."

As the scent of freshly baked bread wafted from the bag, Zoey's heart hurt for everyone. The poor people who'd been hurt, the poor animal who had just wanted to be left alone. And for Graham, who was driving twice the speed limit up narrow mountain roads, just for the chance to say goodbye.

A text came through, and Graham tilted his phone to Zoey, unable to take his eyes from the road.

"It's Easton," she read for him. "He says they darted Ulysses in the clearing behind Rick's back pasture."

Without warning, he pulled off on the side of the road and got out. "We're almost there. It's faster to cut through here."

Trusting Graham knew where he was going, she followed him through the trees on a lightly worn footpath, struggling to keep up in her heels. Even with Graham's hand on her arm, Zoey kept tripping in the underbrush until she finally took them off. Sore feet would be better than a broken ankle.

Lights in the distance told her they were close, and Graham broke into a jog, leaving Zoey to follow at his heels.

Easton stood over a massive, furry brown body, his tranquilizer rifle in hand. At his side, a grim-faced Rick and a second man in a Fish and Game uniform were spreading something out on the ground.

"What is that?" Zoey asked quietly.

"A sling to transport him. You can't just stick a wild bull moose in a trailer. Especially not in a place as heavily wooded as this. You have to airlift them somewhere else."

The second man stood, then walked over to Graham. "Sorry to see you under these circumstances, Graham."

They shook hands, Graham's voice quiet. "Yeah, me too."

"Too bad it had to end up this way. Shame someone got hurt."

Graham nodded tightly. "Zoey, this is Officer Marcus Garcia. He's the one who gets called when stuff like this happens."

"Too many calls from Moose Springs." Officer Garcia shook his head. "I might as well get a satellite station put in there."

Shaking hands with the young Fish and Game warden, Zoey murmured a greeting and stepped back, trying to stay out of everyone's way. Between them, Graham, Rick, and Officer Garcia finished rigging the sling that would take Ulysses away. Easton remained where he was next to Ulysses, tranquilizer rifle at the ready.

"Ash should be here soon. We have to move him before he wakes." Easton rested his palm gently on Ulysses's shoulder. "Took a ton of bricks to drop him. He's a tough one."

Graham cleared his throat. "Yeah. Big weirdo wasn't a wuss, were you?"

Kneeling next to the big, furry head, Graham rubbed the moose's massive nose. The animal was heavily sedated, but he moved a little when Graham touched him, huffing a breath against Graham's hands.

She wanted to touch him too, but this wasn't the time. Not when Graham sounded wrecked at having to say goodbye.

"We had a good run, didn't we, buddy?"

Ulysses huffed louder, his foot twitching.

"It's wearing off already." Easton waved them back, then brought his rifle to his shoulder. The resultant crack of gunfire made Zoey jerk almost as much as Ulysses did, a large dart sticking from his shoulder. When her ears stopped ringing, she could hear helicopter blades chopping through the air, coming closer.

"He's a tough one, isn't he?" Garcia murmured. "How many have you put in him?"

"One more than I should have." Easton grunted. "We need to get him on the sling."

"Just one second." Graham looked around. "I need to... dammit, I forgot the bread in the car."

"I still have it." Zoey handed Graham the bag. Giving her a desperately grateful look, he broke off a small piece, setting it next to Ulysses's nostrils.

"Here you go, big guy. I know it's your thing, you perv." His voice caught. "It's gonna suck. Losing your home is going to suck real bad, but it's better than the alternatives. Ears and eyes up, okay? I want to have lots of your pervy calves giving this town hell one day. Got it?" Leaning over, Graham rested his forehead against the moose's own. "Keep breathing, buddy."

Rising to his feet, Graham's voice hardened. "Let's get him into the sling."

What followed broke her heart. It took all five of them to get Ulysses onto the sling, taking hold of his legs and rolling him onto his back, trying not to get caught beneath his heavy body as momentum caused him to land heavily on his other side. His neck twisted at a painful angle when his antlers caught on the ground, making Graham curse as he helped straighten Ulysses's head.

Officer Garcia took some pictures, making a verbal recording as he did so of the scene and the people there. Then the helicopter above them lowered to just above the treetops, running a cable down to them. Easton and Garcia hooked up the sling, then stepped back. Head and massive antlers hanging limp, Ulysses's body was raised into the air, then flown off into the distance.

The whole thing was awful, and Zoey couldn't imagine how terrifying it would be for him when he woke up, somewhere completely new.

"Can't we go with him? Make sure he's okay?"

Garcia shook his head. "No. My partner and another Fish and Game warden are already en route to where they're unhooking him. If they waited until we got there, he would wake up."

"How far is she taking him?"

"To the base of that big mountain north of here," Garcia said. "Mount Veil. Too far for him to come back and hurt anyone else. If he survives."

Wordlessly, Graham rose and walked away. Not sure what to do, Zoey followed, staying quiet as they backtracked to their truck. Graham drove them to the diner, which was blessedly empty of onlookers. Leaving all but a single light off, Graham went straight to the liquor shelf. She'd never seen him drink anything harder than beer, but Graham poured himself a shot of whiskey and downed it. Then he poured himself a second and threw that back too.

"Is Ulysses going to be okay?" Zoey asked softly.

"Fifty-fifty shot." His voice was harsh, clipped, and angry. "Some get hurt in the move, and some don't come out of the tranquilizers well. He's an easy target until they wear off. He won't know where to get water or find food or shelter. All because some piece of shit wanted to take a picture."

"It could have been an accident."

"No way. I know exactly what happened because I see this crap all the time."

"Graham—"

"No. No, this is exactly what it's like living here. Zoey, you don't have to like it, but *you* are the problem. You, Lana, and all those assholes up there. You come here, you get your kicks, and then you're gone. And screw whoever you hurt in the process. It's all in the name of a good time, right?"

Flinching at his attack, Zoey stood up straighter. "Graham, I know you're upset, but that's not fair."

Inhaling three deep breaths, Graham finally shook his head. "No. It's not. You didn't do anything. But I'm so damn tired of all the people who do."

Clearing his throat, Graham gripped the counter with white-knuckled hands. He walked away, then turned and slammed his fist through the wall. Right next to Barley the Biker Bear. "Zoey," he rasped. "You don't get it."

Except she did. At least as much as she could.

"He was your friend." Coming up behind him, Zoey wrapped her arms around Graham's waist. "You lost a friend today. I'm so sorry, Graham. This wasn't fair to either of you."

He turned, and the hand that had gone through a wall cupped her cheek as carefully as if she were made of glass.

Zoey went up on her toes, wrapping her arms around his neck. "I'm so sorry."

"It's just a moose," Graham finally whispered.

"But he was your moose."

"You're right, Zoey. He was my friend." Leaning his forehead against hers, Graham closed his eyes. Then with a soft noise of surrender, he dipped his head down and kissed her. Just like last time, his lips were warm and soft, but this time, they tasted of whiskey, sweet and strong.

Graham turned, pressing her back to the wall as he deepened the kiss.

A picture frame got caught between her shoulder and his hand fisting into her hair. When the picture fell, Graham ignored it. He ignored two more that hit the floor when he hoisted her up with the strength of one arm, guiding her legs around his waist with the other.

"This stops when you say so," he whispered against her neck. "This doesn't even start unless you say so."

Pulling his face to hers, Zoey crushed her mouth to his, a silent but clear reply. In response, Graham muscled her higher in his arms. But when she started to fumble at his shirt, he pulled back, abruptly releasing her back to her feet.

"Not here, Zo. Not like this. Not some one-night stand."

"We're not—" she started to say, but Graham shook his head, eyes pained.

"But we are. All of this was never a good idea." He braced an arm over her head, resting his forehead to hers. "I can't, okay? This relationship, or whatever it is, is going to end with you walking away. Listen, gorgeous. You and me, this was a mistake. I like you so much, but, Zoey, all of this—"

"A mistake." Just because she understood why he was saying it didn't make those words any easier to hear. "I should go."

He'd been drinking, and he'd been her ride. Even now, Graham wasn't leaving her stranded. "I'll find someone to drive you."

"It's fine. I'll call Lana to come get me. Or I'll call a rideshare."

Ducking under his arm, Zoey took her wounded pride and tucked it into her pocket. She was hurt and still breathless from his kisses, but he was hurt too—more deeply than she was right now, for far more important reasons. Having her feelings hurt was nothing close to losing a friend forever.

And if he could love an animal this much, Zoey had no illusions to how deeply this man could love another person if he gave his heart away.

Graham was right. She was leaving in five days, and she needed to walk out this door. But even as she thought it, she hesitated at the doorway. Graham was watching her leave. The look he gave her...so helpless...so hopeless...broke her heart all over again.

"He'll be okay," Zoey promised softly from the doorway. "And you will be too."

CHAPTER 14

THERE WOULD BE NO SAVING the dress.

Between the hike through the woods, rolling a moose, and multiple encounters of the sexy kind with Graham that evening, the delicate layers of fabric had been ruined.

"I'm sorry, Zoey." Quinn held it up to the light as if better illumination would help her find some inch of fabric not damaged by the evening before. "We can have it cleaned, but this part won't hold a stitch without unravelling more." Turning the dress over, she pointed at the worst of the tearing. "And this can't be stitched without it showing. If you want, I can try."

"It's okay. I won't waste your time."

Disappointed, Zoey accepted the dress back from the hotel's expert seamstress. Quinn was a woman of many talents, including the ability to be truly crestfallen at Zoey's misfortune. If Quinn couldn't save it, it couldn't be saved.

Quinn's domain was a tiny windowless office just off the main laundry rooms. For a resort this big, they kept their laundry machines running nonstop. Detergent, bleach, and heated Egyptian cotton mixed unpleasantly in Zoey's nostrils, but Quinn seemed oblivious to the smell.

"I wish there was more I could do for you." With a wistful sigh, the hospitality specialist turned in her chair. "You looked so pretty in this last night."

Warmed by the unexpected compliment, Zoey sat down in the other chair in the small office. "Thank you. I didn't see you there. I saw Diego, but I didn't recognize anyone else."

"Oh, Diego is in training to be a butler. He and Grass are both in the running." Lowering her voice conspiratorially, Quinn added, "I bet Hannah gives the job to Diego, even though Grass would be so much better at it. Mrs. Harris kept promoting all the out-of-towners over people from here. Hannah is trying to even things out. Which I'm completely in favor of, except have you noticed how Diego bares his teeth at everyone?"

Giggling, Quinn did an impression of Diego that was spot on. Quinn's cheerfulness was infectious. Zoey had been down all morning, distressed beyond what was reasonable for a weeklong pseudo-relationship and unable to get Graham out of her mind, but she felt better being around Quinn.

"Is it like that even here in the resort?" Gesturing to the hotel around them, Zoey turned to Quinn. "Because it seems like out there, it's town versus hotel to the extreme."

"I think it depends on who you talk to. I really like meeting new people all the time. But there's some people in town who are getting really frustrated. It didn't used to be so bad, more like they thought the tourists were an annoyance, but whatever. Then a few years ago, someone got drunk and ran a red light." Quinn's large eyes gleamed in remembrance. "They sideswiped a car coming through the intersection. Killed almost an entire family."

"That's awful. Whose family was it?" Zoey couldn't help but ask.

Shifting uncomfortably, Quinn glanced guiltily at the door as if someone might hear. "Diego's family. He was the only one who survived the crash."

Her heart went out to the awkward, grumpy concierge instantly. "That's so sad. Why would he work here, then?"

"Because there are only so many jobs around here, and the hotel offers benefits a lot of the local businesses can't. Health insurance, retirement, housing. And they pay for career training in the off-seasons. I'd never be able to afford college if it weren't for the Shaws paying for classes. We don't like to admit it, but without the hotel…"

Without the hotel, the community would suffer.

"I shouldn't tease him," Quinn whispered. "He has every reason to be grumpy."

Reaching over to squeeze the younger woman's hand, Zoey murmured, "Thank you. You've been very sweet to try and help me."

When Zoey stood up to go, Quinn popped up to her feet, once more a bundle of energy and enthusiasm. "Are you looking forward to the fireworks?"

"Hmm?"

"Everyone is saying this year will be the best. Although after last night, who really knows what will happen now. Maybe next year's will be even better if more people are around."

"What do you mean?"

Quinn blinked owlishly. "You don't know? All anyone can talk about is Ms. Montgomery's plans for Moose Springs."

"We had to make a dramatic escape prior to the scheduled programming," Zoey replied drolly. "I think I need to talk to Lana. Do you know where she is?"

More than happy to be of help, Quinn immediately said, "Up in her rooms."

Zoey tilted her head, confused by Quinn's certainty. "I was just there. Lana's not inside."

"No, not the one she's staying in with you. The other rooms she reserved. The executive suite and the presidential suite. Ms. Montgomery booked out the entire penthouse floor. Mr. Montgomery—oh my gosh, he is so gorgeous, isn't he—and his companions are staying in one, and she's running the other as an office space."

"Quinn, can you get me into Lana's suite? Her office, not Killian's room. My keycard won't let me access the penthouse floor."

"Sure." Quinn was more than willing to help. "But let's take the staff elevator so no one sees. I'm technically not allowed to let any other guests on the penthouse floors."

Seeming to enjoy sneaking around, Quinn led her to the service elevator allowing staff up to that level. The entire elevator ride, Zoey's heart raced. Graham had been beside himself last night. Knowing something that mattered to him so much had been ripped away by the people visiting this hotel only made Zoey more anxious as they arrived at the suite.

Quinn unlocked the door for her, then disappeared down the hall with a cheery wave, returning to her work.

Stepping inside the hotel suite, Zoey's eyes went immediately to the massive conference table running the length of one side of the suite. Easily capable of seating twenty people with plenty of room, the table had been set up with a miniaturized, lifelike display of the town, resort, and surrounding mountain ranges.

Everything was there. Even tiny places like the daycare and Frankie's bakery had been accounted for. Shops so carefully unmarked and unnamed for privacy were fully disclosed for everyone to see. Places of high traffic were marked with colorful dots, with the largest dots gracing the various coffeehouses and gift shops around town.

The Tourist Trap had the largest dot of all.

"Killian, please warn me of when you're coming over here." Lana's voice came from the other room. "You startle the life out of me every time I'm in the powder room and hear—oh. Zoey."

Zoey nodded at the woman appearing from the suite's far bedroom. "Just me. Lana? What is this?"

Distracted by the display, Zoey had failed to notice the display boards lining the wall, printed with computer-generated, artistic architectural renditions of—

Feeling the blood drain from her face, Zoey stepped back.

"Those are of Moose Springs. You promised Graham you didn't buy the resort."

Lana sighed. "No, dearest. I didn't buy the resort. I promised him I wouldn't, so I didn't. But I might have to eventually. The Shaws don't want to sell, but they're broke. It'll only be so much longer before the resort will fold and take the entire town with it. I care about Moose Springs far too much to let that happen."

Sitting on the edge of a chaise lounge, Lana gave her a sad look. "Zoey, you come from a small farming town. Even without the influx of travelers passing through, your town would survive. Moose Springs is the ultimate tourist trap. A hundred years ago, there weren't enough people to be strained by closing the mining operations. Now the population is too high, and the economy is based on supporting tourism. And unfortunately, for as many bodies as come through here, the resort just isn't making enough money. I give them two years, maybe three tops before they would have to go under."

"Does Jax know?" As Graham's friend, she could only imagine how deep that betrayal would cut.

"No, they specifically wanted Jackson to stay out of it. But his parents came to me with a proposal."

"Why didn't you tell me? Lana, this is huge."

"It is huge, and it's also been a huge pain. Do you know how hard the town will fight me on this? It's not that I didn't trust you, but I couldn't risk word getting out before I had everything in place."

Sashaying over to the table, Lana pointed to a large section of the mountainside abutting the resort. "We build privately owned luxury condominiums here. Each will have all the same amenities available to the owner or seasonal renter as the resort currently offers. That's what the gala was for, showing everyone an amazing time and then selling them on the idea of purchasing a permanent home connected to the resort. Most of them would only come once or twice a year, but it would make a huge difference."

Nudging a folder toward Zoey, Lana sat down at the table, her elbow near Rick's bar. "A construction project this size will bring a lot of jobs to Moose Springs. Annual association fees from the condominiums will provide steady currency to the resort. More employees to take care of guests, more restaurants, healthcare services, better infrastructure...all of which would be needed to accommodate the influx of people from this project. More tax money for the town."

Lana ran a fingernail along the top of the miniature Rick's. "Moose Springs might still be a tourism town, but its wealth will be tied into the permanent establishments of these homes. And that will make the town stronger. Give them a chance when the resort eventually changes hands."

"Are you sure the town will let you? Isn't something of this scale hard to get approved? Won't you need permits or something?"

"That's where the leverage comes in." Lana quirked a tired smile at her. "The bulk of the commercial properties in town are owned by two different investment companies, one out of Anchorage and the other out of Vancouver. A few businesses are privately owned, like the Tourist Trap, but most are rentals. To be able to push this through, I have to have a deep enough sway over the community to get it past the town council."

Feeling her eyes about to pop out of her head, Zoey looked at Lana in shock.

"You didn't buy the resort. You bought the entire town."

The sunlight shining through the diner window had the sheer gall to land right on Graham's face.

"No, quit it." Swatting a hand at the sunbeam, he groaned. "Go away."

Cheerfully oblivious to his self-induced agony, the sun continued its happy path across the sky, bringing more light on his chosen bed. Too drunk to drive and too miserable to call someone for a ride, he slept on top of two tables shoved together, a wadded-up towel as a pillow and a bottle of Wild Turkey tucked under his arm. His suit from the previous night wasn't the most comfortable of sleepwear, but Graham figured he deserved a little pain for making bad choices.

And boy, had he made bad choices. The hard drinking hadn't started until Graham watched Zoey walk out his door.

"Go away, sun." Graham moaned as more poured over his face. "I'm internal monologuing."

"Oh man, he's worse than I thought. It smells like something died in here."

Shoving himself up to his elbows, Graham and what was left of his Wild Turkey stared blearily at the shadows within the diner. "I have resigned myself to the situation and accept all responsibility for my choices."

"Okay, someone needs a trip to the sink."

"I lost my moose," Graham slurred to the people hauling him off his table bed. "I lost my girl."

"I'm really hoping those two aren't the same thing," Ash said. "East, can you help me with him. He's...*oof*. Seriously, Graham. Go on a diet. You are way too heavy to be this drunk."

"Zoey Bear liked me."

"Zoey Bear doesn't have to lug you around." Ash grabbed his chin. "Focus, big guy."

Staring blurrily at her as two Ashes merged into a single one, Graham groaned and dropped forward, his head on her shoulder. "I lost my moose."

"Yes. And Easton tracked him."

"You did?"

Easton grunted an affirmative.

"Is he okay?"

"Better than you."

"Did you see my bed? It was very self-sufficient of me."

"Sure, it was." A hand patting his shoulder became fingers locked in his shirt. "In you go."

Which was how Graham ended up facedown in his diner's dish-washing sink, flailing as Ash held him down and Easton sprayed ice-cold, high-pressured water into his face. Sputtering and cursing, Graham fought his way free, backing away from the sink. He called them both a few names, shaking the droplets out of his face.

Ash raised an eyebrow. "Feel better?"

"A little." Inhaling a deep breath, Graham nodded. "Okay, let's do it again."

This time, Easton held him down and Ash sprayed him, because Easton was much harder to escape from. By the second time Graham emerged from the sink, drenched and frozen, he was wide awake.

"That's a way to sober up." He shuddered.

"Fun to watch too." Setting a hip against the sink, Ash playfully aimed the sprayer toward her twin. "You're smelling a little ripe yourself, East. Want the same?"

"I've been in the woods all night," he rumbled. "What's your excuse?"

"Children, behave." Stripping his now soaked dress shirt off, Graham grabbed a kitchen towel from the stack of freshly laundered ones. Scrubbing the water from his hair and face, he turned back to his friends. "I don't suppose anyone was nice enough to bring me a change of clothes? Or my dog?"

"No, we just figured we should sober you up before the lunch shift. Jake's with Dad right now. We didn't want him to smell you like this." This time, there was only one Ash when she took his chin in her hand, peering up at him critically. "You good in there?"

"Better." Pulling her in for a quick hug, Graham smirked at her noise of protest.

"You smell terrible, Graham." Ash freed herself, then looked at him seriously. "Hey, we need to talk."

"About how my stupid ass broke up with my dream girl last night over an emotionally disturbed moose?"

"Worse."

The news really wasn't good. Graham listened to what Easton and Ashtyn had heard through word of mouth, then he went straight to the source, Jackson Shaw. Graham could have called Lana herself, but he had...feelings...about all this, and he didn't trust himself not to lose another friend and burn a second bridge in the heat of the moment. So he listened to Jax tell him all about the gala's main excitement: the revealing of the multimillion-dollar luxury dream homes that were soon to be a permanent scar on his already disfigured mountain.

"Is there any way we can stop this?" Graham asked, his hangover building into a powerful headache between his temples.

"Mom and Dad already sold her the land. Nice of them to leave me as the one fielding all the calls today. Do you know how many times my ass has been chewed just this morning?"

"We'll block it at the permit stage," Graham decided. "Listen, I've got a line building up outside, and I need to find a shirt. I'll call you later to discuss this some—"

"Why don't you have a shirt?"

"Why do you care if I don't have a shirt?"

"I'm not the one running a restaurant. That's gross, man."

Graham didn't bother saying goodbye before hanging up. Easton and Ash left with a promise to bring Jake by soon. Easton refused to give Graham the shirt off his back, but Graham did find a sweatshirt stuffed in the back of his truck. It smelled like campfire smoke and bread, which wasn't a terrible combination. Better than what was happening with the rest of him. Turning his phone off, Graham stuck it in his truck, the physical distance keeping him from calling Zoey and Lana, begging the first to forgive him for being an idiot and telling the second she had lost extra Growly Bear privileges.

The day was long, the dress shoes hurt as he wore them standing behind a grill, and all anyone coming through the doors could talk about was Lana's condominiums. People wanting to know what they would cost, speculating on the types of floor plans, and buzzing over who would get one.

Graham didn't bother letting himself get angry. The town council would never let this happen. He knew because he was there for every council meeting, and most of the discussion involved how to limit tourism's effect on their daily lives, not increase it. This would be handled. If L was out some money, that was unfortunate, but she had plenty more. She would be fine.

A shower, a change of clothes for both him and Jake, and distracting himself with balancing the business's books killed the time he had between lunch and dinner. As the evening wore on, Graham kept hoping Zoey would walk in and then immediately was grateful when she didn't. He'd hurt her last night, and Graham needed to apologize. But the break had been made, and it was probably for the best. Reaching out to her would only make things worse.

Graham waited as long as he felt necessary before driving the customers out of his diner. Focused on straightening chairs and wiping down tables, Graham didn't immediately notice the woman standing next to Barley the Biker Bear.

Raising his eyes to hers, the tension Graham had carried in his chest all day clenched down painfully tight.

"Hey there, Zoey Bear," he said, voice softening. "I've been thinking about you all day."

Which was brutally true. Even faced with the news about the condos, all Graham could focus on was the hurt in her eyes as he'd driven her away from him. When she gave him a small, worried look, his heart tried to turn itself inside out.

"I know you wanted me to leave. But I need to tell you something really important. I tried to call, but your phone went to voicemail."

"Yeah, I kept it off today. I do that on days I'm hungover and pretty sure I majorly screwed up."

"How are you feeling now?"

"Like I'm an idiot who's sorry. Like my hangover's gone and I really, *really* screwed up." Graham stood close, inhaling the scent of her hair. "Zoey, last night—"

He drifted off, unable to formulate the words.

"Last night was a bad night for you," she said, kindness and sympathy in her eyes. "And I'm worried I'm about to make tonight bad too. I need to tell you what they announced at the gala yesterday. Lana's done something that's going to upset you."

Sighing, Graham stepped back, settling down on a chair and holding out a hand to her. Zoey placed her fingers in his, allowing Graham to pull her onto his lap.

"Okay. Let me have it."

"I didn't know anything until today. Quinn let it slip that Lana had an extra room she was using as an office—"

"No, not about L. You and me first, darlin'. I did you wrong last night, so let me have it."

When she just looked at him, Graham tangled their fingers together. "I'm so sorry, gorgeous," he whispered. "I wanted you so much last night, and it hit me you're leaving. I didn't think I could deal with losing two people…friends…I care about at the same time. I was a stupid, typical guy and pushed you away. On behalf of me and my gender's knee-jerk instincts, I am so, so sorry. You deserved better. Let me have it, Zo. I'm ready and willing."

Instead of yelling at him, Zoey kissed him. It was the best getting chewed out by a girlfriend he'd ever experienced, and Graham'd sure had his fair share.

"Are you okay?" she asked him, running her fingers through his hair the way he loved. "About Ulysses?"

"Easton tracked him, and he's safe." The headache he'd never been able to shake began to ease beneath her touch. "I'm getting better by the moment." Graham squeezed her in a careful hug. "Are we okay, Zoey? Because not seeing you or talking to you today was torture."

Zoey hesitated for a few seconds, long enough for his stomach to end up somewhere on the floor.

"Graham, I know I'm leaving, and this isn't what I planned either. If it means anything, whatever this is scares me too."

Scared wasn't what Graham wanted her to feel, especially not when she was with him. So he drew her closer, finding her soft lips and kissing them, slow, small kisses that made her melt against him. Then he deepened the kiss, all but crushing her to him.

Breathless, Zoey pulled back. "Is that your way of saying I shouldn't be scared?"

"Screw that," Graham murmured. "I'm terrified."

Her laughter was a balm to his soul. Suddenly, his awful day was all okay because Zoey was there, her slender arms around his neck, holding him too.

Clever eyes found the computer sitting on the counter where he'd been working as business died down that night.

"What's the laptop for?"

"I'm trying to balance the books. My numbers this quarter are off, but I can't figure out why. This is the part that I suck at."

"Hmm, I would have thought customer relations was the part you sucked at." Glancing at him shyly, Zoey added, "I always helped with the books back at the truck stop. I can look at it for you if you want. Sometimes fresh eyes help."

He'd let her put on ballet slippers and do pirouettes on his back if she wanted.

"Go for it. Better you than me." As Zoey abandoned his lap for the laptop on the counter, Graham followed at her heels. "Have I ever told you how much I hate running a diner?"

"It's come up a time or two." She sat down, tugging the laptop closer, focusing on his spreadsheet. "For someone who hates running a diner, you're really freaking good at it."

His lips curved despite himself. "That's a complete fluke. Speaking of which, are you hungry? The grill's still hot."

She glanced up at him, and her stomach couldn't have timed its growl more perfectly if it had tried.

"I'm taking that as a yes?" Leaning in, Graham allowed himself the luxury of brushing one last strand out of her eyes. "We could go out somewhere if you want."

"This late in Moose Springs?" Her eyes sparkled in the partial light of the diner. "We'd have to break into the hotel's kitchen or go hunting."

"There's always Rick's," Graham added, knowing he'd offered to cook for her yet utterly unwilling to move away from her side.

He couldn't keep his eyes off her. Graham knew Zoey was focused on the task at hand, but all he could focus on was how her hair kept falling into her eyes, her fingers pushing those errant strands back as she concentrated.

"It's right here. See?" Zoey twisted his laptop, pointing at a column in his spreadsheet. "You added a zero. Unless you spent ten thousand dollars on ketchup this quarter. If you did, you might need to reconsider how many squirts you're adding on any given Rudolph."

"They aren't your thing, are they?"

"They aren't *not* my thing," she hedged, a deer caught in the headlights look on her face.

"Reindeer's an acquired taste. I'm not offended. I'll make you a burger." He pressed a quick kiss to her temple, the action instinctual. "There's a secret to these." Pulling out a small Tupperware container with beef patties, he added two to the hottest part of the grill. Graham washed his hands, then he placed one of the beer-braised reindeer dogs on the grill separate from the raw meat. "I have the local butcher make them with a special blend of spices. They're stronger than most, which is probably why you don't like them."

"Are you calling my taste buds a weenie?" Closing his laptop and setting it aside, she turned on her stool to face him. Her eyes brightened. "Can I drink out of the soda gun?"

"I'd be disappointed in you if you didn't." Holding it up for her, Graham waggled the nozzle. "Open up."

"I want Coke. No! Sprite! No. Better stick with Coke."

Whatever she wanted, Graham was more than happy to soda spray her with it. Most got in her mouth, but enough got in her nose and on her face that she sneezed soda.

"No, don't stop."

"You're drowning," he reminded her, adjusting the angle. "Tilt your head down. Swallow. Faster."

"Stop making this sound like a porno."

"Stop making me think about pornos."

Then, to his utter delight, a soda-drenched Zoey wrapped her arms around his neck and kissed him.

Now, for the record, Graham knew this wasn't going to last. And he was not a vacation fling type of guy. But when a Zoey Bear kissed a guy, there wasn't a Graham alive who could resist her. Especially with her lips sugary sweet and her hands in his hair.

Even though he was sure he'd kissed the lingering soda from her lips, Zoey still stole a dish towel from his stack near the ice machine to wipe her hands and face clean of their game.

"Still feeling the porno vibes."

Zoey wrinkled her nose at him. "You're incorrigible."

"Incorrigible. I-n-c-o-r-r-i-g-i-b-l-e. I was the fifth-grade spelling bee champ." With a twist of his wrist, he flipped their burgers, the patties hitting the grill with a satisfying sizzle. "I'm full of delightful details to impress you. Ask me the square root of any round number between eight and a half and nine and a half."

"You have to beat the women away with boat paddles, don't you?"

"Absolutely." When she settled on her stool, Graham leaned on the counter. "Not really. That's the danger of growing up with everyone you know. They remember you peeing your pants at the Fourth of July Fireworks Festival when you were eleven, and they never, ever let you forget it." Letting his thumb trace the side of her neck, he added, "You want an actual drink? We can try seeing what a Growly Bear on a full stomach does."

She leaned into his touch. "You'd have to baby bear me, because I've never been so sick in my life as I was after that. Besides, don't you sell out every night?"

"Yes, but I make them in huge batches, and I've got the rest of the week's Growlies stored in the back fridge."

Her eyes widened. "You're sneaky."

"Supply and demand. Keeps them coming back through the door."

"But you don't want them to come to the door."

With a dramatic sigh, Graham nodded. "I know. I'm a mystery to even me."

"You know I have dangerous information on you now," Zoey reminded him. "I could leverage it to my advantage."

Graham's eyes dropped down to her mouth unconsciously. And when he realized he was doing it, he didn't try to hide the fact he couldn't stop focusing on that part of her.

"You've had the advantage over me since we met, Zo."

"You're on fire."

Graham slid his fingers into her hair, lips lingering only centimeters from her own. "Yeah, it's one of my better lines," he murmured.

"I mean, you're literally on fire."

"Hmm?"

"Graham." She grabbed his chin and turned it, forcing him to look at his side.

"Aww crap."

He was in fact on fire, although just a little singed around the edges of his apron string, which had gotten too close to the grill while he had gotten close to her. Graham growled playfully, then kissed her one more time.

"You're going to get hurt. Graham!"

It would be so easy to pull her into his arms, to keep kissing her, but her words registered deep in the part of his brain that knew better. A little singeing on the grill didn't matter. But the ability she had to set literal fire to him finally gave Graham the strength to pull away.

The apron string was nice and browned, but so was the reindeer dog. The burgers were dangerously close to being dry, but he managed to save those in time.

"Don't worry. The burgers are ours, but the dog is mine," Graham assured her.

"I'll share it with you," Zoey offered. "You can have half of my burger. If these are an acquired taste, I don't mind trying to acquire it. This place is the town's claim to fame."

Graham glanced down at the grill, feeling his eyebrows scrunch together. "I doubt it."

"Have you ever checked your rating online? Or travel restaurant recommendations? You're actually in Luffet and Mash's book."

"That guy is a disaster. Seriously, don't listen to him. He's got a screw loose."

"You meet a lot of people, huh?"

Groaning, Graham shook his head as he plated their food.

"You have no idea. Some of the crazies that come through these doors..."

Just like every other time, he slipped a pair of antlers on her reindeer dog, drawing a startled face with little soda drops dripping all over the dog.

She giggled when he offered it to her, which only cemented the fact he'd have to do the same to every food product he prepared for her.

Which, unfortunately, would only be a few more days of food products. Graham killed the heat on the grill, then joined her at the counter. She wrinkled her nose at the first bite of her reindeer dog but gamely powered through her half, the half with the soda-covered face.

"Maybe if they were less cute, it would feel less mean."

Graham patted her knee, chuckling. "I'm sure there's a lot of cows out there right now who are very offended by your statement."

"Cows have it coming. They're mean. And they're contributing to global warming. Did you know the amount of methane produced by their flatulence has a direct impact on greenhouse gases?"

"Did you know that one supervolcano eruption will do far worse to the environment than some poor cows eating their greens?"

"Did you know that using theoretical geological events to counter current environmental issues is not only statistically inaccurate, it's also lazy?"

"Are you calling me statistically inaccurate?" he asked, eyes once more on her mouth as she licked the salt from her fries off her lower lip.

"Do you like me calling you statistically inaccurate?"

"It's turning me on, gorgeous. I won't lie."

"You are seriously the weirdest person who has ever lived." Even as she said it, Zoey raised her eyes to his. "Graham? If a drink with you is still on the table, I wouldn't say no."

For a moment, his eyes darkened with the kind of desire she'd seen before he'd kissed her earlier. Then a lopsided smile crossed his lips as Graham leaned in.

"I'm happy to make you a drink, Zoey, but I probably need to pass. I'm not sure my liver would appreciate it after last night."

As he spoke, his hand resting on her knee slid half an inch higher, squeezing her thigh lightly.

"And?" She raised an eyebrow.

"And I don't think it's a good idea," he admitted in a rough voice, sounding unusually vulnerable. "I've had enough emotional whiplash over the last twenty-four hours to last me a lifetime. I'm not sure if mixing you and alcohol is going to help."

"Hey, Graham?"

"Yeah?"

"I promise I'm not going to hurt you. Or...do anything else to you...tonight."

She'd rarely seen Graham blush before, but as his cheeks rushed with color at the idea of "anything else," Zoey leaned over and hugged him. "Why don't you make me a drink, and we'll leave it at that?"

Dropping a kiss to her temple, Graham rolled to his feet. "Whatever you want, Zo."

The way he murmured it, Zoey could believe he meant every word.

The Growly Bear was much better on a full stomach, and the fact that he made her a much smaller one than her first helped even more. To his credit, Graham added several extra gummy bears to the concoction. She left them floating in the drink, soaking up the growly part so that she could munch on them later.

They moved outside beneath the front window, leaning against the concrete blocks that made up the diner's wall. The asphalt parking lot ran all the way up to the building, with faded lines and a cracked concrete bumper, none of which should have been comfortable, but Zoey was more than content to sit with her legs folded beneath her, alternating sips of water with her drink. He was milking a third root beer, and neither one felt inclined to move. Graham had started out next to her, but when she reached over, running her fingers through his short hair, he sighed and flopped down to the ground with the kind of laid-back dramatics he had made his specialty. Apparently, her lap made the perfect pillow.

Every so often, Graham would ask her to count backward from twenty using prime numbers. She was pacing herself, because at some point, Zoey was going to need to drive herself home tonight. And as of right then, she was not going to be in any condition to drive anytime soon.

Even a baby Growly Bear packed a punch.

"Tell me something about you," Zoey said. "Something normal."

Graham raised an eyebrow even though his eyes remained closed. The empty root beer bottles were lined up next to them. To the outside eye, it looked like they had a solid party for two happening beneath stars softened by the midnight sun.

So far, he hadn't choked on the root beer, even when swigging it on his back, which was impressive.

"I wear a size extra-large shirt. And Easton's a jerk who won't share his clothes."

"That's too normal. Give me medium normal. Everyone always wants to know deepest, darkest secrets about each other."

"I have deep, dark secrets," Graham promised.

"Do you?" Zoey ran her fingers lightly through his hair, because she enjoyed it and because he kept making soft little happy noises every time she did. "I get the feeling what's on the outside is your deep, dark secret," she teased. "Either that or you really are a chainsaw murderer, in which case I really don't want to know. Give me something normal."

"Hmm, okay. I have great parents."

"In this day and age, that's pretty abnormal."

"They aren't the normal part. The normal part is that it took me most of my life to appreciate their awesomeness." Graham opened one eyelid. "You'll love them. They're weird."

"Weirder than you?"

"I'll let you decide for yourself."

An uncomfortable pause fell between them. There was no way Zoey was getting to meet Graham's parents or decide she loved them. A sip of her baby Growly Bear smoothed the discomfort away.

"Any siblings?"

"Are we doing the get to know you questions, for real?" Chuckling, Graham reached an arm back and hooked it loosely around her waist. "I can make up a lot more interesting version of myself than the truth."

"What's the truth?"

"I'm just a guy. With my head in the lap of a girl. Asking her not to spill her drink on me."

"Too many pop culture references." Zoey leaned down and kissed him on impulse. "Your parents told you they loved you a lot, didn't they?"

"Every single day," he murmured placidly in agreement.

"I knew there was a reason why you're this ridiculously self-confident and simultaneously desperate for approval."

"Definitely," Graham agreed. "It's hard work trying to live up to that level of acceptance and unconditional love. So I make sure never to tell them if I have a one-night stand or forget to eat my veggies."

"Does that happen a lot?"

"The veggies? Naw, I'm pretty solid in the veggie department."

Zoey kissed him again. "I meant the one-night stands."

"Well...did I tell you I'm good in the veggie department?" Deepening the kiss, Graham sighed in contentment when she finally pulled away. "Tell me something not true about you."

"You know those big dinosaurs they have in that museum in Chicago?"

"I'm aware of their existence."

"I like to sneak into the exhibits and swap the bones. Not the big ones. The little tiny ones no one notices."

"That's…perverse."

"The perverse thing is that I kept one of the bones."

"Have my babies."

"Right now?"

"Or in eight months."

"That's the gestation time of a moose, isn't it?"

Graham groaned in sheer pleasure. "You get me. You really get me, Zoey Bear. Did you actually steal a dinosaur bone?"

"No, they secure those suckers. But I daydream about it every time I'm there."

Graham watched her drain the last of her drink.

"Tell me something real, Zoey." His voice softened on her name. "Not deep or dark, unless you want to share that kind of thing. But something real."

"I made head waitress last year. At least I did before I told the owner that I was taking two weeks of vacation. I got fired, but I'm guessing by the time I go home, she'll be so miserable without me, I'll get my job back. If not, I'll find another one."

"Do you like it?"

"Being a waitress? I'm good at it." Zoey shrugged, her lip quirking up. "Did you ever have one of those jobs where you think 'I'll just do this for now, just to make ends meet'? And then you look up, and it's been ten years, and you're still a waitress at the truck stop down the road from your grandmother's place? But the tips are decent, and the people are nice, so you never leave?"

"Not exactly. But I know what it's like to have a five-year plan grab you by the balls and make you its bitch."

"Graham, you can't actually be this unhappy to have a thriving business." Zoey wasn't buying it. "You probably have a mattress stuffed with twenties to sleep on every night."

"Fives," he murmured. "The profit margins on reindeer aren't as high as you'd expect." Graham looked at her. "I just always wanted to be an artist. A real one, not a guy with a shipping container in the backyard full of untouched cedar logs. I wanted to spend my days with a chainsaw in my hands, carving the most massive, incredible pieces of art. Life-sized bears, moose calves playing, these mountains down to every last perfect detail.

"But I just wasn't good enough," he admitted. "And at some point, programs will drop you and give the space to someone else who is."

"Where did you study?"

"In New York. At the School of Visual Arts."

When Zoey's jaw dropped open, he touched the tip of his pinkie to her chin, closing it. "I know. And I was totally out of my depth. But there's something to being able to get food delivered at three in the morning.

"I missed the stars," he continued. "I missed these mountains. I really missed my friends. The Trap was just supposed to be a small little lunch stop, something to pay the bills. But now..." Graham sounded tired as he confessed, "Now I'm stuck."

"Why not just hire someone else to run it for you?"

"Because as much as I don't want to be here, I really don't want to go back to being the art school dropout. I want to be more than I am. I just don't know what that means yet."

Still playing with his hair, Zoey closed her eyes. "Sometimes life gives us the things we weren't planning on."

"I was just thinking the same thing." A warm hand found hers in the darkness. "You know, the day I opened, I was so worried. Then I went outside to get the bread, and there was Ulysses, trying to get in my truck. And I thought, hey, at least someone likes this place. That was good enough to me."

"Graham? You don't need art school to be an artist. You don't need a studio or even anyone to buy your work. You just need you. And from what I know of you, I can't imagine you being anything less than amazing at whatever you set your mind to."

"What do you want, Zoey?"

"I wanted to come here. That's all I cared about. This was my dream."

Strong fingers gave her slender ones a gentle squeeze. "And it got screwed up from the very beginning. Are you disappointed?"

Was she disappointed?

"Do you hear that?"

"Hmm?" Graham tilted his head, listening. "All I hear are the thrushes singing. They're loud little suckers at night up here."

"Exactly. That's all I hear too." Pushing her glasses up high on her nose, Zoey lifted her face to the sky, a soft purple-gray, still trimmed with blue on the horizon. "I didn't get some of the memories I thought I'd wanted. But right here, just like this, you're giving me memories I didn't know I needed. A girl can go a long time on a night like this. Maybe even ten more years while I save enough to come back."

Even though the idea of returning made her smile, the rest of her words caused the smile to slip from her face. Silence fell between them, a silence she didn't think she had the courage to break.

Graham did. "Ten years is a long time."

"Yeah."

"You'll probably have a potbellied husband and four kids by then."

"You might have a wife and thirty kids by then."

With a low chuckle, he looked up at her. "I might. Poor thing, getting stuck with a guy like me. I've been told I'm a pain in the ass."

"I have physical proof that is one hundred percent true." She hesitated, then added softly, "Graham? I don't want to go home regretting anything. Especially you."

"Meaning what, Zo?"

"Meaning I only have a few days left. I'd like to make the most of them with you."

Drawing her down into his arms, Graham kissed her, with only the silent majestic mountains rising above them bearing witness to the most perfect kiss of her life. As she closed her eyes, letting the warmth of Graham's presence lull her into sleep against his chest, Zoey heard him whisper, "Yeah, darlin'. Me too."

CHAPTER 15

THINGS WERE GETTING SERIOUS WITH Graham, which meant it was time to book an appointment with Grace. Zoey was in need of some ladyscaping.

They were having a fireworks show by the lake that night to celebrate the Fourth of July, and apparently, the resort went all out, setting off a sheer arsenal over the valley. It was one of the few times a year that the town and the resort came together, with the town adding their own supplies to that of the resort, resulting in enough fireworks to blow a small crater in the side of the mountain range.

According to Lana, the Moose Springs fireworks show was absolutely *fabulous*.

Last night with Graham had lasted until dawn, and by the time he walked Zoey to her car, whatever this was growing between them hadn't eased one single bit. She would see him tonight, because the entire town shut down to go watch the fireworks. Like Lana, Graham assured her it was not to be missed. Lingering at the end of their goodbye kiss, Zoey's desire for him skyrocketed. Only when she was back at the hotel, a couple of hours of sleep under her belt and the promise he would come find her as soon as he could get away from work, did it occur to her that she might be in over her head. It had been a while since she'd dated someone and…well…things weren't at their tidiest.

Having her eyebrows already threaded by the resort's expert stylist, Zoey knew Grace was the best. The scariest but the best. As Zoey stood awkwardly in the spa's reception room, waiting for her turn to be tortured, she embraced how utterly intimidated she was by the other woman. There was something particularly horrifying about asking a cover model-beautiful stylist with perfect eyebrows to make sure you don't have errant chin hairs or a mustache.

That had been last time. This time, Zoey had more serious hair issues to attend to.

"Oh, Zoey, there you are."

Zoey glanced up in surprise, not expecting Lana to come around the corner, fresh-faced and dewy, ready for her day.

The fact Lana hadn't woken Zoey to ask her to do her makeup and went to the spa to have it done instead spoke volumes to her level of guilt. Rarely at a loss for something to say, Lana hesitated, fiddling with the delicate diamond bracelet on her wrist.

"I'm getting a wax," Zoey blurted out. "I'm trying not to run screaming."

Lana's eyes sparkled with interest. "Oh really? Things are going that well?"

Grace the follicle extractor appeared at the desk, a hush going through the reception area. Clearly, Zoey wasn't the only one intimidated by the stylist. "Zoey Caldwell."

"That's me." Could her voice have sounded any weaker?

Grace lifted one sculpted eyebrow, and Zoey found herself shrinking beneath her gaze. "Umm, Lana? Do you want to come with me?"

Relief flashed over Lana's face as if she thought Zoey would be angry with her. "Of course I will."

"I don't think she likes me," Zoey mumbled as they followed Grace deeper into the salon, past overstuffed pedicure chairs and someone getting their hair styled for the day. Last time when they had their brows done, it had been from a bright and cheery spot near the pedicure chairs.

This time, they were going to a room. A dark, ominous lady cave where terrible things happened to those with insufficient follicle care.

Upon seeing the table and sheer amount of wax waiting for her, Zoey's body stopped of its own accord, unwilling to move past the doorway.

"On the table." Grace ignored Zoey's internal panic attack. "Are we still doing a Brazilian wax?"

"I think so?"

Raising another eyebrow at her squeak, Grace glanced at Lana.

"Of course she is. Now undress, love. We can't get all spiffy with our clothes in the way."

Nervously, Zoey did as she was told and lay down on the torture table.

"It's nothing to be scared of." Sitting on a chair next to Zoey's head, Lana gave her a reassuring squeeze of her hand. "I do this all the time. All they will do is—"

Grace gasped, mumbling, "What in the world?"

"What?" Pushing herself up to her elbows, Zoey cast about frantically. "What's wrong?"

"I mean, do the words daily moisturizer mean nothing to you?"

"Down there?"

Grace and Lana shared a look. "It's okay," her friend promised. "It's never too late to start wrinkle repair."

"I have *wrinkles*?"

"Well, they certainly aren't laugh lines," Grace said dryly.

"Until recently, that part of you didn't have much to laugh about, did it?" Lana shrugged. "If nothing else, the handsome boy has put a spring in your step. Now, let's make it easier for him to see the forest for the trees."

"That analogy doesn't even make sense—ow ow ow!" With an impossibly loud rip, Zoey saw nothing but stars. "This was a terrible idea."

"Agreed." Nodding, Lana patted her head. "But now that you've taken the right steps, it should be easier next time. I never even feel it when I'm being done. What are you getting?"

"I'm sorry?"

"It'll be a while before it matters," Grace muttered, rolling her shoulders to loosen them before going back in.

"Hey! I'm not that bad."

Lana stole a peek, then clucked her tongue. "You're not that good."

"Don't look!"

"Oh nonsense. It's not anything I haven't seen before. Now, some get a heart, some a little strip, but Grace's claim to fame is the moose."

"I'm sorry?"

"A moose." Lana turned her phone to Zoey, waggling an image of the animal in question. "Tall, big horns, the town is named after them."

"I know what moose are. I just never imagined one...down there."

"Get the moose," Lana encouraged her.

"You're not joking? This can't be a thing."

"Oh, it's not just a thing. Grace's signature moose is Moose Springs' second rite of passage. You should definitely get one." Peeking one more time, Lana's face creased in concern. "Hmm. Might want to brace yourself."

When Grace's brows knitted together in determination, Zoey knew she was in for a rough time of it. Things went downhill for a while, and in between her yelps and several attempts to crawl half-naked from the table, Lana did her best to distract Zoey.

"We're watching the fireworks tonight from the veranda. Killian reserved it. You can bring Graham if you want."

"Lana, why in the world would he want to go? These are the same people you're trying to sell pieces of his home to."

"Oh, he won't be mad forever." Despite her dismissive tone, there was worry in her eyes. "Graham doesn't hold a grudge."

"I don't know. I'm not from here, so I don't have to live with what he does. But I saw him in pain. Real, heart-wrenching pain. And what you're doing is only going to make things worse."

"Worse than letting the town die?"

Another rip had Zoey hiding her face beneath her arm from embarrassment. Lana tilted her head, nodding in approval.

"Stop looking!" Zoey squeaked. "There are friendship boundaries, Lana."

"Are there?" Lana flapped her hand in dismissal. "You know you should have done this days ago. You'll be awfully raw tonight."

"I hadn't really planned on..." Zoey trailed off.

"The delicious diner owner making you swoon? Understandable. I see a moose horn. Oh, well done, Grace. You truly are skilled. She's quite the fixer-upper, isn't she?"

"I'm taking my break early," the stylist said as she started on the final rips.

Lana's phone began to chime, and she hopped up, squeezing Zoey's hand. "I have to take this. Come tonight, just for a little while. I want to clear the air with Graham. He's not returning my calls."

"I'll talk to him," Zoey promised. "But I won't force him to go if he doesn't want to—ahh!"

With an expression of victory, Grace held up a waxing strip. "Finished. I feel like I just came back from war."

"You and me both." Whimpering, Zoey and her freshly minted moose paid and tipped Grace, then they both limped out of the spa.

"Are you okay, ma'am?" Grass asked as she passed through the lobby.

"Yep," she replied through gritted teeth. "If anyone asks, drinking a Growly Bear is the less painful rite of passage."

By the time Zoey made it back to the room and finished getting ready, her phone was already buzzing. Graham was down at the lake, and they were setting up their own fireworks to shoot off. Would she come meet him?

As if he even had to ask.

Moose Springs Lake was a short walk down the mountainside, nestled beneath the resort's shadow. Large enough to boat and fish in but not nearly as massive as the lakes she was used to back home in the Midwest, Moose Springs Lake was the place to go for all Fourth of July festivities. Already the waters were filling with pontoon boats and little fishing boats, people playing music and swimming. On the shore, trucks and cars were parked, blankets spread on the ground, and children ran with sparklers in their hands.

"Someone's going to lose an eye," Zoey murmured.

"Yes, but it'll be fun up until it happens."

Turning around at Graham's familiar rumble, Zoey found herself swept up in the best, most massive bear hug.

"So, are you adding to this craziness?"

"You better believe it." He was practically vibrating with childlike enthusiasm. "Any excuse to close the diner after lunch. Here, I got you something." Graham tossed her a small firework box with a round frog on the label. "It's a frog prince. It matches your little money holder thing."

"You remember my coin purse?"

"It's a sparkly frog. A guy doesn't forget a pretty girl with a sparkly frog in her back pocket. Lucky frog."

Sliding his hands into said back pockets, Graham stole a kiss from Zoey's lips.

"You're trouble."

"Always." He gazed down at her, that look in his eyes.

The look that took the strength right out of Zoey's knees and left her a mess, plastered all over him despite who might be watching. Graham didn't seem to mind the plastering one single bit, not even when their embrace resulted in several ear-piercing catcalls.

"We might need to find a more private spot." Graham hugged her again, pulling her up to her toes. "You look especially great today. Anything different?"

"It's the glow of surviving my last rite of passage," she informed him. Whispering in Graham's ear, Zoey added, "Grace moosed me."

A wide grin crossed his handsome features. "You know I'm going to lose a hand setting off fireworks now. I'm completely distracted by you."

"Good. Keep that up."

"Where's Jake?" For once, Graham's constant companion wasn't with him.

"He's staying with my parents tonight. Anchorage does a fireworks show but nothing like we do here. Jake gets scared of all the noise, and my folks aren't big fireworks people. They'd rather spend time with their grandpuppy."

She arched an eyebrow. "So you're saying we have some alone time without the kids?"

"Better make the most of it." Leaning in, Graham added, "Maybe I got a moose from Grace too."

What was it about him that made her unable to stop smiling? Zoey's face hurt from grinning so much, and she was hoarse from laughter. They spent the afternoon surrounded by his friends, helping the younger kids with the kid-safe poppers and spinners. Zoey happily ate what was offered her, be it delicious potato salads, incredible desserts, or unknown animal flesh formed in hot dog shapes and slathered in ketchup.

The fireworks grew bigger and better as the afternoon turned into evening. Sitting with Ash and some of Graham's friends, Zoey found herself utterly content, watching him lighting off the fireworks, happier than she'd ever seen him. A few mishaps occurred, including one accidental tipping of a mortar. Everyone dove for cover as fiery shells zipped over their heads instead of toward the sky, exploding on the grass frighteningly close. But as she climbed back into her lawn chair, Zoey knew Graham wasn't the only one having a blast.

Surrounded by the warm kindness of Graham's friends, Zoey couldn't remember ever being so happy.

When the resort started their fireworks show, each burst bigger than the last, it seemed to renew everyone's efforts to shoot off more fireworks of their own. Zoey loved watching the colors exploding across the sky, but her eyes kept drifting back to Graham. He must have noticed the way she was watching him, because even as the resort started to roll the big ones out, Graham came over, kneeling next to her chair instead of watching.

"I parked a little way away," he told her. "Want to help me get some blankets?"

Considering he'd waited until everyone was distracted to ask her, Zoey was fairly sure the blankets weren't the only reason why Graham invited her to go somewhere, just the two of them, alone.

Feeling her cheeks flush in response to the heat in his eyes, Zoey nodded. "Absolutely."

They walked around the lake to where he had left his truck.

And yes, it was still near people, because everyone in town was at the lake right then, but compared to where they had spent the afternoon, it was as close to privacy as they were going to get.

Drawing her in close, Graham leaned against the side of the truck bed. Denied his hands on her for too long, Zoey pulled his face down to hers, pressing into his warm, strong body. It should be illegal to look that good, to kiss her like her legs were going to buckle, to steal her breath but keep her desperate for more. By the time it occurred to her she needed to breathe at some point, they were both winded. The air had grown cool, and it felt good on her heated neck.

"I thought we were getting blankets," she panted.

"That was code for 'do you want to go make out with me in my truck?'"

"Yes. We need blankets. All the blankets. Brrr, so cold."

He scooped her up, dropping a giggling Zoey over the side of the truck and into the bed. Without bothering with the tailgate, he swung himself over, joining her. And yes, there were several blankets tucked in there, along with a cooler and some snacks, but Zoey was far more focused on sneaking a blanket over them. She kicked off her shoes for comfort, then snuggled against him.

"Oh, it's like that, huh?" he teased her.

"Only if you want." She watched Graham settle his weight on his elbow next to her.

"Did you have any doubt?" A hand slid down her hip, warm and slow. "Hey there, Zoey Bear." Somehow the greeting was far softer, far sexier than ever, his voice husky in the growing dimness.

"You're missing the fireworks," Zoey reminded him, a shiver of anticipation rolling up her spine.

The lightest touch of his fingertips tracing along her arm caused her to shiver all over again, even as she moved in closer.

"Are you sure you won't miss out?" she pressed.

"You or those stinky old light shows? I'm picking you any day of the week. Although as much as I'd love a recreation of the *Titanic* sexy scene, I don't think we're going to have much privacy in here." Graham's eyes reflected the light of a massive multicolored firework.

"That's what blankets are for."

A mischievous expression spread across his handsome face. "Zoey, you keep getting better and better by the minute."

"I bet you say that to all the girls."

"Only the tourists. They're a dime a dozen. What's your name again? Ingrid? Jessica?"

He deserved the playful slap of her hand on his muscled bicep. "You're a brat," Zoey said. "Someone should pay me for putting up with you all this time."

"Oh, definitely." Then Graham dipped his head to hers. For a man who spent so much of his time pretending not to care, the careful way he slid his hand down her side, squeezing her hip before tracing the length of her leg, told her everything.

"I can't promise we won't have visitors any moment," he warned her.

"I don't care."

He gazed down at her, hunger and a hundred other indecipherable emotions in his eyes. "Zoey? Are you sure about this?"

Graham's thumb traced a circle around her navel, voice husky with desire. Just his thumb. So far, he'd kept his contact with her minimal, but as he opened his hand, covering her stomach with his palm, Zoey wanted to know what it felt like to be in this man's arms, his touch unrestrained.

"I'm surer about wanting you than I've ever been about anything. I'm just worried about what happens after."

Some guys would have told her that didn't matter. If Graham had told her it didn't matter right then, Zoey would have let him convince her. Instead, his eyes shadowed, his expression growing tight.

"Yeah. Me too."

His hair was soft and felt good between her fingers.

"How 'in' are you?" she asked.

"Eighty-twenty," Graham admitted roughly. "The eighty is ready to pull this blanket over our heads, right here, right now."

Eighty-twenty. Which meant twenty percent of him was unsure. It shouldn't have hurt, but for some reason, that twenty burned.

"And twenty wants to go find someone else?"

"You're leaving, Zo. I can't…" He hesitated. "This isn't some summertime romance. I'm not sixteen. I need more in my life, and I can't just fall for you."

"I never asked you to."

"Darlin', you might not be asking me to. But every time you turn those gorgeous eyes my way, you're sure as shit daring me to."

That was as close to a declaration of his feelings as Zoey was going to get. In truth, she wasn't sure she wanted to hear more. Graham wasn't the only one afraid of what falling in love would do to them. He was right, this wasn't a summertime romance. It was a couple more days, and then it would be done.

Graham Barnett would be nothing but a memory. A good memory, but like all memories, he would eventually fade.

Instinctively tightening her fingers into his arms in resistance to his loss, she looked up at him. "Graham? Can we not talk about what we can't have and just enjoy what we do? Because this started out as the absolute worst vacation, but meeting you…"

A sweet smile eased the strain in his features. "It's pretty awesome, right? I'm pretty cool."

"You're actually the biggest dork I have ever met." Zoey leaned in and kissed him. In a soft voice, she added, "Eighty-twenty isn't all that bad."

"No, gorgeous. And if I were being honest, that shit's more like eighty-five-fifteen."

"We're getting closer."

Graham curled his arm under the small of her back, gently drawing her beneath him. "Ninety-two-eight," he murmured huskily, pressing a kiss to her neck, then another to her collarbone.

"Hit ninety-three-seven, and I might pull this blanket up no matter what you say."

Graham kissed her, this kiss deeper, more passionate. Showing her how much he wanted her.

"We're at least ninety-four, six."

Giggling as his warm breath and the stubble from his two-day beard tickled her neck, Zoey wriggled her toes against his ankles, tugging the blanket up higher. "In that case…"

Maybe in another time, in another place, Zoey might have been too shy to wrap her arms around his neck and kiss Graham like her life depended on it, knowing there were people who could walk by. But all eyes were turned to the massive fireworks in the sky. All eyes except for his. The only thing Graham was looking at was her.

When Zoey's phone buzzed in her jeans side pocket, she ignored it, far too focused on the warm kisses trailing a path from her pulse point to the base of her neck. It rang again, then once more.

"The one time my phone actually works up here..." She reached into her pocket and turned it off without looking at the screen.

Lips curving against her skin, Graham wrapped his hand around her hip, pulling her tighter to his muscled form. In Zoey's world, the low fifty-degree temperatures were cool, just on the shy side of chilly, but Graham was born and bred Alaskan. She doubted he even noticed anything above thirty. She slipped her hands beneath the hem of his shirt, sliding her palms across his stomach before tugging lightly at the piece of clothing between them.

"It's like that, is it?"

"Mm-hmm. I'm curious."

"You and me both." His voice deepened with desire as his eyes scraped down her form. Reaching behind his neck, he grabbed the back of his shirt and tugged it over his head, tossing it off to the side. The sight of cut abdominal muscles and a broad, muscled chest greeted her. A little sigh of lust escaped her throat.

"I'm so disappointed," she teased, because there was no way she could be. He made a low noise of masculine approval when her fingernails dug into his hard sides, tugging him back down to her. When his thumb slid along the hem of her shirt, she leaned into his touch.

"We still good?" Graham checked.

"Perfect," Zoey breathed.

His palm spread across her stomach, eyes meeting hers. "Fair's fair."

A massive, sky-covering firework exploded above their heads, casting them both in a flash of brilliant white light, the boom rattling his truck. Jerking at the sudden explosion, Zoey realized she had pressed into him instinctively. Particularly one specific part.

If Graham was startled to find her breast abruptly in his hand, he handled it well.

"I was going to take this slow, but by all means. Lead the way."

Waggling his eyebrows suggestively, Graham ran a skilled thumb over the side of her breast. Unable to keep from giggling at his antics, Zoey sidled out of her own shirt, hoping that his warmth and the blanket would save her from freezing any of her own dangly bits.

She wasn't sure what to expect, but when Graham buried his nose between her breasts and began making rooting, animal noises, she dissolved into helpless giggles. Recognizing the pleased expression on his face, Zoey shook her head, heart full.

"I love you," she said.

The hands on her went still. When she realized her word choice, Zoey bit her lip, wondering if she'd messed things up.

"I mean, I love *this*. Being around you."

Graham's expression was hard to read, and the dim light didn't help much. But when he ran his palm soothingly down her breastbone, Zoey knew it would take more than a wrong—if true—word to screw up whatever this was between them.

He gazed down at her as if memorizing her features.

"Me too."

This time, when he bent his head to hers, all jokes between them gave way to even better things.

———

If she'd had any idea how beautiful she looked, wrapped up in his arms and smiling up at him, nose crinkled, Zoey would have grabbed her blanket and found a better man in a better truck bed to spend her evening with.

Somehow, she'd chosen him, and Graham was trying to keep his gut reactions in a choke hold. Then she'd busted out that word.

The word.

And he didn't blame her one bit, because Graham was pretty sure he loved...*this*...too.

Messing around in his truck was beyond fun, but fun was quickly being replaced with a series of emotions he did not want to share with anyone who might happen to walk past their secluded parking spot.

Now his damn phone wouldn't stop buzzing. So far, he'd managed to successfully distract her, but at some point, it was going to be more than a little inconvenient.

"Zo."

"Hmm?"

Groaning, Graham nipped her lower lip, because not doing so seemed so wrong. "Any chance we can take this back to your place? It's closer."

"Depends on if you tossed my keycard in the grass next to my bra."

Lips curving, he nipped her neck this time, then each of her fingertips. "That wasn't me."

"I'm pretty sure it was."

"Definitely not. L's at a thing, right? The thing we're invited to go to that we don't want to go to?"

Her breath caught, and Graham decided they definitely needed to take this back to her place.

"I can get a new keycard. Grass likes me."

"Grass hates me."

"You probably deserve it."

In the end, they found her keycard after hunting for their clothes. Hastily dressing, they snuck up to the resort. The interior of the hotel was empty, with all the guests and employees outside watching the fireworks. The elevator took twice as long as it should have to reach her floor, or maybe that was just Graham's impatience getting the best of him. Arm around her shoulders, Graham held open the door for Zoey after she unlocked it with trembling fingers. Graham felt the same. His hands might not be trembling, but his entire body was tensed with anticipation. Wanting her was killing him, especially when she kept stealing glances at him from the corner of her eye, unconsciously wetting her lower lip.

Unable to keep his eyes off her mouth, Graham stole her hand as soon as the door closed behind her, pulling her back into his arms. The room was dark, lit only by the low summer light and the fireworks still exploding above the mountainside through the windows. The view was incredible, but all Graham could see was her.

"Are you sure, Zo?" He had to ask one more time because more than her fingers were trembling now. "We can take this slow."

"I'm trying *not* to attack you," Zoey replied, breathless. "How am I doing so far?"

When her hands slid beneath his shirt, tracing his abdominal muscles, Graham groaned, capturing her mouth. Fingers kneading into her hips, he whispered against her lips.

"Bed or couch, gorgeous?"

"Both," she breathed. "Or the window. The shower. Maybe the elevator."

Not asking her to marry him right then and there was only possible because his hands and mouth were currently otherwise occupied.

They were halfway to the couch when Graham heard a small noise that didn't belong. Disengaging Zoey's hands from him, he pulled her behind him protectively, scanning the suite for something out of place.

"What's wrong?"

"I heard something."

Not something. Someone. As he stepped closer to the partially open door to Lana's bedroom, he saw movement next to the bed. This time, the noise was a small sniffle, feminine and familiar in tone.

"It's L."

Zoey pushed past him, turning on a light and making a little noise of distress in her throat.

For the first time since he'd met her, Lana looked rough. She'd been crying, her face and eyes reddened. Hair a mess and clothing—

With a growl of instant rage, Graham realized her clothing was dirty, as if she'd fallen, and there was a scratch on her arm.

"Who did this?" he demanded. "Did someone hurt you?"

"Graham, give her space. Lana, what happened?"

"It doesn't matter. Just a small disagreement, and then I tripped." Lana tried to give them a breezy grin, but it fell flat. "Did you two crazy kids have fun on your date?"

Her shaking hands would have given her away even without her makeup running down her cheeks in thick streaks. Taking Lana's hands in her own, Zoey sat close.

"Lana, it's okay. You can tell us."

"Word about the condos has spread. It appears not everyone is happy about my little investment project." Sniffling again, Lana raised her chin defiantly. "But I refuse to be intimidated."

"Who was it, L? Did you recognize them?"

"No, but that nice boy from town stepped in. The place with the pool tables."

"Rick?" Zoey asked quietly. Lana nodded.

"He should have done more than step in," Graham decided, incensed. Taking Lana's wrist, he gently turned her arm. "That's a bad scratch you have there. Rick should have gotten you medical attention."

"I told him I was fine. I don't need a man to hover over me when I'm more than capable of taking care of myself."

Even as she said it, Graham noticed the empty bottle of wine on the nightstand. She might not need a man, but it was clear she was distraught, half-drunk, and needed a friend.

"Graham, we need to get her cleaned up."

Curling her arm over his shoulders, Graham locked his arm around Lana's waist. Zoey did the same, although the height difference between the two women wasn't going to make it easy for her to help.

"I got her," Graham promised. "Okay, let's get you somewhere more comfortable. Upsy-daisy."

Picking her up, Graham carried Lana to the bathroom, carefully setting her on the vanity counter next to the sink. "You didn't take anything with that wine, did you, sweetie?"

Lana glanced at him guiltily. "Nothing worth talking about."

"Let me guess, more baby aspirin." Sighing, he kept a steadying arm around her as Zoey found a washcloth. It must have stung when they scrubbed the dirt and debris from the scratches on her arm, but Lana was tough. Other than clenching her teeth, she ignored it.

"Was this down in town?" Keeping her voice soft so as not to pressure Lana. "Or was it somewhere on the grounds?"

Staying quiet for a long time, Lana finally whispered, "I went down to the lake because I wanted to talk to you two. I didn't want you to be mad at me."

"We weren't parked with the others. Zo and I were aiming for some alone time."

Graham leaned a hip into the counter next to her, taking Lana's face in his hands. In all their years of steadily growing friendship, he'd never seen her like this. Wiping the tears from her eyes, Graham waited until she was able to look up at him.

"I'm not happy with you, sweetie, but my guess is you won't be happy with me either. But it's not going to change how much you matter to me. I'm not the kind of guy that bails on my friends. Okay?"

She nodded, accepting a tissue from Zoey to blow her nose.

Graham waited for her to compose herself, then continued. "Here's what we're going to do. You're going to take a deep breath, then you're going to tell me what happened. And then Easton and I will take care of it."

"It's not your problem," she whispered. "I can take care of myself."

"I know. I've been watching you for a long time now, and I believe you're capable of anything. But this place here? This is just a bunch of sticks and concrete glued to a mountain pretending to be far more important than it actually is. It's not real, L, and neither are the people. It's not worth getting hurt for, and it sure isn't worth protecting anyone for."

Zoey put a warning hand on his arm. "Graham, not now."

"I'm just saying—"

"Say it later, okay? Not now. Look, she's half-out as it is."

Zoey wasn't wrong. Lana had started to sway, her eyes glazing. The combination of alcohol and who knew what else was quickly taking her down for the count.

"Should we call a doctor?" he asked Zoey, wrapping an arm around Lana's shoulders.

"No, she's done this before when she was upset. I don't know what she takes, but it helps her calm down." Voice clipped, Zoey took Lana's shoes off. "Help me get her to bed?"

"Did I do something to upset you?" Graham couldn't imagine what, but he wasn't imagining her teeth clenched tightly together or the way Zoey wouldn't look directly at him. He chose instead to focus on the woman currently falling asleep against his shoulder.

"We'll talk about it later."

Well. That was never good.

Zoey finished taking off Lana's earrings and necklace, a ridiculously expensive diamond-encrusted set he would have been afraid to touch, let alone stuff in a jewelry box without looking twice. Clearly, Zoey was more used to Lana's jewelry, moving on to shed her of a delicate tennis bracelet worth more than Graham's house and land put together.

Watching Zoey wipe Lana's streaked makeup clean from her eyes with a makeup remover cloth, it occurred to Graham these two made a strange pairing, but their friendship was real.

"She'll be horrified if she wakes up with mascara on her face." Her voice was still clipped, but Zoey's movements were careful. "It always embarrasses her the morning after, when she's been upset. Okay, she's ready. Put her on the left side. That's the side she sleeps on."

"Carrying around drunken women in this hotel is starting to become my thing."

"She's not drunk, she's sedated. And that wine was more than half-empty when I left today. She couldn't have had much more than a glass."

"She had enough," Graham drawled.

They pulled the covers over Lana and closed her door most of the way, leaving just enough room for Zoey to be able to check on her. Grabbing his arm, Zoey pulled Graham toward the hotel room door, as far away from Lana's bedroom as they could get.

"What is wrong with you?" Eyes flashing behind her glasses, Zoey's voice was pitched quiet, but the anger came through loud and clear. "It's not real? Look around, Graham. This place is getting more real by the minute. And it's real enough that some local lowlifes hurt my friend. I want you to get Jonah up here right now and take care of this the right way."

"I don't need Jonah. East and I will put the fear of pain in them."

"I don't want the fear of pain. I want Jonah to arrest them. I want them behind bars for hurting her, all because of this stupid local versus resort bullshit that you are constantly promoting!"

Tightening his mouth, Graham ground his teeth in frustration. "That's not fair, Zoey, and you know it. I didn't hurt her."

"No, but I would put twenty bucks down that you've already started riling everyone up to fight the condos being planned." Busted. She knew it too, because like a spider monkey, she was all over him. "People listen to you, Graham. They follow you. You think I don't notice how people react when you're around? You're an alphahole."

"Excuse me?"

"Figure it out. Everyone follows the alphahole. But guess what? Alphaholes don't get to play innocent when innocent people get hurt. You're not better than her. You're not better than me or anyone, Graham. We're all just people. And tonight, your town took this too far."

Trying to fight his anger, Graham nearly chewed his tongue off to keep from raising his voice. "You don't get it, Zoey."

"No, because I'm not a local. So any loyalty I have known in my life couldn't possibly compare to what you have here. There's no way anyone will ever be good enough or belong. You have made that crystal freaking clear from the beginning. But maybe if a bunch of jerks down there had thought a little less like you, maybe my friend wouldn't be in there like that!"

Graham's jaw rippled. "Tell me how you really feel."

The angry little bit pulled herself up to every inch of height she had, so furious she was shaking. "Oh, trust me, I'm going to. You're not the center of the world. You're not the ultimately wounded, the epically maltreated. You're people, living in a town, surrounded by mountains pretty enough that other people come to see them. And as funny as it is to watch you bitch and moan about it, the result of your shitty-ass attitude is you still take the money they put in your tip jar while spitting in their faces."

Well. That was fun to hear.

"Zoey, you've *seen*—"

"Both sides, Graham. I've seen *both* sides. And no, I'm not comfortable around rich people either. I never know what they're talking about, and it makes me feel small and foolish. And what happened to Ulysses was wrong. I'm sorry about him, I truly am, but what happened to Lana is so far out of control, I'm ready to skin everyone in this town alive. What is *wrong* with you? Everyone else I've met in Alaska has been warm and kind and inviting, but this toxic little town is its own undoing."

"You want me to call Jonah? Fine. He can have whatever's left of these idiots when I'm done. You want me to apologize to L? Sure. But I'm not going to stand here and listen to you rip up something that matters to me."

"You've done that to me since the moment we met! You've shredded every experience I've had here, but it matters to me. *This* was what mattered to *me*."

"It's a *vacation*," Graham drawled, hearing and hating the sarcasm in his voice.

He saw her flinch, and his heart was screaming at him to stop, to shut his mouth and take a step back. Maybe if he wasn't so angry because he damn well knew he'd been inflaming his town over the condos as they set off fireworks by the lake, Graham might have held back. Instead, like the fool he was, his mouth kept going.

"This is your vacation, but it's my life. You're getting on a plane, and *you're* leaving *me*. So no, none of this is real to any of you. It's only real to us. What do you want from me?"

"All I wanted from you was not to be a coward."

This time, he flinched. "You know what, Zoey? I think this thing has run its course. Why don't we save ourselves some heartache and call time of death?"

As he headed for the door, he could hear her choked voice say after him, "For the record, Graham, right now, you're the one walking away. *Again*."

The moment the door slammed shut between them, he heard her burst into tears. Graham stopped in the hall, shaking with anger and the desire to turn around, to go back in and fix this. He didn't want to fight with her, but it was clear Zoey didn't understand. And as much as he cared about her, this vacation romance *had* to end sometime. If walking away and ending this pain for both of them made him an alphahole, then so be it. In the meantime, Graham had something he needed to do.

He had to see some men about a girl with a scratch on her arm.

CHAPTER 16

THERE WAS A CERTAIN AMOUNT of visceral satisfaction in taking a really big chainsaw and attacking an even bigger stump of wood with it. Graham didn't know what he was carving or if he was simply hacking out chunks at random, but for once, he didn't care. Tired of standing around, unwilling to take chances, Graham was ready to do this or be done.

The irony of that train of thought wasn't lost on him, but it sure did piss him off.

Wood chips were flying when a pickup pulled into the drive and a massive figure stepped out of it. Graham ignored his visitor in favor of a vertical cut along the grain of the wood in front of him. If it split, he didn't care about that either.

It was only eight o'clock in the morning, but Easton had a six-pack in his hand. Dropping the beer on the ground next to his boot, Easton settled down in a lawn chair, cracking open a beer, content to wait in silence.

The log had been reduced by more than half its size before the chainsaw sputtered to a stop, gas tank empty.

Graham had been carving so long, his hands had grown numb

from the vibrations. Flexing them to regain feeling, he set the chainsaw on the ground next to the stump.

"You all right?" Easton nodded toward Graham's hands.

"Getting arthritis in my old age."

Easton snorted, stretching an arm out with a beer, waggling the bottle at him. "If I wanted to drink alone, I would have stayed at home and watched a game."

"It isn't even noon." Graham declined the offer, not caring how surly he sounded. "With Ash and your dad there, you're never alone."

"Dad went to visit Grandma in the home. And Ash has a date today, some guy from Whittier."

Dropping down into a second chair, Graham sighed. "Well, that's disturbing."

"The date or the Whittier part?"

"The idea she's capable of having the kinds of romantic emotions that lead to her actually going on a date. Want to go kill him?"

Raising an eyebrow at Graham's tone, Easton drained his beer and opened another. "Like you killed those guys last night?"

Graham grunted sourly. He hadn't killed anyone, but between the two of them, Easton and Graham had put some very serious regret into the people who had messed with Lana. In his frustration, Graham'd had difficulty restraining himself. Easton, however, had been the epitome of cool, calm collectedness.

It was beyond annoying.

"You want to talk about her?"

"Nope."

Graham stared at the stump. Nothing. It looked like nothing

but a busted-up, mangled mess. "The irony of this project isn't just annoying, it's becoming prophetic. Remind me to become a hermit."

There was nothing much to say to that, so Easton didn't. Instead, he looked up at the sky.

"Storm's coming in this afternoon. Gonna be a bad one."

"And?"

"And I saw your woman this morning. I went to the big house to see Jax before he leaves. She looked like she was having a tough time of it."

Grunting, Graham finally reached for a beer, popping it open on the arm of his lawn chair. "Zoey's not my woman. And it ended last night, whatever it was. Or wasn't. Can we talk about something else?"

"She still planning on that ATV tour?"

Apparently, they couldn't.

"She wouldn't go out in that. Zoey's not an idiot."

"She went out with you."

Frowning, Graham took a long pull of his beer. "What's that supposed to mean?"

"It means you're the idiot. You knew what you were doing." Easton leveled a look at him. "When you walked over to her in Rick's, you knew exactly the kind of mess you were stepping in. Punishing her for it now, when things are exactly how you knew they'd be, is cruel."

A muscle in his jaw twitched, but Graham said nothing.

Settling deeper in his chair, Easton scratched a thumbnail under the condensation-softened label. "I suppose picking a fight with her was a lot easier than sticking around until the end. This way, it's on her."

"If you're trying to be an ass, you're succeeding."

Easton didn't even blink at the acid in Graham's tone.

"Man up. If you care about her, then don't let her go home feeling bad. It's not like you can go find her next week and apologize."

"East, buddy, I want to show you something." Pulling his cell phone out of his pocket, Graham smacked it down on the arm of his lawn chair a little too hard. "It's this new technology that somehow manages to connect people all across the world. All you have to do is pick it up and make the call."

"You plan on making that call?"

They both knew he wouldn't.

"The storm's going to be real bad." Easton looked up at the sky as the first streaks of lightning flashed in the distance. "They'll cancel the tour."

Of course they would. And like Graham, it would just be one more disappointment for her.

———————

Zoey had always known ending things with Graham would hurt. How could it not? Whatever this was, it was real. Temporary, maybe, but always real.

Zoey really, truly loved him. Of all the ways she'd thought they would say goodbye, a blowout in her hotel room was not anywhere close to the plan. Instead of bittersweet, there was only bitter tears and pain.

Mostly, there was just pain.

Throughout the worst, Lana stayed by her side. Between the ice cream for breakfast for Zoey and a massive Bloody Mary for Lana, they decided men in general weren't worth half the amount of annoyance they caused. They plotted the havoc they would wreak on the people who had messed with Lana and spent more than the recommended time in the steam room, sweating away the night before. And not a bit of it did any good, beyond increasing her blood sugar and opening her pores, because there wasn't an indulgence in the world as good as having Graham Barnett smiling down on her, his hands in her hair, his lips pressing soft kisses along her skin. Seeing Easton and Jax in the lobby had been awkward and awful, both men giving her sympathetic looks that only made her feel worse.

Sometime in the late morning, a mass of heavy storm clouds rolled in, and by the time Zoey should have been getting ready for her final Alaskan adventure—an ATV tour—she was sitting on hold, trying to find out if the tour had been canceled instead. Logic would have assumed Moose Springs Adventurers would have called to let her know, but the helpfulness would have been inconsistent with their consistently bad customer service.

"Well, they canceled it," Zoey finally said with a sigh, ending the call. "I guess my vacation is officially over."

"You still have today and tomorrow, love," Lana answered. "We'll find something worth doing. What do you think? Should we scooch everything over a bit?"

Lounging in a chair at Lana's conference table in the penthouse suite, Zoey turned a slow, lazy circle. By scooch, Lana meant move the entirety of the planned condominium complex over, cutting into land Zoey was fairly sure was a national forest.

"Maybe not so much," she replied, turning another circle. The shadows of dark grays and even darker blues across the mountainsides were as striking as they were ominous. Still, it burned at her to spend today in a hotel, staring out a window instead of being out there, where all the best experiences were.

"Hmm. Killian, I need your advice."

So far, Zoey had done a decent job of ignoring the three people in the corner of the suite. Like Zoey, they were lounging, but with far more indulgence. Haleigh had called room service twice in the time Zoey and Lana had been there, and Enzo was deep in a bottle of cognac. Sober but clearly bored, Killian craned his neck to see what Lana was doing.

"I'm sure you have it handled." With a yawn, Killian kicked a foot up on the custom-built gleaming cedar coffee table.

"It's your investment too," Lana reminded him. "The Montgomery Group's holdings affect all of us, cousin, so half an interest on your side isn't going to kill you."

"Are you sure?" Killian rolled to his feet. "My father might feel otherwise." Wandering over, Killian dropped down into the chair next to Zoey, giving her a kind smile. "I heard you and your boyfriend broke up. You okay?"

"We weren't…" With a soft sigh, Zoey shrugged. "I'm not great. Wishing I could get out of here and do something fun to distract myself. But they cancelled my ATV thing."

"Then we should uncancel it."

"Never mind. I'll just decide all these incredibly expensive plans all on my own," Lana murmured.

Killian winked at Zoey, knowing he'd annoyed his cousin. The wink was so similar to Graham, Zoey had to look away. Her phone was in her pocket, and she didn't allow herself to check to see if he'd called. The last twenty times she had, the screen had been blank.

"What do you mean, uncancel it?"

Leaning over, Killian dropped his voice low, nodding his chin at Enzo and Haleigh. "At the risk of coming off like my friends over there, some things, money can buy. A quick trip through the woods in the rain is one of those things. I'd hate for you to miss out, and if we make it quick, we should be back before the worst hits. Assuming you won't mind getting a little wet and muddy?"

His suggestion was reckless and maybe even a little scary. Definitely not something she'd planned. But maybe Zoey was feeling reckless today. And mud was not something she'd ever been afraid of.

"I don't have much to help pay for it," she admitted.

"Consider it my way of saying sorry for your bad day. Us guys suck." Patting her hand, Killian stood.

"We were just saying the same thing this morning." Zoey nodded at him in gratitude. "But thank you, Killian. You're kind. And much better than polo Killian."

He blinked in surprise. "You're the only one who thinks so." Taking hold of the back of Lana's chair, Killian tugged her just out of reach of her miniature Moose Springs village. "Come with us. You need a break."

"Sorry, dearest, I have a conference call scheduled with our Realtor. It seems we're already having offers on the new construction."

"By all means," he drawled lazily. "Make us some money then. That's why the family loves you."

Was there a note of discontent in Killian's voice? Zoey didn't know him enough to tell, but she did know him well enough to not be surprised when ten minutes later, they had a car waiting for them downstairs to take them to an off-site four-wheeling company. Zoey didn't even care that Enzo and Haleigh came too, Killian's constant entourage.

Dressed in a borrowed raincoat, her warmest sweater, and a pair of hiking boots, Zoey wished she had something better than a ball cap to keep the light rain off her face. If she'd been thinking clearly—not numb from parting ways with Graham so abruptly and painfully—maybe she would have thought to bring a pair of goggles to cover her glasses. If the rain got worse, seeing was going to be a whole lot harder.

Their guide, Cory, was young, cheerful, and more than happy to take a quick jaunt out into the woods. After explaining how to run the ATVs and giving everyone a few minutes to demonstrate their ability to stop, go, and go faster, Cory led them to a gate. Beyond the gate, a series of trails crisscrossed the mountain's government-protected lands. Killian went first, followed by Haleigh, then Enzo, with Zoey happy to bring up the rear. Without someone behind her, she was in the best spot to see the wilderness around her. And on such tight paths, often she lost sight of Enzo's ATV, meaning for a moment, she could enjoy this incredible place all alone.

The heavier the storm clouds, the darker the woods, enough that the running lights on the ATVs were actually useful. But the wind whipping through her hair, the trees and thick underbrush streaming past as they drove down the path were exhilarating. Every time they hit a mud puddle, splashed through a creek, or got to gun the vehicles around a curve, Zoey felt sheer delight. Only realizing now that Haleigh and Enzo were adrenaline junkies, Zoey could hear them whooping through the worst of the trail's bumps and mud splashes. She couldn't see Killian, but she could hear his voice, sounding just as happy as his friends.

Following Enzo as they turned at a wood marker post, they slowed down. Eventually, the trail ended, and they turned back around. The guide indicated for them to all cut their engines so he could talk to them over the wind blowing through the trees.

"Normally, we go down this trail, down to the river, and then get some pictures by the waterfall," Cory said, clearly unfazed by the rain and wind. "But it's going to get muddy. It's up to you."

They glanced at each other, but Killian only hopped off his ATV when Zoey nodded.

"Let's do this," he said.

The trail was often used by grizzlies, which made it even more exciting. They slipped and slid down a very steep path leading down to a river, and Cory was right. The waterfall was absolutely great to take pictures in front of. Zoey was never going to enjoy the company of Enzo and Haleigh, but she was more than happy to squeeze in with them, enjoying herself immensely as Cory hung dangerously off the side of a tree, taking pictures of them.

Over the rushing of the waterfall, a crash of thunder made Zoey jump, then laugh because Killian had jumped too.

"I hate to say it, but this is getting bad." Their guide cast around. "We need to get in. The lightning is coming."

The path back up the trail wasn't nearly as easy as the way down. The light rain turned heavier, and the slick slope became a muddy mess, requiring linked arms around tree trunks and chained hands to get back up. By the time they managed the climb, it was dangerously dark. Cory pulled out a light, but Zoey caught a glance of his face and saw true concern.

"Come on. We need to hurry," he shouted at them, his voice nearly lost in the screaming wind. "We stayed too long!"

That was when the rain hit. Sheeting so bad Zoey could barely see in front of her, she was grateful for Killian keeping a hand on her arm as if afraid he would lose her over the edge of the cliff they knew was only feet away from them. The exhilaration quickly turned to fear as lighting filled the sky, the thunder rocking them.

They raced to the ATVs, starting them up. "Stay together!" Cory yelled, twisting to make sure they all were there before he stood up, pointed the direction of the trail, and took off. Killian and Haleigh raced after them, but Enzo's ATV stalled. Cursing, he fought it before it caught gear, then he gunned forward, spinning mud and grass all over Zoey.

"Wait, I can't see!" Zoey yelled, slowing enough to wipe the mud from her glasses on the relative dryness of her shirt beneath her raincoat. It was a streaked mess, with splatters of muck mixing with rain on the lenses.

Frustrated, she wiped them again, cleaning them enough so

she could see. Even as she put them back on, her glasses were already covered with more rain. But Zoey couldn't wait any longer. Hitting the accelerator, she took off dangerously fast, barely able to see the trail and hoping to glimpse Enzo's taillights ahead. She never did. Through twist and turn, she tried to find her way, but in the stormy darkness, it was impossible to recognize anything.

Finally, she saw a familiar wooden marker post, but as she paused, trying to wipe the water from her glasses, Zoey couldn't tell which way she was supposed to go. She didn't know if the water rushing past her was because of the storm or if this was even the marker post she thought it was.

And as the storm unleashed itself, the skies opening right on top of her, Zoey knew she was screwed.

Answering a call from this particular person was the last thing Graham wanted to do. But Graham meant it when he said Lana was his friend, and when a friend called, he picked up—most of the time.

Besides, she'd called him three times in a row and seemed determined not to be ignored.

"What is it, L?" Maybe he was a teeny bit grumpy. "I'm busy being brokenhearted over here."

"Graham, something happened." Lana's voice was panicked. "I need Easton's number. He can find people, right?"

Standing up from his kitchen chair, Graham tensed. "Lana, calm down. I can get you to East, but tell me what happened first."

"They went out on a tour, and when they came back, she was gone. They tried to find her, but she's missing."

"Who's missing?"

"Zoey. Graham, she's out in this. Someone needs to find her."

With a curse, Graham told Lana to stay by her phone. This wasn't the first time someone had gotten lost in these mountains. This wasn't the first time this year someone had gotten lost in these mountains. But this wasn't someone, it was Graham's someone, and the storm outside raged. Graham knew far too well how much danger she was in, and his heart stayed in his stomach, twisted up in knots as he called everyone he knew to meet them at the ATV tour site.

Easton and Ash pulled up right as Graham skidded into the drive, both dressed for the weather and grim faced. Jonah, Rick, Marcus Garcia and his partner, even Frankie and Graham's cousin…everyone who knew these mountains was there. Even Lana was there, although she was the last person Graham would send into the mountains to look for Zoey.

They all knew how bad this was.

The kid, Cory, was young and stupid enough to have taken them out. He was also brave enough to have spent the last hour trying to find Zoey, soaked to the bone and pale from cold. He told the same story to Easton and Graham, how he made sure they were all there. How he paused halfway back, thought he saw four sets of lights behind him, and kept going.

The kid was crushed, his hands shivering. "Maybe it was the last guy going over a bump? The rain was so bad. I screwed up, I screwed up. I sent them all to the resort to get help, and I went looking for her. I need to go back out there and keep searching. She's out there because of me."

The storm had whipped itself into a frenzy, with trees bending from the violent gusts of winds and sheets of sideways rain driving into anyone not taking cover. The skies had grown dangerously dark for anyone out in the woods. Streak after streak of lightning cutting through the darkness illuminated Easton's features.

"Cory, you're not going anywhere," Easton said sternly, taking control of the group. "You're dead on your feet, and this will turn into a double rescue instead of just her. We can't risk anyone going out in this."

Graham inhaled a tight breath, drawing himself up furiously, ready to fight, but Easton shot him a look. "Until it clears off, just the three of us will look. Ash, Graham, you follow the trail they were supposed to be on. You both know these woods blindfolded. Don't let a tree fall on you, and keep those radios on. I'll scout wider. But no one else."

"Without a bigger search party, we might not find her." Ash didn't need to add the unspoken "in time." They all knew what she was thinking.

"It's the best we can do for now." Easton turned to Jonah and Marcus. "As soon as the weather breaks, get dogs out here and get everyone involved."

Taking his supplies and a gassed-up ATV, Graham looked at Ash. "We'll find her," she promised.

Sometimes people got lost in these mountains and never came back. But Graham wasn't going to come back without her, weather be damned. He'd left her thinking he didn't love her, and if that was the last conversation they had, Graham would never be able to forgive himself.

"We'll find her." Graham started the engine with a snarl of his own. "And then I'm never letting her go again."

As they retraced the trail Cory had taken, the visibility was nearly nonexistent. Graham bellowed himself hoarse calling Zoey's name, knowing Ash was doing the same just behind him. And still he could barely hear her. Rain and wind beat at them from all directions, and the storm had brought down tree limbs into their path. They rounded a corner and found a huge evergreen had downed across the trail, impossible to get around.

"What do you want to do?" Ash leaned into his shoulder, yelling into his ear to be heard. "Do you want to keep going?"

"I'm not leaving her out here!"

Pink hair plastered to her face, Ash nodded. "I'll radio East and let him know we're going ahead on foot."

The fallen tree was massive, and Graham was still trying to find a good place to go over it when Ash came back, waving her radio in her hand.

"It's Easton! He found her!"

"Is she okay?"

"I don't know. I could barely hear him. But he says come back in."

Zoey stood in the center of the angry mass of people in the hotel lobby, holding a blanket Easton had found her wrapped tight around her shoulders. He hadn't left her side since returning to the resort, standing so close her shoulder brushed his arm.

She just couldn't get warm, no matter how much body heat Easton gave off.

"You need to sit," Easton rumbled, his gravelly voice like a slow rockslide. "You're pale as a sheet."

"I'm fine. Just cold."

Which was mostly true. Zoey was physically fine, if more than a little shaken up. She didn't know how long she'd been lost, trying to find her way back to the trail, but she'd hit deep mud and gotten stuck. Faced with staying on the ATV and in the path of rising water or backtracking on foot, she'd chosen to go it on foot. Terrified and half-drowned, Zoey had turned a bend and there he'd been, a massive, bearded man in the woods. Even if her rescuer had looked like Sasquatch on an ATV, she had nearly cried in relief, desperately grateful to not be alone.

Zoey hadn't even realized until they were in front of the lights of his ATV that Easton Lockett was the one who'd found her.

Once, Graham had told her Easton knew these woods better than anyone, and now Zoey believed it. Arms around his waist, she'd simply held on as he took trail after trail, cut across a field she only vaguely recognized from her horseback-riding trip, and ended up at the barn Mugs had rejected her in. Grateful to be out of the rain, Zoey waited as Easton radioed that she had been found.

Assuring her that no one would mind, Easton borrowed one of the stable's work trucks, driving her back to the resort. He could have left her there, his work done, but the storm had knocked out the hotel's power, and the hotel had descended into chaos as the computer systems went down. Everyone's keycards were no longer working, and no one could get in their rooms. Hundreds of more important—or at least angrier—people than Zoey were screaming at the overwhelmed staff.

Lana was in the midst of it, fighting for their place in line, determined that Zoey was going to get her hot shower before she died from pneumonia. A hot shower or some time in the sauna followed by a change of clothes would be awesome, but Zoey doubted that would happen anytime soon.

She should sit, but Zoey was rattled enough that she couldn't. Besides, there wasn't anywhere to sit but the floor, and she wasn't sure she could find a corner where she wouldn't accidentally get trampled.

Easton moved closer, his heavy hand coming down on her shoulder. Zoey was too exhausted and emotionally ravaged to feel intimidated by his presence. This was Graham's friend, and in this moment, he was her friend too. So she leaned into his hand, thinking she was dangerously close to becoming a pile of muddy Mickey Mouse sweatshirt and muddier jeans on the floor.

"Screw this," Easton suddenly growled. "I'm taking you back to Graham's place."

"I can't. He doesn't want me there."

The mountain at her side snorted. "If he doesn't want you there, he's doing a terrible job of acting like it. Come on."

The hand on her shoulder became a heavy arm around her shoulders as Easton steered her toward the hotel entrance. She was too exhausted to fight him and too overwhelmed by the other resort guests to want to stay in the lobby any longer.

THE TOURIST ATTRACTION 357

"Okay, but I need to tell Lana."

There were so many people in between her and the desk that there was no way Zoey could even start to find her friend.

"*Zoey.*"

A bellman almost lost a limb when one of the entry doors slammed open with far too much force. When Graham's familiar voice roared her name over the angry yelling all around her, Zoey's heart leapt in her chest.

Easton was head and shoulders above everyone else, but Graham was tall and strong and *pissed*, wearing almost as much mud as she was.

She hadn't realized how much she needed him until his eyes locked onto her from across the lobby. Graham didn't part the crowd as he strode toward her...he walked right over them. Ignoring more than one offended look and harsh word, he bulldozed his way to her. He crushed her into his body, arms wrapping around her shoulders.

"Are you okay?" Graham rasped, voice harsh and desperate. "Are you hurt?"

He stepped back a little and ran his hands over her body, checking her for injuries even as he hauled her close.

"I'm okay. Easton found me."

"Thank God." Then those warm, strong hands were tilting her face up, tracing her jaw, tangling into her soaked and bedraggled hair.

"I can't believe my glasses survived all that. Look, the tape held."

Even Zoey could hear the edge of hysteria in her voice. Graham must have heard it too, because he tightened his arms around her even more.

"Zoey. What happened out there?"

Her answer was muffled by his chest as she whispered, "It was a bad morning. Killian was trying to be nice, offering a trip out when mine had been canceled. We knew we were going to get muddy, but we were planning on getting back before the storm hit."

Graham shook his head. "It doesn't work that way. These summer storms hit fast."

"Don't interrupt her," Easton grunted. "Keep going."

"We went down that hill to the waterfall to take pictures, but we stayed too long, and the storm started getting bad. We raced back, and I was the last of the group, and the ground was a mess. They took off, but it kicked mud up into my face. I couldn't see and..."

She trailed off. At her side, Easton went still. Graham's eyes widened, then his tanned features went pale with rage.

"They *left* you?"

Even with her silence, Zoey knew the truth was written all over her face.

"I tried, but I couldn't remember my way back. Then the four-wheeler got stuck, and I scratched up my glasses. I'm so glad Easton found me." She didn't add how terrifying it had been to be lost in the woods alone in such a violent storm. "It's my own fault. My decision to go out in the weather, my decision to stay too long at the waterfall. It's no one's fault but mine."

"I found her on Switchback Trail," Easton growled. "She was headed right for the ravine. In that visibility..."

A shudder of sheer rage rolled through him, and then Graham was twisting on his heel, heading right for Killian.

"Graham, don't!" Zoey tried to stop him, grabbing for Graham's arm, but he ignored her as he stalked up to Lana's cousin.

"You left her?" With a snarl, Graham shoved Killian backward. "She could have *died* out there."

"It wasn't his fault," Zoey tried, but he wasn't listening to her.

"Hey, we didn't even know she wasn't there until we got back." Killian held up his hands in defense, but Graham didn't bother to wait for an explanation. Even over the crowd, Zoey could hear the crunch of a nose when Graham slammed his fist into Killian's handsome face.

Easton breathed out a curse, pushing Zoey behind him just as Graham tackled Killian around the waist. Both men fell into the delicately carved cedar statues decorating that side of the lobby. Killian wasn't going down without a fight, but Graham had lost it completely. He had the other man beneath him, slamming his fists into Killian's face and torso.

"Graham, stop!" Zoey yelled again.

"Enough," Easton barked. "He's *done*, man."

When Graham ignored them both, Easton strode forward, forcefully hauling Graham off Killian. Zoey caught a brief glance of Lana crouching by Killian, helping him sit up, but her attention was diverted as Hannah shoved her way into the mess. Just as the lights flickered back on, Hannah grabbed Graham's shirt, forcing him to listen to her. "Out! Get out of my hotel, Graham. Don't come back here."

For a long moment, Graham just stared in sheer hatred at

Killian, then he stepped back, away from Hannah, away from Zoey, away from all of them.

"Graham," Zoey started, but he shook his head.

"Don't. I knew better than to start this with you. Just don't, Zo."

———————

A hot shower would have been amazing. Theoretically.

Too many guests had the exact same idea as Zoey, leaving the water pressure less than impressive and the temperature lukewarm at best. Still, it was good to wash the mud from her hair, face, and limbs.

Lana was waiting for her when Zoey came out, bundled up in one of the thick bathrobes provided by the hotel. Brush in hand, Lana settled on the couch next to her. Letting her friend brush her already combed hair was incredibly soothing to her frazzled nerves. Even better than a hot shower would have been.

"He was frightened for you," Lana said softly. "I've known Graham for a long time, and I've never seen him so upset. When he realized you were still out in the storm, he went right out there. He'd still be out there if Easton hadn't found you. You should call him."

"Graham doesn't want whatever this is, Lana. He made that crystal clear."

"That boy has no idea what he's doing, but how he *feels* is not up for negotiation." Setting the brush aside, Lana wrapped her arms around Zoey's shoulders, pulling her close. "I know a lot of people, dearest, but I think you're my only real friend." By the softness in her voice, Zoey knew Lana had been scared too.

"And as my only friend, it's my job to tell you that he loves you. If you love him too, he deserves to know. Even if this is done, he still should know."

Zoey nodded wordlessly, then leaned into Lana's shoulder, listening to the rain outside. Trying to find the courage to do something even more reckless than four-wheeling in a storm.

———————

Punching someone hurt like a son of a bitch.

It had been a long time since Graham had gotten into a real brawl. His temper had gotten him in more than one scuffle in high school, but it seemed like the only times he ended up in a full throw down was over a woman.

"Women are rough, Jake. You're lucky you're neutered."

From his place at Graham's feet, the border collie wagged his tail, acknowledging being acknowledged. Graham had been icing his busted knuckles on and off since he'd come home, and the swelling seemed to have reached the worst it was going to get. Two Tylenol had taken the edge off the soreness, but it would be a while before flexing his fingers didn't make him wince.

"Guess I'll have to close tomorrow. I deserve a day off, don't you think? You and I could hang out and lick our wounds together?"

Jake's ears perked, then he whined. His blind eyes followed the path of whatever vehicle was coming down the driveway.

"Whoever it is, they can keep on going," Graham grunted sourly.

Gravel crunched as the car came to a stop outside.

This time, Jake's whine was softer, happier, his tail wagging furiously as he wriggled and scooted toward the door. He only acted like that for one person.

They both only acted like that for one person.

When she knocked, Graham stayed at the table, staring down at the faded yellow tablecloth. Maybe it was time he changed it.

"Graham?" That voice, sweet but strong, was seared into his memory. He'd never forget her, not a single inch of her. "You don't have to let me in. I just need to know you're okay. You weren't picking up your phone."

No. No, he wasn't. Because it was still sitting in his bathroom, bloodied from Killian's face exploding all over them both.

"I just..." Zoey drifted off, then cleared her throat. "I just wanted to say thank you. Thank you for caring enough to look for me. I was really scared, and if it wasn't for you, I'd still be out there, still scared. So...thank you."

When Zoey fell quiet, Graham knew she would leave. If he just stayed in his seat, kept his heart and his eyes and his mouth shut, she would leave and this whole thing would be over. He could go back to life as normal.

That was the problem. Normal would never feel like normal again. Not after Zoey had walked into his life and wrapped her slender fingers around his heart. Right now, it felt like those fingers were squeezing for all they were worth.

But she was going to leave.

Right this instant, she was leaving.

Here, at his kitchen table, the rain thrumming on the metal roof, was where he lost her.

Jake whined again, more plaintively this time, but Graham was already on his feet. The border collie scooted out of the way as he opened the door.

"Haven't you spent enough time in the rain today?" he asked quietly.

She looked tiny on the other side of the screen door, still pale and drawn, but the fear no longer lingered in her eyes. It was the fear that had flipped his rage from barely contained to unreasonable in the big house. Graham couldn't stand it, the idea that she would ever be anything but safe.

Her palm was against the screen door. And when Zoey saw him, she sighed with the same longing that was tearing him apart and leaned her forehead against the screen.

"Thank you, Graham. For everything."

Closing his eyes, Graham placed his hand to the screen opposite hers, resting his forehead to Zoey's own.

And when her thumb pressed into his, the lightest of touches, Graham was done.

"I can't do this anymore." His words a desperate rasp of misery as all reason abandoned him.

"I know. I just—"

Jerking open the screen door, Graham took her face in his hands and kissed her. He kissed her because not kissing her was like trying to swim backward in a riptide. Whether he liked it or not, his heart had pulled him to her, and there was no going back now. She was leaving, and Graham couldn't do a damn thing to stop that.

All he could do was make the most of what time they had left.

When Zoey pulled away, breathless and eyes wide, Graham

allowed himself a moment to let this sink in. To enjoy the anticipation of having her in his arms. Running a thumb along her jaw in silent question, he waited for her. And when she nodded, reaching for him, wrapping her arms around his neck, Graham picked her up, walked a few steps, and set her on the counter.

He closed the door with his free hand, locking it this time because he was *not* getting interrupted. Wanting her was like breathing, an involuntary reaction necessary for survival. Touching her was coming home. Never had Graham known how lost he was, but he was lost without her.

Tonight proved it.

"You're breaking my heart, Zoey Bear. You know that, right?" Those gorgeous eyes gleamed with instant tears. She started to pull back, but Graham shook his head, smiling against her lips. "You're worth it. You've always been worth it."

"Graham? I love you."

Brokenhearted wasn't anywhere close to what this felt like. With four soft words, she had *destroyed* him.

And as he drew her into his arms, into his bed and too deep into his life, Graham knew that no one else would be able to fix what loving her had done to him.

CHAPTER 17

THE SUN NEVER REALLY SET up there, leaving a soft glow of gray light around the edges of the window shade. After two weeks of sleeping on a couch, it felt good to curl up on a real bed, a pillow beneath her head that wasn't starched and perfectly pressed. This pillow was soft and lumpy and real. It smelled like shampoo and Graham, deodorant and bakery bread, and was warm like the space next to her in the now empty bed.

For a moment, it hurt like nothing had ever hurt before, waking up in his bed alone. But then Zoey opened her eyes and saw the small take-out bag on the nightstand next to her, with the label marked from that morning. Opening the bag revealed a cinnamon roll from Frankie's.

He'd snuck out of bed and gotten her favorite breakfast. A whole different kind of warmth filled her, and Zoey rolled onto her back, wriggling deeper in the bedding.

"You get points for that one," she decided.

He got points for more than breakfast. As she closed her eyes, memories of last night curled around her as pleasantly as Graham's arms had as she slept. Being with Graham was a perfect combination of sweet kisses and soft teasing, tempering an otherwise unbridled passion that left her shivering in remembrance. He'd put it all on the table, letting her see how much he wanted her.

The sound of a chainsaw was muted enough she almost didn't notice it, so lost in her memories. Curious, Zoey rose out of bed—nearly stepping on a snoozing Jake.

"Sorry," she murmured, patting his head before peering out the window. The large door to Graham's workshop was swung closed but still slightly ajar.

"What's he up to, Jake? Or did he just wander off on you like normal?"

The border collie wagged his tail adorably in answer.

After dressing, Zoey found a sticky note on the bathroom mirror pointing at a still packaged toothbrush sitting on the counter. Smiling to herself at his thoughtfulness, she finished getting ready, then headed outside.

Graham had moved outside his workshop, chainsaw in hands and welding mask over his face. There was a looseness to his stance, a relaxation to his shoulders that matched what Zoey felt. Circling the log, Graham seemed to consider it, tilting his head to the right for a moment. Then he lifted the chainsaw higher and started carving.

Watching him work fascinated Zoey. By the time he was done, little bits of wood and a thin coating of sawdust clung to his arms and chest. Graham set the chainsaw aside, pushing the welding mask up from his face. He eyed his work critically but for once seemed pleased with the result. As Graham ran a careful thumb along the newly carved lines in the log, Zoey couldn't help but remember the night before.

That was how he touched her too.

"Hey there, Zoey Bear," Graham murmured sweetly. "Did I wake you up?"

"Only in the good way."

Meeting him at the log, Zoey went up on her toes and kissed his cheek. The corners of his eyes crinkled as she made a face, wiping her lips to remove sawdust from them.

"The fiber's good for you," he reminded her even as he peeled his shirt off and used the inside of the fabric to scrub his face and neck clean of debris.

The view around her was fabulous, but the view in front of her was good enough to leave her mouth watering.

Remembering those same broad shoulders and muscled arms from last night, she closed the distance between them. Tracing her palms over his stomach, Zoey felt his muscles contract beneath her touch. When she glanced up at him, Graham was watching her with heat in his eyes.

"Sorry, not sorry. The goods were on display."

Snorting a laugh, Graham wrapped his hands around her hips and pulled her closer. "Voyeur."

"Maybe."

They snuck into the workshop, craving privacy even though they were alone. The steel shipping container that had once freaked her out was now the perfect place to wrap her arms around Graham's waist. This time, there wasn't sawdust when she kissed him, only the hint of coffee and the same minty toothpaste she'd used herself. Graham deepened the kiss, taking a step forward so that her hips bumped his work bench. Sitting on top of the bench worked a lot better. Zoey didn't have to crane her head back to kiss him, and his muscled torso was far more accessible.

Graham kissed his way down the side of her neck, nipping lightly at the junction of her shoulder and making her tighten her knees into his hips.

"Here?" she murmured.

"Why not?"

"Because I'll get splinters in my butt. And other places."

He hoisted her off the bench, turning and settling down on a cheap folding chair with her on his lap. "There. Safe and sound."

"Aren't we too heavy for this?" she asked.

"Naw." His mouth pressed slow, deliberate kisses along her pulse point, leaving her heart racing. Safe and sound wasn't the descriptor Zoey would have used for how Graham made her feel. Burning alive from the inside out was far closer. And as she leaned in to kiss him again, she knew she never wanted this feeling to end.

Eventually, she abandoned his lap for his artwork. Or what he hoped was art.

Graham watched Zoey move about his workshop, slender fingers tracing the lines of his most recent failure like it was something precious. "This is beautiful."

"It's better, but it's not..." Graham trailed off, swallowing the knee-jerk reaction to joke about what was wrong with the carving. "It's better," he finally said. "Zoey?"

"Hmm?"

"Did you ever watch *Ghost*?"

She snickered, moving deeper into the workshop. "If you're suggesting we recreate the pottery wheel scene with a chainsaw and wood chips flying, you're reaching high."

"It's not my fault you're top shelf."

Her cheeks flushed at the compliment, eyes dropping down to what was supposed to be a chair. It was more like a butt-sized bowl chopped out of a stump.

"I love this."

Graham loved her, but he had absolutely no idea what to do about it. The only logical option was to follow her around the shop, a puppy on a string that she had no idea was tied to her pinkie finger. She rounded the table and ended up back at the butt stump. It didn't fit Graham at all, but it was perfect for her. When Zoey wriggled in delight when the seat ended up holding her curves perfectly, Graham was done.

"Hey, Zo?"

"Hmm?"

"I like your glasses."

"No one likes my glasses."

"I do." He gently took them off her face, leaving her blinking owlishly at him. Smiling, he replaced them on her nose. "That's why I don't want to scratch them."

"Why would you scratch them?"

"Because I want to recreate *Ghost*." Graham covered her glasses with his welding mask.

"You want to carve things with a chainsaw all sexy like with a half-blind woman in a welding mask?"

"Well, when you put it that way...yes. Absolutely."

He led her outside where they clipped Jake to his tie-out on the porch so he wouldn't be in reach of any flying wood chips. Then, in the exact same place where she'd once kicked him and run screaming because of his chainsaw, Zoey hefted her own chainsaw and gave him an excited grin.

Teaching Zoey to carve was fun, even though it was louder than pottery, and they didn't have a killer theme song. Arms around her to guide the movements of the saw, Graham helped her carve her name into a chunk of cedar. Then, because he was an absolute idiot for her, he added Jake's name too with a few three-dimensional hearts surrounding both.

"Don't tell anyone I'm this lame," Graham whispered against her neck when they'd turned off the saw.

"Oh, I'm telling everyone," Zoey promised.

She squealed when he made a playful grab for her. This time, Graham didn't suffer any physical pain or have the cops called for running after Zoey in his yard. Instead, he ended up with the woman of his dreams in his arms as Jake barked from the porch, whining because he wanted in on the fun.

"House?" he asked her, because she had that look in her eye, the one he couldn't say no to.

"I have a better idea." When she dragged him back into the workshop instead, Graham remembered all over again why she was perfect for him.

There were logistical issues with making love in a woodworker's workshop. Still, Graham didn't think he'd made too much of a mess of things. Afterward, Zoey curled up on a bench he had made, her head pillowed on his balled-up, sawdusty shirt as she

THE TOURIST ATTRACTION 371

took a nap, simultaneously the cutest and sexiest thing Graham had ever seen.

He didn't blame her for being exhausted. Yesterday's ordeal would have been enough for anyone to be worn down, but Graham had spent the night showing her how much she mattered to him. He'd taken his time, careful to make sure their passion wasn't one-sided. Watching her fall apart in his arms had been one of the best experiences of his life.

Now the little tourist who had stolen his heart had also stolen his bench. And he didn't mind one single bit. Unwilling to wake her up, Graham untied Jake and went about organizing his shop instead of continuing to carve. Jake had been napping at her feet, but at the sound of gravel crunching beneath tires, he lifted his head and gave a warning woof.

"I know, buddy. I'm not sure who thinks it's a good idea to bother us right now."

Us. Him and Zoey and Jake. Graham's little island of happiness that he didn't want invaded just then.

She could sleep through anything, even Easton's hulking figure appearing in the doorway. "We need to talk." He must have noticed her—how could he not—because Easton kept his voice low.

"Then talk." Graham continued wiping down a smaller half-finished piece of art, considering his next cuts.

"In private."

Glancing at Zoey, Graham nodded and followed his friend outside. It took a lot to rattle Easton, but he looked shaken.

"Lana's got too much sway. The council is going to agree to the project."

Inhaling a deep, steadying breath, Graham counted to three. Then ten. Then thirty. "So that's it?" he finally asked.

"That's it."

Exhaling explosively, Graham folded his arms over his chest. Two days ago, it was the worst news he could possibly have imagined. But compared to what he was about to lose, Graham struggled to find the emotions he normally would have felt on hearing his town was about to be ruined.

"Maybe it's for the better." Nudging a cedar chip with the side of his work boot, Graham looked at the trees rising around him. "Maybe L will do this right."

Easton didn't seem convinced, but there was nothing either of them could do at this point. Discussing it only left them both without any ideas, so they talked about Easton's climbing season instead. He was considering taking one more group up Mount Veil, the beast of a mountain not far from Moose Springs, but it was risky. This late in the season, the cold weather could hit fast and hard up there. Eventually, Easton went home, leaving Graham to consider his little home and what would become of it.

He went back inside his workshop, because contemplating his future felt a little rough right now. It was easier, better to contemplate her. Zoey was awake, sitting up on his workbench when he returned. Graham went to her, gazing down, memorizing her in that moment.

"You leave tomorrow morning?"

She nodded, sadness in her eyes. That just wouldn't do.

"We'll worry about tomorrow when it happens." Graham kissed her again, soft, slow kisses, then he pressed his face to her neck, stealing one more kiss as he murmured, "This is your last day in Moose Springs. How do you want to spend it before we say goodbye? What is the epic adventure of your dreams?"

Anything. He'd do anything she wanted.

"No goodbyes. From now until I leave, I just want to do this."

Smiling against her skin, Graham nodded. He'd always known she was perfect.

———————

Zoey's bags were packed. Her heart was shattering, but she'd wrapped cellophane and duct tape around what pieces were left, and she'd packed that too. It was time to go home, away from this amazing, wild place that had crawled into her soul.

It was time to leave the man who'd done the same.

"When will I see you again?" Lana asked, unusually subdued as she watched Zoey double-check their room for any forgotten items.

"When are you heading down the highway at midnight again?" Zoey shot Lana a little smile. "I'll keep the coffee on for you."

"Zoey? Be my assistant. Or just be my friend, and we'll work out the finances later. I hate that we can't spend the time together I want to spend with you. You're the only real friend I have."

Reaching out her arms, Zoey hugged her tight. "We both know that's the best way to mess up a good thing. Let's just stay in touch and see each other as often as possible."

Lana hugged her right back, and when she pulled away, there were tears in her eyes. "Well, I don't know about some people, but I adore the truck stop in Mudgeton. It's the place to go, so of course I'll be there."

Deeply grateful for having Lana in her life, Zoey hugged her again, whispering goodbye.

The valet would have carried her suitcase, but Zoey only had the one. She wheeled it down the hall where Graham had asked her out to her favorite cinnamon roll breakfast, into the elevator they had used to escape the gala, across the lobby where Graham had lost his mind at the thought of her being left alone in the woods during a storm.

So many memories, too many memories. Good and bad and amazing and heartbreaking.

They'd already arranged for her rental car to be returned, so Zoey went to the desk instead.

An exhausted Hannah welcomed her. "Good morning, Ms. Caldwell. I hear you're leaving us today."

"I'm just Zoey," she replied softly. Just Zoey. Just a tourist who was destined to leave. Maybe Graham's ex would help him pick up the pieces of what this vacation had done to them. Maybe when Zoey got back home, she'd meet someone who could help her do the same.

"Are you okay?" Hannah asked, reaching out and squeezing her hand. "I know goodbyes are hard."

Overwhelmed by Hannah's kindness, Zoey had to fight not to cry.

"Some more than others." Hesitating, she asked, "He'll be okay, right?"

Intelligent eyes searched Zoey's face, and Hannah's expression softened. "He's tough. A big marshmallow, but he's tough as any of us up here. It's not an easy life, but Graham's made for it."

THE TOURIST ATTRACTION 375

Nodding, Zoey wiped at her eyes with the heel of her hand. "Good. Thank you. Umm, I need to have a car drive me to the airport, please. I called down yesterday to be put on the schedule."

"I would, but I think I might get in trouble for letting you." Hannah tilted her head toward the valet pickup. "He's been out there for an hour, waiting on you."

Through the windows, Zoey could see a moose-loved Dodge pickup truck was parked out front. A man who had changed her life, even as he opened her eyes, leaned against the hood. Gripping a single flower in his hand, he stared at the ground beneath his feet. Shoulders slumped, body language defeated.

Then Graham looked up, meeting her eyes through the glass. His gaze raked over her, his expression shifting to hunger, to pride, to so many amazing things as his body language changed.

Loving her hadn't broken him. Her leaving, that was what was crushing them both.

"For what it's worth, I was rooting for you two," Hannah told her, smiling sweetly.

At her side, Quinn's large eyes were gleaming. "I was too!"

Quinn burst into tears, leaving a groaning Hannah to attend to comforting her and Zoey to head outside.

"I thought we weren't saying goodbye," Zoey said, unable to keep from wrapping her arms around his waist.

"I couldn't let the B team of Moose Springs' rideshare drivers take you to the airport," Graham told her, voice husky as he leaned down and rested his forehead to hers.

"What about the Tourist Trap?"

"What about it?"

Zoey exhaled a breathy laugh. "You're incorrigible. You don't deserve that awesome place."

"Not at all." Graham slipped the flower into her hand before kissing her. "I'm not letting someone else take my last moments with you."

As she opened the passenger side door, Zoey found a roly-poly little stuffed moose sitting in the passenger seat, safely buckled in. Jake was in the back seat, his muzzle on his paws as if he knew something bad was happening.

"Jake picked that out. Something to remember us by," Graham told her. The softness of his voice and the pain in his eyes couldn't be hidden behind a plushy.

"He's a happy moose." Zoey climbed in the truck, hugging the moose to her stomach. "Thank you."

She didn't say that she didn't need a happy moose to remember him. Forgetting Graham would be like forgetting how to breathe…impossible and painful when tried.

The drive to Anchorage was quiet. Every time Zoey opened her mouth to tell him they could stay in touch, they could text or call, they could visit…she closed her mouth again. They could, but all that would do was delay the inevitable.

Graham's calloused, work-roughened hands gripped the steering wheel too hard, even though he smiled at her with that same lazy smile she loved when he caught her eye. Reaching over, he threaded his fingers through her own.

Unlike the poor steering wheel creaking beneath his clenching fist, he held her hand like it was as delicate as the flower he'd given her.

Rubbing his thumb across her knuckles, Graham pulled her wrist to his mouth, pressing the softest of kisses to the sensitive flesh. Then he pressed their entwined fingers to the top of his thigh as if holding her close just a little longer.

"Gonna miss you, darlin'."

Four words, and they cut into her soul.

"You're going to have a lot more free time to harass the poor tourists that come after me," Zoey joked.

He opened his mouth to make a joke, then closed it. "You know what? They're not so bad."

Counting to three silently in her head, Zoey waited for the pinched expression to come to his face, as if his words tasted of sour lemons. "You're so full of it," she teased.

"Yeah, I hate them. Super-duper can't stand them." Shooting her a grin, Graham shrugged. "Sorry, Zo, I can only make exceptions for you."

"Graham? People love you. It's okay to let them."

A pained expression crossed his handsome features, but Zoey plunged on, twisting to face him as the airport came into view at the end of the road.

"It's okay to be good at something you weren't planning on, and it's okay to enjoy being successful." She squeezed his fingers, hard. "Maybe it wasn't the plan, and it wasn't the dream, but you have a good life. You don't have to be embarrassed by your success. Use it to make your dreams happen. Let the masses buy a million reindeer dogs and then go attack cedar logs with your chainsaw like a crazy guy. You've earned the right to have the things you want."

Nodding, Graham didn't say anything. But his eyes said it all as he pulled up to the curb in front of the airport and turned to her.

"I can park in short-term parking," he offered, voice quiet, gaze scraping over her form. "I can wait with you for a while."

Zoey shook her head. "And drag this out? I'm barely keeping from bawling like a baby right now."

She turned around in the seat to say goodbye to Jake, running her fingers one last time through the border collie's silky coat. "Take care of him, Jake."

When Jake whined, Zoey dropped a kiss to the end of his nose. "You're a good dog. And he's a good man. Don't let him forget, okay?"

Zoey could feel the heat of tears stinging her eyes, even if she'd managed to keep them from falling. That lasted up until the moment his strong hands carefully cupped her face.

Gripping his biceps for strength, Zoey closed her eyes. "I don't like this part," she whispered, voice catching on the words.

"Me either." His thumbs brushed the wetness sliding down her cheeks. "Zoey? Some women walk in a room and turn a guy inside out. You turned me inside out, and I've never enjoyed anything more. Losing a woman like you screws a guy up good and hard." Graham's arms shook, but his hands slid into her hair, his forehead against hers. Voice thick with emotion, he said, "Screwed up or not, I wouldn't change the last two weeks for the world."

This kiss, their last one, lingered too long. A security guard started toward the truck, waving them on.

"Goodbye, Graham," she whispered.

"Goodbye, Zoey."

And then he let his hands drop.

There was nothing left to do. Zoey grabbed her Alaska bag and her suitcase and got out of the truck. By the time she reached the sliding door of the terminal entrance and looked back over her shoulder, Graham was gone.

———

As love stories went, Graham was pretty sure this one sucked.

The gas pedal wasn't his friend, and the planes coming in low over the inlet just rubbed this deeper into his soul. But he couldn't ask her to stay. Zoey was a strong, beautiful, independent woman, and he couldn't ask her to give up her life for his, no matter how much he wanted her. Even if he did, she'd say no. This wasn't a movie, there wasn't anything he could do, and adding that bit of rejection would only sour what had been the most bittersweet goodbye of his life.

There was a long drive between Anchorage and Moose Springs, and it was probably going to take every single one of those miles to convince himself that this was the right thing. He'd had to let her go. And after her, there would never be another tourist. Locals only, he was done. Graham couldn't do this to himself again. After her...

The road blurred, and Graham cursed, pulling over into the bird sanctuary just south of Anchorage. Across the road was a gun range, and the dichotomy of the two normally made him snort. Right now, nothing seemed funny. Nothing was right, nothing was good, nothing in his life fit anymore, not the way they'd fit. Somehow, for some reason completely beyond him, Zoey had fit him, and he'd fit her perfectly.

He wanted her shyness, her enthusiasm, her bravery, her recklessness, her strength. Her atrocious attempts at karaoke. Her arms around him as he slept. Zoey had the kind of drive Graham had never had in his own life, an ability to keep pushing on where he would have—where he *had*—rolled over and given up.

Inhaling a hard breath, Graham rubbed his fist over his chest. He hoped she found someone who loved her this much. Someone who thought it was cute when her glasses slipped on her nose. Someone who liked her tucked beneath his arm. Someone who gave a crap when those gorgeous eyes filled with tears. Someone Graham would have to kill, because the idea of her with someone else made him want to punch something.

The heart in his chest was clawing its way out, abandoning him for her. And his ass was sitting in his truck, doing nothing.

Paralyzed. Torn between fighting for what he needed and the fear of losing his dream again. She was art school all over, and he was sitting here and just taking it.

"Jake, I think I need a little help here." At Graham's soft whistle, the border collie hopped the seat divider, wiggling into his lap. Wrapping his arms around his puppy as tight as he dared, Graham picked up Jake and hugged him for a really long time, face buried in a furry neck.

After he had been thoroughly bathed in kisses, Graham sighed and returned Jake to the back seat.

"Get yourself together." Dragging his palms over his face, Graham shook his head. "It's just a girl."

His girl. The only girl he ever wanted for the rest of his stupid, freaking life.

Hands shaking, Graham set the hazard lights and pulled out his phone. It rang twice before she picked up. "Hey, Ash, I need a wingman right now. I just dropped off Zoey." Graham's voice was ragged and harsh in his ears. "Tell me to keep driving."

"Are you asking me for permission to be an idiot? Because you've never needed my permission before."

He didn't say anything, unable to formulate a sentence that didn't start and end with how messed up this was.

There was silence, then Ash added softly, "Graham? You love each other. It's okay to be upset. She's probably crying right now too."

Well. It was one thing for him to be upset, but when it was her? That just wouldn't do.

"Ash, I think I'm going to go do something stupid."

"Thank goodness." She exhaled heavily. "What took you so long? Easton put a hundred down that you wouldn't even make it to the airport."

"I like to draw things out and make it hard on everyone." Graham spun a three-point turn in the gravel, his suspension system protesting when he backed over a curb.

"Go get her, cowboy," Ash said, hanging up the phone.

That was exactly what Graham was planning. He had no idea what he was going to do when he got to her. He had no clue what to say, but he figured he'd start with, "Here's my heart and guts on a silver platter" and go from there.

"Come on," he snarled as the traffic grew heavier as he got closer to the airport. "Come *on*. How many people are leaving today? Is it mass exodus from Anchorage day?"

The airport was small, but this was the height of the tourist season. With so many visitors taking morning flights, the single road in and out of the airport was jam-packed with cars.

Smacking his hand on the steering wheel in frustration, Graham was forced to slow to a crawl. "Seriously? There was no one here before!"

Her plane was leaving soon, and he didn't have time for this Graham's heart buried itself somewhere below the bench seat. Finally, he'd had enough. Pulling to the side of the road, he hit the hazard lights.

"Come on, buddy," Graham said as he got out and opened the door. Slipping a leash on Jake, he tucked him into the crook of his arm and started running.

Graham was more of a stand and chop things type of guy rather than a sprint half a mile type of guy, but he wasn't too out of shape. Breathless but still alive by the time he reached the terminal, he ignored the long line of people waiting to get their tickets and cut his way in front.

"I need to get back to the gates," Graham told the airline attendant at the desk. "It's an emergency."

"I'm sorry, sir, but you're going to have to wait in line like everyone else. And you can't have that dog in here unsedated and uncrated."

"Don't worry, he's chill. And I'm talking an actual emergency."

"What's the emergency?"

Graham smacked his palms down on the desk. "Love story shit. Please, help a guy out."

"Sir. End of the line."

Well. This was about to get ugly.

It was a well-known truth for any traveler that jumping a security line was "frowned upon" and would probably result in consequences that Graham wouldn't enjoy, but he was kind of on a deadline here. So without further ado, he did just that.

Thank goodness the line was guarded by only two people, and both only blinked in surprise instead of tasing him when Graham hopped the gate holding Jake under one arm like a football. He flattened himself along the side of the tube-shaped X-ray machine, startling the poor man already standing inside.

"Good morning. Nice jacket. How you doing? Don't worry, guys. I'm not a terrorist. Jake, say hi."

With a bark, Jake did as he was asked. Graham bolted for the terminal, taking the stairs two at a time because there were way too many people on the escalators. Graham wasn't stupid. He knew he was in trouble, so he embraced his inner spy movie hero, stealing a shirt from the outside of the gift shop that he definitely would pay them back for. Pausing to pull on the bright orange and slightly too-tight shirt then stuffing his baseball cap in his back pocket, his disguise was complete.

"Try to be cool, boy," Graham muttered as he scooped up Jake again. In an airport this small, there were only two options: terminal to the left of the ginormous stuffed moose and terminal to the right of the ginormous stuffed moose. Dropping down to a fast walk to not draw any more attention, Graham took a chance and turned left at the moose, down the direction it was facing.

"Show me the way, big guy," Graham murmured, patting it

on the nose as he passed, ignoring the cries of dismay from a blond and a brunette as he stepped through their selfie shot.

"Anna, he ruined it," the blond wailed as Graham checked the departure screen and saw Zoey's plane was boarding from gate three. But gate three was right in front of him.

He didn't see her.

She was flying to Chicago via Seattle, and it only took Graham a moment to double-check her flight on the departures screen. He was at the right place, but that gate was empty of people except for a lone flight attendant still manning the ticket counter.

"No." He ran over, but the door was already closed and locked. "No no no, it's still here. Let me in."

"Sir, you can't go in there," the flight attendant told him. "Sir. The plane's leaving."

"I need to talk to someone on that plane. Just for a second, that's all I need. Can you radio the plane?"

The flight attendant kept shaking her head. "Sir, I'm sorry. It's too late."

It was too late. He'd waited too long. He should have just taken her hand and pulled her back into the truck, back into his arms. Jake whined, wiggling, so Graham set him down.

He never should have left Moose Springs that morning. He should have done so many things...

"I need a flight to Chicago. I need—"

"There are no more flights to Chicago today. That was the only one on the schedule. If you go back to the ticket counters, they can help you arrange a flight."

Standing at the floor-to-ceiling windows, there was nothing

Graham could do but watch Zoey's plane pulling away from the gate, taking his heart along with it. Jake pulled hard at the leash, trying to get to something behind Graham, but his eyes stayed glued to the plane.

"Zo…"

"Graham?"

That voice. The perfect voice seared into his soul. Heart jumping into his throat, Graham turned around.

She was sitting on a bench next to the cinnamon roll stand, the little stuffed happy moose he'd given her tucked against her hip and the largest cinnamon roll one could find until they got to Moose Springs balanced on her knee. Letting go of the leash, Jake bolted for her, a wiggling mass of happiness once again.

If only it were that easy for people.

Face red and splotchy from tears and arms full of Jake, Zoey raised her eyes up to him.

"I had my moment," she whispered. "I was waiting for the plane, and there was a car out there, just past the runway. This guy was parked next to a moose, trying to take a picture of it. And I got so mad because he should have known better. Moose matter. They're not cute, cuddly stuffed things. They matter. People love them and care if bad things happen to them. I care if bad things happen to them."

Zoey squeezed the stuffed toy, adding softly, "And I realized I couldn't leave."

"Because of the moose."

"Yeah. Because of the moose." She gave him a watery smile. "And because of the bears and the whales, the ice caves and the mountains. The bonfires and the cinnamon rolls and little horri-fied faces made of ketchup on reindeer dogs. I can't leave. This is where I want to be." Her smile strengthened. "That's a really tight shirt."

"I like the color," he admitted.

"I do too."

"Zoey, I want you." Inhaling a deep breath, Graham took a step toward her. "Darlin', I *need* you. What will it take to make us happen? Because I would do anything—"

When the three-hundred-pound security guard hit him, it was with the force of a freight train and the determination of a man who had never saved his airport before and was damn well going to save it today.

Graham didn't have a chance.

Face to a carpet that had seen the bottom of way too many people's feet, Graham's arms were wrenched behind his back, the guard using his greater weight to pin Graham in place. Jake started barking in alarm, but Zoey was quick enough to realize what was happening, keeping his leash too tight for him to reach the guard.

"Is this really necessary?" Graham grunted, the breath squeez-ing out of his lungs.

"Trespassing—" Wheeze wheeze. "In an airport—" Cough cough choke snort. "Is punishable—dang it. *Graham*?"

"Yeah, man." He eyeballed the guy on top of him. "Hey, Joey, do you think you can arrest me in a minute? I'm trying to win my dream girl here."

"How's it going?"

"Well, I'm getting spooned by you and not her, so you tell me."

The security guard groaned, shook his head, and then climbed back to his feet, allowing a squashed Graham to do the same. Joey bent over, hands on his knees, wheezing hard. "That's a long way to run. I should've turned left, not right."

Patting Joey on the back, Graham nodded. "Yeah, got to always turn left. And maybe focus on the cardio, buddy."

Joey gave him a thumbs-up, then lumbered over to a bench seat, dropping down. Waving off a pair of additional security officers, he flapped his hand at Graham to continue.

"As I was saying, I want you—"

Then Zoey's mouth was on his, tasting of icing and cinnamon, sweet and soft as she melted in his arms. Her eyes gleamed with held back tears. "Keep going. You stopped at the best part."

Groaning, Graham kissed her again, whispering against her lips, "I need you." Hands in her hair, he lingered over her mouth, adding, "And I will do anything to keep every inch of your perfect self in my life."

"I'm not going to be perfect for long." Zoey glanced ruefully at the plane taking off on the runway. "All my underwear's on that plane."

He couldn't help but kiss her again. "I'm probably about to get arrested."

When she laughed against his lips, Graham didn't care one bit if he ended up in jail for the second time over this one.

The life he wanted—the one he'd been waiting for—had started the moment she walked into it.

———

As love stories went, it wasn't the worst. Graham spent the day being questioned by airport security, the night in a little room while TSA checked and rechecked his credentials. Eventually, he was sentenced to serving thirty hours of community service for his crimes. They let him keep the shirt, as long as he paid for it.

Considering everyone in Moose Springs knew Graham and his reason for getting himself into trouble this time, he never lacked for company or a cold beverage as he ambled down the road on his off hours between lunch and dinner shifts, spearing any trash he could find. And if he spent more time sitting in Jonah's squad car than ambling, well, Jonah was a busy guy. He enjoyed having a moment to sit and talk about love too.

Zoey didn't mind the bright orange of the safety vest Graham wore on his community service time, but she quickly grew to hate the orange "Anchorage or Bust" shirt he'd procured at the airport gift shop.

"This is our love shirt, Zoey Bear," Graham told her just to tease her. "If I take it off, the romance will be over."

She took that shirt off often. From where they were both sitting, the romance between them was doing just fine.

Moving to Alaska for a moose wasn't really a thing. At least not a financially legitimate thing. But Zoey was a planner, and she could plan on the fly with the best of them. She never asked Graham to use his influence with the town to help her find a job. Zoey marched straight up to Jackson Shaw and told him exactly why the resort needed her as a tour guide. Sold on her drive and enthusiasm, Zoey walked away with the job of her dreams—and Graham's nightmares. Graham had never seen anyone as happy as she was, a headset tucked behind her ears and a group of wide-eyed tourists hanging on to her every word.

At night, curled up in his arms, Zoey whispered her plans against his skin. When she'd saved up enough money, she was planning on taking flying lessons, opening her own business, and running her own flight tours. Graham had absolutely no doubt she'd do everything she dreamed of.

And while Zoey slept in—exhausted from taking on the world—Graham stood outside his workshop, chainsaw in hand, and he finally carved that sucker.

A moose curled up around a bun. He'd never been so proud of anything...except for winning her.

Four months, twenty-one days, and three hours from the night Graham had looked up from a hoagie and met the eyes of the woman he'd love forever, he stretched out in the back of his pickup truck, bundled up in a blanket and a thick winter jacket, that same woman and a second sandwich tucked in close for warmth.

"You're getting crumbs on me," Graham warned her, even though he didn't mind.

"No, I'm not." Zoey swatted away his tickling fingers. "Are you sure?"

"About the crumbs? I'm pretty sure those aren't my crumbs."

"No, goofball, about the—"

Her voice slipped off into silence, eyes wide as she stared up into the night sky. Taking her hand, Graham relaxed back, content to watch the woman he loved living her dream. Knowing she was his dream and all he would ever need. When she leaned into his shoulder, inhaling a soft sigh of happiness, Graham whispered in her ear.

"Darlin', I've never been surer of anything in my life."

As the northern lights danced and played across the stars for her, Graham kept the little ring box in his pocket awhile longer. This was Zoey's moment, not his.

She'd always been worth the wait.

KEEP READING
FOR A SNEAK PEEK AT
MISTLETOE AND MR. RIGHT
BY SARAH MORGENTHALER,
COMING OCTOBER 2020!

CHAPTER 1

SOMEONE HAD DRAWN A GIANT penis in the snow.

"At least it's anatomically correct." Newly minted Moose Springs, Alaska property mogul Lana Montgomery tilted her head to the side, considering the artwork carved so precisely into the mountainside.

"A snow angel might have been more appropriate." Ben, her construction manager, scratched the back of his neck, trying and failing to keep a professional tone. "It is two weeks until Christmas."

"Yes, but then the message might have been lost. At least the mistletoe is a nice touch."

Nothing said *screw you* like an acre-wide penis pointed at a future construction site.

Ben exhaled a breath into the cold winter air, as if trying to cover a snort. "The locals are consistent, I'll give them that."

The penis was causing problems, as penises tended to do. The artwork was an eyesore, and the most recent in a long list of attempts by the Moose Springs locals to halt her luxury condominium project. At least the snow penis was refreshingly different from her normal issues: an accountant stealing from the family company here, insufficient returns from an ill-advised investment there, bad PR from someone in the family playing too hard with the Montgomery money.

A cheerful approach at life meant Lana was good at smoothing things over, but cheerfulness didn't help the slight crow's feet at the corner of her eyes or the permanent stress line trying to carve itself into her forehead.

Thirty-two was too young to feel the weight of her responsibilities this heavily.

"I can get a snowcat out here to level this out," Ben offered.

"Let's leave it for a while." Lana smiled congenially at her contractor. "Let them have their fun. Someone went to an awful lot of effort to put this here without being seen. I'd hate to disappoint them. Plus, who knows what they might choose for the follow-up pièce de résistance?"

"They don't get to you at all, do they?"

"I'm not *completely* immune to the attention." Lana scooped a handle of snow into her gloved palm. "I'm also hoping it won't take too much time before they stop being angry with me."

"You did buy up the entire town," Ben reminded her with an amused look. "Folks in a place this small don't take that sort of thing lightly."

"It's only a few properties, just enough to give my company the votes to force through this development. Property owners hold a lot of political sway in Moose Springs. We can't build a condominium on a mountainside without the town council's approval."

"And you wonder why they don't like you." Ben softened his

teasing with a good-natured chuckle. "Don't worry. As soon as the place gets built, they'll get used to it…in a couple dozen generations or so."

Montgomerys didn't snort. At least, they didn't in public, but what happened on a penis-carved mountainside stayed on a penis-carved mountainside.

"Be careful, darling, your optimism is showing."

Ben barked out a laugh then waved his hand for her to follow him. She lobbed the snowball toward the closest mistletoe leaf before heading back to her snowmobile. It slipped and slid on the loose powdery snow until she maneuvered into Ben's tracks. They circled the mountainside property the Montgomery Group had purchased from Moose Springs Resort and then tightened the circle to where her eventual luxury condominiums would be built.

Key word: eventual.

Among the top of today's to-do list was checking on the construction site progress. As sites went, this one was sorely lacking. So far, they'd only driven tall stakes with bright orange plastic flags on the tops to mark the boundaries of what would soon become the riskiest venture Lana had ever started.

The condominiums were meant to lure the rich and powerful from all over the world into permanently sinking their wealth into the town of Moose Springs, not simply arriving for a two-week ski-vacation at the resort every other year. New residents would enjoy all the amenities of the resort with the permanence of a personal vacation home.

If Lana could just get the darn place built.

As they reached the top of the site, highest on the mountainside, the town was at its best view. The lake below Moose Springs Resort had frozen over, now crisscrossed with tracks from snowmobiles and sledding children. Nestled in the bottom of the valley were tiny buildings set among thick stands of evergreen: the homes and businesses and people of Moose Springs. The lifeblood of this town.

Lana loved Moose Springs in a way she'd never loved anything before. It had stolen her heart and soul since her first visit as a young child, and she was determined to drive a stabilizing steel bar through the picturesque Alaskan town's shaky, tourism-driven economy no matter what. But just because she believed in what she was doing didn't mean the town did too.

Lana hadn't given up hope she could get them on board with her plans, but as of yet, she had very little support in the community or her holding company.

"Ask for forgiveness, not permission," she murmured to herself as they slowed. Calling forward over the rumble of the engines, she asked Ben, "Are you sure we can't break ground sooner?"

"Not unless we want to be digging through eight feet of snow."

Lana's work schedule limited her time in Moose Springs, but she was invested in doing this project right. For months, she and Ben had been up to their elbows in architect plans, zoning requirements, and a sleigh full of red tape. She'd hoped their progress would have been further by now.

"I thought construction during winter was the norm in Alaska," Lana said.

"Yeah, if you need a roof replaced or a kitchen remodeled. Not this behemoth."

Lana pursed her lips. "I don't suppose anyone would be willing to pay top dollar just to slide right on down the hill, would they?"

Ben jutted his chin towards the snowy penis. "They wouldn't want to pay top dollar to sit in the resort and see this lovely beast either."

"I know, Hannah's been blowing up my phone." The newly promoted General Manager of the resort had been emphatic Lana take care of it, or Hannah was hopping in one of the resort's ski-slope-smoothing snowcats to do it herself.

"Listen," Ben grunted. "It's not impossible, but the costs for site prep are going to skyrocket and there's not much we can do about getting material in until the access road up here gets widened and gravel down. Ever tried to off-road a semi loaded down with heavy equipment?"

"Point made. We wait until spring." When Ben opened his mouth, Lana added, "*Early* spring. I'm getting this project done as fast as humanly possible. And Ben? When you start hiring day labor, supplement your crew with as many local hires as you can, please. It'll save us on per diem."

He gave her a knowing look but didn't call Lana out on her decision. Her construction manager knew exactly why she wanted the locals to benefit from the jobs this project would provide.

She loved Moose Springs. Which only made it worse knowing they hated her.

In the distance, a heavy cloud clung to the top of the highest peak, one usually obscured by the weather on less clear days than this.

"Mount Veil is looking particularly ominous today," she mentioned.

Ben glanced at the giant hovering in the distance. "Veil's not Denali, but it's one badass monster. You've never tried to climb it?"

"I'm more of a snowmobile girl." Lana patted the handle of her ride.

"If you're going to be a resident of Moose Springs, you're going to need to use the right lingo. This is a snow machine."

"I'm not a resident," she informed him. "I stay in the resort."

"You own property, don't you?"

"The company owns property, not me."

Chicago, London, Singapore, the Virgin Islands...the Montgomery Group had their hands everywhere. But just because it was easier to stay at her family's holdings didn't mean she belonged in any of them. In the first thirty some years of her life, Lana had learned a lot from the company. Negotiating a million-dollar deal over cocktails was a normal Thursday for her. She could out-maneuver veteran CEO's while making a single martini double twist to perfection. But she'd never learned how to feel at home.

"Buying land doesn't make you part of a town, Ben. I wish it were that easy."

"Well, ma'am, either way, you had better get down to the town hall meeting."

"Why is that?"

Ben grinned at her. "Because they're still trying to figure out how to get rid of you."

Most town hall meetings were held in, well, a town hall. But not Moose Springs.

In Moose Springs, town hall meetings were held in an abandoned barn on the far side of town, complete with snow piled up around the building to near impassability. If one wanted to get to the barn door closest to her parking spot, they better have some gumption and a sturdy pair of shoes.

Lana had the first but not so much the second. She spent too much time in boardrooms to remember that Moose Springs liked to make things as difficult as possible.

When she reached the door, it stuck, so Lana put her weight behind her pull. Apparently someone had stacked a pile of three-foot-tall plastic Christmas elves against the other side of the door, because when it finally swung open, the elves saw their chance to make their escape. She jumped back to avoid the avalanche, ending up in a snowbank halfway to her now very cold knees. The closest elf was facedown in a boot hole, looking like it had officially given up on making it through the holidays with a semblance of dignity.

As everyone in the back few rows turned in their seats to stare at her through the open doorway, Lana knew the feeling.

"There's another entrance on the other side," someone muttered.

Well. That certainly would have been informative.

Rescuing half a dozen cheap plastic elves from a snowy death wasn't the worst thing Lana had ever done, although she would have appreciated a few less smirks aimed her way. Lana never had liked it when everyone looked at her when she stepped into a room. She was used to it, but she didn't like it.

She'd learned a long time ago to compensate for that

discomfort by throwing her best and brightest smile to the room. Usually it worked to take the attention away from her, but not this time. The gathered townsfolk most definitely didn't smile back.

"Tough crowd," she murmured to the plastic elves in her arms.

As meeting halls went, the barn worked well. A wooden stage had been built on the end furthest from where Lana had made her less than grand entrance. At least most of the people present hadn't witnessed her faux pas. They'd scooted the chairs around to form rows facing the makeshift stage up front. If Ben hadn't told her where they held town hall meetings, she never would have been able to find it. By the looks she received when she headed toward the front of the barn, more than a few people wouldn't have minded her absence.

They'd tried to make the barn seasonally appropriate, filling it with a cheerful if haphazard assortment of holiday decor. Most was fairly innocuous, but liberties had been taken with Rudolph's antlers, and something seemed to be going on between Mrs. Claus and Frosty the Snowman, if the twinkle in her eye was to be believed. The pile of elves had been hanging out near the rear escape exit, the one Lana had unwittingly entered. They'd probably had the right idea.

The combination of strings of blinking Christmas lights, red and green plastic ornaments, blue and white papier-mâché snowflakes, and gold sparkles painted on popcorn balls was somewhat jarring. Someone had mounted a star on the top of a cardboard cutout of a lamp made out of a woman's stockinged leg, with several presents stuck underneath, although no one had informed Lana that this was the gift-giving type of meeting.

Drawing her coat close to chase away the chill, Lana scanned the room, searching for a friendly face among the familiar ones. She breathed a sigh of relief when she spotted a short, slender brunette in glasses seated off to the side, across the room from a folding table loaded with coffee urns and holiday treats. Zoey Caldwell glanced up from the book in her lap as Lana approached, brightening when Lana waved at her in greeting.

"I saved Graham a seat, but you can have his," Zoey joked. "He's been a brat all day."

"Is he ever not a brat?" Lana replied, sitting down next to her best friend.

"Hmm, good point."

The constant good mood Zoey had been in since moving to Moose Springs still hadn't faded, and she gave Lana an enthusiastic hug. A hug Lana happily returned. It was embarrassing to admit how much Lana wanted those hugs...and needed them. They had met years ago at a truck stop diner outside of Chicago. Zoey had been Lana's waitress, and something between them had simply clicked. If Lana had to be honest with herself—which was more of a pain than she wanted to think about at the moment—her relationship with Zoey was the healthiest human interaction she'd experienced in her entire life. And it meant more to Lana than Zoey realized that they would be spending the holidays together.

Lana glanced around. "I was hoping Jake would be here."

Jake was originally Graham's dog, but all three of them worked equally hard at securing the blind border collie's affection. So far, Zoey was winning.

"We asked him if he wanted to come, but he preferred to sleep by the fireplace." Adjusting her glasses, Zoey said, "I think he was done being dressed for the day. Graham changed his outfit four times."

"Jake's wearing pajamas right now, isn't he?"

"His Christmas Ninja Turtle pj's." Zoey rolled her eyes. "They're his *favorite*."

They both knew whose favorite those pj's actually were.

"How did the meeting go?"

"Festively phallic," Lana decided. "Almost as festive as this place. How did it go meeting Graham's parents?"

"They're just like him. Loving, wonderful, excessively loquacious. Their place in Anchorage is right off the inlet, and it's very cute."

"But?"

"But that's a lot of Barnett humor in one room." Zoey shuddered. "I might need to crash with you tonight, so I don't murder him."

"My couch is always yours." Lana squeezed Zoey's hand, briefly leaning in her friend's shoulder companionably. "I don't think the heater is doing much to help."

"Graham is bringing another one and some more chairs. I guess people always show up when his cousin's wife, Leah, makes her holiday mix."

As Zoey expounded on the deliciousness of holiday mixes, Lana made a mental note. Leah, Graham's cousin's wife, owner of a local car rental business and one of Lana's recent acquisitions. These days, it seemed like everyone was either directly or indirectly affected by the mass purchase.

"You have your work face on." Zoey nudged Lana with her elbow. "You've been running a hundred miles an hour since this summer. You need a day off."

"If I took a day off, I wouldn't know what to do with myself," Lana joked. Zoey wasn't wrong, though. Lana was dying for a day of no phone calls, no emails, and no penises.

"Have you ever been to one of these things?" Zoey asked.

Lana started to answer, but Zoey was immediately distracted as her boyfriend arrived. Graham's best friends—the very tall, very man-bunned Easton, and Easton's heavily-tattooed twin sister Ashtyn—were in tow. All of their arms were full of space heaters and extra folding chairs. Where one found a Graham Barnett, one usually would find the Lockett twins, although it was impossible to identify the leader in their little trio. Easton's expression was hidden behind his reddish-brown beard, but Ashtyn's super short, multi-colored spiky hair was both visible and fabulous.

"I wish I could pull off that style," Lana murmured as she watched Ash, fingers absently touching her shoulder-length auburn locks. The closest she'd come to exciting was freshly redone lowlights for the winter.

"I wish I was brave enough to," Zoey sighed. Then she quirked a grin at Lana. "Brace yourself. A Moose Springs town hall is nothing like what you'd expect. They get a little weird."

"Quirky weird or get-out-of-the-room weird?"

"It's more like...do you remember that guy who always came in at the end of my shifts on Friday nights?"

"The one with the underwear or the one without?"

"The one without." Zoey rubbed her hands together to warm them. "This will be worse."

Not for the first time, Lana's overwhelming affection for her friend rushed over her.

Lana wasn't the only one overwhelmed with affection for Zoey Caldwell. After setting the heater down, Graham Barnett turned, his eyes searching for Zoey in the crowd. Beside her, Lana could hear Zoey's breath catch. Graham's face split into a broad, almost silly grin as he strode across the room, ignoring the leg lamp and heading straight for them. Dropping down into the seat Zoey had saved on her other side, Graham kissed her.

"Hey there, Zoey Bear." He wrapped his arm around her shoulders, giving her the perfect place to snuggle for warmth into his side. Over Zoey's head, Graham offered Lana an amused look. "Greetings, supreme overtaker."

"Graham, stop." Zoey frowned at him, poking his stomach with a finger. "You're going to make her feel bad."

"He's just teasing me," Lana promised. "Graham only teases people he likes. I'm going to get myself a treat. Would you like anything?"

"Usually I'm the one tossing food your way." Graham flashed her that charming look of his, the one that always got him out of trouble. "I'm happy to sit back and let you be the bearer of delicious things."

"Just a coffee, please," Zoey decided.

"A complicated, no-one-can-get-it-right, super-coffee with the exact right amount of everything or she'll give you hell for it."

"Lana will get it right."

"Einstein couldn't get it right." Graham winked at Zoey, knowing he was ruffling her feathers but doing so anyway. "I don't know, darlin'. You're super particular. You should probably remind her."

"Lana's much smarter than you, and even if she did get it wrong, I wouldn't say anything. Unlike you, who has deliberately screwed up my coffee every day this week because you think it's funny."

"You get the cutest little scrunchy face when it's too sweet—"

"Graham."

"Or not sweet enough."

"*Graham*."

"Or forbid there's *regular* dairy instead of non-dairy creamer—"

Lana left them to their conversation, having been exposed to their antics enough to know how this would progress. Graham's particular brand of affection was exactly what Zoey needed in her life. And if Graham following her around like a love-smitten puppy was any indicator, she was exactly what he needed too.

Lana didn't know what she needed, but some eggnog would be a pleasant start.

A table had been set up along the wall, complete with coffee urns and cookies, the little hard ones from a Christmas-themed tin. So far no one was eating the cookies, preferring a large Tupperware container full of homemade party mix. Sadly, there was no eggnog and not enough hands, so Lana fixed coffees for three instead. Taking a small portion of party mix and two cookies out of politeness instead of any real desire to consume either, Lana turned and bumped cookie plate to cookie plate into the man behind her.

"Oops, sorry. *Oh*. Hello, Rick." Lana glanced up at the only person in this town who made her heart skip an extra beat.

"Hey." The quiet, rumbled word was nice, especially from a man more known for nodding than talking.

Hazel eyes just a shade greener than she remembered gazed down at her over his own coffee. Normally clean shaven, Rick Harding must have slept in late that morning, because the light stubble on his face was as unusual for the pool hall owner as it was attractive.

There had been a time when Lana had considered Rick somewhat average. Average height, somewhat larger than average muscular build, with a strong jaw on a pleasantly attractive face.

Then he'd come to her rescue the previous summer, after some disgruntled and inebriated townsfolk had taken her to task for announcing the condominium project. Someone had caused her to deliberately fall, hurting her arm. After helping her off the ground, Rick had promptly punched the lights out of the man who tripped her.

There were many people in Lana's life, but very few heroes.

"It's really good to see you again," Lana told him sincerely.

"I didn't realize you were back in town," Rick admitted in his low, rich voice.

She'd never been able to decide if he was quiet or shy, or maybe both. But the fact that he'd noticed she was gone somehow warmed her far more than the coffee cups she was balancing.

"I had to meet with my general contractor. We start construction soon."

Rick nodded, shifting on his feet and glancing down at the coffee in his hands.

Lana liked how his hands were strong, and how his

fingers—calloused from work—wrapped around his coffee cup. She liked his broad shoulders and the way his jeans were worn from use, not styled to look that way. The flannel-lined hoodie he wore reminded her of the woods, and being warm, and Christmas time. Back when she was young enough to believe Christmas was reindeers and mistletoe and lists to Santa, not emotionally charged dinners with an extended family more interested in profit margins and expensive cocktails than truly enjoying each other's company.

They hesitated, an awkward moment where Lana wasn't sure what to say and Rick stood there saying nothing. Then of course they spoke at the exact same time.

"Are you—?"

"Do you—?"

A flush reddened his face beneath the scruffy beard. "Sorry," Rick mumbled. "You first."

He looked so cute, shifting on his feet.

"I was just going to ask if you're ready for Christmas. The presents, the tree, all of that stuff."

A soft snort was his answer. "It's not really my holiday," Rick admitted. "Are you staying around?"

He sounded almost hopeful. Lana wasn't a blusher, but something about the way he was looking at her made her cheeks heat. "I was hoping to."

A loud clearing of a throat pulled their attention to the stage, and the tired-looking officer standing on it. Jonah wasn't the mayor—as far as Lana was aware, there was no mayor—and the members of the town council all collectively slouched in their seats, refusing to meet Jonah's eye. Which left their poor overworked police officer to deal with running the meeting alone, like he dealt with protecting the town alone. Jonah was going to need some backup if her condominiums brought more residents permanently to Moose Springs.

"More police," Lana murmured to herself.

"You don't like Jonah?" Rick asked, glancing at the officer curiously.

"Actually, I like him a lot," Lana admitted. "I'd like him even more if he wasn't stretched thin enough to see through. I'm hoping to talk the new mayor into giving him a little help."

"We don't have a mayor." Rick's eyebrows knitted together in confusion.

"I suppose I could always run."

She'd meant it as a joke, but the look of horror on his face almost managed to hurt her feelings. Then abruptly he chuckled.

"You'd be good at it." Those greener-than-normal hazel eyes crinkled with amusement. "Better than I was."

Hmmm. Why was it a compliment from him felt like a warm brownie and a mug of hot tea in front of a fireplace? Then suddenly what Rick had said registered.

"Wait, you were mayor?" Too bad Rick wasn't the mayor now. Lana could only imagine how much easier her life would be.

"Only for a month, a few years back. We all took a turn, and none of us wanted anything to do with it. This town is a pain in the ass."

Lana couldn't help her laugh.

"L, you can flirt later," Graham called from their seats on the other side of the barn. "Rick, be careful, buddy. She's a piranha in sheep's clothing."

"Pariah, dearest," Lana joked back.

She turned back to Rick and saw a deeper flush had reddened his face. Rick opened his mouth, as if to continue the conversation like a normal human being, then promptly shut it again. He glanced down at his coffee cup, clearing his throat.

Lana knew she made him nervous, and while it wasn't a first for her, she wished that Rick found her more approachable. It was nice having someone to talk to. Feeling as if perhaps she'd overstayed her welcome, Lana took an awkward step back.

"Well, I better take my seat."

"Do you need help?" Rick started to ask as she turned, juggling her off-balance coffees, but his helping hands only jostled them more. "Oh, sorry."

He cursed when the closest coffee spilled on the sleeve of her coat. The poor man grabbed some napkins from the table, dabbing them at her arm while pouring coffee all over his own hand in the process. The only way to save him from more scalding was to take another step back.

"Thick jacket," she promised, trying to ease his discomfort with a smile. "Did you burn yourself?"

"Naw," Rick mumbled, still holding his handful of coffee-soaked napkins. "I have thick arms. Skin. Arm skin. Damn, I don't even know what I'm saying. Are you sure I didn't burn you?"

"I promise."

He looked like he wanted to be anywhere else at that moment. Since Rick had saved her once, Lana was happy to save him in return, even if it meant denying herself his company.

Still, she couldn't help giving him a flirty wink. "I'll see you later, Rick."

ACKNOWLEDGMENTS

IN THE FALL OF 2018, I took a trip to Alaska to research the area for another series. The last thing I expected was to walk into a little tourist trap souvenir store and walk out with the idea for this book. In all the amazing time since, my life has been a whirlwind of moose, romance, and having far more fun than I ever thought possible. There are so many people who helped *Tourist* come into the world, and I'm so overwhelmingly appreciative to all of you.

Thank you to God for giving me a life I love and definitely do not deserve.

This book wouldn't have happened without my husband, Kenney. Thank you so much for your endless patience, love, support, and willingness to hug me when I cry after I hit Send. To my mom and dad, the most amazing parents a girl could ask for. I'm so proud to say you're my best friends. My brother, for always giving me the books you loved to read when growing up and for making "moose-tastic" a part of my vocabulary.

To Sara Megibow, for not only being an incredible agent but a wonderful person and the best cheerleader for your clients. Working with you is a joy, and I'm grateful every day.

ABOUT THE AUTHOR

GEOLOGIST AND LIFELONG SCIENCE NERD, Sarah Morgenthaler is a passionate supporter of chocolate chip cookies, geeking out over rocks, and playing with her rescue pit bull, Sammy. When not writing romantic comedy and contemporary romance set in far-off places, Sarah can be found traveling with her husband, hiking national parks, and enjoying her own happily ever after. Sarah is a two-time Golden Heart Finalist and winner of the NOLA STARS Suzannah award.

Cat Clyne, thank you for being the editor of my dreams. For your relentless positivity and support of these books, for always emailing me moose pictures, and for letting me keep the barfing scene. You're truly the best. Also thank you to the entire Sourcebooks team, including Stefani Sloma, Rachel Gilmer, and Sarah Otterness, for all your hard work. You have been amazing.

To Leigh Sullivan and Catey Escobar for always believing in my writing, for lovely walks on beaches in Washington, and for my favorite plot hunting ever. To my Golden Heart sisters, the Persisters and the Rebelles. Words can't express how your support, friendship, and advice have changed my life. You are talented and wonderful and truly the best group of women.

To my amazing critique partners, C. R. Grissom and Christina Hovland. This book wouldn't be here without you. To Alexis Daria, for your wisdom, your support, and your incredible friendship. To my mentor, Sarah Andre, for always being there with your enthusiasm and guidance.

To Grace and Michael Esquivel, Chuck and Marcella Heh, and Jeannine Segatto for always believing in me. Justin and Sophia, I love you so much. Anna Penn, thank you for the *best* Alaskan research trip and more adventures than I could ever put into writing. To the Penn family and Tyler Shiver, for letting me steal Anna for that trip.

And lastly, to my son, Kyle. Every day I write, I know you're with me, in spirit and in hope.